Isdria

A Tale of the Fromryr

Book 2

Sam Middleton

Darkenheit Publishing

Isdria: A Tale of the Fromryr

Cover design by Charles Utting
ISBN: 978-1-7393742-1-1
First edition: October 2025

Special thanks…

…to Charles Utting, who once again turned my mad science-fiction fantasy blend into one hell of a cover, Luan Bittencourt, who created masterpieces from my rough sketches, and Daniela, whose steady hand cleared the way for the words…

A note to the reader

There's a glossary in the back – you're probably going to need it. It **does not** contain spoilers.

Pronunciation:
Aetraya: *EE - tray - uh*
Aeturnum: *EE - turn - uhm*
Formaria: *For - mare - ee - uh*
Fromryr: *Fruhm - rear*
Gyre: *Jy - er*

Other stories set in the world of the Fromryr
The Lazarat Moon (Book 0.5)
Eluthienn (Book 1)

If you like the world of Aetraya, you can find out more at www.instagram.com/sammiddletonbooks/

Kelej-Irok
Troll Ken
Shale of the Moon
Kelej-Itan
The Knor-Dan Mnts.
Etherlain
Kelej-Orst
The Lilac Coast
The Amarant Sea
Fal'Hannar
Anslyn
Sorren
Myrtle
Kern Moor
Lemos
Myrin
Celboryn
Onia
Celmyr
Moech
Taeoch
The Jungle's Teeth
Elliptica
The Fenn Sea

a
Nexoria
Helmharothell
endergaarden
Pelothrian Mnts
The Old World
ania
Pontifax
noclen
Mord-Gonn
Toinar
Helispont
Vakersreach
Fion
Ylstgaar
Fiondagaard
Alstgaar
Ekersreach
Voygerburg
Vallorandyl
Zymifar
Vroyker Marshes
Thanead
Estar
Lyle Marsh
Syracuta
Kainburg
N
W
E
S

Lucretia
Omega
Xeron
Ilantia
Maylanese Gulf
Thela
Kyor
Sep
Vypora
Calanthis Major
Asteron
Grindle
Calaxis
Everaux
Verax
Map Key
Maw
Vault
Cauldron
Spire
Cradle
Cove
Calanthis Minor
Ersana

FORMARIA
Kronos
Talon
Acheron
Maledus
Teuron
dergaarden
Taranis
Talisor
Reantha
KLIOXIES
Theselan
Baron
Pheobe
Hyralian Gulf
Tia
Pontifax
Damoclen
Helispont

EPISTOLAR MESSAGE VALLORANDYL TO FION

A telling in Fion.

The teller is Vermillies Sidtch, Lord Regent of Ravinica and Absolver General.

The witness is Emries von Cadst, Duke of Ylstgaar, Adjutant to the Fion Throne, and Marshal of the Western Front.

The telling concerns the Sorel Tan Captain, Isdria Laanorath, son to the elven queen Elspeth Laanorath, scourge of the underground realms of Formaria, and declared terrorist of the Fromryian state.

My agents captured him near the Hyralian Gulf in a desperate condition, having fled battle upon, of all creatures, a cicadron. The details of why he rode a goblin mount remain obscure.

This fortunate event brings clarity to my suspicions: despite your doubts, my Duke, I believed Laanorath possessed critical knowledge concerning Eluthienn's fate and the Ecclessius' involvement in it. His capture, as you will discover, dispels any notion of the rogue prince's survival; the absence of Eluthienn even as Alstgaar fell and Fiondagaard marched across eastern Ravinica confirms his demise.

Yet, from Isdria emerges darker news: your suspicion the Fromryr sought a weapon are confirmed. It appears this weapon is of immense, ancient power, unseen since the days of Redcrosse, a threat capable of overturning our ambitions in Ravinica and striking even Fiondagaard itself.

However, opportunity accompanies dread. The underground factions fracture, weakened by the supposed vampire attack and internal strife, perhaps even civil war, as they contest this weapon's ownership.

Remarkably, Isdria spoke of the Gyre Gates, claiming the Sorel Tan had rediscovered the means to rebuild the ancient world portals. Though I cannot yet confirm this account's authenticity, our interrogators spare no method in extracting every detail from the elf, whom I assure you endures discomfort suitable to his kind. He is, as we speak, standing manacled in the dungeons, never able to sit, afforded no respite.

If true, this intelligence holds grave implications and perhaps an advantage we might exploit. My Duke, I present this tale for your contemplation and the emperor's wisdom. A tale, it transpires, occurred less than one week past. May it serve the empire's glory and your everlasting favour.

One
Kathryn

Kathryn Stryker stood at the end of the corridor, watching a dull grey pulse creep along its ceiling canal toward the sealed portal. She wondered, and not for the first time, how likely it was that she'd die in the chamber beyond.

A single exit, from a room barely bigger than a cruiser's nav deck. So far down Ilantia's chute, the ice ghosted its veins, the corridors were spectral black, and the air so thin no one would hear a cry for help. Not the kind that would come to save her, anyway.

Likely, then, she thought. *Very likely.*

But whatever the odds, she was walking through that door. Because Kathryn was out of options. She *had been* for some time—a reality only now catching up with her.

The pulse overhead revealed black grime clawing at the corridor's corners and staining the Formarian alloy flags. Where they should have reflected polished silver, there were only murky dark stains.

Unbidden, perhaps because of the ugliness around her, her mother's voice rushed through her thoughts, angry and laced with judgment.

There's always options!

Words said to her so many times as a child. Hawkish eyes never leaving Kathryn's notes, hands clasped behind her back, ruler clenched between them, a silent threat held so tightly Kathryn hoped it would snap.

Good officers create options, her mother continued. And

Kathryn knew exactly what came next.

Scribbling so hard her quill's nib cut lines into the parchment, she tried not to think about the words. She tried not to care. But they always came, and were spoken with so much seething anger, it was all Kathryn could do not to cringe into her writing desk.

But you will never be good enough!

Kathryn flinched at the memory. The fixer had known. She saw that now, as she cast her mind back to the previous night, if only to rid herself of her mother's voice. He had known she was out of options, even before she did.

Human, like her, they were the same height. But his thin frame filled the seat. He spread one arm on the table and draped the other across the back of his chair. It made him seem taller.

Desde Harada had turned to face the thousands passing by the Esteemed Crystal Prospector's Lounge. The Cradle's upper levels, and far above them, the arteries of blue ice cutting through the rock ceiling, produced a sapphire glow. It poured onto dock workers, miners, and free traders. Fromryr starting night shifts, or spending enough coin to forget they lived in Ilantia, the overcrowded spit of rock jutting into a bottomless cavern.

The Formarians had built here, everyone agreed, purely for its strategic value as a junction connecting three more important installations. A waystation that had become a city. A city that had become a smuggler's paradise, and all the nastiness that came with it. Kathryn hated the place. Even more than she hated Harada.

Wearing his faded red mining gambeson, the links worn smooth, his hair shorn into a single messy strip, he blended right in. If Kathryn hadn't known exactly who he was, she might have found it convincing.

He gave her no empty promises this time, no baseless assurances, no drug-addled monologues punctuated by vague commitments. Just a name. And not the one she wanted.

"Seyuda Veers," Harada said, calmly. *Soberly*, Kathryn thought. And just loud enough for her to hear above the city's crowds. "He has what you want."

"Seyuda Veers wants me dead," she replied.

"He wants you gone. Dead is bad for business. Gone is better. Gone is better for everybody."

"And what does he want in exchange?" she asked. "Other than me gone." No way she was getting off that lightly. Not when a man like Veers was involved.

"You give him what he needs. He gives you what you need."

In her imagination, she grabbed the front of Harada's gambeson, yanking that stupid strip of hair until she got the answers she wanted. Half tunnel-gang affectation, half mining-crew signifier, it was neither and both at the same time. It made her hate the man even more. She'd pressed both palms into the table, thinking she almost preferred the overconfident, drug-induced assertions.

"What does he need, Harada?"

"You just got to meet him," he replied. "Tomorrow night. Down the chute. Kaborachi District, Level Sixteen."

"Sounds like a trap," Kathryn said.

"Your choice," Harada said, and stood, becoming another body in Ilantia's night traffic. Kathryn had watched him go, wanting to drag him back to the table but knowing it would do no good.

Now it was tomorrow night, and the tiny grey star was at the end of the canal. It flickered, dimmed, and like Kathryn's options, died just above the triangular portal at the corridor's end.

Looks like you were right all along, mother. The thought was bitter and defiant. Her mouth tightened to a thin line. *I really wasn't good enough after all.*

She pulled back her black coat and gave her sword belt a reassuring tug, tightening it across her leather cuirass. It was five strides to the portal. One hand found the pommel of her blade, and the other reached for the waist-high terminal.

It was empty of hex.

Guess I'll knock then. But the portal clicked. Its three triangular partitions creaked like rusted gears. They retracted into the ceiling. There was a faint warmth, the smell of leather and bodies. Parchment-yellow light spilled from the chamber's ceiling ducts.

Three dwarves stood around a single grey block. They wore dark, thigh-length gambesons. From their bulk, Kathryn guessed they wore chain vests and skirts beneath.

Each dwarf carried a compact repeater, the shoulder stock removed, flight chamber reduced by a third. They were wildly inaccurate at range but deadly at close quarters, the kind that could punch through plate and mail before her sword even left its scabbard. Her eyes lingered on the repeaters' gyre cartridges. They smoked hard teal beneath the chamber's bleached light.

Then she saw the man sitting behind the grey block. Seyuda Veers was bald except for a ring of white hair. He wore a grey coat with a maroon lapel. It looked imported, and expensive.

He leaned to one side, favouring it like he was taking the weight off an old injury. His eyes, hidden deep within weathered folds of skin, watched her closely. On the block sat a bronzite chest, its lid shut.

She took another step, then froze. A tremor made her head snap right, where a gnome leaned against the wall. His crimson jacket blended into the gloom—one arm folded across his chest, the other held aloft, fingers twisting slowly in the air. Behind her, the portal slid shut.

"Our situation dictates that we must be separated from the network," Veers said. His voice was precise, each syllable meticulously shaped, and he hit the 't' hard. It was a foreign accent. "I am sure you understand."

"Desde Harada said you wanted to meet me," Kathryn said, taking another step forward. Her fingers ached from gripping the sword's pommel.

"He also said it was a certainty you would come. That despite our opposing professions, what we possess is too valuable to you," Veers said.

He wasn't wrong. If, against all odds, he really did have what she needed. But Kathryn wouldn't begin a negotiation with Seyuda Veers by acknowledging her desperation.

"Giving away your position to me was a risk," she said

instead.

"A risk many of my associates believed too great," Veers replied. "That your agreement to meet was only to flush me out. That someone such as yourself would not compromise themselves by working with us. They are limited in their vision."

"But you're not," Kathryn said, making it a statement, not a question.

Veers placed a liver-spotted hand on the bronzite chest.

"It was curious to me why you would need this. Why an elite officer of the Custodia would seek such an obscure substance. A medicine, as it turns out. But after some investigation, it became perfectly clear why someone with your condition would require Veskanca."

Kathryn fought to maintain her composure, knuckles whitening on the pommel. Two thoughts collided: she'd finally found Veskanca, and Veers knew far too much.

And if he knew too much, he held all the cards in the game they were about to play. Somewhere in the recesses of her mind, her mother berated her. Kathryn tried not to flinch.

"What condition?" she asked, trying to keep her tone flat, trying to give nothing away. It was a wasted effort.

"Please, Ms. Stryker. I am a thorough individual," Veers said. "I would not have invited you here unless I possessed indisputable knowledge of your circumstances."

He gestured to the chair in front of the desk. "If you wouldn't mind."

Kathryn glanced once more at the dwarves, then pulled the chair out and sat.

"You suffer from a rare form of abhorrence," Veers said. "One that induces regular and severe hallucinations. But with the administration of certain elixirs, these side effects are perfectly manageable and render the condition all but benign."

He paused, chin dipping a fraction.

"But the condition is old. Obscure. Ecclessiarchal healers declared there was no permanent cure, only ongoing treatment. An oversight that proved fatal for your career, as the Fromryian Navy does not tolerate such corruption in its captains."

A string of profanities tore through Kathryn's thoughts, followed by her mother's voice: *Never give away your strength! Never let the enemy know.* Kathryn had the sudden urge to flip the table and cut Veers' throat. It was a stupid thought. She wouldn't be an inch out of the chair before they stuck her with bolts.

"As you can see," Veers continued, neither gloating nor threatening. He was just a professional explaining the facts. Kathryn was starting to feel out of her depth. But she shouldn't. She'd dealt with worse.

"We are not the Church. When we heard what you were looking for, we conducted an investigation into your background."

Carefully, he opened the chest and pulled out an ampule no longer than his index finger. It held a clear liquid.

"I was not aware of Veskanca myself," Veers said. "But it appears it is no longer produced in Formaria."

"So where did you get it?" Kathryn asked, surprised by the calm in her voice.

"We have access to jurisdictions most do not," Veers replied. "It was exceptionally costly to locate and required particularly unpleasant and lengthy negotiations with a one-eyed and legless dwarf."

"And you went to all that trouble for little old me?"

"Your diligence as Palatine has been most detrimental to our operations here," Veers said, a hint of annoyance slipping into what had, so far, been a measured tone. "It is in our interest for you to leave Ilantia and return to your position in the navy."

Kathryn stopped herself from laughing.

"That seems overly generous," she said. "You could have just had me killed. Same result."

"Believe me, Ms. Stryker, the thought crossed my mind. But such an act would fail to take advantage of your position and your talents."

Here it comes. It couldn't be that easy. If it wasn't going to be her death, it was going to be something worse.

"Veskanca must be taken nightly over the course of four

weeks," Veers went on. "During this time, we will enter into a partnership of mutual benefit. That partnership begins in two nights."

Kathryn's imagination conjured her mother like an apparition: hands clenched around a ruler, leaning in, inches from her face, eyes wild with smug satisfaction. *Why aren't you good enough, Kathryn? Tell me. Why?*

"A miner by the name of Orphan Guyan will arrive at Ilantia's western dock," Veers continued.

Kathryn ground her teeth, banishing the vision of her mother. *Concentrate. You need this.*

"It is carrying cargo of the utmost value to me. It must be allowed to dock and unload unimpeded by local officials. Most importantly, it must avoid scrutiny from the Cradle's Custodia troopers."

Something you and every other smuggler in this city wants.

"Ilantia is a gateway for major smuggling operations, as you well know," she said. "The local detachment spends half their time at the docks trying to impound unregistered cargo."

"Which is why the Orphan's flight path and docking schedule must be approved in the local network," Veers said.

He pulled a vial of black and silver filaments from inside his coat pocket.

"This contains the flight path and docking clearance for the Orphan's gyre signature and its captain's identification script," he said, holding the vial between thumb and forefinger. Its contents looked like any other collection of hex reduction. "You will ensure this makes its way into the local network."

"Corrupting the hex network is a serious crime," she said.

"You would not have come here without knowing a certain moral flexibility would be required on your part," Veers said.

In other words, she had no choice.

"Whoever made that for you would need to be a military-level caster to break the Custodia script and go unnoticed," she said.

A cold weight settled at the back of her mind. She imagined herself caught, dragged in, and exposed in some short-lived attempt to infiltrate the network.

"It will go unnoticed," the gnome said behind her, his voice strangely serene.

She turned back to Veers. "Even so, the Custodia on dock duty will impound anything they don't like the look of—clearance or no clearance."

"We are well aware of your colleagues' scrupulousness in upholding the law," Veers said, with a note of irritation. When Custodia officers took a cut of an illegal shipment's black market value, even someone like Veers felt the sharp end of the law.

"Other precautions have been made. Shortly before the Orphan is scheduled to dock, the Agreiga Barons and the Void Born Collective will engage in a territorial dispute across levels thirteen and fourteen. You will inform your superiors that you've received highly reliable intelligence that senior members of each organisation will be in attendance. To avoid missing such a rare opportunity to capture their leadership, you'll request that all unengaged officers be reassigned to your detail."

"You've convinced the Barons and the Collective to fight a skirmish?" Kathryn asked, unable to keep the astonishment from her voice.

"The whys and wherefores of these events are of no concern to you," Veers said. His dark eyes betrayed more impatience than his voice.

"And after tomorrow night?" Kathryn asked. "What else are you going to need?"

"Nothing that would result in your death or incarceration," Veers said. "Both outcomes would bring unwanted attention to our operations. Better that we reap the benefits of your position, and then you leave quietly without anyone knowing we managed to infiltrate the Custodia at such a high level."

Those final words hit like a blade to the gut. They pierced through her, breaching the wall she'd built around herself. All she could see was her mother's vindicated smile.

That was all she was good for now, a tool for criminals. She'd failed, just as her mother had always predicted.

"Do we have an agreement?" Veers asked.

Kathryn held his gaze, losing herself in those dark irises. Every fibre of her body screamed at her to tell this cavern-crawling scum to shove his Veskanca into the darkest orifice he could find.

Instead, she reached into the crate and pulled out an ampule at random. Veers didn't take his eyes off her hand.

"If this isn't what you say it is. If this doesn't work. I will…"

Veers raised a hand, cutting across her. "There is no need for anger or threats, Ms. Stryker. We are well aware of your capabilities."

By the black void, you better be. Kathryn almost hoped he was lying, just to give her an excuse to throw him off the nearest edge.

"And the rest of it?" she asked.

"A single dose will be here for you to collect each night," Veers said.

"Then we have an agreement," she said, pocketing both the ampule and the vial of hex. "You'll have your cargo."

Veers' mouth softened. It was the closest he came to smiling, she suspected. Then he nodded at his caster. The air around the gnome's fingers shimmered, and the portal opened.

Without another word, Kathryn made her way toward it.

"In such times of disarray," Veers said, just as she was about to step into the corridor, "it is good that those who once considered themselves foes can forge a new order."

She paused but didn't look back. *Oh, we're still foes*, she thought. *And don't you for a second think I'll be leaving Ilantia quietly.*

Let him gloat; it didn't matter. She was alive, and she'd found Veskanca. She'd found the cure.

And that gave her options again. They were bad options: the kind of options her mother would've laughed at her for. But they were options, nonetheless.

Two
Brazier

Brazier lay in his cot, one arm behind his head, his wrist soaking in the gentle vibration of the *Anchorite's* engines, while a pleasant ache spread from his groin. He watched Freyen pour water from a jug, his gaze tracing the soft curve of her backside and the shadow it cast at the top of her thigh. Deep inside him, something resembling bliss threatened to become a real feeling. He ignored it, focusing on Freyen.

She probably knew he was watching. She probably didn't care. Probably, she was standing there on purpose, taking all the time in the world to pour that water. The thought made Brazier smile, and just for a moment, he really did feel bliss.

"I'm going to hit the head," she said, placing the cup she'd poured on the side table. "Get in there before Switch gets back."

"Good idea," Brazier replied, reaching for the cup and taking several gulps.

"I'm also borrowing this," she added, picking up his white undershirt and slipping it over her head. Far too big for her, it hung off her shoulders, the hem falling to just above her knees in a way that reminded Brazier of the ache between his legs. Clutching her clothes, she pushed a stray curl behind one of her bat-like ears and flashed him a shy smile before leaving.

Brazier leaned back in his cot, trying to hold onto that blissful feeling. The dim blue glow of the cabin's ambient channels cast long, lazy shadows across his sparse quarters, making his eyelids heavy and drawing him into the comforting haze of half-sleep, where consciousness blurred with dreams. There, on the edge of wakefulness, his mind slipped the leash. His thoughts ventured forward, toward a future he usually tried his best not to think about.

For Freyen and him, that future was carved in the cold, hard stone of inevitability. In the tangled web of Fromryian society, interspecies relationships, while not explicitly banned, hovered in a grey area: tolerated but never encouraged. Theoretically, such unions were meant to strengthen bonds between the allied races. Yet they stood in stark defiance of one of the underground's unwritten tenets: procreate a lot, and provide warriors for the Bellum Infinara, the Endless War, to ensure the people's survival.

Freyen and Brazier would never have children. No two people of different races ever had, and not for lack of trying. Couples like them were common, but their relationships were typically fleeting. Eventually, driven by need or duty, people wanted children and that meant finding someone of their own kind. Perhaps Freyen harboured dreams of parenthood. Perhaps she didn't. Hell, he wasn't even sure of his own feelings on the matter.

What they had, this fledgling thing between them, was still raw, undefined, too new to burden with thoughts of a future already denied them. And truth be told, he wasn't sure it was even an idea worth entertaining. They were mercenaries, a warship for hire, working jobs for people on the fringes of Formaria, flitting from one shadowy contract to another. It was hardly a life for children.

That thought led his slumbering mind to darker places. Officially, the vampire had been summoned by an unusually powerful Mirrovinjin witch. That witch had met her end at the hands of witch hunters, bringing about the destruction of the spawn. No mention was made of a pact with a prince, a former First Champion, or the crew that flew with them. Unofficially, there were rumours, tales growing wilder and more unbelievable with each telling.

And somewhere between it all, the *Shian Anchorite* and her crew had been quietly listed as outlaws. There was no reason given, no link to the vampire ever mentioned. Orders to Navarch ships were simple: apprehend or destroy on sight.

Such was the life of a criminal.

And it was a reality that came with a deep unease for Brazier. Not because they no longer fought for the good of Formaria, though that gnawed at him daily. It was because of how easily his crew had slipped into life on the run.

He'd thought he would need to hold them together, to be their lodestone, the one who wouldn't let them dwell on what they'd become. He'd thought he would need to remind them outlawed was better than dead. But if anything, they seemed perfectly content.

Mathias, and to a certain extent Switch, he understood. Outlaw was better than the state they'd found the navigator in. And at any rate, Mathias had come into his own, introducing the crew to a whole network of nefarious people and places Brazier could hardly believe existed. A free trader operation smuggling weapons into Ravinica. Mining captains selling black market gyre ice to bandits in the Pelothrian Mountains. An elderly gnome running illegal substance shipments out of Calaxis, and who had quickly become the crew's friend.

Many of their contracts now involved protecting unregistered haulers, vessels so beaten-up Brazier sometimes wondered how they managed to stay airborne. Switch was in her element, offering a kind of complimentary repair service on the side. He'd never seen her so happy.

But what troubled him most was Freyen's perfect adaptation to this fringe existence. A silent reminder they still hadn't had the conversation about her past. Somehow, it had become entangled with the one about their future—the conversation they both seemed to avoid, as if speaking it aloud would break the fragile magic between them.

He sighed, realising he was now fully awake. Still, at least there was no shortage of work. The vampire attack had left the Fromryr vulnerable. Engagements across the underground had doubled. The Navarch was stretched to its limits, and Formaria's criminal class had been quick to capitalise. Unregistered miners, free traders, and scavengers looking to avoid the Church's new taxes all needed protection. With attacks on the rise, few crews wanted to travel without firepower. And as a top-of-the-line Navarch frigate, the *Anchorite* had firepower in buckets.

It wasn't bliss, but it was stable. And that gave him some comfort.

"Captain, you awake?" The terminal in his room vibrated with Mathias' gravelly voice.

Brazier swung his legs over the side of the cot. He planted his feet on the warm bronzite floor and pushed his mane of hair from his eyes. "Sadly," he said.

"Say again?" Mathias asked.

"I'm awake," Brazier repeated, loud enough to carry to the hex.

"Okay, you're going to want to come up and see this."

"See what?"

"We're getting a distress signal from a lander about a league out. Says their ship was destroyed."

Every trace of sleep fled him. He was suddenly wide awake.

"Destroyed?" he asked. "What was the ship?"

"Miner. Cauldron-class. Called Hayley's Gambit."

A weight settled on Brazier, thin as silk and heavy as dread. It was somewhere between instinct and premonition. That fleeting sense of bliss, he suddenly suspected, wouldn't return for a long time. Rubbing his eyes, he shook the thought away, ginger strands tumbling forward as he reached for his trousers.

"I'm on my way," he said.

Three
Kathryn

She could feel cold iron digging into her thighs, the backs of her arms, clamps encircling her wrists, ankles, and forehead. The only part of her body that moved was her chest. It rose and fell in shallow, panicked breaths.

Because she knew what was coming.

Instinctively, she felt it was only moments away. It wasn't death. She knew it wouldn't be death, but pain and change. Her change. And there was nothing she could do about it. The loss of control, the knowledge of the coming violation she was helpless against, obliterated every memory of her training.

She was an animal in a snare, consumed by her rapid, panicked inhalations and made worse by the heat. A heat so oppressive it suffocated her lungs, made bile rise in her throat, and sent sweat running down her neck to pool between her collarbones.

Then fire.

Blue columns of flame billowed at the corners of her vision. Ragged bursts so ferocious they momentarily stunned her, like a hundred furnaces drowning her out.

And the Mirrovinjin stepped into view, a grotesque mimicry of the human form. An open wound split the centre of its forehead, blistering and festering with black corruption. Its eyes were sunken in dark pits, the sclera yellow, the veins writhing like eels in a bleached swamp. Its teeth were jagged and blackened with rot.

But it was the ravine down its skull, and the thought of it

bearing down upon her, close enough for her to smell the decay, that made her fight against the restraints. She gritted her teeth, tried to turn her head.

But the Mirrovinjin stopped before her. And then turned.

Into her vision stepped the one-eyed elf.

Cruelly handsome, the line of Isdria Laanorath's mouth bore its own version of the Mirrovinjin's corruption. Those perfect red lips, glistening with a kind of sneering malice that always made Kathryn want to spit in his face, to kick, to bite, to punch.

Then a shape drifted across her horizon, a black behemoth that dwarfed all other thoughts, making her feel small and powerless. Its hull was a latticework of ruts and crevasses, jagged trenches pitted with spikes and snares: a hell ship, trailing wisps of smoky abhorrence.

From within its trenches, Fromryr writhed and screamed. Their bodies were pinned to the hull, their flesh grey with death, kept alive only by the ship's dark sorcery.

All she wanted was to disappear into the iron chair, to become insignificant. But the hulking form of black death was inescapable, and its presence struck such violent fear through her that her limbs went numb.

She was unable to fight and unable to flee. Consumed by panic, she writhed and thrashed against her restraints. Drawing on her rage, she screamed. She screamed so hard it drove the fear and revulsion from her veins, drowned out the gyranic bursts, and eclipsed everything until there was only darkness.

She noticed her breathing first, the slow, deep inhalations. Then she felt the damp cool of her back and legs. The darkness turned charcoal, then grey, as her eyes adjusted to the silver light of her quarters.

She rolled onto her side, sheets tangled around her, clinging to her skin, and pushed herself upright. Veers' vial sat on the knee-high table in the centre of the room, the corrupted hex almost indistinguishable in the low light. Next to it lay the ampule, a sliver of translucent Veskanca pooled in the bulb. Watching it glint, she wanted to smash it against the wall, to watch it shatter, to make a mess.

Instead, she drew a deep breath and let her body feel the sweat cooling her skin.

Whether the hallucination had been triggered by the Veskanca, like so many medicines before their cure, or by the absence of her regular formula, she didn't know. *But if you've played me, Veers*, she almost said aloud, *there's no abyss deep enough in all of Formaria that could hide you from me.*

She kicked off the sheets and rose from the cot, making her way to the bathing room adjoining her chamber. Dark grey walls enclosed a small hexagonal space. A grey sink was set into one wall, a grey toilet against another, ceiling jets protruding just above a shallow depression in the floor. They were all as immaculate as the day they were built. The only thing that wasn't Formarian was the mirror above the sink.

Once upon a time, Kathryn would've thought that an endlessly wonderful mystery. An ancient forgotten race that had needed bathing rooms and toilets perfectly fitted for Fromryr, but no mirrors?

But mysteries were no longer things to marvel at. Now, they were to be ignored or distrusted.

She shovelled a fist-sized diamond of ice from a bucket, then tipped it onto a waist-high platform with a cross-hatch of thin channels. The shards hissed and simmered, then melted. A blue-white pulse ran down the platform, along the floor, and up the wall. She stepped into the depression and turned the wall nozzle. Magically heated water sprayed from the jets above.

As it washed the night's sweat from her skin, she walked herself through the steps she'd need to carry out Veers' plan, counting them like a banker counting Vidicks with the utmost concentration. She had a focus so sharp there was no room for her mother's voice to slip in, no room for doubt or second-guessing.

First: a distraction in the Custodia command centre, allowing her to corrupt the network unnoticed.

Then: lying to the Captain, persuading her to redirect all Custodia officers to a fabricated gang fight.

She would need to find the Dreggs brothers; only they could pull off the kind of diversion she needed at such short notice.

With the plan taking shape, she focused on the water heating her skin, not on how ugly the coming acts made her feel, or the judgment she could already feel brewing in the back of her mind.

#

The maintenance bay repair chambers sat directly below the hangar, surrounded by a maze of corridors and smaller shafts used for specialised repairs and transporting parts. They were the guts of the installation; antechambers and connecting rooms that most people would never see. They were cramped, hot, and stinking of scorched metal and cleaning fluid. But the solid grey walls, slick with sweat and oil, were strangely comforting, like a fortress surrounding her.

Still, she would've preferred a ship.

"Too much," Kathryn said, shaking her head at the dwarf. "Way too much."

Standing in a secondary repair chamber no larger than her bedchamber, Azomanda Dreggs crossed his bulky arms, his frown adding a fresh layer of wrinkles to his bald head. Even for a dwarf, he was massive. Muscles built from a life spent beating bronzite and hauling engines in and out of ships. And, from a life of petty violence and criminality.

"Now you said you wanted a diversion," he replied. "That's what we charge for a diversion."

His brother, Kazanda Dreggs, also crossed his arms and also frowned. If it weren't for Kazanda's braids, they would've been indistinguishable. Both shared a thick Harothellian accent, black beards, and bushy eyebrows. Their orange maintenance coveralls were rolled up to the exact same spot on their arms. Even the black Araknors tattooed on their necks were identical.

"Aye," Kazanda added, looking up at her. "That's the market rate, minus some for a friend."

"You're forgetting who you're talking to, Kaz," she said, then paused. A metallic screech rang from several chambers down, followed by the rhythmic pounding of hammers against bronzite.

"I know how much a diversion costs," she said, once the hammering stopped.

Azomanda snorted hard enough he may as well have blown his nose. "Noncy toncy fist-kissing," he said. "Bit of street theatre."

"That's all I need," she replied.

"Except it isn't," Azomanda countered.

"You want the rough and tumble in worm territory," Kazanda said. Then, with no indication he meant it: "No offence."

"None taken," Kathryn said. The slur referring to the Custodia's gold wyvern insignia didn't bother her, probably because she wasn't really Custodia.

"Anyway," Azomanda said, shooting his brother a look. "This isn't the street and they're not going to be playing around."

"They're going to mean business," Kazanda added. "Big risk for us."

"And the bigger the risk for us," Azomanda said, jabbing a finger at Kathryn's chest, "the bigger the cost for you."

"Alright," she said, raising both hands in placation. She knew she wouldn't get a better price at such short notice. "Twenty gold Vidicks."

"Plus thirty silver Knortes for the bailout," Kazanda added.

"Don't push your luck, Kaz," she said. "I'll be the one processing you. There's no need for bail. You don't need to worry about that."

Kazanda winked at his brother. "Worth a shot."

"Aye," Azomanda agreed. "Now come here, it's your turn."

"Don't try that on me," his brother snapped, suddenly serious. "It's your turn, not mine."

"What are you talking about?" Azomanda said, turning to face him and throwing up his hands in what Kathryn thought was a poor attempt at disbelief. "I did the one for Brazag."

"Our mother didn't push me out yesterday, brother," Kazanda said, jabbing a finger into Azomanda's chest. "Brazag was six jobs ago. The last one was the Kneldeirian tunnel runner outside the Blue Hammer."

"The Bountiful Vein," Azomanda corrected, his voice exasperated. "Who are you trying to fool? That wasn't the last one. The last one was—"

"We'll flip on it," Kathryn cut in, not entirely sure what they were arguing about but already losing patience.

"Sounds fair to me," Azomanda said.

"Only because it's your turn," Kazanda muttered.

"Crowns or crosses?" Kathryn asked before Azomanda could restart the debate.

"Crowns," they both said in unison.

Black void. She sighed and reached into her jacket pocket, pulling out a bronze Lycal. "Az—you're crowns," she said. "Kaz—you're crosses. No arguments."

Before either could respond, she flipped the coin. It spun in the air, she caught it in her right hand, slapped it onto the back of her left.

"Crowns," she said, looking up at the pair, half expecting another round.

"Well, deal's a deal," Azomanda said.

"Fair's fair," Kazanda agreed.

"But not the teeth this time," Azomanda added. "You know they're a pain to grow back."

"Cheek it is," Kazanda said. "Bit of nose to add some colour?"

"May as well," Azomanda replied.

"Ready?"

His brother took a deep breath and nodded. "Ready," he said. And just as the hammering started again, Kazanda began punching his brother in the face.

Once upon a time, Kathryn had been a Navarch commander at the helm of a warship, leading a crew who respected her. Now she was paying criminals to beat each other in the lower levels of a Cradle city. From where she'd been to where she was now, she'd fallen far and she'd fallen hard. But she would climb her way back up, even if it took everything she had.

She would be free of the abhorrence. She would command a ship again. She knew this to be true.

At the back of her mind, her mother's laughter rose sharp and mocking, drowning out the hammering, drowning out the beatings.

Four
Brazier

The lander looked like a beetle with a broken leg. Brazier didn't think he'd ever actually seen a beetle with a broken leg. But, he decided, this was what it would look like. Its front aft thruster was bent inward at an odd angle, the disc devoid of gyre light. Occasionally it would dip before righting itself, as if it were limping, just like a beetle with a broken leg.

"Give it to me again," he said to Matthias.

The navigator knelt in the pit, head cocked. One of the command terminal's wells trembled. The girl's voice trembled with it, quick, distressed, and out of breath.

"My name is Ariadne Ambertine. Our ice miner, Hayley's Gambit, was attacked and destroyed by an unknown enemy ship. We are requesting immediate aid. I repeat, our ship has been destroyed, and we are requesting immediate aid."

Brazier found himself glaring at the hex, as if staring long enough would somehow make what he'd heard make sense. *Destroyed*. There was no mistaking it. She'd said destroyed.

The voice echoed with a familiar desperation. It reminded him of the last time he'd faced a distress call. His brother's final moments clawed their way to the surface of his conscience, the old wound torn open afresh. And yet, he was fairly certain he was considering charging off into the black again. Apparently, some lessons he refused to learn.

There had been maybe fifteen incidents in the past century where a Fromryian ship was actually destroyed.

Perhaps a third occurred during the vampire attack, and in all those cases, the captains had overloaded the core, taking the enemy with them. Just like his brother had.

The rest happened during the last Heiron campaign, which, according to his brother, had involved drake battalions, skavriin breachers dropping from tunnel ceilings, or entire warbands of witches. Or all of them combined. Other ships didn't destroy ships, because their enemies, for all their might, didn't possess ships.

The Mirrovinjin, and on occasion a goblin warband, might commandeer a Fromryian vessel. But they never got far.

They literally, never got far.

It took navigators years to master the complex chemistry of a ship's hex network and gyranic systems. As far as the Fromryr could tell, their enemies' genetic makeup lacked the specific variant of gyranic sorcery required to pilot large ships. At best, they could achieve what a non-magical Fromryr could: pilot a lander through a haze, and even that took years of flight school.

That meant *Hayley's Gambit* had been destroyed by another Fromryian ship, a thought that nearly made Brazier laugh. Even in the rare moments of civil conflict, there were lines they didn't cross. A tacit understanding lived deep in the Fromryian consciousness, so ingrained even the worst criminals abided by it.

Destroying a ship was like amputating a limb. It was an act of self-mutilation that threatened the people's collective survival. Everyone lost when ships were destroyed, so you didn't do it.

Except now, someone had.

"What other ships are in the area?" Brazier asked, knowing it was a futile question. Acting as security for the mining op, they'd been monitoring their surroundings for hours.

"There aren't. Just us and the Atache," Matthias said.

Brazier glanced at the hex well to his left, showing a sculpt of their frigate floating above the tunnel floor, with fifty miners scattered beneath it. That complicated things.

As if reading his mind, Matthias added, "They're not going to like it if we leave."

"Who said anything about leaving?" Brazier replied.

"You did," Matthias said, voice like smouldering embers. "In your mind."

Brazier was about to retort when the nav deck doors slid apart and laughter rolled in like a wave. Switch entered first, her usual black coveralls unbuttoned just enough to reveal an oil-smeared white shirt. Freyen followed, boots soft on the deck, her curls still damp from bathing. She wore slim-cut leather trousers, a forest-green shirt, and the brown jacket she'd picked up last time they docked in Calaxis.

Apparently they could read his mind too. One look at him, and their laughter vanished like air escaping a chamber. Freyen met his gaze with quiet concern.

"We have a problem," he said as they joined him around the command terminal. "Matthias, run the message again."

Ariadne Ambertine's voice called out again from the hex. When it ended, Brazier said, "Other than the Atache, we're the only ship in range."

"Have they contacted us?" Freyen asked.

"Nope," Matthias said, walking barefoot to stand across from Brazier. "Probably waiting for us to make the call."

"One question," Switch said, staring at the hex the same way Brazier had. "When was the last time a ship destroyed another ship?"

"Six hundred years ago," Brazier said. "House Kastrian blew the core in House Strigori's cruiser." He'd memorised the tale at the Navarch academy. It was both history lesson and cautionary tale. There was a reason those two houses no longer existed.

"Precisely," Switch said. "That not a little odd to you?"

"It's especially odd to me," Brazier replied. "And all the more reason to render aid."

Freyen twirled a damp strand of hair between her fingers. "Can we confirm their ship was destroyed?"

Matthias shook his head. "I didn't pick up a gyre spike."

"Then how are they close enough for us to pick up the distress beacon?" she asked.

"My guess: they burned long and hard getting away," Matthias said. "Probably on their last reserves."

But Brazier understood what she was getting at, and he wasn't convinced.

"If I were setting a trap," he said, "I wouldn't claim to have been in the sort of engagement that hasn't happened in half a millennium."

"I was thinking more that whatever got them might still be out there," she said. Then, hesitantly, "Last time we answered a distress call…"

She trailed off, her eyes edged with caution and concern.

"Last time, we didn't have a spire-class battle frigate," Brazier said, a little harder than he meant to. "If there's something nasty out there, we can outfight it or outrun it."

"I'm all in favour of a little ship-to-ship action," Matthias said. "But last I checked, we were trying to keep a low profile." He added, "On account of being fugitives."

"And on account of the illegal security services we're providing, for illegal mining ops, in our illegally commandeered gyre ship," Switch said.

"Changes nothing," Brazier said. "They don't need to know who we are or what we're doing here."

"And once we pick them up?" Matthias said. "What's your plan? Not like we can drop them at the nearest installation."

"We take them to Calaxis," Brazier said. "Karenna will get us in without alerting Spire command, like she always does."

That was life now: relying on criminal friends just to find a place to dock.

"And what are we telling the Captain of the Atache?" Switch asked.

"That we're answering a distress call," Brazier said. "Because it's our duty as citizens of Formaria and as people with common decency."

"Times like these," Switch muttered, "I'm glad you're the Captain, Captain."

Brazier resisted a sigh. The *Atache's* captain, Rendick Fowler, was short-tempered, ill-mannered, and, Brazier suspected, half-mad. This would not be a pleasant conversation.

"Arm up," he said to Freyen and Switch. "Just because we have the Anchorite doesn't mean we take chances."

They gave him curt aye, sirs and left for the fuselage.

"Matthias," Brazier said, "tether me to the Atache."

"I am going to enjoy this," the dwarf muttered, returning to the pit.

One of the wells gave a single pulse, fell flat, then vibrated with Fowler's voice: "Veranquis, you better not be about to do what I think you're about to do."

#

"Vector of approach?" Brazier asked.

"We'll be coming down on top of them," Matthias said.

"Let me know when you get a read on the lander."

A moment of silence followed, as Brazier, Freyen, and Switch all watched the *Anchorite's* hex sculpt descend bow-first, threading through the narrow shaft. Its thruster arms looked like insectoid feelers, groping at the rock around them while Matthias reoriented the ship around looming deposits and jagged protrusions.

"Got it," Matthias said. "Four gyre signatures. If we're going to do this, we better move fast. They've got less than five percent reserves."

"Can they land?"

"Sure," Matthias said. "Not in one piece, though. It's half a league drop. And that's not even the bottom."

"We're doing this in the air, then," Brazier said. Then: "You can do that, right?"

In their short time together, Brazier had learned to trust Matthias' uncanny ability to coax the *Anchorite* into manoeuvres that defied the normal rules of flying. Still, linking two ships mid air was something even seasoned pilots avoided.

"You really got to ask?" Matthias replied, and even from behind, Brazier could tell he was smiling.

"Then tether me to the lander," Brazier said.

The well pulsed beside him.

"Lander crew of Hayley's Gambit, are you receiving?"

There was a beat of silence, followed by a familiar female voice, hurried and breathless: "We're here! Yes, thank the abyss."

"Is this Ariadne Ambertine?" Brazier asked.

"It is. Who's this?"

"Navarch intelligence," he said, hoping the phrase would shut down any follow-up questions. "We're above you and pulling alongside. When we give the signal, open your hatch."

"Wait," Ariadne said. "Wait a minute. You want to do this in the air?"

"You're about to drop into the abyss," Brazier said. "It's this or the black."

She must have turned from the terminal. Her voice dropped to a murmur: "They're coming up alongside us." Then louder: "Okay. Alright. Tell us when."

"Matthias?" Brazier prompted.

"Just bringing her around now."

On the hex, the *Anchorite* dipped out of the shaft into the main tunnel, rotated 180 degrees, and brought its stern in line with the lander's hatch.

"We'd better go welcome our new guests," Freyen said.

Brazier nodded. A mechanical shunt echoed through the ship.

"Fuselage ramp is down," Matthias said. "Tell them to open their hatch."

"Ariadne," Brazier said, "open your hatch."

Through the hex, he heard the lander door open, then a distant voice: "Go—go on!"

A pause.

"They're all aboard," Matthias confirmed.

Brazier heard the ramp close with another soft shunt.

"Nicely done," he said. "I'm going to say hello."

In the fuselage, the survivors of the *Gambit* wore the fevered expressions of people still caught in a nightmare. Their eyes darted between Switch and Freyen, trying to convince themselves they were safe. A gnome, a dwarf, and two human women were all covered in sweat that made their skin glisten beneath the blue lighting. Three wore striped red-and-purple gambesons. The fourth was a woman in purple enginator's coveralls.

They were arguing.

No, Brazier realized, they were arguing with Switch.

"Listen," said the woman in purple, her fists trembling with panic. "We need to get out of here now."

From her voice, Brazier knew it was Ariadne. A foot taller than Switch and taller still than the other woman, a deep V of sweat had stained the front of her coveralls. Her shoulder-length black hair clung damp to her neck and temples, framing a face that was almost elven, with eyes the colour of honey. It was a face many human men, and probably a few Ilvalien and Kneldierian males, would find attractive. But right now, that face was drawn and stricken with terror.

"You don't understand," she said, voice cracking. "Whatever attacked us is still out there."

Freyen raised her palms in a calming gesture, her voice gentle, like speaking to a frightened child. "You're safe now. We've searched the area, there's nothing out there."

"And we're not going anywhere until we refuel that lander," Switch added.

"Please!" Ariadne begged. "There's no time. We need to warn the Navarch!"

"Ariadne," Brazier said, stepping beside Freyen, keeping his tone level. "Our navigator's been scanning the area for the past hour. The hex shows empty tunnels for leagues. There's nothing out there."

"That's what it showed us," the dwarf said, his east Formarian accent heavy with disbelief. The others nodded frantically. "There was nothing on the hex, then it just appeared, half a mile off."

Brazier exchanged a look with his crew. They all knew things could hide from the hex. But this was a ship. As far as they knew, the *Anchorite* was the only vessel with stealth capabilities.

Unless someone else had it now. But even then, why

attack another ship?

"Why would a Fromryian ship attack a mining vessel?" Brazier asked.

Ariadne blinked. Her desperation gave way to stunned confusion.

"It wasn't one of ours," she said. "It was Mirrovinjin."

Switch's expression transformed all at once: forehead wrinkling, nose crinkling, mouth twisting into a scowl. "Mirrovinjin can't pilot our ships," she said, almost insulted by the idea.

Ariadne shook her head. "They weren't piloting one of ours. They have their own."

Her words hit like a slap. Brazier felt the idea rise in his mind, as if it had always been there: *They've found the shipbuilding installation.*

Looking at Switch and Freyen, he saw the same fear dawning behind their eyes. But that couldn't be. Even if the Mirrovinjin had found the installation, how could they build something so quickly?

Unless... there were other shipyards, and they had found those.

Before he could speak, Matthias' voice cut in from the terminal, sharp and tight:

"Captain, we've got company."

The dwarf's voice had lost all its usual humour. Brazier didn't like that.

"What kind of company?" he asked.

"Pretty sure it's the bad kind of company."

Brazier's heart thudded.

"Matthias," he said carefully, "I need you to be very specific about what you're seeing."

"I don't know how else to say it," Matthias replied. "But there's a Mirrovinjin ship heading straight for us."

Brazier felt a chill bloom in the warm fuselage.

"Get us out of here," he said. "Get us out of here now."

FIVE
KATHRYN

"I don't see how any of that was necessary," Kathryn said, as the lift to the Custodia command chamber slowed and the shimmering black-and-purple walls gave way to polished slate.

"Gotta look authentic," Azomanda said, wincing. One eye was already swelling shut, and a deep bruise had begun to bloom across the bridge of his nose.

"Why does only one of you get hit?" she asked.

"So we can do more jobs," Kazanda said. "And the anomancer doesn't charge us twice."

"Remember," Azomanda said, jabbing a thick finger at her, "you're playing along too. Gotta make it look real."

"Don't worry about me," Kathryn said, just as the lift doors opened into a corridor shaped like a semi-octagon. Like all Formarian architecture, it was composed of grey alloy tiling with narrow blue channels pulsing along the centre of the floor, ceiling, and walls. "I'll make it look real."

Directly opposite, a set of double grey doors led into the Custodia command centre. She stepped out of the lift and placed her hand in the hex terminal beside the entrance. In her mind, she gave her name, rank, command script, and reason for requesting entry. A subtle click at the base of her skull signalled that the request had been accepted—a sensation that always felt like a tight muscle releasing.

"Show time," she said, grabbing the dwarves by the backs of their collars. As the doors slid apart, Azomanda and Kazanda launched into their performance.

"You were the one who gave me the fabricator torch!" Azomanda bellowed, pretending to struggle in Kathryn's grip. His squat dwarven build made him easily twice as strong as the average human. That both brothers also spent most of their time lifting ship parts made the notion of her restraining them laughable. She hoped the Custodia officers would be too distracted by the noise to notice.

"Why would I give you a bloody fabricator for the outer hull, you brainless tunnel lump?"

"I said the inner bulkheads! I never said anything about the hull!"

"Well maybe you should've been paying attention before you used the thing!" Kazanda shouted back, letting Kathryn shove him through the doorway.

"Maybe you should've been paying attention when you gave it to me! That's a week's pay you lost us!"

"I lost us?" Azomanda roared, rounding on his brother. He jabbed a stubby finger into Kazanda's chest. "If it wasn't for our mother, I'd 'ave beaten you bloody!"

Kazanda shoved him. Azomanda grabbed the front of his shirt. Kathryn, still holding each by the collar, made a show of trying to pull them apart.

"A little help here!" she shouted.

The Custodias descended in a blur, five officers throwing themselves into the scuffle. One tackled Azomanda around the waist while another swept out his legs, the two of them slamming the dwarf to the floor with a thump.

"Says the dwarf who took the beating!" Kazanda yelled, his face pressed against the tiles as two dwarven officers locked manacles around his wrists.

"Get them into the cells!" barked Sergeant Ridger, a slab of a man with messy blond hair. He and two others hauled Kazanda upright and dragged him around the command terminal toward the doors at the far end of the chamber. Kazanda kicked out at the frame in a last act of defiance, but was promptly shoved through. Azomanda, with a Custodia arm hooked around his neck, was dragged after him, both dwarves still hurling curses amid the officers' grunts.

The moment the doors closed, Kathryn reached into her

coat and pulled out the vial. She uncorked it, held it over one of the command terminal's hex wells, then hesitated.

If Veers is wrong, she thought, *it's all over*. The network would flag the corruption, alert the nearest Constructii, and identify her as the one present at the time of the breach.

She would be caught.

But somehow, that risk felt smaller than the shame of the act itself. She was about to commit a criminal act for a smuggler who gave nothing to Formaria, who undermined the very laws that had kept her people alive. It ran against everything she believed in, everything she'd once stood for.

All to command a ship again.

But the thought of it, the vibration beneath her boots, the weight of the bronzite hull around her, the pulse of a living ship wrapped around her and her crew, nearly drowned out the guilt.

You were never good enough! her mother's voice rang out from the corners of her mind. *I knew you'd never be good enough!*

Her hand trembled.

Then she thought of the ship again, of home, and everything it meant to her.

You're right, Mother. But you never gave me any lessons for this.

With that, she tipped the vial. The black-and-silver filaments tumbled into the well like a spray of falling stars. They shimmered briefly, then vanished into the hex, indistinguishable from the rest.

She slid the empty vial back into her pocket just as the detention doors hissed open.

Ridger marched into the room, breathing hard. "Those two have more fight in them than a skavrinn tunnel brawler," he said, adjusting his black gambeson and smoothing down the gold wyvern on his chest.

"Thanks for taking them off my hands," Kathryn said, her heart still hammering in her chest. *Abyss*, she thought, *he could've walked in seconds earlier.*

"Always happy to lock those two up."

"Reckon they can cool off for the night," she said.

"They won't be going anywhere."

She nodded and made for the lift, knowing the hard part was still ahead. Inside, she inhaled slowly and tried to bring her heartbeat back under control.

The lift rose three levels, then moved horizontally. It deposited her into an empty antechamber. Blue channels were carved through the grey walls like a luminous crosshatch, converging in a triangular portal at the opposite end. It might've just been her nerves, but the chamber felt more like a prison cell than a reception room, reminding her that anyone the Custodia Captain didn't trust could be trapped here indefinitely. Whoever the Formarians had been, it seemed they'd shared the same fears their descendants did.

Kathryn stepped forward and placed her hand in the terminal, giving her name and command script. She felt only partially ridiculous for the wave of relief that washed over her when the portal accepted her entry and released her hand.

Captain Lauren Demina sat behind a dark grey desk of Formarian stone, hands cradling her forehead as she pored over a piece of parchment. She wore a collared black doublet with plain cuffs, grey buttons, and the gold Custodia wyvern stitched over her breast—a style Kathryn always thought perfectly conveyed the captain's austere professionalism.

Next to her elbow, a bronzite cup steamed with Kyora tea, wafting vanilla and bitter wood. The mushroom blend cost about a tenth of real tea imports, maybe even one twentieth, since the Fiondagaardian invasion of Ravinica.

Cloth banners bearing the Custodia wyvern and the Rosantz eagle hung from the walls, and a longsword in an orange-and-green animal-hide scabbard leaned in the corner. A pale blue haze flooded the room, creeping in from the embrasure that overlooked Ilantia's ground level and the forking tunnels leading to Omega and Lucretia. It was an enviable view, and not one usually afforded to a Custodia captain. Kathryn always wondered if it was a way of softening the blow, a kind of compensation for being tasked with maintaining law and order in one of Formaria's most crime-ridden cities.

"The system just notified me of an arrest," Demina said

without looking up. "Dreggs brothers are a waste of time. I thought someone would've mentioned that by now?"

"I was on my way to see you and found them causing trouble," Kathryn said casually, making it sound like a throwaway comment. "Thought I'd bring them with me."

Demina looked up. "You've got nothing to prove here, Stryker. I hope you know that."

She thought Kathryn was overcompensating by arresting the Dreggs brothers, and was trying to be nice about it.

"Just doing my job," Kathryn replied, knowing the guilt and shame she heard in her own voice were imagined. She stared somewhere over Demina's shoulder, not wanting to see the pity she was sure would be in her eyes, even if the woman meant well, in her abrupt and unsubtle way.

There was an awkward pause before Demina asked, "Any more episodes?"

She just had to ask, Kathryn thought. *No, no more episodes, Demina. Just a bad dream that felt horribly real, but I'm going to pretend it wasn't*—something she could almost convince herself of, because the real thing had been worse. Much worse.

Three months into her Ilantia posting, just as the grief of losing her former life had begun to fade, just as the other officers were starting to accept her, just as the abhorrence in her veins began to feel dormant, it had reminded her it wasn't.

It had been her fault.

Asked to join a two-day operation in Ilantia's lower levels, she'd forgotten the elixirs that kept her condition at bay. She might've gotten away with it, if the mission hadn't led them into local tunnels, stretching two days into four.

So focused on the task, so happy to be part of something that felt remotely like her navy days, she forgot she was sick at all. That was until she collapsed in the tunnels, frothing and convulsing so violently they had to evacuate her immediately. Unbeknownst to her, she'd babbled the entire flight back about secret ships and terrorist groups colluding with Formaria's enemies.

Recovering in Ilantia's vulnerum, she had begged

Demina not to report the incident to central command. For reasons still unclear, Demina had agreed. She'd saved Kathryn from an excruciating round of purification and probably the loss of her post.

But Kathryn had worked alone ever since. No matter how many arrests she made, the Custodia treated her like someone about to crack. Some looked at her like a dying infirmary patient. Most looked at her like an untrained evocator, liable to pull on too much gyranic force and explode, taking everyone else with her.

The isolation felt eerily similar to the solitude of command, except without the quiet respect or the unspoken bond of shared purpose. The part she missed most wasn't the control; it was the weight of decisions and the burden no one else could carry. Now, she was just responsible for herself, and she wasn't sure that was going all that well.

"Those days are far behind me," Kathryn said.

Demina gave her a smile that said she didn't buy that for a moment. "Then what do you need?"

"Got intel," Kathryn said, pushing the loneliness from her mind and summoning something closer to professional calm. "Agreiga Barons and the Void Born Collective are organising a skirmish to settle a territorial dispute."

Demina's smile disappeared and she was all business. "Where and when?"

Kathryn felt her shoulders relax. She might be seen as unstable, but her record still spoke for itself. Demina didn't question the intel, she just accepted it.

Too easily, Kathryn thought, shifting uncomfortably.

"Tomorrow night. Levels five and six."

"The Barons stick to the drinking holes near the eastern docks, and the Collective runs the gambling district. We'll have half of them in lockup by dawn," she said, snorting a mirthless laugh. "The black gall of these people—organising a war on my streets. They think they're untouchable."

"Problem there, Captain," Kathryn added quickly. "We can't move on them yet."

Demina's brow creased so hard it could have been etched into stone.

"This one's serious for both sides," Kathryn said, her heartbeat climbing. If she pushed too hard, Demina might start asking why.

"Word is, upper echelons will be in attendance."

"How upper?"

Two extra heartbeats now.

"Upper enough that it's worth letting this play out."

Demina stared at her over laced fingers, expression unreadable. *Too vague*, Kathryn thought. *Too presumptuous*.

"If that's true, they'll turn out in force," Demina said. "Full criminal complement."

Kathryn's pulse eased to only one extra beat again. The cold stare hadn't been for her.

"We'll need everyone we've got," she said, pressing the advantage.

Demina shot her a sharp look. For a moment, Kathryn thought she'd gone too far. But then the captain said, "You bet the black-damned abyss we will. Off-duty officers, patrols, dock security. The lot."

Kathryn nodded, hiding her relief. But Demina leaned back, her energy draining. She suddenly looked ten years older.

"This is not the time for this," she muttered.

Kathryn stood still, unsure what the remark meant, and afraid of saying anything that might change her mind.

Demina held her gaze, then said, "I know this is your find, and by all rights, you should take point. But I need you on something else."

The surprise stunned her, briefly. Then she thought: *Maybe this isn't so bad*. She didn't need to be at the skirmish; she just needed to make sure officers were pulled from the docks. Still, it was a shame. Cracking criminal skulls was always a bonding experience. She might've made a friend.

"What is it?"

Demina placed a hand into the well and mouthed something Kathryn couldn't hear. The hex filaments vibrated, rising into the floating sculpt of a young woman's head.

"Ariadne Ambertine. Fifth and youngest daughter of

Luanne and Marianne Ambertine. She's been missing six months."

"Ambertine?" Kathryn asked. "As in House Ambertine?"

Demina nodded. "Merchants out of Tia. Luxury foodstuffs, southeast trade lanes. Tied to House Angelaux."

Wealthy, Kathryn thought. If there was one thing Fromryians paid good coin for—if they had it—it was food that wasn't made from the same reconstituted mushroom as Demina's tea.

"And they misplaced a daughter?"

"Seems she ran off. Wanted to play explorer, jumping between free trader crews," Demina said. "The family humoured her for a while. Now they want her back."

"And what's that got to do with us?"

"She was last seen boarding a miner in Reantha. Ambertine pulled strings and got its flight path. It's inbound."

"Still don't see how that's our problem," Kathryn said, voice cooling. She knew where this was going and she didn't like it.

"We're to detain her and ship her home," Demina said. "And by we, I mean you."

"Since when does the Custodia accept private contracts?" Kathryn asked. "This is a kidnap job."

In her mind, Ariadne was a determined young woman who knew she was made for more than logistics. Kathryn felt an unjustifiably strong sense of empathy and protection toward her.

"Look around, Stryker," Demina said. "The vampire attack gutted Formaria's defences. Our best officers reassigned to the front. Half the fleet gone. Ecclessius coffers empty. We're on our own. We don't have the luxury of navy protocol. We take the Vidicks where we can get them. And right now, that's from Luanne Ambertine."

The heat in Kathryn's chest cooled fast. *Looks like I'm not the only one being pragmatic*, she thought. But it didn't make her feel better.

In her book, kidnapping was higher up the ladder of wrongdoing than helping smugglers. A lot higher.

It's all wrongdoing! her mother's voice shrieked. *That's all you're good for now!*

Kathryn tensed. To banish the voice, she blurted, "I thought we were getting reinforcements from the south?"

She hoped the rumour she'd overheard Ridger tell a pretty new Custodia wasn't just an excuse to flirt.

"We are," Demina said. "Someone decided to pull the whole squadron from the Gate south of Calanthis Major and reassign it to us and Kyor."

"No one's guarding the Gyre Gate?" Kathryn asked, stunned.

While mostly ceremonial, the Gyre Gates were always watched. Just in case.

"'Guarding' is generous," Demina said. "They're old soldiers who didn't save enough to retire. That's why none of them can do the job I'm giving you."

"Give it to Garlon or Bransig," Kathryn snapped. "They barely know Custodia from mercenary work."

"Perhaps," Demina said. "But their corruption doesn't put them in a coma."

The threat rang out like a blast of gyre light. Do this, or I'll report your condition. But before Kathryn could respond, Demina softened. "There's a lot riding on this. I need someone I can trust not to drop it over the edge."

And someone she could trust to stay silent. That was the real reason Kathryn was chosen. She had no leverage. She had no choice if she wanted to avoid purification.

"She'll be back playing lords and ladies before you know it," Kathryn said.

"Knew I could count on you," Demina said, smiling again. "Free trader is Hayley's Gambit. Scheduled arrival: tomorrow night, western docks. Let's bring Ariadne home."

Tomorrow night. Western docks.

All the feeling drained from Kathryn's limbs. That complicated things. Tomorrow night, the *Orphan Guyan* would also arrive at the western docks.

Of all places…

Veers would have people everywhere. They'd see her. They'd suspect. And they'd be right to.

Maybe if she was seen making an arrest, it could be dismissed as coincidence. But she knew better than to count on luck.

She'd have to explain to Veers that she was on a separate op, and one she hadn't chosen.

That was it. That's what she'd tell him.

It would muddy the waters, though, right when she needed them crystal clear.

"Problem, Stryker?"

"No problem, sir, I'll get it done."

Demina smiled and placed her hand into the well. Her eyes fluttered. The sculpt disintegrated and the hex fell back into the terminal.

"I've sent you everything we have on Ariadne. Maybe it'll help."

Then she went back to her parchment, dismissing Kathryn with silence.

So much for those options, Kathryn thought. And in her mind's eye, her mother's smirk returned, self-satisfied and seething.

There was no getting away from it.

SIX
BRAZIER

"You three, strap in," Brazier said to the *Gambit's* crew. To Ariadne: "Come with us."

He practically ran up the fuselage stairwell, Ariadne, Freyen, and Switch close behind. Their boots thudded on the metal rungs, punctuated by the double doors shunting open.

On the nav deck, the sight of the hex display stopped him so abruptly he nearly stumbled. The Mirrovinjin ship was enormous, easily the size of a Cauldron-class cruiser. But it was the shape that horrified him. An elongated, oval-like hull was pitted with shallow trenches and spiked protrusions, as if spears had been welded to its exterior. Its aft was made entirely of long, slim, curved fins extending outward, tapering to wicked points. They looked like a collection of sword blades, each easily twice the length of the hull itself. It resembled some twisted, mechanical squid.

Watching it, a sick dread stirred deep in his gut, a sensation he hadn't felt since losing his brother. For just a heartbeat, he felt powerless again.

He shoved the feeling aside. There was no time for weakness, not now.

"I've seen some ugly ships, but that," Switch said, pointing at the sculpt, "is just wrong."

On the hex display, the *Anchorite's* thrusters were angled behind it, the discs vibrating with so many grey and silver filaments they appeared twice their normal size. Matthias had rerouted all power to propulsion.

And it still wasn't enough. The Mirrovinjin ship was

gaining on them.

"Do you think the Mirrovinjin found—" Freyen started, glancing at Ariadne. But the girl didn't seem to notice; her gaze was locked on the display.

"We'll figure that out later," Brazier said. "Switch, if there's any way to make this ship fly faster, now would be a good time."

"I'll see what I can reroute from auxiliary," she said, darting back through the double doors.

Freyen's eyes snapped to Brazier, disbelief flickering across her face. He caught the question in her expression: *Are you sure?*

It was only a moment, but it made him hesitate.

"Get on the aft turrets," he ordered, stamping out his uncertainty. "With power rerouted, you'll need to take manual wield. As soon as they're in range, target the hull repeaters."

Freyen nodded, stepping around the other side of the command terminal. She placed her hands into adjacent wells and closed her eyes.

"Tell me everything about the ship," Brazier said to Ariadne. "How did it destroy the Gambit?"

She didn't respond. Eyes wide, shoulders drawn inward, she stared at the sculpt like it was tearing her apart.

"Ariadne," he said again, sharper this time.

Startled, her amber eyes snapped to his. Her hands shook. Her breathing came in short gasps.

"I need to know about the Mirrovinjin ship."

"Witches," she said. "They killed our navigator straight away. Blew through the hull. Then they got to the engines."

Brazier nodded slowly, hiding his shock.

The Formarians had designed gyre ships so that gyranic power flowed through them like blood. Navigators could shield themselves and the vessel with minimal use of ice reserves. Only multiple witches, or a powerful blood maiden could breach such a defence.

It happened, but rarely.

"Matthias," Brazier called.

"Watch out for the witches," the navigator growled. "Got

it."

Brazier glanced at the display. It wouldn't be long before the Mirrovinjin came into range and their witches started hammering the *Anchorite*. Or worse, they started hammering Matthias.

Switch's voice came through one of the wells. "Cap, I can give us maybe fifteen percent more power."

Even through the hex, he heard the hesitation.

"What's the problem?"

"I'll need to release the spatial anchor. Route its power straight to the thrusters."

The spatial anchor kept the ship's interior stabilised, ensuring the crew didn't get flung around during evasive maneuvers. Without it, any sudden movement would toss them like dice in a gambler's cup.

"Do it," Brazier said.

The effect was immediate. It felt like shedding armour. He stumbled, suddenly lighter, and caught himself on the edge of the command terminal. Ariadne and Freyen did the same.

On the display, the *Anchorite* accelerated, not by much, but enough to slow the enemy's approach. Still, the Mirrovinjin continued to close the gap in a steady, nerve-rattling crawl.

Brazier ignored the tension rising in his chest and plunged a hand into the nearest well.

"Scope out three-tenths," he said.

The sculpt expanded, zooming out to reveal the snaking network of surrounding tunnels.

"Scan south. Maintain scope aperture."

The sculpt rolled southward. Filaments on the left cascaded into the well like a waterfall, reformed on the right, and brought more tunnels into view.

They needed an escape route, probably a tertiary or quaternary shaft. It had to be something narrow enough that the Mirrovinjin ship couldn't follow them down, and one that didn't lead back to a primary tunnel where they'd be rediscovered.

The sculpt continued to roll. A secondary tunnel jutted

out like a bent arm but rejoined a main artery. Another shaft shot east, then southeast, before circling back to their current route.

Formaria's a maze. There has to be something...

He was so fixed on the display that Ariadne's voice made him jump.

"There," she said. "I've got one."

Brazier looked up. She'd activated a separate hex display in a smaller well. Instead of tracking horizontally, she'd brought up a vertical sculpt. It showed a shaft plunging straight down for miles, ending on the roof of a vast cavern. On the display, it looked like an axe wound, a long ravine with a single tunnel at its southern end, diving deeper into Formaria's depths.

There were no adjoining passages.

"Matthias, are you seeing this?" Brazier asked.

Instead of answering, the navigator growled. Short and gravelly, it was somewhere between a snarl and a groan. His arms were stretched out, muscles taut like rope. Sweat beaded at his neck, running in rivulets down his back.

Knowing what he'd see but needing confirmation anyway, Brazier placed his hand in the well.

"Track Anchorite."

The filaments shifted and reformed into the two ships. The gap was halved. Tiny needles launched from the *Anchorite's* repeaters, embedding in the enemy's hull or bouncing off and falling out of view.

In front of him, Freyen stood with her eyes shut, mouth a tight line. Her muscles twitched as she focused.

"Matthias," Brazier said again. "We have an exit. Two-tenths of a league ahead."

"Found it," the navigator muttered through clenched teeth.

Brazier connected to the engine chamber. He opened his mouth to relay the plan but a sudden barrage of metallic thuds slammed against the hull.

On the hex, the Mirrovinjin ship returned fire. Their volley was triple the size, launched from more repeaters than the *Anchorite* possessed.

The ship echoed with the impact. Brazier tore his gaze from the display.

"Switch," he said. "We have an exit. When I give the word, re-engage the anchor."

"Aye, sir."

Brazier pulled his hand free, leaving the connection open. Then the cabin lurched.

A sharp crackling hiss erupted outside. The floor dropped beneath him. He reached for the terminal, misjudged, and smacked his wrist against the edge, nearly falling.

He pulled himself up. Ariadne and Freyen were doing the same.

"What in the abyss was that?" Ariadne said, rubbing her ribs and pushing damp strands from her face.

"Second portside thruster," Brazier said, eyeing the hex. A bolt had pierced the disc, with more were wedged into the arm crook.

"Switch," he said. "Reroute any power going to the second portside thruster. It's done."

Switch responded with a string of expletives and a challenge for the Mirrovinjin to board the ship, only to be drowned out by another round of, *crack crack crack crack crack.*

"Black abyss," Freyen muttered, arms tensed, eyes still closed. On the display, Brazier watched as the remnants of one aft repeater slid down the hull, crumbling away.

At least it wasn't a thruster, he thought, a flicker of relief rising, only to curse it as premature a second later.

Another wave of bolts struck the hull. A sharp crack echoed from their aft, and the deck lurched again.

He and Freyen managed to stay upright. Ariadne wasn't so lucky. She hit the ground with a thump, groaning as he helped her up.

"Something's wrong," she said.

He opened his mouth to ask what hurt but then realised she wasn't talking about herself.

The nav deck was sloping. It was subtly, but unmistakably tilting toward the bow.

He checked the display.

The rear starboard thruster was gone. Its disc had been obliterated. The ship, their home, was being torn apart, piece by piece. And every crack in the hull felt like a blow to the heart.

It wouldn't matter, he told himself, eyes flicking to the shaft ahead. They weren't far now. They were going to make it. They were.

"Switch?" he called out.

"I'm here," she replied. Then, "Just about."

"Get ready with the anchor. We're almost there."

"Ready when you are, Cap."

"Matthias," Brazier said. "Tell us when."

But there was no response.

Brazier looked up. Smoke curled from the tops of the navigator's outstretched arms. His black shirt was drenched with sweat and clung to his back. He was trembling, every muscle pulled so tight he looked carved from stone.

Back on the hex, the shaft was coming up fast. They were hurtling toward it at breakneck speed.

Too fast, Brazier thought. They were either going to overshoot it, or crash straight into the wall.

"Matthias!" he shouted, panic sharpening his voice.

A growl rumbled from deep in the navigator's chest. "I heard you the first time," he rasped.

Thank the endless black void.

"Switch?" Brazier barked.

"Still ready, Cap."

Brazier gripped the command terminal, tension mounting as the shaft drew closer—half the distance now, then the length of his wrist, then his hand, then his little finger. They were almost there.

"Now!" Matthias roared.

"Now, Switch!" Brazier shouted.

Even with the spatial anchor engaged, Brazier, Freyen, and Ariadne were slammed against the terminal as Matthias pulled the ship to a jarring halt. At the same time, he spun the *Anchorite* 180 degrees and dove the bow downward.

They shot into the shaft, bow-first, a hail of bolts skittering off their aft plating as the Mirrovinjin ship sailed overhead.

Matthias' arms dropped to his sides. His head sagged forward, shoulders heaving. Smoke cloaked him, thick and acrid, filling the nav deck with a bitter, oily stench that clawed at Brazier's throat.

He swallowed hard. "Freyen," he said, hurrying to the navigator's side. He knelt, gripping his friend's shoulder. "We've got Tutela Animata in the vulnerum."

The elixir would help mitigate the damage from Aeturnic sorcery. But judging by the smoke curling off him, Matthias would need more than a precautionary dose. He'd need an anomancer.

"On it," Freyen said, and dashed from the deck.

"Those four-armed freaks are running with a whole damned cadre," Matthias muttered. He sat back on his heels, then forced himself upright with a grunt of pain. "Good ones, too." He met Brazier's gaze. "They've got something new. Something different."

"Different how?" Ariadne asked. Her face remained fierce, but her eyes were glassy with exhaustion.

"Don't know," Matthias said, shaking his head. "But it's powerful."

Not only did the Mirrovinjin possess stealth ships, they now wielded stronger sorcery. A crawling dread began to rise in Brazier, only held back by the adrenaline still coursing through his system.

"Not powerful enough," he said, with more confidence than he felt. "You good?"

The navigator offered a faint smile. "Still alive, aren't I? Ship's not looking pretty, though. Internal gyre system's fried. Half the reductors are spent."

"Switch might finally have something to fix, then," Brazier said. Even to him, the attempt at levity sounded hollow. He masked it by clapping a hand on Matthias' shoulder. It burned with feverish heat.

"That was some serious flying."

Behind them, the nav deck doors hissed open. Freyen stepped through, a small vial in her hand. But before she could round the terminal, she froze, her eyes locked on the hex display. A look of alarm swept across her face.

Brazier turned to follow her gaze.

They were halfway down the tertiary shaft, but that wasn't what had stopped her.

A cruiser, so massive it could only be Maw-class, was slinking out from the tunnel at the cavern's southern edge. Sleek and predatory, its slim hull flared into curved midsection flanges. A circular command spire rose from its dorsal frame, and five thruster arrays widened its rear like a clawed tail. Two smaller frigates flanked it, like hatchlings swimming in their mother's shadow.

Brazier's heart sank. The brief relief he'd felt froze solid.

Matthias dropped to his knees, palms splayed wide above the hex pit. Filaments swirled beneath his hands.

"They know we're here," he said.

"Is it Fromryian?" Ariadne asked.

Matthias nodded. Ariadne exhaled in relief, her shoulders relaxing.

"They're requesting a tether," he added.

Brazier stiffened. He knew what was coming and there was nothing he could do to stop it.

The memory of his brother's death flickered in his mind. Those final, helpless moments when he could do nothing.

"On the hex," he said.

The well beside him pulsed. A male voice, deep and stern with a gravelly edge, filled the nav deck: "Battle frigate Shian Anchorite, this is Captain Philip Sourant of the Sovereign Eclipse. Your ship's gyre signal is registered as pirated, and its last known crew listed as fugitives. Float down to our position and prepare to be boarded. Noncompliance with these orders will result in your destruction."

They were caught.

And again, Brazier could do nothing to stop it.

SEVEN
KATHRYN

Ilantia's western docks were a smuggler's paradise, Kathryn decided, as she looked out over the sprawl of berths, cargo lanes, and refuelling stations.

Miners, merchants, and free traders became indistinguishable from dock workers, hawkers, and Navarch crews the moment they stepped onto the silvered alloy platforms. They moved between lines of bronzite crates, either fed into or disgorged from the gyre ships' open feranium bays.

A dropped sack of Vidicks, an extra crate in the manifest, or a whispered word from a persuasive trader to a tired official could all slip past unnoticed. Everything was drowned beneath the winding whir of gyre thrusters and the thousand Fromryian voices merging into a hive-like thrum.

And that was to say nothing of the dock's layout. It connected directly with the city. There were no lifts, no gates, no junctions. It was impossible to tell where the docks ended and the city's concourse began. It was a nightmare to police. Something would always get through.

Thinking like a criminal, Kathryn. Is this how it begins?

She pushed the thought away. She told herself she was just tired, and she was. It had been another night of blue fire, hideous ships, and the one-eyed elf, but worse. She'd woken dazed, half her mind still in the dream, skin burning, the air in her quarters so tight it felt as if the nightmare had bled into her waking world.

"Everything alright, Palatine?" the dock master asked.

"Like a surface sunrise," she replied, smiling at the gnome. "Just been a long day, and that dock's making it feel longer."

"Can we help you find something?"

She shook her head. "Routine flight check and inspection."

The way his face relaxed told her he believed the lie, or didn't care enough to question it.

"She's all yours, then," he said.

Kathryn reached into a nearby hex well and requested the docking schedule for the next three hours. The grey-white fog of the well turned into a rolling script. *Slower*, she thought, and the script crawled down her mind's eye at half speed: mostly miners and haulers, a cruiser making an overnight resupply, and the occasional personal transporter returning from Thela.

Then: *Hayley's Gambit*, Eron Davonati listed as its captain. Expected arrival: fifteen minutes.

Then it scrolled off her mind's eye.

More ships and more captains followed. Then, fifteen minutes later: *Orphan Guyan*, Shyora Long at the helm.

Kathryn severed the connection and pulled her hand from the well.

She'd follow the *Gambit's* crew when they docked, trail them to wherever they were staying, then isolate Ariadne. There would be no confrontation on the pier. It was too exposed, and without Custodia backup, too risky. It would be better to wait. Most free traders in Ilantia ended up in the watering holes. It would be easier to separate Ariadne there.

And with luck, she'd be gone before the *Orphan* arrived. If Veers' people saw her leave following another crew, they'd assume it was routine. There'd be no confusion, no suspicion, no loss of trust. Their arrangement would continue, and she'd get the rest of the Veskanca.

Her heart fluttered at the thought, while darker doubts pressed at the edges of her mind like a magical charge in a sealed chamber.

Would Veers accept that? Would he believe her?

Then, from deep within that pressure, her mother's voice

rose, venomous and seething.

I knew you wouldn't be good enough... A captain never second-guesses. A captain creates options. She doesn't rely on hope.

Then, something new.

A captain doesn't put faith in criminals!

Kathryn clenched her eyes shut and dug her nails into her palms, driving the voice back down where it belonged. When she opened them, the dock master was watching her, brow furrowed.

But before he could speak, a female dwarf called from across the terminal: "Sir, I've got the Fortune of Orias tethered. Captain says he wants immediate berth and access to an unloading bay."

"When's the Orias scheduled?"

"Not for another twenty minutes."

"Everyone wants to jump the queue," the dock master muttered, heading over to the dwarf's terminal and leaving Kathryn alone with the view.

A transporter zipped past the tunnel mouth, its gyre thrusters flickering like a cluster of tiny blue stars before vanishing into the black. Three miners emerged one after the other, their bronzite hulls gleaming like sea beasts surfacing from the depths, ponderously slow and triumphant with their catch. They descended lazily toward their berths. All three looked spire- or cradle-class.

Five more minutes passed. There was still nothing that fit the *Gambit's* description.

Kathryn's eyes narrowed. She scanned the tunnel for signs of movement, then checked the docks again, jumping from one miner to the next, trying not to let the doubt creep in, trying not to let her mother creep in.

Maybe the *Gambit* had already arrived? Maybe she'd misidentified it? Or perhaps it had changed docks at the last moment.

She pulled up the schedule again. *Hayley's Gambit* was still listed and still in-bound.

But it was late.

She removed her hand from the well and waited, resisting

the urge to pace. It would be just her luck that the two ships arrived at the same time, on the same pier and docked side by side.

As the minutes dragged on, she crossed her arms. Then her foot started tapping. Realising it, she planted her feet firmly and fixed her gaze beyond the docks. She could already imagine the conversation:

What were you doing at the docks? Veers would ask, the 't' sharp as always.

On another op, she'd say. *Just a coincidence.*

Very likely, he'd reply. *Are you sure you weren't observing my operation?*

And that was exactly how it would go, because just then, the gleaming hull of a miner emerged from the tunnel.

She knew, instinctively, before it was fully visible. The shape alone told her that this was Veers' ship.

It formed from the darkness: short-nosed, a wide midsection, and an even bulkier stern. It looked like some sort of surface insect, its gyre thrusters sprouting like antennae.

Endless void, you're ugly.

She found herself staring, unable to pull her eyes from its slow descent. The thrusters flared in unison, and the ship hovered just above its berth.

Kathryn slipped her hand into the terminal, confirmed the ship's signature. It was the *Orphan Guyan*. The *Gambit* still showed as overdue.

She disconnected and turned her full attention back to the miner. She should have looked away. She should have kept her eyes on the tunnel, watching for the *Gambit*. But she couldn't. The *Orphan* pulled at her, its presence almost hypnotic. It was too enticing to ignore.

You don't know what's good for you!

But her body seemed to. Her heart kicked into a quick, insistent rhythm. A rising apprehension filled her chest, warning her to turn away, to ignore the ship, to not do anything stupid.

This doesn't matter to you, she told herself, echoing the warning.

Then the crew appeared from beneath the hull.

There were eight in total, two in black mining gambesons while the rest wore long brown travelling cloaks. The gambeson-clad men were clearly human, with brutish, spade-like faces and cropped hair.

Of the six in cloaks, only two pulled back their hoods, revealing aquiline features and shoulder-length hair: Elves.

They do not matter to you.

But her eyes weren't listening. They stayed fixed on the group as they marched down the pier.

She saw now that of the four still hooded, one kept to the centre. The others flanked them, crowding in protectively. The figure in the middle held their head low, shoulders slumped, moving with a pained, unnatural gait.

But it was the one at the front that kept drawing her gaze. The way they moved, confident and authoritative, felt disturbingly familiar—unnervingly so, as if she knew them. And yet, something about them felt... wrong.

Without thinking, she slid her hand back into the well.

Track Hayley's Gambit and crew arrival. Send updates to my quarters. She gave her command script, restricted access to Palatine-only, and disconnected.

The crew reappeared from behind a repeater tower, heading toward the main docks.

Compelled now, instincts overriding every rational warning, Kathryn moved. She shot down the steps, rounding the base of the command tower, boots thumping against the tiling.

All that mattered was finding out who the leader was. There was something wrong about him. She needed to know what. She could deal with the consequences later.

The sounds around her, her mother's laughter, maybe, or just the ever-present hum of the docks, blurred into the thrum inside her skull.

She slipped between a line of crates, then around an enginator team inspecting a damaged Constructii, before passing a group of Navarch officers arguing with an inspection team over manifests and schedules.

Up ahead, the *Orphan's* crew pushed toward the

concourse. Kathryn angled her route to intercept. She picked up her pace, hoping to get far enough ahead to find a vantage point, somewhere she could watch without being seen.

Her eyes darted across the concourse.

There, a group of miners huddled around two maintenance officers. One of the officers had her hand in a terminal; the other logged the report on parchment. The *Orphan's* crew would pass right beside them. Kathryn could position herself on the edge, hidden among the miners.

Coat whipping at her ankles, she moved quickly, careful not to draw attention. She slid into position next to the group. No one noticed. The miners were too absorbed in the damage report, eyes fixed on the growing repair bill.

Kathryn pretended to study it too. She angled her body toward the officers, mimicking their stance. But her gaze stayed fixed on the docks, watching from the corner of her eye as the *Orphan's* crew drew closer.

The two human men came first. They were tall and broad-shouldered, their jaws set in stern lines. The leader remained obscured by a group of soldiers ahead of them.

Then the *Orphan's* crew slowed, pausing to let a line of miners carrying repeater magazines pass. The gap widened, and through it, she glimpsed the one in the middle.

The prisoner.

She was certain of it now. He had a black beard, unwashed skin, and unfocused eyes sunken in dark rings like he hadn't slept in weeks.

Is that your cargo, Veers?

But she barely registered him. Her attention snapped back to the leader, the one her body recognised, even if her mind refused to.

The group was nearly upon her.

Her eyes jumped from figure to figure, searching for the face. The last of the miners passed. The *Orphan's* crew cleared the crowd. There was nothing between them now.

And then the leader turned.

He looked up, straight ahead.

She saw the face beneath the hood, and her heart slammed into her throat.

Her breath caught. The sweat running down her spine turned to ice. She forgot the *Gambit*. She forgot Veers, forgot Demina, and forgot the Veskanca. Even her mother's laughter and the thrum of the docks disappeared.

Because beneath that hood, framed in shadow, jutted a prominent jaw and a sneer she knew all too well.

She couldn't move. Her breath came in shallow gulps.

It can't be. It just can't be.

But she knew the red kerchief. She knew the faint scar running beneath it. She knew the remaining eye that glared at the world with unrelenting contempt.

It was the elf responsible for the rot in her blood, the reason she could no longer command a ship, the reason her entire world had collapsed.

It was the elf who haunted her nightmares.

It was Isdria Laanorath.

Eight
Brazier

The *Eclipse's* interrogation chamber was four equilateral bronze walls and a ceiling slanted at a 45-degree angle. A deep blue channel cut through the floor's centre, glowing faintly and casting Brazier's shadow across the solid bronzite desk he sat behind. With no terminal, the desk dominated the space, making the room feel cramped and oppressive.

If someone had asked him to imagine an interrogation chamber, this is exactly what he would have pictured. Just as the man who stepped into it was exactly what he would have imagined if asked to describe an interrogator.

Tall and oddly muscular, he filled out his blue military doublet with crisp precision. His receding hairline was slicked back over pale, angular features that bordered on brutish, and his dark eyebrows brooded over even darker eyes. They regarded Brazier with a mix of indifference and amusement.

He sat opposite, and the insignia on his chest caught Brazier's attention. It was a thumb-sized silver diamond overlapping a spearhead, marking him as a lieutenant.

Still holding Brazier's gaze, the man reached into his breast pocket and retrieved a vial no longer than a little finger. The black substance inside gleamed oily under the chamber's blue light. With a soft pop, he uncorked it and downed it in one smooth motion. His pupils dilated.

Vide Omnius, commonly called *see all* by Navarch

sailors, heightened visual and auditory perception, and gave a black hell of a hangover once it wore off.

"It seems your bloodline is treasonous," the lieutenant said, smiling faintly. His tone was almost friendly.

"Excuse me?" Brazier said.

"You are Brazier Veranquis. Brother to Torquen Veranquis, the disgraced Gyre Star Admiral. Son of Edmerin Veranquis, traitor to Formaria. Correct?"

Heat flared in Brazier's chest. "Where are my crew? And the crew of the Gambit?" he said. "My navigator needs immediate medical attention."

"Answer the question. Are you Brazier Veranquis?"

"Yes," Brazier replied.

The lieutenant held his gaze, pupils dilating slightly.

Then, without breaking eye contact: "Large holding in Thendergaarden. Balasque district. Family mining business. Owned mining fleet, including personal transports and landers, as well as inherited artefacts from prospector ancestry. All seized under Ecclessiarchal directives. You must feel some resentment toward the Church?"

"We're not on the best of terms," Brazier said, not bothering to hide the sarcasm.

"Is that why you enlisted a Donnie Shied operative?"

"What?" The question caught him completely off guard.

"How long have you known your First Officer is a member of the Kneldierian branch of the Sorrel Tan?"

"Freyen is an operations and logistics specialist," Brazier said. "She joined our ice miner, the Chalice of Amaranth, six months ago."

"We've been through the Anchorite's hex logs," the lieutenant said. "Freyen Fortigris holds guild degrees in advanced script writing and hex design. She has turret defence training, and according to the ship's engagement logs, experience in war walker combat. Did you ever wonder why someone of such obvious skill and intelligence would waste her life running a mining crew?"

"My brother didn't ask," Brazier said. "And neither did I."

"She's trained in multiple combat specialisms and

developed cloaking technology from Aeturnic magic. These are the hallmarks of a terrorist."

Brazier had suspected the cloaking script would be discovered the moment they stepped off the *Anchorite*. But right now, that was the least of his concerns.

"Freyen isn't Donnie Shied," he said flatly. "I don't believe you."

The lieutenant's gaze sharpened, but his expression remained unreadable.

"You're aware your navigator is considered highly dangerous by the Ecclessius, and escaped from a high-security Custodia transport vessel?"

"I should be," Brazier replied. "I helped him escape."

"Matthias Phaser is an errant-class navigator," the lieutenant said. "Along with Freyen Fortigris, you stole a Navarch frigate."

"We didn't steal it," Brazier said.

A flicker of something passed across the lieutenant's face, but the eye contact never broke.

"Then how do you explain your possession of it?"

"We were given it by the Ecclessius. As part of our mission."

The lieutenant's pupils expanded, then contracted. "What mission?"

Brazier exhaled a slow, weary breath that turned into a sigh. What he was about to say would not be believed. It would almost certainly make their situation worse. But he had no better option.

"We were sent to destroy Lokul. A Lord of the Eternal Hunt."

He watched the lieutenant's face for any sign of emotion: a smirk, a twitch, maybe disbelief. But there was nothing.

Then came the question: "Was Eluthienn Leonette, Prince of Ravinica, with you?"

Brazier recoiled. "How do you know that?" he asked, too surprised to stop himself.

"Confirm or deny."

"We escorted the prince to Lokul's location. Eluthienn was the only one who could destroy him."

The lieutenant's eyes widened, just slightly. It was the first crack in the mask. Brazier pressed the advantage.

"None of that matters now. We were attacked by a Mirrovinjin warship. We were fleeing when we ran into you—that's why the Anchorite is damaged."

The lieutenant's brow twitched. "You're lying," he said. But it didn't sound like he believed it.

"They have a Cauldron-class vessel, supported by a full cadre of witches. And it can cloak itself from navigators."

The lieutenant's expression barely changed, just a slight furrow of his brow. The chamber filled with silence, punctuated only by the low hum of the ship's thrusters and the steady rhythm of Brazier's heart.

"If the Mirrovinjin had such a ship," the lieutenant said finally, "more powerful than any we possess, why would they attack a single frigate of no apparent importance?"

Brazier shook his head. The question made sense. It was a stupid move.

"I don't know. Maybe they were testing it."

"In a southern quadrant?" the lieutenant asked. "Why risk passing our northern defences?"

He shook his head again and looked around the chamber as if the bronzite walls might offer answers.

"I don't know," he repeated. "But it's still out there. You need to warn your superior and ready the crew for combat."

The lieutenant stared at him for a long moment, his eyes cold and calculating. Then, without a word, he stood so abruptly Brazier flinched.

"Where are you going?" Brazier asked, as the portal cycled open.

"To speak with your crew, and the crew of Hayley's Gambit," he said, and disappeared behind the closing partitions.

#

Brazier could only measure the passage of time by the growing numbness in his arse and the frequency of his stomach growls. But he barely noticed either. Two thoughts warred for his attention: the anxiety-inducing image of the Mirrovinjin ship stalking Formaria's tunnels, and the unsettling idea that Freyen might be a terrorist.

His mind replayed their earliest conversations, searching for any clue that she might have ties to the Donnie Shied. But every attempt at reflection was interrupted by the ship's faint creaks and shifts, each one sending his heart racing in anticipation of an announcement, the Captain's voice echoing down the corridors: "Unknown vessel on attack trajectory." But it never came.

Instead, Brazier spiralled back into uncertainty. Was the lieutenant lying? Had he used standard interrogation tactics—separating the crew to pressure them into revealing hidden truths? Yet the lieutenant hadn't lied about Matthias, and he had known about Eluthienn.

How had the crew of a Navarch cruiser learned of the prince, when most of Formaria knew nothing about his role in the vampire king's destruction? And why hadn't they been handed straight over to the Ecclessius?

Brazier sat in frustrated silence, questions circling endlessly. The uncertainty gnawed at him worse than fear or anger, because at least those emotions had shape. But now, with Freyen's loyalty in doubt and his crew's fate unclear, he felt something darker. It was the same hollow weight he'd carried after his parents' executions: powerlessness and betrayal.

The one thing he could be nearly certain of, though, was the Captain of the *Sovereign Eclipse* suspected the Church was lying. Otherwise, they'd already be in an Ecclessiarchal cell, which meant they might not be in as deep a mess as he feared. He clung to that thought instead of thinking about Freyen.

The portal cycled open.

"Come with us," the lieutenant said. Two other Navarch officers, a human male and female with repeaters slung across their shoulders, stood behind him.

"And what happens if I do?" Brazier asked.

The lieutenant produced an iron key from his trouser pocket and held it up. "The Captain would like to speak with you."

Taking this as another good sign, Brazier stood, sidled around the desk, and stepped into the corridor. He held up his manacled hands.

"Your crew and the survivors you rescued have been moved to larger quarters," the lieutenant said, unlocking the restraints.

"And my navigator?"

"He's been treated by our war casters and is perfectly well," the lieutenant replied.

Brazier felt some of the tension drain from his shoulders. His crew was alive. They weren't in Church custody.

"This way," the lieutenant said.

He led Brazier to a set of double doors, and the four of them stepped into a lift. They travelled in silence.

When the doors parted, they turned right into a long corridor with bronze-gold bulkheads every ten feet. At the far end, the lieutenant placed his hand in a terminal, and the portal cycled open.

He stood aside. Brazier entered alone.

The Captain's chambers were shaped like an elongated octagon. On one side, three crimson couches surrounded a low bronzite chest that served as both table and storage. Opposite them stood a compact command terminal, about half the size of those found on navigation decks.

Captain Philip Sourant stood behind it, back to the room, studying an obscure map of a Formarian subsection. His short, dark hair and average human height gave him an unassuming appearance, but the rigidity of his posture marked him as a Navarch officer. Unlike most, though, he had the soldier's build more common among infantry.

As Brazier waited to be acknowledged, his gaze drifted to the alcoves lining the walls. They held an eclectic array of pre-migration weaponry, stacks of books, and preserved taxidermy monsters. Among them—much to Brazier's disgust—were a Tyragast Flayer, a stubby, pale snake-like creature with filmy, exoskeletal wings protruding from either side of its head, and an adolescent Kastigor Wurm, about the length of Brazier's arm, its shell-like plating ribbed in sharp curves. Currently, its hundreds of finger-length teeth were bared in a permanent snarl.

"The Wurm's been hunted to near extinction by the Tyragast."

Sourant remained planted behind the terminal, gazing at the creatures with unsettling intensity.

"Wasn't always that way," he continued. "The Wurm used to hunt the Tyragast. But the Tyragast has no shell or plating. It's slower and smaller. The only reason it survived in Yeggardania at all is its blood, which can process gyranic energy strong enough to melt a war caster from the inside."

"Let me guess," Brazier said. "It adapted to the thing hunting it."

Sourant smiled as if they shared a private joke.

"At some point, a Tyragast sired an offspring that could absorb that energy, not just process it. Most people think those are wings, but they're frills lined with gyranic membranes. They use the absorbed sorcery to hypnotise the Wurm. Or they surround it and vibrate their frills, creating a localised gyranic storm that sickens and paralyses it."

Brazier was reminded, yet again, of why he hated Yeggardania. "And now the Wurm's no longer the predator," he said, his appetite officially gone.

"Now the Tyragast dominates a species it once fled from," Sourant said. "Just one of thousands of adaptations driven by the chaos raging across the surface. Funny to think all that's happening above us, while below we never change. We endure, but never dominate."

"I think our situation's a bit more complicated than the Wurms'," Brazier said.

"Perhaps. We're not even one species, after all," Sourant said, shrugging. Then, as if explaining the tangent: "The need to adapt comes naturally to me. I failed the Navarch Academy tests. Most go into the army after that. I went to the surface. Survived long enough to learn the rules are different up there. What saves you one day might kill you the next. I embraced the chaos. Eventually, I earned a second shot at the navy."

"Looks like you picked up a hobby in the meantime,"

Brazier said.

Sourant barked a laugh.

"They remind me nothing is guaranteed. The game can change, and you must change with it," he said. "And thanks to you, the game just changed."

Brazier blinked. "I think you're overestimating me."

"I'm talking about your ship," Sourant said. "We found an unidentifiable script buried in its core. My navigator assures me it's cloaking technology."

Created by my First Officer, the terrorist, Brazier's mind whispered. He shoved the thought away.

"You've got a good navigator."

"I have the best," Sourant said. "How did you come by the technology?"

"My First Officer developed it. She used vampire sorcery to mask us from detection. The Anchorite can stay hidden if it doesn't move. Same goes for when it's powered down."

Brazier expected some reaction—shock, maybe, or a comment about Freyen's skill. But Sourant just rolled up his sleeve.

"We had the misfortune of encountering the vampires ourselves," he said, revealing a white scar in a jagged circle around his forearm. The skin below, including his hand, looked younger.

"Had to fight left-handed," he added. "Was about as useful as a troll with cutlery."

He tugged the sleeve back down. "Luckily for me, you and your crew killed the maker. Turned our opponents into dust."

"Actually, Eluthienn killed the maker. We just gave him a ride," Brazier said. "But you already knew that."

Sourant nodded. "I know you were acting on orders from the Church."

"They needed a crew. We were available."

"And once your mission ended, they labelled you outlaws and pirates. Why?"

"After Eluthienn destroyed the maker, our witch hunter killed him. On Church orders."

"So they wouldn't have to honour the pact with

Ravinica," Sourant said. "The one that promised to support Eluthienn's war against Fiondagaard."

"That's the best explanation we've got," Brazier said. "Only the High Lords of Thendergaarden would've known about the pact."

"And they didn't know about the Anchorite or her crew," Sourant said. "So the Church covered it up."

"Apparently not as well as they thought," Brazier said. "How do you know about Eluthienn?"

"Some of the High Lords are curious about the prince's death. They, and a number of Navarch officers, are investigating."

A knot twisted in Brazier's stomach. The High Lords investigating Eluthienn's assassination should have been a relief. But all he could think was: *What have we stumbled into?*

"Still doesn't explain how you knew we were involved," he said.

"I didn't. Not for sure, until now," Sourant replied. "But the brother of Torquen Veranquis made quite the name for himself at Teuron. And so did a certain nameless warrior among his crew."

Brazier knew where this was going.

"And now you're taking us to these High Lords."

"They'll want to hear what you've told me," Sourant said. "In the meantime, your First Officer will replicate the cloaking script for our hex network. It will be indispensable to the war effort."

"My First Officer," Brazier said, "the one you accused of being a terrorist?"

"Former terrorist," Sourant said. "Our intelligence shows she left the Donnie Shied years ago."

"No one leaves the Donnie Shied."

"No," Sourant agreed, giving Brazier a knowing look. "But sometimes they escape and join mining crews whose captains don't look too closely at backgrounds."

"Even former operatives are to be killed or apprehended on sight. That's the law."

"You may not have noticed, but we're not operating

under legal jurisdictions. And there's more at stake here than one ex-Donnie Shied who changed her mind."

Brazier suspected there was more to it. Sourant's charitable framing likely concealed a harsher reality. But he couldn't shake the memory of Freyen saving them, fighting beside them, joking through long nights aboard the *Anchorite*. It hurt to think those moments might have been lies, or worse, half-truths.

"She's useful to you," Brazier said.

"You're all useful to me," Sourant replied. "A state of affairs you'd do well to maintain, starting with the script."

Brazier hesitated, a sinking feeling rising in his chest. Giving up the cloaking technology felt like betrayal, not just of his crew's wishes, but of the fragile trust they'd built. But refusing would doom them.

He finally nodded. "She'll give you the script."

This had been a long and bitter debate among the crew. Brazier recognised the technology's value. But Switch and Matthias had fiercely opposed handing it over to other Fromryr. They feared it would allow the Custodia, and others, to hide just as easily. For fugitives like them, that was suicide. Freyen had offered a compromise: they'd share the technology only when they no longer needed it to stay alive. She'd been the voice of reason. Had she only told him what he'd wanted to hear?

"Outstanding," Sourant said, snapping Brazier from his thoughts. "Your crew will have access to the officer's mess. Let Lieutenant Anson know if you need anything. The survivors from the Gambit will be taken to other quarters. They may ask questions we don't want you to answer—best if we keep you separated."

"Wait," Brazier said, Freyen momentarily forgotten. "You know we were attacked by a Mirrovinjin vessel? Your casters must've detected the signature."

Then, anticipating doubt, he added, "Check the Anchorite's engagement history. You'll see the hex activity."

Sourant let him finish, studying him with an expression Brazier couldn't read.

"The High Lords will tell you about the ships," he said.

NINE
KATHRYN

The lift shot through Ilantia, ascending and descending, shifting course with a smoothness Kathryn barely registered. The walls, blurred shades of amethyst and wet slate, pulsed and flickered in rhythm with the cascade of her thoughts.

She needed to inform the Ecclessius that Isdria Laanorath was in the city. She needed to let Demina know. Demina would have to alert central command in Thendergaarden. Demina needed to send it up the chain, and fast—epistolar fast. That would mean full-scale military mobilization, with troops marshalled from Thela. There was no way the Ecclessius would let its most notorious traitor slip through its fingers.

Yet amid the mental whirlwind, another thrill crashed through her, euphoria rippling through every limb. Isdria's capture meant her return to the navy. The Ecclessius would torture him. She wouldn't be losing any sleep over that. They'd extract every ounce of information about his operations, his alliance with the Mirrovinjin, and the grotesque new warships they'd engineered together. Finally, they would know it wasn't just the aftereffects of Mirrovinjin sorcery, that her memories weren't hallucinations born of lingering abhorrence, but real events. Finally, they would know she'd told the truth.

And maybe, just maybe, with knowledge of the sorcery Isdria had used on her, the Ecclessius could develop Veskanca. She wouldn't need to make deals with criminals.

She wouldn't need Veers.

The name hit her like a bolt to the chest.

So focused on Isdria, she hadn't even registered the connection between the smuggler and the Sorel Tan captain. They were working together. Veers would know she'd followed them off the *Orphan*. If they captured Isdria, Veers would realise she was behind it and any hope of securing Veskanca from him would be lost.

The lift doors parted onto the antechamber outside Demina's office. The shunt snapped Kathryn back to reality. Bells rang in her ears, her heart pounded, and her limbs tingled with post-battle mania. But it was dying quickly beneath the weight of the decision before her.

Isdria's capture meant losing the only known source of Veskanca. But it might also mean her absolution. If the Ecclessius could replicate Veskanca, she'd be reinstated. Her story would be believed. And she could stop the Sorel Tan and the Mirrovinjin from building their nightmare fleet.

If the Ecclessius could develop it. If.

Kathryn stared at the portal to Demina's chambers, drawing deep breath after deep breath. Her heart still thundered. In her mind, she was back at her writing desk, her mother leaning in close.

A good officer's mind is like a river, she'd said. *It flows over their choices, dispassionate, logical, removed from emotion. That's how they take the right course.*

Her mother had leaned even closer, nose almost touching hers as Kathryn scribbled the words, too afraid to look up.

But you won't be good enough, will you, Kathryn? she'd said with such venom that Kathryn had flinched, snapping the nib of her quill.

The memory shattered, flinging her back to the present.

We'll see about that, Kathryn thought, striding toward the terminal. The portal cycled at her request, and she stepped inside.

Demina stood with her back to the room, hands clasped, gazing out over the city. She turned as Kathryn approached, expression inquisitive but not unwelcoming.

"Didn't think you'd get it done that quickly," she said.

"Impressive, even for you."

"Isdria Laanorath is in the city," Kathryn said flatly. "He just got off a ship called the Orphan Guyan."

Demina went very still. Her chin dropped a fraction, her body tensed. "Why would Isdria Laanorath be in Ilantia, Kathryn?"

She used her first name. She never used her first name.

"He and seven others disembarked. Looked like they were guarding someone. Could be a prisoner. Maybe a caster they've snatched. Point is, he's here."

Too late, she realised she was speaking too fast. The words tumbled out in a rush. Even to her, they didn't sound convincing.

Demina watched her carefully, unblinking. "Have you found Ariadne Ambertine?"

"What?" Kathryn blinked. "No. Hayley's Gambit never arrived. Listen, Isdria Laanorath got off a ship named the Orphan Guyan, and he's here. Right now!"

Demina placed her hand into one of the wells on her desk. Her eyes fluttered briefly.

"You're right," she said, disconnecting. "With any luck, Ariadne will be someone else's problem. And Ambertine has already paid up. That's better than we could have hoped for."

Kathryn clenched her fists, stopping herself from pounding them on the desk. *Why in all the endless dark is she ignoring everything I'm saying?*

"This has nothing to do with Ariadne!" she snapped. "Isdria Laanorath is in the city, and you need to alert central command. He probably has forces here. We'll need a detachment from Thela. We–"

Demina raised a hand, cutting her off. "You've had another hallucination," she said. "This is just like last time."

She exhaled, then added, almost gently, "I can't let this one go unchecked, Kathryn. You need to submit yourself for purification."

Kathryn's mind reeled. This wasn't a nightmare. This wasn't like before.

"I'm telling you, Isdria Laanorath got off that ship. He's in Ilantia."

"Why would the most wanted elf in Formaria travel on an ice hauler?" Demina asked. "Why would he arrive with only seven guards? He knows he's to be killed or captured on sight. Why would he risk it?"

Because I corrupted the hex network and helped him enter Ilantia unnoticed.

For one brief second, Kathryn considered admitting it—her deal with Veers, the gang war diversion, everything. She opened her mouth.

Then closed it again.

Even if Demina believed her, she'd have her arrested on the spot, right here, right now. She'd lose any chance of capturing Isdria. There'd be no Veskanca, no navy, no future.

"Listen, Cap," Kathryn said. "Isdria is here, and he's planning something."

"That's exactly what you said last time," Demina replied. "Those exact words: Isdria Laanorath is planning something. That he's working with our enemies to bring down Formaria." She gestured broadly. "And yet here we are."

Demina's voice softened. "Submit yourself for purification, or I'll have no choice but to inform the Church you're compromised."

Kathryn was dimly aware of her own trembling. Rage coursed through her at Demina's blindness, at the life slipping from her grasp. But it burned brightest for Isdria black-damned Laanorath, for what he had done to her, for the abhorrence.

For several seconds, she could only stand there. Arguments, justifications, even begging, anything to make Demina believe her, flashed through her mind. Not even her mother's voice could get in.

But in the end, all she said was: "Yes, sir. I understand."

Demina held her gaze, eyes searching. "If I don't have an interrogation report within thirty minutes, I'll alert the Church."

The words hit like a punch to the gut. Demina no longer trusted her, and that stung worse than the threat, even if it was justified.

"I'll go there straight away," Kathryn lied, her voice laced with resignation that wasn't entirely false.

She turned and left, barely registering the chute doors opening or that she'd summoned a lift. Her mother's cruel smile was background ambiance to the plan dominating her thoughts, a plan involving nothing even remotely resembling purification.

Ten
Brazier

The officer's mess was like any other on a ship of its class: walls of polished bronzite, a low ceiling that made the room feel smaller than it was, and three bronzite tables with a handful of chairs.

Brazier and Matthias sat at one, while Switch perched cross-legged atop another. A selection of tools was arranged on her left, an untouched plate of hard-baked mushroom cakes and a cup of beer on her right. She pushed a thin wire brush through her augmented wrist joint, eyes screwed up in concentration.

"A group of High Lords and Navarch officers know the Mirrovinjin have their own ships," she said, giving the brush a twist. "Why aren't they warning the rest of Formaria?"

Brazier, whose own wrist ached with phantom discomfort just watching her, ignored the question and asked, "What does that even feel like?"

"Exactly how you'd imagine," she said. Then, catching the look likely written across his face, added, "You get used to it."

Brazier rubbed his wrist.

"Well, they probably don't want to spread panic," he said, though he could hear the lack of conviction in his voice. If the *Anchorite* had been attacked, other ships would be too.

Switch seemed to be thinking the same thing. "Mirrovinjin with ships isn't something you can hide for long," she said, blowing through her wrist joint. "And why would that same group of High Lords and Navarch officers be secretly investigating Eluthienn's death?"

"Probably because they suspect the Church of doing what the Church does best," Matthias said. He'd already finished one plate of mushroom cakes and was now working through his second. Apparently, getting scorched by witches made you hungry. The dark rings under his eyes were the only clue he'd recently fought off an entire cadre. To Brazier, he looked like he could go another round.

"And what's that?" Brazier asked.

"Serving its own interests," Matthias said.

"But those interests also serve the High Lords," Switch countered. "Eluthienn's death means they don't have to fight Fiondagaard."

Matthias chuckled, a dry, mirthless sound, then broke one of the rectangular cakes in half. "If I were a High Lord," he said.

"That'll be the day," Switch muttered under her breath.

"And I'd just made a deal with a foreign prince," Matthias went on, acknowledging the jab with a wry smile, "and that prince died right after fulfilling his end of the bargain, I'd want to know what happened."

"Even if that outcome played in your favour?" Brazier asked.

"Especially if it played in my favour," Matthias said, voice low and gravelled. "They believe the Church betrayed Formaria's ally right under their noses. If the Church is willing to do that, you wonder what they'll do to you."

"You think they want to overthrow the Ecclessius?"

"Wouldn't you, if you were one of the great houses?" Matthias said, tossing the half cake into his mouth.

"Maybe," Brazier said. The centuries-long power struggle between the great houses and the Church ensured no single house could ever achieve absolute control over Formaria. While they might resent the balance, it guaranteed their survival—a status quo Brazier doubted any of them would jeopardise.

"What are the odds the Mirrovinjin found the shipyard?" Switch asked, returning the brush to her tool belt and flexing her augmented wrist.

"And built a ship in less than two months?" Brazier said, shaking his head. "Very low."

"Then they found another one," Switch said. "One they've controlled for a while."

"Or they didn't build the ship," Matthias said.

Brazier frowned. "If they didn't build it, who did?"

"Could be something they've had from the beginning," Matthias said. "And they're only using it now."

"You're saying the same sorcery that created the Mirrovinjin also created their ships?" Brazier asked.

"All I know is that ship was drowning in Aeturnic energy," Matthias said. "Felt like pure sorcery itself."

"You sure that wasn't just the amount of witches?" Switch asked.

Matthias shrugged. "Maybe. But I've never seen witches create that kind of power."

"The Fromryr nearly destroyed the Mirrovinjin during the Moranthian Wars," Brazier said. "If they had ships, they would've used them then."

Two hundred years after the Fenn had been driven from Formaria, they invaded again. The second time, they came prepared to win above and below ground. Facing defeat after defeat, Lucienn Moranthia, heir to the Ilvalien throne, sought out a power to save the races of Aetraya. No one knew where he found it, but he emerged from the depths of Elliptica at the head of the Mirrovinjin, who then swept aside the Fennian armies.

But when Lucienn's father ordered him to destroy his creations, he refused. War broke out instantly, and the Mirrovinjin, already crippled by their battles with the Fenn, were driven nearly to extinction. If there was ever a time to deploy ships, it had been then.

"What if Lucienn only made a few?" Matthias said. "If I had just one or two, I wouldn't have thrown them at the Fromryr navy to be destroyed. I'd wait until they were weak."

"Nearly a thousand years?" Switch asked. But before Matthias could reply, the mess hall door slid open.

Freyen stepped through, massaging her right hand with her left, wearing the look of someone who'd just explained something complicated, repeatedly. She dropped into the chair beside Brazier and gave him a warm, if slightly weary smile. Staring at her, it was hard to imagine she'd once belonged to a faction most would consider extremists.

Lieutenant Anson had kept her past a secret from Switch and Matthias. Brazier still hadn't decided whether to tell them. But like many things involving Freyen, it was a conversation for another time.

"How'd it go?" he asked.

"It didn't," she said, reaching for his plate. He'd barely touched it.

"Thanks," she added, breaking off a piece. "Turns out it can't be replicated in other systems."

Brazier leaned back, arms folded. He should've felt relief at that. It meant no one else could use the cloak. But all he could think about was how easily they might lose the only ship that had ever felt like his.

Freyen hesitated, then added, "There's something else. The Eclipse's navigator can't use the cloaking script, even when inside the Anchorite's nav pit. It's like the script is locked behind a protocol she doesn't have clearance for. She can see it but she can't activate it. The cloak seems tied specifically to the Anchorite and Matthias."

Matthias paused mid-chew, slowly breaking into a satisfied grin. "Now, isn't that interesting?"

Switch rolled her eyes. "Great. As if he didn't already think he was Formaria's best navigator."

Brazier tried to keep his face neutral, but a cold weight settled in his stomach. It was great for them, of course. Freyen's solution had made it harder for the *Anchorite* to be taken from them. But he felt a sharp, unexpected stab of annoyance at how impressed he was with her.

"Locked specifically to Matthias?" he asked.

"I think it's how he first activated the script," Freyen said. "He should be able to grant access to other navigators, though."

"Does Sourant and his navigator know that?" Brazier

asked.

Freyen shook her head. "Thought it best to keep that to myself."

"Good call," Brazier said. "But why can't the script be transferred to another ship?"

Freyen shrugged. "The script I created using the vampire's signature doesn't work in the Eclipse's system. It seems to only function aboard the Anchorite."

"She is one special lady," Switch said, smiling as if recalling a fond memory.

Freyen chewed, twisting a curl between her fingers. "I don't think it's the Anchorite's network. I think the sorcery embedded in the script is no longer accessible."

"How's that possible?" Brazier asked.

"Maybe when the vampires were destroyed, their sorcery was destroyed with them," Freyen said.

"Don't think so," Matthias replied. "We used the cloak two weeks ago. I can feel it crawling up my neck every time we do."

"What if the sorcery was destroyed," Freyen said, "but we managed to trap it while the vampires were still alive—encase it inside the ship's hex network?"

"What, like we preserved it?" Brazier said. Then to Switch: "Is that even possible?"

Switch scratched the top of her ear with her augmented hand. "The way a hex network interacts with a gyranic core does create a kind of contained magical environment. Maybe it captured the vampire's sorcery, and if you remove it, it dies." She shrugged. "It's just a theory. Scholars in the Artificium spend entire careers debating this. The Fromryr just don't know enough about the gyre ships."

"So we're the only ones who'll ever have the cloak," Matthias said, grinning. "Good to know."

Brazier was surprised by how hard the truth hit him, gutting a hope he hadn't realised he'd clung to: the hope that the technology might be their salvation. Replicated, it could have meant freedom from war, a future unshackled from the Bellum Infinara.

"That's if they let us keep the Anchorite," Freyen said,

watching him sidelong.

Switch had been about to start polishing her augment but stopped, looking up. “Cap?”

“That decision’s probably down to the people we’re about to meet,” Brazier said.

A silence followed, one he felt more than heard.

He looked at each of them: Switch, Matthias, Freyen. They were his crew, and it was his responsibility to keep them fed, safe, and alive. Whatever the High Lords wanted, the *Anchorite* wasn’t just a ship, it was their home.

His voice was steady. “The Anchorite belongs to us.”

Saying it out loud made him realise how angry he was at the thought of losing her. “We’re the ones who flew her against a Lord of the Eternal Hunt. She’s ours. And no one’s taking her from us.”

Switch had crossed her arms and was nodding defiantly. Matthias’ moon-grey eyes glinted with mischief. Freyen smiled in a way that made Brazier question everything Sourant had said about her.

They all turned as the portal shunted apart, and Lieutenant Anson stepped into the mess.

“We’re here,” he said, standing aside and gesturing toward the door. “The High Lords are waiting for you.”

ELEVEN
KATHRYN

Even before the lift decelerated, Kathryn could hear the sounds bleeding in from the corridor surrounding the Custodia command centre. It was a muted cacophony, like musicians playing in another room. The sounds grew louder, morphing into something sharper, until, when the doors finally slid open, the melodic illusion shattered. What remained resembled a skirmish.

Fromryr filled the octagonal corridor. Custodia in black and yellow gambesons, worn beneath breastplates and greaves, moved among others similarly dressed for war. Except the others wore a rough assortment of armour: mostly cuirasses and mining gambesons. Down the right wing, they wore solid black or black and brown. Down the left: striped red and yellow. Some were bare-chested, showing gang tattoos across their shoulders or over their hearts—the slashed circle of the Collective, or the key and upside-down triangle of the Barons. All had manacles around their wrists, except for those deemed higher risk, who had them clamped around their ankles too.

They were a mix of dwarves, humans, and gnomes, all covered in blood.

Ridger nodded as she stepped out of the lift, one eye swelling shut, blond hair matted across his forehead, then turned back to the dwarf he was questioning.

Looks like I really did miss out, Kathryn thought, silently thanking the abyss for the chaos. With every Custodia officer occupied, no one would question her walking out with half the armoury.

It was worse inside the command centre. She sidestepped a Custodia officer taking names from two gnomes sitting on the floor, then stepped over a dwarf pinned beneath a knee. She nearly tripped over three humans lying face down, hands clasped behind their backs, before reaching the armoury doors.

"Palatine," Orla Nygen said as the doors slid shut behind Kathryn, cutting off most of the noise. The gnome sat behind a long, dark desk. It served as both workstation and barrier. "Doesn't look like there's a scratch on you. Either you missed all the fun, or you're as good as they say."

"I'm as good as they say," Kathryn said, "and I missed all the fun."

Orla laughed.

"I'm on an opp," Kathryn said.

"And this requires weapons," Orla replied, more a statement than a question.

"Lots of weapons."

"Well, you came to the right place. Just let me know what you take. Cap's been a little tetchy lately."

"What's new in the dark," Kathryn said, drawing another laugh. *Let's hope she stays friendly enough not to ask questions.*

A regal blue ceiling canal guided her to a portal at the far end of the corridor, the chamber where the Custodia held its military-grade weaponry. Some of it was owned, most of it was confiscated. Ash-grey partitions slid open, revealing an octagonal chamber filled wall to wall with armour and weapons: tactical breastplates with helms, greaves and vambraces; light and heavy cuirasses, hauberks, reinforced gambesons, even an aged scale shirt. Along the far wall were long and short-range repeating crossbows, racks of inactivated gyre cartridges and magazines, long swords, short swords, hand and a half swords, falchions, daggers, knives, axes, and even a Gorefelder—the two-handed blade as long as Kathryn was tall, propped in a corner.

Don't know what it is, Kathryn thought, *but there's*

something about all that steel that makes a person feel better.

She chose a tactical breastplate, backplate, and a matching steel helm, cuisses, spaulders, greaves, and vambraces. Moving quickly, she removed her coat and cuirass, pulled on the heavier armour, and tightened the straps. She'd pick up the leather gear later. For now, she shrugged her jacket back on over the plate, then turned to the weapons. She fastened a leather sheath belt, sliding in a combat knife beside her short sword. At the crossbows, she selected a close-quarters repeater, along with gyre cartridges and magazines. She looped a leather shoulder strap through the sling mounts, slung it across her back, then looked at the rack again. *Don't think I'm going to have time to reload*, she thought, grabbing an identical repeater, loading it, and slinging it over her shoulder.

Clanking back down the corridor, she found each rhythmic clink and clonk oddly satisfying. *If this plan ends up in the abyss*, she thought, *at least I'll go out with a bang.*

Orla gave a long, low whistle. "Someone's in trouble," she said. "Let me see what you've got."

Leaning over the counter, she scanned Kathryn's gear.

"Full tactical. Dagger. Short sword's yours. Two close-quarter repeaters, because why take one when you can take two. Body straps. Reinforced stocks. Fast-fire gear wheels. No optics, because who needs to aim, and two gyre cartridges and six magazines."

"Better safe than sorry," Kathryn said.

"I hear that," Orla replied, opening the doors. "You have fun out there."

You know what, Orla, Kathryn thought, *dragging Isdria Laanorath back here might be the most fun I've had in a long time.*

Pushing past officers and detainees, she earned several raised eyebrows and questioning glances. She avoided eye contact, striding with purpose, making it clear she wasn't in the mood for conversation.

Then she stopped dead in her tracks.

The man being escorted by Isdria's crew, the one with

the pallid complexion and dark circles, was being taken to the interrogation chambers by Jace Redolin, a young gnome with messy dark hair.

What in the black abyss is going on there? Kathryn thought, watching Jace open a chamber door and guide the man inside. He wasn't manacled. So, he wasn't in custody.

She caught up with them as they entered one of the side chambers.

"You take a seat in there, sir," Jace was saying. "Someone will be back to talk to you soon."

Then the man, voice cracked with fatigue and sorrow, said something that made Kathryn's heart freeze: "Tell them about the ships."

"Don't worry, sir," Jace said, stepping out and catching Kathryn's eye with a look: *We've got one of those*. "I'll tell them all about the ships," he promised. "You just take a seat and we'll be right back."

"You need to tell them about the ships," the man called again, as the door closed behind him.

"Where'd you find our friend?" Kathryn asked. Was that a tremble in her voice?

Jace didn't seem to notice. "Handed himself in to a Custodia officer on level two, Segora district," he said. "Says he's Erin Carmowright."

"Who?"

"Navarch liaison to Everaux. Been missing six weeks."

"And is he?"

"You think if I knew high-level Navarch officials, I'd be working here?"

Fair point.

"All I know," he added, "is there are some ships, and they're real important to him."

That makes two of us.

"Look, I've got an ongoing opp—smuggling ring, suspected trafficking. Real nasty types," she said. "You say he's been missing? He might be relevant."

"Be my guest," Jace said, nodding back toward the command centre. "No one else is talking to him any time soon."

She watched him leave, then stepped into the chamber. The man, Erin Carmowright, if that was really his name, looked up as she sat opposite him. She placed one repeater on the floor beside her, resting the other across her lap. Up close, she saw his cracked lips, the glassy sheen to his eyes. He looked almost blind.

Looking at him sparked a contradictory rush of emotion. A part of her wanted to fetch water and clean clothes. Another part wanted to be anywhere else, anywhere but here, facing this hollowed shell of a man.

"Get it together, Stryker," she muttered, tightening her grip on the stock and forcing herself to meet his gaze.

"Are you okay?" she asked at last.

His mouth twitched, and his brow creased as if confused by the question. "I have important information for Admiral Sozart La'Zeen."

"The quadrant commander?" she asked.

He blinked. "He must be warned."

"About the ships?" she asked, carefully.

It didn't work. He leaned forward, gripping the table, knuckles white. *Too fast*, she thought. *Back it up*. But before she could respond, Erin's eyes burned with sudden, manic intensity.

"They're coming," he said. "The enemy are coming. You need to warn them. You need to tell the Admiral—to warn the Navarch!"

Kathryn felt like she was staring into a mirror. Someone else had been through what she had. But another thought cut through the turmoil: *Without Isdria Laanorath, you can't prove anything.*

"I'm going to tell them about the ships," she said.

"You must tell them," he said, cutting her off.

"I will," she said, raising a hand. "But I need to know who brought you here. Where are they?"

He opened his mouth, then closed it, shaking his head.

Come on. Give me something. "Did they take you to a man named Veers?"

His gaze drifted past her, vacant again. She was losing him.

"To a small chamber," she said. "No hex. Disconnected from the network?"

His mouth twitched. His right eye did too. His brow creased. Whatever answer he wanted to give, it was costing him. He shook his head and looked to the ceiling.

Kathryn leaned in. "Where is Isdria Laanorath?"

His eyes snapped to hers, the intensity returned. "Gone," he said.

"Gone where?"

He shook his head, mouth trembling. "Gone back," he said. "Gone back to the ships."

"Is he still here? Still in the city?"

The man shook his head, eyes wet. "Gone back," he whispered, again and again. "Gone back, gone back, gone back."

Kathryn grabbed the crossbows and stood. "I'll make this right," she said, glancing back. But he was mumbling now, eyes fixed on the empty chair.

I promise I'm going to make this right.

Twelve
Brazier

The lander's hatch opened with a hiss, revealing a bridge of rock so dark it merged with the blackness falling away on either side. In the far distance, the bridge widened into an island cradling Formarian architecture. Angled rhomboid pillars jutted from the ground at precise 45-degrees, leading Brazier's eye to a multi-level pyramidal structure large enough to house a thousand Constructii. It looked fossilised, almost completely devoid of gyre light, leaving behind only bone and shadow.

Lieutenant Anson stepped onto the bridge, and the crew of the *Anchorite* followed close behind. Outside the lander, the air hit them all at once, cold, wet, and dense. It felt like standing beside a subterranean waterfall.

Brazier glanced up, and the source of the chill became immediately apparent. They stood inside a domed cavern, or so he guessed. The vastness and depth of shadow concealed its far walls. Above, the slopes of the dome curved inward, the ceiling lost in thick, hanging mist.

Suspended in the gloom above the Formarian complex hung two Gyre Stars and a pair of Maw-class cruisers. They were leviathans asleep in the dark. Each Gyre Star resembled a colossal armoured worm, their curved central hulls massive and joined to long oval spines. On either side jutted colossal, slightly ovoid hangar bays, like the arched wings of a bird. At the rear, barrel-like thrusters glowed faint blue, like embers burning low in a forgotten furnace.

The cruisers, smaller but similar in shape, included the *Sovereign Eclipse*. All were enormous, each one capable of repelling a Mirrovinjin war host. Yet the cavern made them seem small. Brazier had never seen two Gyre Stars in one place, not outside Helmharothell at least.

"We're near the surface?" Switch asked as they made their way toward the installation. Though she spoke clearly, her voice seemed to vanish into the void around them.

"I don't think so," Freyen replied. "Feels like it's got its own atmosphere."

"Agravata Eukatoria," Anson said. "You can't see them from here, but fungus lines the cavern's lower walls. Releases and absorbs water during its lifecycle. It's one of the largest growths outside Everaux."

"And no one's farming it?" Freyen asked.

"No one knows about it," Anson replied.

Behind them came a metallic cycling sound, a rhythmic *clink, clink, clink*, like a massive gear biting through its links. The final shunt echoed so loud it felt like the entire cavern had drawn breath. They turned together.

High above, a set of gates large enough to admit a Gyre Star, had closed shut. Debris and ancient dust drifted from the ledges, falling slowly through still air. Staring up, Brazier felt like he'd just been sealed inside a tomb. Then it clicked.

"This is a cache," he said.

"Former cache," Anson corrected. "It's been empty of Formarian treasure for centuries."

"And now the Navarch use it as a secret hiding place," Matthias said, his silver eyes locked on Anson.

"During the mapping of Formaria, an early iteration of the navy excluded this cache from most hex network maps," Anson said.

"Just in case they ever needed to plan treason," Matthias said. Brazier thought it needlessly antagonistic. Then again, they were, in all but name, prisoners of House Angelaux. That might provoke one of Formaria's most wanted criminals. Then he remembered being sardonic was hardly out of character for Matthias, prisoner or not.

Anson ignored the jab and continued toward the

installation. “The High Lords are waiting.”

They walked in silence until they reached the end of the rock bridge. Without any visible gate, they slipped between seamless walls into a courtyard surrounding the pyramid. The rhomboid structures rose at sharp angles, positioned roughly fifteen feet apart. Each bore a straight gyre channel bisected by a central node, and at their bases, faint outlines marked rectangular doors in the shadowed alloy.

Looking around, Brazier could picture ranks of Constructii arrayed in formation, officers and officials presiding from the pyramid’s steps.

“This would’ve housed Constructii,” Brazier said.

“As well as ships and other artefacts of war,” Anson added.

“Who found them?” Brazier asked.

Anson glanced down at him. “The predecessors of House Angelaux,” he said, then began climbing the pyramid’s steps.

They reached a set of wide double doors. Anson placed his hand on the terminal to their right. A silver pulse shot down its vein, then across the floor channel beneath the doors. Slowly, the doors shuddered apart, grinding into the walls with a heavy groan. Ahead lay a hall lined with rectangular pillars, leading to another flight of steps.

As they advanced, a low murmur of voices drifted toward them. Climbing the steps, the murmurs sharpened and were punctuated by the harsher tones of a heated conversation.

“You’re correct, Your Highness,” a woman said. “The northern passage into Maw Grindle might provide cover for a single ship. That’s why it will be heavily patrolled. We cannot risk it.”

A murmur of assent followed, then Sourant’s voice.

“Not to mention the Rosantz capital,” Brazier heard him say. “For all we know, Varkoneth is with the Church.”

“Speculation, Phillip,” the woman said. “We may soon be calling on his support.”

Someone snorted thickly.

“Varkoneth Rosantz will wait for every speck of dust to settle before he picks a side,” a gruff male voice said. Brazier pictured a large human male. “We’d be fools to expect his support.”

“The passage is closed to us nonetheless,” the woman said.

“Then we have no option but to employ this Brazier Veranquis and his ship,” the gruff voice replied.

The crew shared a look. Sourant hadn’t mentioned being employed by the High Lords.

“And if he and his crew refuse?” a third man asked. Brazier was happy to hear refusal was still on the table.

“Then we descend upon the drift with our entire host,” the gruff voice said. “Everything we can muster. We attack in force.”

A pause.

“What’s the likelihood of Veranquis agreeing, Phillip?” the woman asked.

“I believe we’re about to find out,” Sourant said.

They ascended the final steps and entered a grand chamber. Each of its four sides opened onto broad balconies overlooking the cavern, admitting a soft, slate-blue light.

At the centre stood a solitary grey terminal. Around it clustered seven figures: two Navarch officers—one a squat, scarred female dwarf, the other a female gnome with sharp, restless eyes; a human in a red and green officer’s doublet, his face drawn tight with military rigidity; and Sourant, tall and composed as ever.

Beside them stood two human men with the unmistakable bearing of royalty. And finally, the last figure: cloaked in dull green, unmoving, face concealed behind a bronzite mask. Cast in the likeness of a Constructii, Brazier had only ever seen the masks worn by war casters disfigured by magical wounds.

The masked figure held a gold pipe, short and slim. As they neared, he brought it to the mask’s mouth slot and exhaled a plume of crimson smoke flecked with glinting silver motes. Whoever he was, and whatever he was smoking, projected a disconcerting aura. Brazier felt as though he could only perceive him from the corner of his eye.

"Your Highnesses, Sirs," Anson said. "Brazier Veranquis and the crew of the Anchorite—Matthias Phaser, Freyen Fortigris, and Daniella Gundrisson."

"It's Switch," Switch said.

Anson glanced at her, his eyes lingering briefly on her augmented arm.

"Thank you, Lieutenant," Sourant said. Anson stepped back, standing at ease with hands clasped behind him.

"May I introduce His Royal Highness, Marcus Angelaux, King of Pontifax," Sourant said, gesturing to the man at the head of the terminal. Despite his middle years, Marcus Angelaux retained the frame of a warrior and the rugged features to match. Thick, unruly brown hair fell to his shoulders, framing a square jaw and intense, dark eyes. He wore an enamelled green-and-gold breastplate over a beige gambeson. Despite, or perhaps because of the armour, Brazier thought he looked more like a warlord of the Old World than a king of the new. He would've bet gold Vidicks this was the source of the gruff voice.

"His Royal Highness, Aymeri La'Voline, King of Sephera," Sourant continued, nodding to the man at Marcus's side.

Every inch a king, Aymeri had short, greying hair, high cheekbones, and a proud brow. Like Marcus, he was dressed for war, in dark leathers beneath a steel breastplate bearing his house's sigil.

"Admiral Katrina Zarlow," Sourant said, indicating the gnome opposite the terminal. She wore the dark blue doublet of the Navarch, black epaulettes on her shoulders. Her long brown hair cascaded freely, and if not for her broad features, bat-like ears, and wide eyes, Brazier might've mistaken her for a human. Standing nearly a foot taller than any gnome he'd met, she exuded presence, and Brazier guessed she knew it. The proud, mildly amused expression on her face suited a commander of a Navarch capital ship.

"Admiral Benera Korst," Sourant said, gesturing to the dwarf beside Zarlow.

Golden hair spilled over the collar of her Navarch doublet, but that was where the beauty ended. A scar ran down her left eye, leaving it a cloudy grey beside its sharper blue companion. Her cheeks were ruddy and lined with age, her nose large and slightly crooked, and her heavy brow left her eyes in permanent shadow. Unlike Zarlow's hardened, aloof pride, Korst gave the impression of an admiral who inspired loyalty through warmth and quiet strength. Torquen had always seemed somewhere in between: hard steel tempered by rare but meaningful heat. Brazier wondered if he was either of those things, but the thought vanished as quickly as it had come.

Sourant turned to the man wearing the red and green La'Voline doublet.

"Captain Nathanial Rook," he said.

Rook had the slender build of a man born into the navy. His greying hair was slicked into a quiff that made him look younger than Brazier suspected he was. He smiled with the boyish confidence of someone who'd always known his place, and that place had always been secure. He was likely born into privilege, not that Brazier could judge.

"And lastly, Guilfier Forain, head of House Angelaux's royal household casters," Sourant said, nodding at the masked figure beside Marcus.

Brazier stared into the mask's metallic features, struck once more by the unsettling sense that the man behind it might not truly exist.

"Now we all know each other and have seen each other's faces, let's not waste any more time," Marcus growled. He leaned forward, fists pressed to the terminal, turning his head from side to side like a bear sizing up prey. "Philip tells us you've got a ship that can hide itself from navigators. Is that true?"

Brazier was grateful to look away from the masked figure. But he was far less grateful for the question.

"I thought you wanted to know about Eluthienn, Your Highness?" he said.

"We'll get onto that," Marcus snapped, eyes narrowing. *Clearly a king not fond of being tested.* "Can the ship hide itself or not?"

"*Our* ship can," Brazier replied, stressing their ownership of the vessel.

Marcus grunted with satisfaction.

“And this technology can’t be replicated elsewhere in the network? And it’s only your navigator who can use it?” Marcus asked, turning to Matthias. The navigator smiled, clearly enjoying himself.

“Seems that way, Your Highness.”

Marcus looked to Sourant, who gave a silent nod in confirmation.

“So yours is the only ship, with the only navigator, in all of Formaria able to hide itself,” Marcus said. “Not ideal. But it’ll do. It’ll do just fine.”

Brazier felt a mix of pride and apprehension. Next to him, Switch tensed, then said what he was thinking.

“Do just fine for who?” she asked, scowling so fiercely Brazier wondered if it hurt. She added, more begrudgingly: “Your Highness.”

“For those of us determined to stop the Ecclessius from dominating all of Formaria,” said Katrina Zarlow, her voice soft and husky, carrying an effortless gravitas. She spoke with the calm authority of someone used to being obeyed. It made Brazier want to agree with her. But that didn’t mean he did.

“The Ecclessius already dominates Formaria,” he said, frowning.

“The Ecclessius,” Marcus interjected, voice thick with disdain, “relies on influence, alliances, and subterfuge. It rules by pulling on the levers of bureaucracy and administration.”

“Fine,” Brazier said, not sure where this was leading. “But it still rules.”

“Because we, the Royal Houses, let it rule,” Marcus snapped, as if that settled it.

Brazier wasn’t so easily deterred. “Because without a central authority, the Houses would devolve into civil war.”

Marcus straightened, fists clenching, and for a moment Brazier thought he was about to pound the terminal. But instead, he slowly rested his knuckles against the surface.

Aymeri La’Voline stepped in before his fellow king

could say more.

"That is correct," he said calmly. "A delicate balance of power has ensured the unity of disparate races and the survival of the Fromryr."

"Then what's the problem, Your Highness?" Brazier asked, baffled. Everyone seemed to be agreeing on known facts.

"The balance is shifting," Aymeri said. One hand rested on the pommel of his sword like a royal sceptre. "We believe the Church has found a weapon."

The Church had no shortage of weapons. Brazier failed to see why one more was a crisis.

"What kind of weapon?"

Aymeri nodded for Zarlow to explain.

"The kind you and your crew recently encountered," the Admiral said.

Brazier blinked. *They think we were attacked by an Ecclessiarchal ship?*

"We were attacked by a Mirrovinjin ship," he said.

"Did you see it with your own eyes?" Zarlow asked. "Not just through the hex?"

"We didn't need to," Matthias said. "I know Mirrovinjin sorcery when I smell it, and that ship reeked of it."

"Aeturnic sorcery?" Zarlow pressed.

"Never known them to use anything else," Matthias said.

"There was nothing odd about it? Nothing different?" she asked.

Matthias shrugged. "It wasn't their usual flavour of darkness, I'll admit. But that was probably down to the brand-new ship they were flying."

Zarlow shook her head. "This might be hard to believe, but we don't think those ships are real. Not in the usual sense of the word."

Matthias let out a laugh, like he was humouring a child. "Felt pretty real to me."

"And we lost two thruster discs to their repeaters," Brazier said. "How was any of that not real?"

"It was real for you," Sourant said. "But a ship of that size and with that much sorcery should have lit up the minds of every war caster in range. Yet they detected nothing."

"With all due respect, Captain," Matthias said, tone entirely lacking respect, "maybe employ better casters. That ship nearly crippled a top-of-the-line frigate."

"With a top-of-the-line crew running her," Switch added.

Sourant raised an eyebrow at her, a flicker of amusement tugging at his lips.

"Be that as it may," said a soft, breathless voice.

It took Brazier a moment to realise it was the masked caster, Guilfier Forain. His voice was strained, as though speaking itself was a chore.

"That is the nature of Obliquency," Guilfier said. "Misdirection. Manipulation. When powerful enough in the target's mind… illusions become reality."

Brazier remembered his academy days, watching a novice Obliquencer convince her bunkmates there were three white rats scurrying around their chambers instead of just one. She hoped to be attached to a ground unit where she could make a Fromryian squadron seem like three or the gleam of ice deposits look like the thruster discs of reinforcing gyre ships. But she would never make those ships a reality.

Freyen clearly thought the same.

"No one, not even the Church, has casters powerful enough to make illusions real."

"Not until now," Guilfier said. "Obliquency draws from the darker side of the gyranic force. To untrained minds, it resembles Aeturnic sorcery."

He paused to catch his breath.

"Many believe it originated in the Aeturnum and bled into the gyre. We believe the Church has found this original strain of Aeturnic Obliquency."

"This is the weapon we believe the Church now possesses," Zarlow said.

"Even if that strain exists," Brazier said, "how do you know it's the Church using it? Why not the Mirrovinjin? Or some goblin death cult?"

"Because we know things about the Church that you don't," Marcus said. "They've been searching for a way to consolidate their power. Now they've found it."

But it all sounded like the usual Royal House paranoia to Brazier.

"The Church using Aeturnic sorcery would be apostasy," he said. "They're… the Church."

"Desperate times," Marcus growled, "call for desperate measures. Or so the Grand Ecclessian believes."

Brazier opened his mouth to argue but Freyen beat him to it.

"Your Highness, why would the Church be so desperate they'd conjure Mirrovinjin ships?"

"Because their authority has been called into question," Marcus said.

"How so?" she asked.

"On their watch, an Aeturnic demi-god returned," Marcus said, jabbing a finger toward the terminal. "Entire installations lost. Thousands dead. Our survival depended on a pact with a foreign prince, whom the Church betrayed. The Houses are whispering. Even Thendergaarden's court questions the Grand Ecclessian's ability to rule."

Brazier wondered if Marcus was one of those whispering but saw no point in asking.

"No matter how discontented the Houses become," he said, "you all know what happens without the Church. Civil war."

"True words, Brazier Veranquis," Aymeri said. "Yet the Church does not take chances with its survival. If it sees a threat, it will destroy even the possibility of rebellion, before it takes root."

"And it would do that how?" Brazier asked. "By helping the Mirrovinjin?"

"By weakening the Royal Houses. By attacking our fleets, reducing our armies," Marcus replied. "And doing so in a way that convinces us the Mirrovinjin are the threat. With no other option, we remain united beneath the Ecclessiarchal heel, while it grows ever more powerful."

"And in so doing, weaken Formaria," Freyen said. Brazier was glad someone else thought this theory bordered on madness. "The Church takes its tithe from the Great

Houses in soldiers and ships. It relies on you as much as you rely on it."

"The Ecclessius," Marcus spat, "plots its survival across centuries. Their plan may cost installations, ships, Fromryian lives, but to them, what is lost now can be regained in a hundred years. They look to themselves, first and always."

Brazier, having witnessed the Church's self-interest first hand, couldn't deny it sounded plausible. But there was one variable no one had mentioned.

"Fiondagaard has invaded Ravinica," he said. "And from what we've heard, they're likely to win. The Church wouldn't let a weakened Formaria face Fiondagaard alone."

"Bah," Marcus scoffed, waving a hand as if brushing off a fly. "Fiondagaard will be weakened, too."

He leaned in over the terminal, eyes narrowing. "They could bring a hundred times our numbers and still not conquer Formaria. They lack ships and navigators. Half our installations would be unreachable. Their armies would march in darkness, their baggage trains stretched across hundreds of miles while we rained death upon them. They are no threat to Formaria, and their Emperor knows it."

"And what about food?" Freyen asked. "We rely on Ravinica for what we can't grow ourselves."

"Which is a lot," Aymeri admitted. "But we are self-sufficient when it comes to feeding Formaria."

"If you don't mind eating reconstituted mushroom for the rest of your life," Switch muttered, then added, "Your Highness."

"The Ravinican and Formarian economies are deeply entwined," Aymeri said. "They buy our gyre ice; we buy their grain and livestock. But if Fiondagaard takes Ravinica, they'll quickly realise the country's economy depends on us. They'll be forced to treat with us."

"And if they decide they're happy to rule over poverty?" Matthias asked.

"We've already sent ambassadors to Celmyr," Aymeri said. "Their land isn't as fertile, and transport across the Amarant Sea will be costly. But it means we won't be eating reconstituted mushroom forever." He looked directly at

Switch as he said it.

Brazier considered. Everything they said sounded both plausible and wildly implausible. He simply couldn't believe the Church would use an Aeturnic weapon against its own people. Freyen seemed to share that disbelief.

"This is all speculation, Your Highness," she said. "You have no proof linking the Ecclessius to these ships. You don't even have evidence this is Obliquency—ancient strain or not."

"Actually, we do," Marcus said, turning to his caster. "Guilfier?"

The caster removed the pipe from his mouth. Crimson smoke drifted from the mask.

"I have a disposition toward Obliquency," he said. Brazier thought he heard sadness in the breathless voice. "Not by choice, but by circumstance. Prolonged exposure during my naval service. My body can no longer maintain a stable form, hence the mask. I'm... difficult to look at."

He held up the pipe. "Vide Fundatum keeps the condition at bay. Even so, I remain highly sensitive to Obliquency."

"Thanks to the Church," Marcus growled.

"The Church's role in my condition is... a story for another day," Guilfier said.

"The Church's negligence," Marcus muttered.

"Regardless," Guilfier went on, "my sensitivity means I can detect Obliquency from great distances. Lately, I've felt massive spikes—Obliquency laced with traces of Aeturnic sorcery. Like purple flares through the gyranic maelstrom."

"We're also tracking disturbances elsewhere," Zarlow added, her voice low but commanding. "We believe the Church's weapon is triggering Aeturnic activity across Formaria, above and below ground. Our scouts report at least one powerful Aeturnic being active on the surface, likely connected to these manifestations." She met Brazier's eyes. "And it isn't alone. Time is against us."

"You think these disturbances are the Church creating illusions of Mirrovinjin ships?" Brazier said. Saying it aloud made it sound even more far-fetched.

"We do," Guilfier said.

"And how do you know it's not the Mirrovinjin?" Brazier asked. "Why assume it's the Church?"

"Live long enough as a caster," Guilfier replied, "and you learn to distinguish the signatures of different races. It's more taste than sight. These casters are human. And they're operating inside Formarian territory."

"Where?" Brazier asked.

Zarlow placed her hand into the well, summoning a map of Formaria. It rotated northwest and stopped at Maw Grindle.

"The Cawdora surface drift," she said, pointing to a cluster of hex filaments floating near the Maw's northern tip.

The crew leaned in. The display showed clusters of various shapes drifting, merging, and breaking apart. They looked serene from a distance, but in reality were the cataclysmic movement of mountains larger than most Gyre Stars.

"That's where Guilfier detected the latest activity," Zarlow said. "And within the last twenty-four hours, a no-fly perimeter was placed around the drift."

"By who?" Brazier asked.

Zarlow shrugged. "Someone with high enough hex clearance to make the command, and erase their tracks."

"Hex corruption?"

"Or someone with the authority to wipe the logs," Rook said casually.

"Or that," Zarlow admitted.

"Whatever the cause," Marcus said, fixing Brazier with a steady gaze, "we need to reach that site, capture the Church's casters, and seize the weapon. Before your arrival, a direct assault was our only option. Now, a better plan presents itself."

"We're just one extra ship," Brazier said. "That's not much of an advantage in a fight."

"We don't want you to fight," Marcus said. "We want you to investigate cloaked and undetected."

Zarlow shifted the display, showing the drift's edge.

"The interference within the drift hides us from navigators. But our ships would still be visible on approach," she said. "From what Phillip tells us, the Anchorite can remain cloaked if fully powered down."

"That's correct," Brazier said.

Zarlow nodded.

"There's enough space aboard for your crew and a team of ours."

"Absolutely not," Brazier said. "We operate better on our own."

"You accusing us of being thieves?" Marcus growled.

"If you took the Anchorite, I think that would make you pirates," Switch said.

The shadow above Marcus' eyes seemed to deepen as he glared at her.

"The cloaking depends on your navigator," Zarlow said. "We couldn't fly her even if we wanted to."

"All the same," Brazier said. "We work best as a four."

Even if they couldn't use the ship without Matthias, Brazier had no desire to invite a Navarch team aboard. He'd learned not to trust that easily.

Zarlow exchanged glances with Marcus and Aymeri before returning her gaze to Brazier. He suspected she was weighing whether they could simply seize the ship and coerce Matthias into cooperation. Not that it would go smoothly.

"We'll accept those terms," she said at last, and to Brazier's relief. "Now explain how the cloaking works."

Brazier let out a breath.

"Originally, we thought the ship had to be completely powered down and stationary," he explained. "But we've since learned we can move while cloaked, so long as all systems remain powered down."

"Which means you can hard sprawl toward the drift," Rook said, tracing a path on the display from the Maw's eastern edge. "Then cut power before entering range of enemy navigators. You'll coast into the drift unseen, under impulse."

"It's possible," Brazier said.

"The fleet will await your return along the Maw's eastern border," Zarlow said.

“Which fleet?” Brazier asked.

“Everyone here,” she replied. “And trusted captains from House Angelaux and House La’Voline.”

“And assuming we find whatever it is the Ecclessius is using to create these ships?” Freyen asked. “What then?”

“We intend to capture it,” Marcus said. “And put it before the other great houses as proof.”

“And if the site is heavily defended?”

“That’s why we need the Anchorite,” Zarlow said. “We need to know what we’re up against. We’ll decide whether to engage based on your reconnaissance.”

“If the Ecclessius outnumbers us,” Sourant added, “we’ll alert the other Great Houses. We may have to engage to hold them in place while aid arrives.”

“Sounds risky,” Freyen said, crossing her arms. Of all the crew, she was the one Brazier trusted to think tactically. It was comforting and unsettling. How many recon plans had she drawn up for the Donnie Shied? Every time she’d helped Brazier and the others… had that been as First Officer, or as a Donnie Shied agent?

“It would be chaos,” Aymeri admitted. “Better to gather evidence and present it. But we must act as circumstances demand.”

“And circumstances demand we act now,” Marcus said, glaring around the terminal. “Decisive action, to prevent the Church from tightening its grip.”

Freyen twisted a curl around her finger, her expression distant and calculating. Brazier found himself staring, and grew annoyed at his own distraction.

“Let’s say you capture this weapon,” she said. “The other houses believe you. What then? You march on Thendergaarden?”

“If we must,” Marcus said. Then, softening: “It won’t come to that. Lother Dillendwan resides in Thendergaarden. He’ll see this for what it is and arrest Cadarasta. That bloated pig will be tried, executed, and replaced by someone less prone to self-interest.”

“And more amenable to the Royal Houses,” Matthias said, smiling. “I’m sure.”

Marcus smiled back.

"In this world, navigator, you take the advantages where you can."

"I couldn't agree more," Matthias replied, silver-grey eyes glinting. "Which brings us to the important question: what do we get for risking our lives?"

Brazier struggled to maintain composure. They were walking a fine line between getting hired and walking away with the *Anchorite*, and losing the ship and being thrown in a prison cell, regardless of whether the cloaking could be used by others or not. Matthias either didn't grasp the gravity of the situation or, more likely, didn't care. Apparently, Switch didn't grasp it either.

"We're taking all the risk," she said, gesturing to their crew. "What's to stop the Church ambushing us in the drift?"

"They don't know you're coming," Zarlow said, voice flat.

"And if you do this," Marcus growled, "we might just let you keep your freedom."

Out the corner of his eye, Brazier saw Matthias dip his chin ever so slightly, like a fighter sizing up his opponent.

Aymeri broke the tension.

"We will revoke your criminal statuses," he said. "Provide full and unconditional pardons. The new Grand Ecclessian will publicly award each of you the Saviour's Cross for destroying a Lord of the Eternal Hunt, and for this mission."

Brazier sensed Matthias go very still at that.

"The Anchorite remains yours," Aymeri continued, turning to Brazier. "But under the condition that you accept Navarch employment, subject to orders against Formaria's enemies. And we want a full written report on Eluthienn, including the shipyard coordinates and how the prince died."

Brazier felt like a child handed a gift he'd begged for, only to find another, even better one hidden inside. Not only would they keep the *Anchorite*, but they'd no longer be outlaws. They would serve Formaria once more. They would be part of the Belum Infinara.

Then the weight of Aymeri's last words landed.

"You believe us? That the Church orchestrated Eluthienn's death?"

Silence fell over the room. Finally, Benera Korst spoke. Brazier had nearly forgotten she was there, she'd stood so still, hands clasped behind her back.

"Those of us here," she said, her voice warm but granite-solid, "formed this organisation to investigate Bork the Borken's supposed revival of a Lord of the Eternal Hunt, and the suspicious nature of Eluthienn's death. We already suspected the Church. Your story confirms it."

"Organisation?" Freyen asked, raising an eyebrow.

"A covert intelligence branch," Korst replied.

"I hate to break it to you," Matthias said, with a grin that made it clear he didn't, "you're not an intelligence branch. You're rebels."

"We are," Korst said evenly. "And you will be too, if you accept our offer."

Of all the outcomes possible after being captured, this was better than Brazier had dared hope for. Still, he knew his crew didn't share his longing for a return to military service.

"It's a fair offer," he said. "But I need to speak with my crew before deciding."

He turned to Freyen, wanting to guage her reaction, but she was looking at Sourant.

"What will you do with the survivors of Hayley's Gambit?" she asked.

"They're already on their way to Pontifax," he said. "We can't have them talking to anyone about us, or you, until this is all over."

"They'll be kept in the royal palace," Marcus said, his tone closing the matter. "Now, make your decision a quick one."

"I'm sure the lieutenant can find a chamber," Zarlow offered.

Marcus grunted, nodding to Sourant.

"Anson," Sourant said. "Level below will do."

Then to Brazier: "Remember, we're only asking for reconnaissance. Just find out what's there. Tell us what we're up against. We'll take it from there."

"You won't even have to fight," Rook added, flashing a boyish smile.

Switch snorted.

"Yeah," she muttered. "That's what they said last time."

THIRTEEN KATHRYN

Isdria Laanorath had left the station and wherever he was going, Kathryn was going too.

Back in the command centre, she sank her hand into one of the terminal wells and tethered to dock command on the western pier. Around her, the cacophony of Custodia and criminal voices dulled to a murky echo, as if she were hearing them underwater.

"Western dock command receiving," a female voice said in her head. "Please provide identification."

Kathryn gave her name, rank, and command script.

There was a pause. Then: "Confirmed, Palatine. How can we help?"

"I need the flight path for the Orphan Guyan."

"Transferring."

By law, every captain had to submit a flight path to any installation they departed from or arrived at, ensuring that if their ship was lost, the Fromryr could locate it again. In theory, the *Orphan* could provide a false path but doing so risked inspection by dock officers or interception by Navarch patrols, especially along the busy transit routes between Thela and Ilantia.

As the line appeared through the white-grey fuzz overlaying her vision, Kathryn felt certain the *Orphan Guyan* fully intended to follow its submitted path.

Because it ended in Maw Grindle.

The route began at Ilantia, curved southwest around the

edge of the massive space containing Thela, then dipped into a lower tunnel shooting south from the cavern, straight into the Maw's northern tip. Briefly, it crossed the Maw's void before cutting into the Cawdora surface drift. There, it wove between the floating mountains and stopped in a dead space near the drift's centre.

She hadn't realised how hard her heart was beating until she could hear it, blood pounding in her ears and drowning out the world. The last time she'd commanded a ship, the last time she'd faced Isdria Laanorath, it had cost her everything.

And now she would face him again. But this time, on her own and outnumbered.

The panic caused her mind to slip. She was back at home again in her mother's quarters in Thendergaarden. Her mother: tall, blonde hair tight in a regulation bun, and her Admiral's doublet so crisp it looked like it could cut skin. She prowled the chamber like a shark circling prey, ruler clutched behind her back, knuckles white.

Why are you such a disappointment, Kathryn? Why do you never learn?

Kathryn knew what was coming. She always knew, just as surely as she knew her own name, that the sky was blue, that the abyss was black. But it didn't stop her from hoping, from praying her mother wouldn't say the words, the words that were worse than the ruler, worse than all the other words combined.

I can always send you back.

Her mother leaned in. *They'll give me another one. A better one.*

And Kathryn's heart stopped. Her limbs turned to ice.

A better child.

"Palatine?" a voice said. "Palatine, are you receiving?"

"Sorry," Kathryn heard herself say. "Sorry, yes. Say again, dock command?"

"I said we're getting a no-fly zone alert around the surface drift," the officer replied.

Kathryn inhaled slowly, forcing herself to focus. "From who?"

There was silence, then: "I'm struggling to find a

command entry."

"Does it say why the area is restricted? Is there enemy presence?"

"There's no reason given. The hex is just telling me no ships are to go near the area."

"Then how is the Orphan going there?"

"Clearance script," the officer said. "Navigator provided one."

How would Isdria Laanorath gain a clearance script for a no-fly zone? A zone with no recorded command script or justification?

Then it clicked.

The no-fly zone and the *Orphan's* clearance for it were part of the hex corruption she herself had fed into the command terminal. Veers just hadn't told her. Isdria Laanorath had clearance because she had given it to him.

Kathryn had to stop herself from punching the terminal.

"When does the Orphan Guyan depart?" she asked.

"Fifteen minutes."

Kathryn clenched her jaw, suppressing the curse rising to her lips. "Give me the crew manifest for arrival and departure. How many logged in versus how many are departing?"

Isdria Laanorath would be registered under a false name, but she could still confirm whether he was leaving with the ship.

"Transferring," the dock officer said. Two lists unspooled across her mind's eye, nearly identical.

"Thirty-four crew accounted for," the officer said. "One original crew member not listed on departure."

"Prep a lander for immediate departure," Kathryn ordered. "Include additional ice reserves. Transfer it the Orphan's flight path."

As a Palatine, she enjoyed privileges most officers did not—something Demina had often complained about. Chief among them was the Right of Passage. Like witch hunters or exorcists, Palatines were entitled to transport upon request, provided a vessel was available.

Fortunately for Kathryn, Ilantia was the busiest transit

hub in the quadrant. There would be a spare ship somewhere.

"Destination?" the dock officer asked.

"Thela," Kathryn lied.

Another pause. "Okay, we've got one. Lander prepped and ready. Pier Seven, fourth on the line."

"Thanks," she said, disconnecting from the hex. The chaos of the station crashed back over her like a wave.

Despite the crossbows slung at her hips and a collection of hand weapons strapped around her waist, no one stopped her as she summoned a lift to the western docks.

Descending on the platform, she finally had space to think, to let the mystery growing like a tumour in her chest take shape.

Focus on the facts. Focus on what you know. That's what they taught you in the academy.

The Sorel Tan had released one of their prisoners. They were a high-value target, someone who'd seen their secret fleet and knew the elven terrorists had allied with the Mirrovinjin. Veers had helped smuggle him in. Veers, who was working with Isdria.

But she shelved that last part. Veers was just a criminal. He probably had no idea what he was tangled in and probably didn't care, so long as he got paid.

Back to the Sorel Tan.

But the facts just raised more questions. They were secretly allying with the Mirrovinjin to build a fleet of ships. Drastic, but believable for a group dedicated to rebuilding the Gyre Gates. But why let one of their prisoners leak that information? Why allow someone like Erin Carmowright walk free and reveal the truth to the Fromryr?

It made no sense. *You didn't tell your enemy what you were building in secret. Not unless...*

The lift shifted direction, a jolt of momentum providing a new angle.

What if sharing that intelligence was the point? What if it made the Fromryr act in a way that benefited the Sorel Tan? But how?

From any perspective, sharing that information would only prompt the Fromryr to find and stop Isdria. How would that benefit the Sorel Tan?

There was only one way to know for sure.

The lift doors opened onto the concourse. Along the pier, waves of heat from gyre thrusters rolled through the air, mingling with the smell of bodies, foodstuffs, and the nauseating sweetness of raw ice.

To her right, she saw the *Orphan Guyan* rise like some creature roused from deep hibernation. Its thrusters gave a short blaze of light, thrummed low, then quieted to a pulsing hum as the ship hovered above its berth.

Then it turned its nose to the abyss.

Kathryn's lander hovered nearby, hatch open, gyre thrusters glowing with soft azure light. She ran to it and confirmed her identity in the terminal beside the pad. A pulse of light travelled from the node down the floor channels and around the octagonal platform. Like the *Orphan*, her lander's thrusters gave a single flare, the release confirmed.

She jumped aboard.

Inside, she racked her crossbows and checked the storage compartments for inertial mutagenis. Opening a shallow cabinet, she found six vials of viscous gold potion. That would be enough.

Satisfied she could follow the *Orphan* into the Maw without suffering temporal displacement, she closed the cabinet and placed her hands into the control terminals at the bow. A second later, a grey-white snowstorm filled her mind's eye.

She focused on her breathing, blanking thoughts and emotions—something she'd done a thousand times before.

Through the static, a tunnel appeared. As her awareness aligned with the ship, the tunnel widened until her senses encompassed the lander's entire periphery, then the docks and tunnels beyond. Her chest eased with a long exhale. She could see it all, the world around her reduced to a palette of grey and white.

Out past the docks, the *Orphan Guyan* was a solid grey mass, its thrusters vibrating disks of silvery white. She imagined her own thrusters surging with power, and they did. The ship rose, and she sent it after Isdria Laanorath.

To the *Orphan's* navigator, she would look like any other lander travelling between Ilantia and Thela. But she'd need to dock at the Cauldron and let the *Orphan* continue alone into the Maw. It would mean losing sight of the ship but it was the only way to follow without alerting its navigator. It was a risk she'd have to take.

She let the ship shrink to the size of her thumb and matched its speed. Without a navigator, it was guesswork. If she didn't focus, she'd lose it in the grey-and-white blur of passing vessels.

But it wasn't hard.

Out in the abyss, with the thrusters' hum thrumming through her body and melding with the bronzite shell, Kathryn felt soothed. She was anchored in the nothingness, and for a little while, she could pretend she was a pilot again.

Six other ships passed her, three ice haulers, two cruisers, and another lander. Through the hex, the cruisers were grey behemoths, great aquiline predators. Their gyre light streaked behind them, glowing slipstreams etched in white.

The haulers looked like some hybrid of larvae and catfish, their thruster arms like mechanical antennae feeling through the dark. The smallest was a firefly by comparison, a pale spark that droned past her unnoticed.

Flying among them, she felt part of something again: the great underground flow, the arterial network that sustained the Fromryr. It was the lifeblood of the people she'd once fought for.

If only it could last longer.

The tunnel's mouth into Thela's cavern complex loomed ahead, hazy like a distant grey sun. The *Orphan* was a tadpole swimming toward it, dwarfed by the tunnel's yawning rim. Then it passed through.

The ship dipped south, heading toward the tunnel that would take it to Maw Grindle. Kathryn kept going, maintaining her heading as she exited into the cavern.

Ahead, Thela, the Cauldron City and capital of House Rosantz, dominated the western side. It looked like a diamond cut in two, with an octagonal wedge driven into its centre. Each triangular half, several miles long, shimmered with geometric white gyre light. To Kathryn, it resembled a crystal spike driven upward from the cavern floor, its peak grazing the ceiling.

Hundreds of ships clustered around the octagonal hub. Each face held its own dock, while smaller personal hangars dotted the diamond's sides. The ships buzzed like bees around a hive. Some shot into the void, others descended onto piers and landing pads.

As Kathryn drew closer, she spotted a Maw-class gyre star floating north of the Cauldron, its bow just visible from behind the far side of the city. Normally, the sight of such a ship would bring comfort. But here, it was like glimpsing the snout of a Mydradyl shark breaching the depths of the Fennian Sea.

That's what you get for disobeying orders and going rogue, she thought. *Suddenly everything's out to get you.*

"Lander, please identify," a voice said in her head, startling her.

Kathryn gave her command script. "Thela Command, I'm requesting emergency docking as befits my rank."

A long pause followed. Anxiety tightened her chest. Had Demina already reported her missing?

Then: "Received, Palatine Stryker. You are cleared to land. Refuel crews are at the ready."

She exhaled slowly. "Negative, command," she said. "I won't be staying long."

"Understood."

She guided the lander to the designated pad, powered it down, and summoned a map of the local tunnel network. The *Orphan's* tunnel began near the base of Thela's cavern complex, like a rabbit hole at the foot of a tree. Three secondary shafts branched from it: one dropped vertically into deeper Formaria, the others ran off horizontally.

Find nearby ice deposits.

The map zoomed out, then back in. Two locations blazed white. One ice shelf ran along the main tunnel into the Maw; another glowed at the end of a secondary shaft.

Smallest deposit.

The map honed in on the secondary shaft.

Location marker on deposit.

A grey dot appeared, flared once, and dimmed. Target locked.

She disconnected from the hex and rubbed the stiffness from her hands. After pacing the cramped lander, just four strides back and forth, she requested a departure window, giving the marker as her destination.

A dock officer confirmed clearance. She fired up the thrusters and sent the lander over the edge of the dock, diving through the cavern, then lit the engines to full sprawl, hurtling through the tunnel after the *Orphan*.

Nearly thirty minutes later, she flew over the secondary shaft she'd listed as her destination. Below, the mouth of the tunnel vanished behind her, and only then did she register what she was about to do.

Taking a lander into a Maw without support was like rowing into open ocean. Doing so and then crossing a surface drift was like braving a midnight storm through a maze of shoals and razor-sharp reef beds. Even for her, it was reckless.

Look on the bright side, at least they won't see you coming.

Like all surface drifts, Cawdora had formed when gyranic energy leaked through great rents in the Yeggardanian surface. The energies, combining with the Maw's sorcerous properties, had gathered tunnel debris to create leagues-long strips of floating rock. Some dwarfed Cradle cities. Others were no bigger than her lander. All of them endlessly collided and reformed, then crashed apart again.

Navigators hated them, and not just because piloting a large ship through the chaos all but guaranteed a beating. Drifts also scrambled hex networks, making mapping and ship detection a nightmare.

Fortunately for her.

With the tunnel's exit in sight, she gave the hex temporary control and disconnected from the terminals. She grabbed a stoppered vial from the cabinet, popped the cork, and drank. The inertial mutagenis scorched down her throat like molten metal, the taste acrid, somewhere between bitter resin and licking cold bronzite.

She had just enough time to return the vial before the potion hit. Biting pain raced through her muscles, from calves to neck. She grabbed the edge of the terminals, knuckles cracking as she braced against the lancing aches.

Then it was gone so quickly it felt imagined.

She exhaled and sank her hands back into the control wells. The snowstorm in her vision cleared with every breath, revealing a view of pure grey, an endless abyss in every direction.

Track *Orphan Guyan* flight path.

There was no visual marker, just instinct, a deep, intuitive pull. The direction was ahead.

She set the thrusters to maximum and plunged into the void. More void, and more, until at last, a faint outline appeared. It was a scattering of triangles that slowly resolved into a distant wall of dark grey mountains wreathed in white haze.

Then the wall fractured. The haze split into veins of light, and she was close enough to make out the individual bergs: mountainous rocks adrift in slow chaos.

The hex showed her where to go, but it didn't make the journey easy. The guidance was broad; the path was hers to cut.

Before her rose a massive formation of shifting rock, its ravines and gorges glowing like halos. A large mass drifted solemnly left, opening a temporary gap. She banked hard to port, guiding the lander through.

The rock walls closed in, tight and tighter. She rolled the ship sideways and squeezed through the narrowing ravine. The white slit of light became a blade's edge, then vanished. Behind her, the mountains slammed shut with a deafening rumble that echoed along the hull.

A boulder, twice the size of her lander, summersaulted across her view. She dove sharply starboard, dodging it. Just as she levelled out, another rock, larger still, rose toward her like a fist from the dark.

She angled the thrusters down, shot the ship up, then

ducked into another dive.

A field of spinning debris spread ahead. Smaller chunks this time, dozens she could weave between. She darted through them, banking left and right. Then—

Crack.

A sharp blow against the hull made her flinch. The ship bucked starboard, but she corrected it.

Don't get cocky.

The hex flagged hairline fractures. Minor damage, it said. Still, she couldn't stop herself from grinning. The last time she'd flown like this was at the Navarch Academy, racing classmates through the southern tunnels of Thendergaarden. That was before the weight of command and before her mother—back when flying had meant freedom.

It was only a spectre of that feeling but she relished it.

She reduced speed by a fifth and pressed on. The topography thinned, the debris fell away, and she entered a pocket of clear space.

Towering mountains of rock rose around her, forming a giant, cavern-like arena. On the far side, her intuition told her, was the *Orphan's* destination.

She brought the lander to a halt. With thrusters on standby, she could hear it: the grinding, creaking clash of mountain-sized bergs jostling for space.

Wait for the gap, she told herself, sweat trickling down her back. Her hands ached from the terminals. A knot tightened in her lower spine. *Wait for the gap.*

Then there was movement.

Two mountains parted with agonising slowness, creating a passable ravine. She surged forward. The walls loomed again, jagged and uncertain. Ahead, a white slit of light widened. This time, the gap grew.

She slowed.

Beyond the ravine lay the *Orphan's* destination.

Like a predator slipping through the grass, she inched forward, thrusters barely aglow. The ravine opened into a wide expanse, dominated by a single massive berg. A mountain range of strange, billowing formations like bulbous tubes, sprawled across its plateau. They blocked her view of the far side. Debris circled the berg in a slow whirlwind, while distant bergs collided in thunderous crashes that rang even through the hull.

Somewhere on the other side, Isdria Laanorath waited. There was nowhere else for him to go, no other place for the *Orphan* to land.

The thought had simmered beneath the surface of Kathryn's mind. With the thrill of flight fading, it came rushing back, seizing her chest in a vice of anticipation.

He was close, so close she could almost taste the victory. Through that mountain range was her chance at redemption, her return to her old life.

Do not mess this up.

FOURTEEN
BRAZIER

Lieutenant Anson led the crew of the *Anchorite* into a small antechamber with a broad balcony overlooking the courtyard below. Somewhere above them, the capital ships hummed into the vastness surrounding the installation. The sound was a low drone, broken now and again by the groan of ancient bulkheads, hulls, and keels echoing into a cavern older still.

At the balcony, Brazier let his gaze drift across the expanse. He wondered if this installation had witnessed the kind of plot now unfolding within it. Knowing the Fromryr's bloody, thousand-year history, it almost certainly had. And before that... who knew what it had borne witness to, across the untold eons of the Formarians. Whether that thought made him feel better or worse, he couldn't say. It definitely made him feel small.

"So we're going to help a couple of High Lords and rebel Navarch officers overthrow the Grand Ecclessian," Switch said, as the doors shunted shut behind Anson. "This might actually be more insane than hunting down a Lord of the Eternal Hunt."

"Except we're not doing the overthrowing part. That's on them," Matthias said, grinning. "Sadly."

"Not unless you count our testimonies against the Grand Ecclessian," Brazier said, voicing the thought that had been bothering him. "That's why they were so quick to accept all our conditions."

"That, and they need me to fly the ship," Matthias added, smiling.

Freyen turned to Brazier. "Handing us back the Anchorite is a risk for them," she said.

"They're attempting to overthrow the Grand Ecclessian," Brazier replied. "Even if they manage to capture this weapon and present it to the other houses, it's a gamble. For all their talk of discontent, the great houses won't rebel lightly. If they fail, it's a death sentence. Our testimonies about Eluthienn's betrayal will help sway them."

Freyen frowned. "And they're letting the people with those testimonies sail off into the dark?"

"I'm guessing that's what the pardons are for," Brazier said.

Freyen raised an eyebrow. "You think they'll let us keep the Anchorite? Once this is over?"

"Aymeri La'Voline is widely reputed to be a man of his word," Brazier said. "I think he means to honour that promise."

"And Marcus and the others?" Switch asked.

"I don't know about the others," Brazier said. His father and brother had never mentioned Admiral Korst or Admiral Zarlow. But his tutors had forced him through endless lessons on the Fromryian royal houses. "Marcus Angelaux is the fourth son of Cornelius and Arabella Angelaux. All three of his brothers died fighting the Mirrovinjin. Of his three sons, one was killed in an ambush, another by goblin raiders."

"That'd explain the permanent bad mood," Switch said.

"He's bitter over how the Church is running Formaria," Brazier said. "But whether that makes him trustworthy, I don't know."

"Doesn't matter if he isn't," Matthias said, voice rich with mischief. "A lot can happen between entering that drift and exiting it. Who knows where we might end up."

"On the run, working for criminals," Brazier said. "Not something I want to go back to if I can help it."

"No different from how it's been," Matthias said. "And as I recall, we had a good thing going."

"You're going to throw away your chance at redemption that easily?" Switch asked. "Full pardons. A clean slate. You'd toss that aside?"

"Redemption?" Matthias chuckled. "I don't need redemption from some king. And you're assuming we actually get those pardons. The Ecclessius aren't in the habit of letting people like me go free. No matter who's in charge."

Or people like Freyen, Brazier thought. Sourant would have shared her past with the others, and none of those officers struck him as the forgiving type—even for *former* Donnie Shied operatives. And Matthias, well, they needed him for now. But that might not last.

The clause binding them to serve the Navarch after this didn't feel like a trap. But it could be just plausible enough to convince them. Was he about to risk his crew's lives again? Was he about to make another mistake?

He thought back to the vulnerum in Thendergaarden, agreeing to escort Eluthienn to destroy Lokul. That had been another decision, another gamble.

This time, he would need a guarantee.

Matthias said something that made Switch laugh, and Brazier realised he'd stopped listening. Freyen caught his eye. She gave him a small smile that made his heart ache, another problem he couldn't think about right now. *One thing at a time*, he told himself. Her smile turned quizzical as she studied his face.

"We need a guarantee," Brazier said abruptly, almost without meaning to speak. Switch and Matthias fell silent, looking at him.

"What if those pardons were guaranteed?" he asked. "If our ownership of the Anchorite was guaranteed, would you agree to fight for the Navarch?"

Matthias studied him for a moment, the cache's blue light gleaming in his grey eyes.

"More interesting than babysitting miners," he said with a shrug. "But there's no way to guarantee those pardons."

"No," Brazier admitted. "But a trial involving the Grand Ecclessian will be public, as will our testimonies. All of Formaria will know about it. I'll make sure they know about the pardon offer too. Neither Aymeri nor Marcus will want to break that promise in front of the entire country."

"Announcing the pardon offer at the trial?" Freyen said. "Won't that make it look like our testimonies were bought?"

"Doesn't matter," Brazier said. "The Anchorite's hex network has our entire engagement history. It'll back up everything we say."

"Aymeri and Marcus won't like it," Freyen said. "But it could work."

Switch nodded. "Not the worst idea I've heard today."

"Well," Matthias said, silver eyes gleaming. "If anyone can pull that off, it's probably you, Cap."

"Then we're agreed?" Brazier asked.

All three nodded.

"Alright then," Brazier said. "Let's go see what the Ecclessius is up to in that drift."

As they left the antechamber, Brazier paused, his gaze sweeping once more across the vast, ancient expanse of the installation. Its history lay buried beneath the weight of forgotten millennia and the world pressing down from above.

But this time, he didn't feel quite so small. Not because the weight was lighter. But because this time, he was choosing to carry it.

Fifteen
Kathryn

She floated down to the berg, keeping the thrusters at minimum sprawl. With the mountain's symphony of crashes rumbling in the distance, she doubted the lander would be heard but she wasn't taking any chances. As carefully and quietly as she could, she settled the ship on the berg's edge, power reduced to minimum while the hex system remained active. The thrusters were just a whisper outside the hull. If she needed a quick getaway, there'd be no time to power up the ship.

The hatch hissed open. Kathryn shrugged off her coat, folded it, and shoved it in a corner. She grabbed the crossbows from their racks, activated both gyre cartridges, then primed the firing wheels before slinging one repeater across her back. It clinked lightly against her armour.

Only when she tried clipping two spare bolt magazines onto her already crowded belt did she realise she'd come equipped for the wrong fight.

Back in the Custodia armoury, she'd imagined storming a chamber barely bigger than a nav deck. Now she was about to fight across open terrain, likely facing multiple enemies spread out and at range. *You'd better get up close and personal then*, she thought grimly. *I don't think Isdria Laanorath is going to come to you.*

Pulling the repeater stock tight into her shoulder, Kathryn stepped off the ship, boots crunching onto rock the colour of rusted steel. All around her, the groan and grind of colliding formations sounded like a ceaseless thunderstorm. The air smelled faintly sulphurous, tinged with the sharp sweetness of raw gyre ice.

Turning toward the tuberous rock formations, paler than the berg's dark reds and ochres, she spotted a gap midway up the mountain, perhaps a hundred feet above. It looked like a pass through to the other side.

She started climbing.

The mineral deposits rose around her like a miniature forest, barely reaching her shins at first. The incline steepened until it felt like climbing stairs. She reached for the deposits with her spare hand, pulling herself upward. Sweat broke across her back beneath the tactical armour. The heat seemed native to the drift, but it had also been some time since she'd marched anywhere in full kit. Being a Palatine in Ilantia, she mostly took lifts.

Hauling herself past another deposit, Kathryn reached the gap. The passage wound through the formations like a trail in a forest. She followed it, repeater tucked into her shoulder, eyes scanning ahead.

Then she heard it: a ship on the float, thrusters at minimum, just audible beneath the background cacophony. It was joined by armour clinking, boots thudding, and the low murmur of voices.

Moving carefully and hunched low, she crept forward. The passage narrowed and opened onto a small landing where the slope fell away. Kathryn knelt between two waist-high deposits.

Below her, the berg mirrored the side she'd landed on: tuber-like formations cascading down toward the edge. The *Orphan* hovered there, boarding ramp lowered. Fifteen, maybe twenty, Sorel Tan elves stood guard around it.

But her gaze didn't stop there.

At the heart of the slope, a raised circle of rock stood like a natural dais. Stacks of glowing blue gyre ice were piled at its edges, some shards as large as her head. But it was the black iron reclining chair set at the circle's edge that seized her attention.

Cold sweat traced her spine. Her breath caught in her

throat.

And then she was sitting in the chair.

She was bound by leather straps and paralysed with fear. Her breath was ragged, sweat pouring from her brow, arms and legs straining, trapped. Blue fire rose in columns around her, raw magic twisting and pulsing. The Mirrovinjin stepped into view, corrupted and grinning. She recoiled, trying to turn away, eyes squeezed shut so hard pain flared at her temples.

When she opened them, she was back, kneeling among the rock formations. Shaking, she clutched the stone for balance.

Not now. Not when she was this close.

Staring at the ground, she forced her breath into something resembling control. Sweat dripped from her temple onto the dusty floor. *Find the elf. Find Isdria. Get out.*

She looked again.

Sorel Tan led blindfolded prisoners down the *Orphan's* ramp, their hands bound behind their backs. They were being marched toward the circle.

Kathryn shifted position, trying to spot Isdria. But then there was buzzing close by, like an insect's wings. She caught a glimpse of a bloated brown abdomen, half the size of a lander, and held aloft by webbed wings. Instinctively, she ducked as the giant wasp-like creature landed nearby.

Boots crunched on the rock below and to her left.

"Your affinity for those creatures is most disturbing, Gabriel," a male voice said, just within earshot. Kathryn inched forward, head low, straining to hear. "As is your relationship with the goblin."

The boots stopped below her.

"I seldom allow others to oversee my plans," the same voice said.

"Oh, I wouldn't dare to supervise," Gabriel replied, mocking.

"Then, Gabriel, your presence here seems somewhat unnecessary."

"Consider it professional curiosity."

There was a snort. “You can tell our mutual friend his sorcerers are most effective. I’m impressed.”

“And yet you burn through them,” Gabriel said. “Some might think you’re thinning your ally’s ranks.”

“Losses no higher than anticipated.”

“And the subjects—how many survive the transformation?”

“One in five.” The words were cool, detached, as if discussing missing cargo.

“And the source?”

“Its power grows with every new crop of harbingers.”

“Does it?” Gabriel said. “I hear one of the first, a woman, was thwarted at first contact. Then another gone missing. Embarrassing for the great Isdria Laanorath.”

Kathryn’s heart somersaulted. Isdria was here, separated from his crew, perhaps even close enough for her to strike.

“We believe the harbinger survived the attack on the Gambit, and remains valuable,” Isdria replied.

The Gambit? Hayley’s Gambit? The thought flashed through her mind but there was no time to dwell on it.

“I do hope so,” Gabriel said. “The source may grow, but it cannot sustain itself yet. One misstep, and it all fails.”

“I hardly need reminding of what’s at stake,” Isdria replied, voice edged with steel.

“Oh, undoubtedly.” Gabriel’s voice dripped with mockery. “Isdria Laanorath, finally the main player. No longer on the fringes. No longer an anecdote in others’ stories, but the lead character. The protagonist. Is that what you think you are?”

There was a pause.

“It matters not what I think I am,” Isdria said, voice sombre. “Now, witness our progress. Then you may report to our ally that the Sorel Tan are upholding their end of the bargain.”

A scuffle broke out near the circle. There was the sound of protest, a shout, then a yelp of pain.

Kathryn eased out for a better view.

Three elves forced a gnome into the iron chair. They tightened leather straps across his ankles, wrists, and chest.

He fought wildly, kicking and thrashing.

She knew what was coming.

Her breath shortened. Her lungs pumped frantically. The sharp pain blossomed in her chest again. Her body screamed warnings.

Forget what's happening! It doesn't matter. You're here for Isdria! The elf—that's why you're here!

She wrenched her gaze from the circle and found what she was looking for.

Isdria and the man called Gabriel stood on a landing further down the slope, roughly ten feet away. The cicadron squatted among the rocks just off to their left, wings folded, forelegs cleaning its large, oval eyes.

Both men had their backs to her. Isdria's black hair was bound with a red kerchief, his cloak discarded. Now he wore Sorel Tan armour openly. Gabriel stood tall and lean, dirty blond hair tied back, posture deceptively relaxed. But his stance radiated readiness, as if poised to strike. The tight leathers and reinforced mail across his back and shoulders only amplified the impression.

Nothing a repeater can't handle, she told herself. *One bolt in his neck. One in the cicadron. One in Isdria's ankle.*

She forced herself to focus on the plan to distract from the gnome's cries rising below. Peering through the rocks, she traced a path that would bring her closer unseen. The formations stood high enough to shield her approach. She could reach Isdria. If needed, she'd ditch the crossbows and carry him on her shoulder, or drag him. Elves weren't that heavy.

But before she could move, a new sound cut the air: a scream.

The elves had cleared the circle. In their place stood a human man in black and red robes, facing the iron chair. He held a book, its withered, bone-white pages scrawled with arcane writing. The man traced a line with one finger, reading quietly. Kathryn couldn't hear a word.

Not that it mattered. The gnome was thrashing now, wailing with such raw terror that it knifed straight through her, seizing her chest with despair.

Get Isdria and get out! she ordered herself. *This is your chance—he's right there! Move!*

But the gnome shrieked again, shrill and unbearable, and Kathryn's body betrayed her. Teeth grinding, limbs shaking, she fought not to cry out herself.

A low chant began, inaudible words in a language she didn't know. It was quiet at first, then louder. A spark flared, like flint on steel. There was another, then another, then the rush of wind, gathering like a storm.

The gnome's screams rose higher, drowning out even the crashing mountains.

Now! Now's the time! she screamed at herself. *Move! Take him while they're distracted!*

She fought the paralysis in her limbs. She tucked the repeater stock into her shoulder. She turned to ensure Isdria was still there.

But just as she looked, the gyre ice ignited. Blue columns of fire burst from the shards, forming towering maelstroms of light that stunned her, momentarily robbing her of all will.

And into that stunned silence came her mother's voice.

You were never good enough! it screamed. *Never going to be good enough!* The ruler crashed down—*crack!*—against the wooden desk, inches from her fingers. Kathryn flinched. Again—*crack!* Her mother's shrieks: *Don't you know what that does to me! Crack!*

She jerked back to the present just as a sphere of darkness formed above the circle. The swirling black mass was nearly the same width as the dais. Black tendrils smoked from its edges. Purple energies cracked like whips from within.

Every spark made Kathryn flinch anew, fighting her mother's voice, fighting the old fear. Below, the gnome was howling now, pleading *no, no, no*, begging for it to stop.

Kathryn felt his terror as if it were her own.

You were never going to be good enough! her mother screamed.

The words ignited something deeper in her. Rage blossomed. A molten, pulsing fire rose in her, a hate that obliterated every shred of fear: hate for her mother, for being forced from the navy, for the abhorrence poisoning her body, and the sorcerer down there inflicting the very torment she had barely survived.

She screamed, raised the repeater, and fired.

Click twang. Click twang. Click twang.

She didn't stop.

Bolts shot wild, ricocheting off rocks, skittering through the air. Some vanished into the dark mass above. But three struck true, burying themselves in the sorcerer's chest and stomach, flinging him to the ground in a crumpled heap.

More bolts flew, pinging around him. Shouts erupted from the Sorel Tan. The swirling darkness above ruptured, belching and thrashing. Gyranic flames roared.

But to Kathryn, it was all background noise. All she heard now was the mechanical rhythm—*click twang, click twang*—blissful, delirious, and drowning out the gnome's screams and her mother's voice alike.

Sixteen
Brazier

The *Sovereign Eclipse* flew toward Maw Grindle's eastern border. It was a single ship, alone in the dark, racing through the tunnels north of Spire Calaxis.

To Brazier, the *Eclipse* vaguely resembled a whale shark. It was flat-nosed, its hull broadening before narrowing at the midsection, then flaring again at the stern where five cylindrical gyre thrusters gleamed: three across the top, two beneath. Two launch bays flanked the ship's middle. Like elongated ventral fins, they were narrow, oddly triangular, and curving back into the hull.

The *Shian Anchorite* and her crew waited in one of those fins, listening to the creaking echoes of a ship under maximum sprawl. Every time the *Eclipse* gave a particularly loud groan, Switch would shake her head, dark eyes crawling the ceiling.

"Ship that beautiful shouldn't be allowed to make those noises," she said. "That's structural damage. Probably stress fractures along the inner bulkheads."

"You have my permission to fix her up," Brazier said, eyes on the display. "Once all this is done."

Switch only crossed her arms and glowered at the hex.

"Tether request from Sourant," Matthias said from the nav pit.

"Go ahead," Brazier said.

The well nearest him pulsed, then carried Sourant's voice: "We're five minutes out from the maw's relative horizon."

"Understood," Brazier said. "Standing by."

They would depart the *Eclipse* just before the relative horizon, entering the Maw alone. As Captain Rook had suggested, the *Anchorite* would max sprawl halfway across the Maw, build enough speed, then cut all power and go dark, shooting toward the Cawdora surface drift cloaked from sight. Unless they were unlucky enough to fly straight into a Church patrol, the *Anchorite* would slip through unseen. Once inside the drift, they could reengage engines; the gyranic chaos would obscure their signature from any navigator.

Or so the plan went.

And plans, in Brazier's experience, rarely survived contact with reality. A horrible feeling stalked him, like a shadow in the dark. It was the sense that he was missing something, that he was about to fly the crew straight into the unknown.

It's just command, he reminded himself. *Everything is an unknown until it happens. You're used to this by now.*

"Shuttle bay doors opening now," Sourant said, as a shunt echoed somewhere outside the *Anchorite*. Beside him, Freyen knocked back her vial of inertial mutagenis and braced against the terminal while the potion took effect.

"Remember," Sourant said. "Do not engage under any circumstances. We need you and the Anchorite for what comes after."

"We are in full agreement with that strategy," Brazier replied.

"And if you're not back within three hours, the fleet is coming to get you."

"I'm not going to let it come to that."

"Good hunting, then," Sourant said, dropping the tether.

On the display, the *Eclipse* slowed to a halt just before the tunnel's mouth. Brazier felt the hum of power as the *Anchorite* rose from her landing pad. A moment later, a small shape, just a cluster of filaments, floated out from the port hangar bay. The hex zoomed in, bringing the *Anchorite* into sharp relief.

Sleek and deadly, yet muscular in design, the ship always made Brazier think of a predator carved from stone. Thruster arms jutted from either side. Two repeaters flanked the bow, a third perched behind the nav deck, another further down the stern. More jutted from beneath the hull. Whatever lay ahead, they would face it aboard one of the deadliest ships the Fromryr had ever inherited.

As they crossed into the Maw, Brazier felt the temporal shift. Pins and needles flared in his extremities. His limbs grew heavy, chest tight, as though bound. Something inside his gut twisted unpleasantly.

Then it passed.

The *Anchorite* cleared Maw Grindle's relative horizon, and the crew exhaled in unison.

"Maximum sprawl," Brazier ordered.

"Aye, Captain," Matthias replied.

The thruster discs spun up, silver filaments shimmering as the ship surged forward. Matthias expanded the hex display, showing the maw's northern half and the surface drift beyond. The *Anchorite* was a single dust mote on the vast map, racing northwest.

"Black void," Switch muttered, one hand in the well, her eyes fluttering. Her mouth curved downward. "Whatever sorcery hit us caused internal displacement."

"How bad?" Brazier asked.

"Maybe ten percent bleed into the ship," she said. "Nothing I can't fix."

"Anything else?"

Her eyelids fluttered again. "Engines are purring. New thrusters putting out at max capacity, fully responsive." She frowned. "Hex system's clean, but some of the protocols look... different."

Freyen slid a hand into her well. "Must've happened when they were analysing the cloaking script."

"Problem?" Brazier asked.

"Just need to reroute some of the internal tethering in the fuselage and vulnerum," Switch said. "One of the repeater magazines is showing a feed error, too."

"Alright," Brazier said, rubbing his brow. "We've got

things to fix. Switch—engines. Freyen—start with the hex. Run the new protocols from here. I'll check the fuselage."

He descended the fuselage stairwell, feeling the thrusters pulsing through his boots, their silent gyre light propelling them through the dark. Placing a hand in the terminal, he tethered to the nav deck.

"Got you," Freyen's voice sounded in his mind. "Running new script now."

Letters, numbers, and symbols cascaded through his mind's eye in a blur of greys, too fast to interpret. He focused on his breathing.

"It's complete," he said, when the cascade ended.

"Running a diagnostic," Freyen replied. "New protocol's integrated."

"I'll check the vulnerum." He dropped the tether and moved aft.

Inside, he repeated the process. As the script ran, his thoughts drifted to the shadow still stalking him. It was the unknown. The thing they were hurtling toward, and what would come after.

When he'd agreed to Aymeri's terms, Brazier had felt lighter, had caught a glimpse of the old confidence he'd once known back when Torquen was alive, when the rules were clear and he knew what side he was fighting for. But since returning to the *Eclipse*, the rules felt less clear, and so did the sides. Because on his side was Freyen.

When the script had run its course, he mumbled something about checking the bulkheads before starting on the repeater feed, and untethered from the terminal.

He found himself pacing down the fuselage, running a hand through his mane, sighing deeply. He'd been so consumed by their capture, and the rebellion they'd been thrust into, that he hadn't realised for the first time ever, he was angry at Freyen. He was angry that she'd been a member of the Donnie Shied, angry that she'd kept it from him, and angry at the doubt it now seeded in him.

What gnawed at him most wasn't that Freyen had lied. It was that he hadn't seen it. How many other mistakes had he made? What else was he blind to? A creeping fear whispered that he wasn't fit to lead. The wrong choice wasn't coming; it had already been made.

And that so-called "guarantee" he'd proposed in the cache? How secure was it really? Even if he publicly announced their pardons, would the High Lords view a high-security prisoner and a former Donnie Shied operative as too dangerous to release? Too dangerous to trust?

"The destruction of Formaria." Now at the end of the fuselage, staring at the weapon racks, he said the words again.

The Donnie Shied were the Knelderian arm of the Sorel Tan, breakaway paramilitaries dedicated to rebuilding the Gyre Gates in their vain attempt to reconnect with ancient kin across the realms. Their aim: to undo the Sundering that had severed the Immuratum from the material realm, and to rearm the Fromryr with sorcery so immense it could poison continents, spawn new races, and, lead to Formaria's destruction.

And Freyen had stood among them. And she had kept that from him. That was what sent the heat prickling across his chest. That was why his jaw clenched.

Half-consciously, he'd disassembled one of the crossbows. It lay scattered around him now, like bones in a wolf's den. He sighed, annoyed at himself for letting his emotions run loose. Slowly, he began reassembling the weapon.

Halfway through, footsteps approached behind him. He half-turned to see Freyen holding out a bronzite mug, steam curling in slow swirls. She wore tight brown leathers and a sleeveless blue-grey shirt, her curls loose around her shoulders. With one leg bent casually, she looked effortless.

It was the unadorned simplicity of it, her posture and her ease that had always drawn him to her. And it was a lie, a front constructed for others. That's what hurt the most. The very thing he loved wasn't real.

He remembered the first time he'd heard her laugh—pure, sing-song, and full of joy. It had seemed so full of possibility, so true.

But now he wasn't sure what was true anymore. That

laugh? The warmth it had sparked in him? Or the lie that had carried it?

It made him doubt everything, including himself.

"Thought you'd want something that wasn't made from reconstituted mushroom," she said, offering the mug.

"You mean while we still have it?" he replied, taking the mug and setting it on a patch of floor clear of repeater parts. Notes of fennel, aniseed, and lemon rose from it.

"Everything okay?" Freyen asked.

No. Not really. Not at all, actually.

For months, he'd sidestepped the question of her past. Now, when he wanted answers, it was the wrong time to ask. Even if he had the right, pressing her now would accomplish little and risk much. It was a poor captain who created a rift with his First Officer in the middle of a dangerous mission.

"Just fine," he said, managing a smile. "All things considered."

She frowned, glancing at the half-finished crossbow in his lap.

"You're distracted," she said.

"I just needed to clear my head."

"No." Freyen nodded at the crossbow. "You're distracted. You fitted the flight chamber the wrong way round."

Brazier looked down. The cylindrical tube jutted awkwardly from the gear housing. With a grunt of agreement, he pulled it free and rotated it into place.

He reached for the mug, glanced up as he blew on the tea. "I don't know if announcing our pardons at the trial will work," he said, skirting the edge of truth. "For all I know, I might not even get the chance. They might limit our testimonies to a smaller court."

"Not too late to bail," Freyen said. "We could find out what the Church is up to in this drift and just send the information over long-range hex cast to the Eclipse."

"Then slip back into the drift and make our escape," Brazier finished for her.

"We'd be long gone," Freyen said. "They wouldn't be able to find us."

"And we'd have done our part."

But the words left him hollow. He sipped the tea, tasting nothing but hot water.

"One problem though," Freyen said. "We made a deal with a king. And I know Brazier Veranquis doesn't renege on his promises."

He gazed at her, into those deep brown eyes. He studied her broad face, angular chin, the pointed tips of her ears peeking through a cascade of curls, and the subtle curve of her mouth. It was a quiet expression, yet it radiated encouragement, confidence, and trust.

For a moment, he entertained the idea of never asking about her past, consigning himself instead to blissful ignorance.

"You know that whatever you decide," she said, "we're all with you. You're our captain. You've been our captain since the moment we escaped on that prison transport."

"Not quite how I remember Matthias' feelings at the time," Brazier said.

"He's come around," Freyen replied, squeezing his shoulder as she turned to leave. "Speaking of, he thinks we should cloak soon."

"I'll meet you up there."

"Oh, by the way," she called back. "You might want to check the gear wheel, too."

Brazier turned the crossbow over in his lap, gave another grunt, and refitted the palm-sized gear wheel. It took him less than a minute to reassemble the rest and slot it back onto the wall rack.

Picking up his tea, he climbed the stairwell one-handed, mind turning over her words, trying them on for size.

Whatever you decide, we're all with you.

"What's our ETA?" Brazier asked Matthias as the nav deck doors slid shut behind him.

"We're two minutes out," the navigator replied, head bowed, arms outstretched. On the hex display, the *Anchorite* shot across a vast expanse of emptiness. The lack of a tunnel floor, of any topography at all, gave Brazier the unsettling sense of being adrift in a great ocean, with no land visible in any direction.

He placed a hand in a well, connecting to the engines. "How are we looking?" he asked Switch.

"I've rerouted the displacement," she said. "But I'll monitor the cloak from here. Make sure it doesn't affect the throughput."

"Good idea," Brazier said, dropping the tether. Then to Matthias: "Open internal doors and cut power when ready."

The nav deck's doors slid open with a mechanical hiss, echoed throughout the ship as compartments and cabins unlocked. The *Anchorite's* cloaking system required a full power-down, including all internal systems. To retain access, they opened everything in advance.

"One minute," Matthias said.

Brazier rested his hands on the command terminal's cool surface, the deep thrum of the thrusters vibrating through his palms and up through the soles of his boots. On the hex, the *Anchorite* was a shooting star, streaking across the void, through a space beyond time and beyond understanding.

"Cutting power now," Matthias said.

The hex display flattened, becoming featureless as a lake in dead calm. The blue gyre channels along the floor and bronzite wall panels dimmed, then winked out, turning ghostly ice-white. Beneath Brazier's feet, the loss of the thrusters' thrum left a void of silence, as if they were adrift in an empty husk, not a ship.

"Auxiliary override complete. Ship's systems at one-tenth power output," Matthias said. "We're flying dark."

And they were flying blind, or as good as. When the ship was stationary, Matthias could use the hex to project his mind and keep them cloaked. But under motion, every system, including the hex, had to shut down to maintain the cloak. He was navigating like a non-magic user, barely able to sense what lay ahead.

In the weeks after their escape from Lokul's lair, they'd dissected Freyen's script, but none could explain the cloak's limitations. The vampire's sorcery had one thing in common with all the Fromryr's scavenged technology: they could use it, but no one knew how it worked.

"How long to the drift?" Brazier asked.

"On last estimate," Matthias said, "we'll reach the drift's eastern wall in just under two hours."

"Nicely done," Brazier said, draining the last of his tea.

"I'll go see about that repeater feed," Freyen said, leaving him and Matthias in a thoughtful silence.

With nothing to fly, the navigator leaned back, arms loose in his lap. Brazier leaned on the terminal, stretching out the stiffness in his lower back. It was time to address the other thing gnawing at him.

"So, when this is done, you'll be wearing Navarch blues," he said.

"Black's more my colour," Matthias replied. "But I've always fancied one of those buttoned doublets."

"Won't bother you, fighting for the ones who imprisoned you? Fighting for the other side?"

Matthias chuckled a low rumble, like stone grating on stone. He turned, sitting cross-legged in the pit. There was something about his stillness, the calm, the faint edge of a knowing smirk, that reminded Brazier of a warrior monk.

"You're good at the captain thing," Matthias said. "But you keep getting the rest of it wrong."

"The rest of it?" Brazier asked, confused.

"There's no this side or that side," Matthias said. "There's only *our* side. The ones in this ship."

"It's only by choosing a side that the Fromryr have stood for a thousand years against its enemies," Brazier said.

"And it'll stand for a thousand more, with us or without us," Matthias said. "Makes no difference."

"And if we won?" Brazier asked. "If we actually won?"

"Deliverance from the dark." Matthias gave a dry chuckle, then grew serious: "What makes you think we'd be any good topside?"

"What makes you think we wouldn't?" Brazier asked.

"Before I became intimately acquainted with the Solace of Iron's holding cell," Matthias said, "I stayed in Crawforge."

Brazier looked up, surprised. Matthias rarely spoke about his past. "Stayed?"

"They keep a cell free for me," Matthias said with a smile. "Just in case I stop by."

"Crawforge is supposed to be inescapable," Brazier said. The prison installation, located far to the west of Calanthis Minor and buried deep beneath the surface, was carved into a network of naturally formed burrows, many of which opened onto vast underground caverns. From what Brazier had heard, it was plagued by Dire Amibrodons, 20-foot-long salamander-like creatures that migrated from the Amarant Sea every five years to nest in Formaria's warmer tunnels. Their young, it was said, hunted the prisoners, keeping the population at manageable levels.

"Supposed to be," Matthias said. "Last time I visited, I shared a section with a professor. At least, that's what he claimed. Liturgic purification had made him mad and bald. Any chance he got, he'd tell me we belonged in the dark. That when the Fenn first invaded, they didn't just force us underground, they helped us rediscover our home."

"That's Velgavinian theory," Brazier said. "That we are the Formarians."

Matthias nodded. "Didn't know it had a name. This professor said believing the Formarians were some long-dead race who left technology perfectly suited to all four species of the Fromryr, relied too much on coincidence. He thought the simpler explanation was that we are their descendants. Same as the ancient techno-barbarian humans are the ancestors of today's humans."

"And you believe that?"

"Doesn't matter what I believe." Matthias' moon-grey eyes gleamed. "Point is, we've been doing this so long we've forgotten who we are. Formaria's just the same old story, playing out again and again. Those at the top, moving those at the bottom."

"For the survival of the people," Brazier said.

"If that's what keeps you going," Matthias said, eyes glinting, "then that's what keeps you going. Me? I can go either way. You want to make us heroes of Formaria? Fine. You want to take this ship and get rich running protection contracts? That's fine too. Just don't expect me to become a believer. Because there was never anything to believe in."

Brazier stared at him, unsure if he was annoyed or depressed by the navigator's relentless cynicism. "I'm going to find something to fix," he said at last.

Matthias shrugged and stretched out in the pit, looking for all the world like he might fall asleep in it.

Brazier left the nav deck, the fuselage suddenly claustrophobic, eerie without the hum of the thrusters. He descended to the engine room, found Switch elbow-deep in the core, engine parts sprawled across the floor.

He tried to make conversation, but Switch wasn't having it, whether because she was focused or because it was clear he was at a loose end. When she asked what she could help him with, he took the hint and moved on, avoiding the landing where Freyen worked on the repeater feed.

He thought about making tea, then remembered there was no hot water with the ship powered down. Sighing, he decided the swords in the armoury surely needed whetting.

Despite himself, he kept drifting into the future, imagining possible outcomes. In most of them, they sent a long-range hex message to the *Eclipse*, shared what they'd learned, then slipped away into the drift or rendezvoused with the fleet. Again and again the scenarios played out, each dissolving into a swirl of conflicting outcomes that left him more confused.

By the time Matthias called down from the nav deck, the short sword on Brazier's knee was sharp enough to cut bronzite.

"We're coming on the drift," the navigator said.

Brazier re-racked the weapon and climbed the stairwell. The rest of the crew was already gathered around the command terminal.

"Looks like we're on our own out here," Matthias said, peering forward as if trying to look through the bronzite walls. "Guess the Ecclessius are counting on the no-fly zone."

"Or the Cawdora drift is too big to patrol," Brazier said. "Let's not take any chances. Engage engines and reverse thrust only when we're in range of the drift's sorcery."

"Aye, Captain," Matthias said. "One minute to the drift wall."

They watched him, arms spread, fingers splayed wide, like he was gripping two great invisible spheres.

"Twenty seconds," he said, shoulder muscles taut. Then: "Engaging engines."

He rotated his hands behind him, and crystal blue nodes shot along the floor and up the walls, the deck shivering beneath their feet. A ripple coursed across the display, then the hex rose up, forming a sculpt of the Cawdora surface drift.

Half the display remained flat, showing the maw's void. The other half rose into a shifting, ancient wall of rock, mountains, bergs, boulders grinding and crashing in eddying currents.

When Brazier made it out, the *Anchorite* was a speck of filaments, an ant staring up at something vast and ancient.

"Take her in when you're ready," Brazier said.

The ant floated through a ravine in the drift wall. The hex rescaled; the floating mountains expanded, covering two-thirds of the display.

"Anyone see where we are?" Switch asked, leaning over the terminal.

"That's us," Freyen said, pointing to a vague shape amid the chaos. The *Anchorite* looked like any other drifting boulder, only its clean flight path marked it as a ship.

Outside, the grinding echoes and crashes of colliding mountains shook the hull. To Brazier, it sounded like giants fighting.

"Err, Matthias," Switch said, eyes narrowing. "You're not about to go where I think you're about to go?"

Brazier followed her gaze across the hex. Two bergs, each half a mile wide, spun directly in front of their flight path, grinding together like massive gear wheels, locking, parting, then locking again.

"We can go around, Matthias," Brazier said, watching the bergs with apprehension.

"We could," Matthias replied, and Brazier's grip on the command terminal loosened in relief. "But where's the fun in that."

And Brazier's grip turned vice-like in an instant.

The *Anchorite* climbed, then dove through the temporary gap in the bergs, its thrusters tucked neatly behind it. The ship vanished between the two mountains. The noise was like a barrage of sorcerous detonations, a small war conducted between titanic stone adversaries.

Only when they were out the other side did Brazier hear Matthias' low chuckle roll across the deck.

"I would've paid gold Vidicks to see your faces," the navigator said.

"If there's so much as a scratch on her," Switch muttered, glaring at the back of Matthias' head, "you will become intimately acquainted with my augment."

"That's an outcome I condone," Brazier said, exhaling. "How long until we reach the target?"

"We'll be coming up on it shortly," Matthias replied.

The hex display rolled westward, new bergs and boulders forming on its far edge. Even with the hex sculpt struggling to hold its form, Brazier quickly spied a ring of mountains encircling a central berg, like a palisade around a keep. The berg itself bore its own jagged mountain range, running through its heart and widening to the west.

"That's the location of the gyre signal," Matthias said. "But if there's anyone on it, the interference is too strong to tell."

Like the rest of the sculpt, the surrounding mountains fought to maintain their form, filaments trickling down their edges before reforming. The berg suffered the same instability, the filaments spilling over the surface like cascading water.

"The surrounding mountains will give us good cover," Brazier said. "But you'll need to find a ravine open long enough for us to get a look. If there isn't one, we go over the top."

"Aye, Captain," Matthias said. The navigator flew the ship toward the circle of mountains, weaving around boulders and larger debris. But the field was too dense to dodge everything. Knocks and thuds echoed off the hull.

Occasionally there was a sizzling crackle, like fat burning, when rocks struck the thruster discs and disintegrated in the gyranic fire.

"Too much of that and the feedback will burn out the reductors," Switch warned, arms crossed, giving Brazier a look that said: *you'll be to blame.*

"What's the eastern face look like?" Brazier asked, ignoring her.

On the hex, the thumb-sized *Anchorite* floated toward the ring of mountains. But with mounting interference, the ravines and gullies opening between the rock faces flickered uncertainly and none lasting long enough to guarantee safe passage.

"I'm not seeing a gap on this side," Matthias said. "Bringing us around."

The *Anchorite* tracked portside, following the mountain ring's southern edge, dipping and rising to avoid rogue debris.

"Nothing," Matthias said.

"Keep following," Brazier replied.

The ship skirted the southwestern perimeter, dodging splintering rock as bergs ground against each other.

"Got something," Matthias said. "Probably a two-minute window."

"We'll take it," Brazier replied. "Take us in."

Standing at the command terminal, Brazier could only see the eastern and southern edges of the mountain ring. The *Anchorite* slipped from his view as Matthias swung them around the western face and into a ravine.

"Coming to a stop," Matthias said. The deck's vibration faded; the groaning of surrounding mountains filled the silence. "We're floating dark."

"What can you see?" Brazier asked.

Somewhere between two of those titanic monoliths, Matthias had edged the *Anchorite* close enough to the ring's inner perimeter to glimpse the central berg, though too much gyranic interference still clouded the hex.

"Single ship," Matthias said. "South side of the berg. Looks like a miner. Cauldron class."

"Anything else? Anyone on the berg?"

Matthias shook his head. "Could be. But we're too far out."

"What's the Ecclessius doing with a single miner?" Freyen asked.

"Inconspicuous ship," Brazier said. "Maybe they pass it off as a free trader, use it as transport."

"Transport for what?" Switch asked.

"Matthias—any sign of what they're doing?" Brazier asked.

"Looks like they're on the float," Matthias replied. "No way to tell if they're shifting cargo."

"We'll need to get closer," Brazier said, studying the berg. The mountain range running through its centre spread westward to a vantage point they could use to observe the south side undetected.

"Can you land us on the western edge, among that range?" Brazier asked.

"I'll need to pull us out and come back in from the north," Matthias said. "But I can get us down."

"Then do it," Brazier said. Then to Switch and Freyen: "We'll go on foot. Use the mountains as cover and take a look. Then we leave."

Matthias trickled power to the engines, coaxing the *Anchorite* back through the ravine with just enough sprawl to remain undetected.

Then there was a crashing rumble so deep it sounded like the world's foundations shattering and the *Anchorite* shook. Vibrations rode up into Brazier's shins. The hex sculpt shuddered, lost cohesion, then reformed in rippling waves.

"That didn't feel like a two-minute window," Brazier said.

"Two minutes was the optimistic end of the timeline," Matthias said. Then: "We've got another opening."

"Do we have two minutes to get through it?" Switch asked, arms crossed again.

"This one's a little tighter."

"Can we make it in one piece?" Brazier asked.

"As long as we don't hang around," Matthias said.

"Then we'll take it," Brazier said.

Matthias' arms tensed, fingers splayed wide. Twin whirlpools swirled beside him in the hex pit. The thrusters pulsed to life beneath their feet.

"Cut sprawl once we're through," Brazier said. "And float us down dark."

Moments later, the *Anchorite* appeared from the western face of the mountain ring. Brazier moved to the terminal's far side, watching as the ship glided toward the berg. As it neared the mountain range, Matthias re-engaged the engines, bringing them to a stop among the jagged formations.

"All right, maintain position here," Brazier said. Then to the others: "Let's see what we can see."

He followed Switch and Freyen down to the armoury, where he took a repeater, spare magazines, and a short sword from the rack. Switch did the same, while Freyen opted for her long knives instead of a blade. Placing his hand in the hex terminal, Brazier called for Matthias to open the boarding ramp. A moment later, it descended onto the berg with a crunch. He led them down.

A forest of stone formations surrounded the ship. They were pale, bleached structures with swollen, rippling edges. They varied in height, some as tall as Brazier, others eight or nine feet, ending in spiralled peaks. He picked a path through them, heading south.

Whatever sorcerous current had swept up this berg and the surrounding mountains seemed to conjure a pocket of warmth. Soon, he regretted the weight of his gambeson and plate armour. The floating mountains made distant, grumbling noises. Underfoot, the pale stone crunched and sent up clouds of dust.

"Anyone else hear that?" Freyen asked. Brazier stopped, watching her bat-like ears twitch.

"Thrusters," Brazier said, hearing what must be the miner Matthias had spotted.

"That," Freyen said, frowning. "And someone shouting."

"Let's move," Brazier said, suddenly gripped by the feeling that whatever was happening, they were already late to see it.

They picked up the pace, weaving through the spiralled stone, climbing steadily. Soon, Brazier made out the mountains floating beyond the southern side of the berg. He slowed, then brought them to a stop, kneeling between a cluster of formations that overlooked the entire southern side.

The stone forest thinned down the slope, formations growing smaller and more scattered. A miner hovered at the berg's edge. Soldiers in ochre and ruddy-brown gambesons stood around one of its boarding ramps. Near the bottom of the slope, a raised circle of cleared stone struck out among the formations to form a natural dais. Someone was being dragged onto it.

Two soldiers held a male gnome between them. The gnome struggled, kicking and shouting, as they hauled him onto an iron chair. Another figure in long black and red robes stepped onto the dais, a book in his hands.

"Sorel Tan," Freyen said. At the name, Brazier's head snapped toward her. For a heartbeat, he thought he saw a flicker of fear in her eyes. He forced his expression to become neutral.

He turned back to the scene below. For a moment, he thought Freyen meant the gnome, that the Ecclessius had captured a terrorist and were about to torture him, until he recognised the Sorel Tan colours: shin-long gambesons the colour of chestnuts and sun-baked earth.

"What in the abyss are they doing here?" Switch said.

Before Brazier could answer, Freyen spoke: "Fifteen feet left of the circle, up the slope."

Brazier followed her instructions, spying two figures on a small promontory overlooking the dais. Then he blinked in surprise, resisting the urge to rub his eyes. A single cicadron sat to their left, its riding harness strapped to its abdomen. The giant wasp, the goblin-tamed mount, was entirely out of place here.

Nearby, one figure wore tight-fitted leathers reinforced with mail. But even if he'd worn priestly robes, Brazier would have recognised the feline posture of the man they once called a crewmate.

"Tell me both of you are also seeing Gabriel down there?" Switch said.

"If he's there, does that mean the Church is working with the Sorel Tan?" Freyen asked, voicing exactly what Brazier was thinking.

"I can't think of a better explanation," Brazier said.

"And the cicadron?" Switch asked.

"Must be Gabriel's," Brazier said. But before he could say more, the man with the book began to chant.

Blue flames erupted around the dais, spiralling columns rising from piles of gyre ice Brazier had only just noticed. The gnome screamed, thrashing against his restraints, his terror a raw, gut-wrenching sound that set Brazier's teeth on edge.

The chanting grew louder. Sparks crackled above the caster's head, one, then another. Then reality split open. A black and purple mass formed from a rent in the air above the dais, Aeturnic energies swirling within, thin tendrils curling outward. The gnome's screams rose, piercing and unendurable. Brazier clenched his jaw.

"What in the black hell are they doing to him?" Switch said, scowling hard.

"I don't know," Brazier said. "But we need to put a stop to it."

"You want to go down there?" Switch asked, though her tone suggested she wasn't entirely against it.

"And what do we tell Sourant?" Freyen said. "We have no idea what's going on here."

"This might be how they're creating the illusions," Brazier said.

"And it might not," Freyen countered. "Do not engage under any circumstances. That was the plan."

Even as the screams rose higher, Brazier knew she was right. They needed to see this through, to learn how the false ships were being created. If they attacked now, they'd blow whatever advantage the rebels had. But standing here, hearing the gnome's screams and doing nothing, felt wrong.

The crew waited for him to choose, not to consult, not to agree, but to lead.

You don't have time to doubt yourself. Or her.

"New plan," he said, voice sharper now. "Matthias brings the Anchorite around for suppressing fire. We go for Gabriel and drag him back to Sourant. We end this and we find out how they're making those ships."

Freyen gave him a hard look, one that said we're not supposed to be doing any fighting. But before she could speak, chaos erupted.

The sound of repeating crossbows clacked and twanged from somewhere along the mountain range. A hail of bolts thundered into the rock, the floor, then the caster, flinging him to the ground.

The Sorel Tan reacted instantly, drawing swords and knocking bows, pointing toward the source of the fire. Without the caster, the black sphere of sorcery began to rupture. The blue flames guttered and died.

Brazier stared, stunned. Someone was already moving down toward the dais, firing, shifting, hugging cover. Each movement was smooth and precise, both professional and deadly.

As they sprang out again, Brazier caught a glimpse: blonde hair beneath a helm, a human face, full tactical plate. Two repeater crossbows, one in each hand. The cicadron lay on its back, abdomen studded with bolts.

"Looks like someone's beaten you to it, Cap," Switch said. She sounded impressed.

"Freyen—get back to the Anchorite. Have Matthias bring the ship around and target the Sorel Tan and the miner's turrets. Force them to disengage," Brazier said. His heart ticked up with anticipation. "Switch—we're going for Gabriel."

"And what about the one-woman army?" Switch asked, nodding toward the battle below.

"Assume she's here for the same reason we are," Brazier said. "She's on our side, for now. But our priority is Gabriel. We bring the witch hunter back alive."

Freyen nodded and dashed off toward the *Anchorite*. Brazier activated his crossbow's gyre cartridge and turned to Switch.

"Let's do this."

Seventeen
Kathryn

The columns of blue fire crackled and petered out. The dark sphere of sorcery disgorged black tendrils and lost its mass. The Sorel Tan's shouts became clearer, somehow louder in Kathryn's ears.

Move, she told herself, stunned by her own actions. *Move*, she repeated, her inner voice rising. *You need to move! Now!*

She flung herself down the slope, darting between rock formations, taking any path that would let her stay moving and provide cover. Skidding to a stop behind a wall of chest-high nodular stone, she ducked and reloaded her crossbow with a fresh magazine.

"I'll deal with this," she heard Gabriel say from somewhere close. "Get out of here, now!"

Kathryn peered over the rock wall. Sorel Tan soldiers, many with swords drawn, others with bows nocked, were edging toward the ritual circle, keeping low. Isdria Laanorath was heading for the *Orphan*. To reach it, he would have to cross through the circle.

She could cut him off.

She swung the second repeater across her body, nestling both stocks in the crooks of her elbows. Blood pounded between her ears. *Get out there and get Isdria! It's now or never!*

She sprang from behind the wall, firing indiscriminately. Moving and firing, leaping from cover to cover, she loosed bolts as fast as the repeaters could cycle.

Elves dove for cover as shards of yellow-grey rock flew into the air. Grunts and curses blended with the rhythmic *click twang*, *click twang* ringing in her ears.

Out of the corner of her eye, Kathryn saw Gabriel scrambling toward her down the slope. She spun, turned her repeater on him, and fired a burst of bolts, forcing him to throw himself flat.

Without missing a beat, she turned her other repeater back on the elves, forcing them back.

But Isdria was nearing the circle, his ochre gambeson billowing around his legs as he cut through the stone forest. She wouldn't reach him in time. He was too quick. The gap between them was too wide.

With no other choice, Kathryn lowered one repeater and aimed for his lower body. She squeezed the trigger. Bolts spat out, cracking stone, spitting up dust, ricocheting through the air.

Isdria stumbled. The elf tried to limp on, then collapsed just before the circle. With no triumph or hesitation, Kathryn spun back toward Gabriel, firing up the slope. But instead of bolts, her repeater clicked a *clack clack clack clack clack.*

Gabriel heard it. He sprang from cover and sprinted toward her, closing the gap fast.

Kathryn ran, bolting toward the ritual circle. She let the empty repeater drop against her shoulder strap, its weight bouncing against her armour. With her free hand, she unclipped a fresh magazine from her belt, swapped it with practiced ease, and jammed the empty back into her kit.

She spun and fired at Gabriel again, forcing him behind cover. Then she turned back toward the circle, but even before she moved—*ping, clatter, ping!* A bolt skittered off her armour. Another struck her helm, ringing in her ears and jolting her head.

She threw herself to the right and pressed forward, firing intermittently. The elves, now returning fire, darted for cover, buying her another few seconds.

Isdria had pulled himself onto the circle. He limped toward the opposite edge, dragging his leg, one bolt pinned his gambeson to his thigh.

Kathryn ran after him, sweat pouring inside her helmet, her heart hammering. She reached the edge of the circle, dropped to her knees, and reloaded her second repeater with her last magazine.

Scrambling onto the rock dais, she saw Isdria at the far edge. He half-stepped, half-fell from the circle, soldiers rushing to his aid. Panic coiled in her gut. *You're going to lose him. You're going to lose your chance. Your future.*

She sprinted across the circle, dodging the dead sorcerer, and firing both repeaters. One elf helping Isdria gasped as Kathryn's bolt slammed into his back. He crumpled. Isdria collapsed again.

But the Sorel Tan were closing in, fanning out around the circle. Kathryn turned one way, fired a burst, then turned another. Cries and shouts rose with the crack and thud of crossbows and the constant rattle of her repeaters.

Move! she screamed at herself. *You're being surrounded!*

Then, mid-sweep, something made her freeze. Gabriel was pulling himself onto the rock dais, sleek and fluid, his movements unnervingly precise.

Except there wasn't just one of him.

Three Gabriels climbed the dais, each a perfect mirror of the other, each with sword drawn, each with the same smile on their lips. They closed in from different angles, like wolves circling prey.

"You know," the one approaching on her right said, voice full of cruel amusement, "this little interlude has really made my day. A shame I'll have to bring all the fun to an end."

Not before I bring you to an end.

Kathryn fired straight into his chest, close enough that she barely needed to aim. Five bolts hammered out—

—but hit nothing.

Instead of striking the man to the ground, the bolts flew through him, leaving only curling tendrils of smoky black vapour in their wake. Kathryn spun and fired at the next one, only to see him vanish in another cloud of smoke.

All her instincts screamed. She whirled left, bringing her repeater up. But she was too late. Gabriel's sword came crashing down on the crossbow, driving its nose to the floor. Kathryn brought her other repeater around, but his blade was faster. The sword knocked the weapon from her grasp, a sharp sting lancing across her wrist.

Without hesitation, she drew her short sword, her fingers slick with blood and her grip already weakened. Wetness slicked her palm, but she forced her fingers tighter around the hilt.

Backing away, careful to avoid the dead sorcerer, Kathryn tugged the other repeater strap over her head and let it fall to the floor. With her free hand, she drew her combat knife.

Gabriel paused, glanced at her dual weapons, raised an eyebrow, and tilted his head in a small, mocking nod. Then he sprang, faster than she'd thought humanly possible.

Her body reacted on instinct. She brought her sword up. *Clang*. The steel clash rang out. Gabriel flowed through a figure eight motion, slicing down on her other side. Kathryn parried, the blow forcing her back.

She sidestepped, ducked another swing, pivoted behind him, but Gabriel spun, a backhanded strike catching her off-guard. Her sword came up, but instead of steel-on-steel, his blade slammed against her helm.

Her ears rang, her eyes watered, and her vision swam. Barely conscious of her actions, she parried an upward swing with her knife, then blocked a cross-arc with her sword while falling back, defending, defending, defending.

Then came a bite. A cold numbness bloomed in her left arm, steel parting flesh at her elbow. Her knife fell from numb fingers.

Breath heaving, she readied her sword for the next strike.

But it didn't come. Gabriel kicked out, his boot slamming into her sternum, sending her tumbling backward.

She hit the floor hard, somehow keeping hold of her sword. She tried to breathe but only wheezed, her lungs refusing to draw air. Panic surged through her like water through a breached hull. Rolling onto her back, she scrabbled away from Gabriel, who now approached, sword at his side, almost lazy in his gait.

"I applaud the effort, whoever you are," he said. "But you're surrounded. It's over."

Like black hell it is, she thought, fighting for air.

Raggedly gasping, Kathryn pushed herself upright. The Sorel Tan ringed the dais, two, three, four of them, edging closer. Isdria was lost; he would be boarding the *Orphan* by now.

But she could still reach the lander. She could still get out. She didn't need to fight them all. If she could just slip past one—

Then the elf exploded.

He actually exploded.

Chunks of gore spattered the nearest rock deposit. An arm, still attached to the shoulder, cartwheeled into the air. The rest of him simply vanished.

Kathryn froze. Then another sharp whistle and *crack!* Another elf burst into red mist. Then the thrumming drone of gyre thrusters filled the air. More whistles and cracks. Elves screamed, diving for cover as deposits shattered under repeater fire.

Kathryn whirled just as a frigate drifted overhead, low enough to churn grey dust clouds, its repeaters unleashing hell on the Sorel Tan below. She turned back to Gabriel. He glanced at the approaching ship, then back at her, his arrogance replaced by a determined scorn.

Kathryn shifted her stance, raised her sword. It wouldn't be enough, she knew. This man vastly outclassed her. But she stood her ground anyway.

Then—*thud!* A crossbow bolt slammed into Gabriel's ankle. He stumbled and cried out. Another bolt struck his thigh. He growled, but still limped toward her, sword raised, grim and relentless.

Kathryn readied herself.

But Gabriel's sword clattered to the floor. He dropped to one knee, clutching his wrist, another bolt lodged clean through it. His face twisted in pain, his breath rasped in low, angry growls.

A female dwarf hauled herself casually onto the dais. Sleek black hair framed a wolfish grin.

"Well, well, well," the dwarf said, audible even over the repeater barrage. "Who'd have thought we'd see each other so soon."

Gabriel scowled. In a growl, he rasped, "Hello, Switch."

The dwarf knelt to retrieve Gabriel's sword, her bronzite-augmented arm gleaming as she tossed the weapon across the dais. Kathryn tracked it, saw it land at the base of the iron chair.

And saw the arrow embedded in the gnome's side.

Oh no.

Hoping it was just a lung, she ran to him.

"Ships," he moaned, eyes rolling, blood frothing at his mouth.

Just a lung. Please just a lung.

"I know about the ships," Kathryn said, sheathing her sword and fumbling with the wrist clamps, her wounds and shock making her fingers clumsy.

Chaos reigned behind her: the thud of repeaters, the shouts of the Sorel Tan, the miner's thrusters screaming, the grinding of the floating mountains. But all Kathryn cared about was saving the gnome.

"They're coming," he gasped, eyes wide now with fearful intensity. "They're coming."

"I know, I know," she said, finally prying open the first clamp.

"The Mirrovinjin are coming in ships," the gnome said, his face pale, lips grey. Kathryn reached for the second clamp, and cried out as her wounded arm spasmed. Gritting her teeth, she forced her other hand to free the lock.

"They're coming," he whispered. "They're coming."

"No one's coming," Kathryn lied, tugging the clamp free. "You're going to be okay. I'm getting you out."

"They're already here," he gasped. His eyes, still locked on hers, went glassy. His jaw slackened. His body seemed to melt into the chair.

"Damn the black abyss," Kathryn swore, gripping her sword hilt to keep from slamming her fist against the iron chair. "Damn the black abyss."

She spun, rage surging.

Gabriel still knelt, breathing hard. Another dwarf, red-haired and flame-bearded, stood over him, questioning him. Switch hovered beside them, crossbow trained on Gabriel but her eyes were on Kathryn.

Kathryn stepped toward the kneeling man.

Then a gust of wind kicked up choking dust. A thrumming drone drowned out every other sound as the frigate pivoted overhead, coming to hover behind the dwarves.

A female gnome stood at its ramp, one hand braced on the hull, reddish-black curls whipping around her face.

"Brazier!" she shouted. "We need to leave."

The gnome pointed out toward the floating mountains.

Kathryn squinted, and saw it.

A spike-studded hull of eerie black alloy. Coiling spines twisted from its stern. A Mirrovinjin ship surged from a ravine, like a demon rising from hell.

They're already here.

"Come with us if you want to live!" the black-haired dwarf shouted.

EIGHTEEN
BRAZIER

Sorel Tan bodies lay scattered across the rock forest, blood splattered across shattered formations, viscera staining the rubble. The *Anchorite's* onslaught had left much of it in ruin.

The ship's gyre thrusters roared close by, their vibrations pulsing through the stone and into Brazier's feet. Dust and debris whipped in a frenzied storm around him.

But he barely noticed.

His attention was locked on the black shape hurtling toward them, on the thing Marcus Angelaux, Aymeri La'Voline, and their band of rebel commanders had promised him was an illusion.

Tearing his gaze from the Mirrovinjin ship, he seized Gabriel's unwounded wrist and wrenched it behind his back, forcing the witch hunter to limp toward the fuselage ramp. If Gabriel protested, Brazier couldn't hear it over the din, or he just chose not to.

Behind him, he heard the women clamber aboard, just before the ramp began to rise.

"I've opened the cargo hold for him," Freyen said, nodding toward the open compartment behind the stairwell.

"Thanks." Brazier shoved Gabriel toward the room. "Tell Matthias to take any opening and to put as much distance between us and that ship as possible."

The ramp clanked shut, silencing most of the chaos.

"That was rather risky of you, Brazier," Gabriel said through gritted teeth, as Brazier drove him into the hold. "Any longer and I would have dispatched your new crew member. I do hope you're not getting complacent."

Brazier ignored him, shoving the witch hunter to the floor with a boot to the back of his knee. He was turning toward the armoury to find manacles when he heard: "Not until I've had a word with your prisoner."

The woman came storming into the hold, clutching her right bicep with her left hand, blood soaking her gloved fingers.

She was blonde, fair-skinned, and average build for a human female. Her features would've been indistinct if not for the piercing blue-green eyes and the hard angles of her cheekbones. Paired with her tactical armour and sweat-slicked hair, she exuded hardened resilience. It was an officer's bearing.

"Where is Isdria Laanorath going?" she demanded.

"Oh, I think he's probably off to one of his favourite hiding places," Gabriel said.

"Who's your mutual friend?" she asked. "Isdria's ally?"

"More a marriage of convenience than a true ally," Gabriel replied, half-smiling, half-grimacing up at her. "But then, I'm hardly in a position to judge."

From the look on her face, Brazier almost stepped in, thinking he might have to stop her from beating Gabriel bloody. But she seemed to restrain herself, just.

"What's the source?" she asked. "Where is it?"

For the first time, Gabriel hesitated. Uncertainty flickered across his face, then vanished behind his familiar, pain-racked smirk.

"You know, it's rude to eavesdrop," he said.

Brazier remembered, with fresh irritation, how much he disliked the man's sly mockery. But if he disliked it, the woman standing beside him hated it with her whole soul.

"So is this," she said, and without warning, stepped forward and drove her knee into Gabriel's face.

Steel-plated knee met cartilage with a wet crunch. Gabriel grunted, his head rocking back as blood spurted from his nose. The woman cursed, clutching her wounded arm again.

Brazier raised his crossbow instinctively. "Stand down," he ordered, voice firm.

Only then did he notice the blood dripping from her other wrist. She was in worse shape than he'd realised.

"He has information I need," she growled, glaring at him. "And I don't have time to play nice."

"He's our prisoner," Brazier said, aiming down the sights. "And I will decide how he's questioned." Without looking away, he said: "Switch, take her to the nav deck. Grab a numbing draught and stabilising potion."

"How thoughtful of you, Brazier," Gabriel rasped through broken teeth.

"That's for her, not you," Brazier said. "Have Freyen bring a clotting elixir for Gabriel. He'll make do without the numbing draught."

"Come on." Switch clamped her augmented hand around the woman's arm. The woman eyed the metal grip, then allowed herself to be steered out. Brazier sealed the hold behind them and turned toward the armoury.

He'd barely reached the weapons rack when the hull echoed with a sharp *crack crack crack*. The ship lurched despite the spatial anchor, and Brazier slammed against a bulkhead.

Another volley struck. The ship shifted again, throwing him against the armoury wall. His head smacked something hard, his crossbow clattering from his grip as he crumpled among the scattered weapons.

Groaning, he rubbed his ribs. Through the mess, his boot clipped something metallic. It was a set of iron manacles, the key already slotted.

"That was easy," Brazier muttered. He tucked the manacles into his belt, stood, shoved his hair from his eyes, and began hastily re-racking weapons. Freyen would scold him for the disorderly job, but they had bigger problems.

Crossbow in hand, he marched back to the hold.

"Put these on," he said, tossing the manacles at Gabriel's feet.

Deathly pale now, the witch hunter struggled to keep from trembling.

"It's not like I'm going anywhere," he said thickly, blood streaking his face.

"If you don't put them on, I will," Brazier said. "And I won't be gentle."

Gabriel shot him a glare, then reluctantly secured the cuffs. Brazier knelt and locked them.

Switch stomped back into the room.

"Found the clotting elixir," she said. Looking down at Gabriel: "And here was me thinking I might be too late."

"Sorry to disappoint," Gabriel croaked.

Switch uncorked the vial, brought it to his lips. Thick, dark liquid flowed down his throat. He grimaced, wiping his mouth with a shaky hand.

"This compartment will be sealed by my command directive," Brazier said. "Don't even bother trying to get out."

Without waiting for a reply, he sealed the hold and headed up the stairwell with Switch.

"Tactical update," he called as they entered the nav deck.

Freyen and the woman stood on opposite sides of the command terminal, watching their desperate escape on the hex.

The *Anchorite* was weaving through drifting crags, the Mirrovinjin ship pursuing like a possessed beast and smashing aside boulders with no concern for its own path. Brazier tried, futilely, to convince himself it was still an illusion.

"Heading north," Freyen said. "Four minutes to drift exit."

"Can we lose them before then?" Brazier asked.

Matthias grunted. "I can lose them."

Switch approached the woman. "This'll stop the bleeding," she said, holding out the dark elixir. "And this'll stop the pain." The second vial shimmered faintly. "Sort of."

"Thanks," the woman said, downing the clotting draught in one gulp, her nose scrunching. She took the stabilising draught, drained it, and Brazier saw the tension ease from her shoulders.

"You'll need these as well," Switch said, producing bandages and folded cloth. The woman rolled up her sleeve, removing her vambrace and rerebrace, laying them on the terminal.

"You'll need to cut the rest," she said, handing over her knife.

The ship shuddered again and everyone grabbed the terminal for balance as Switch worked.

"Okay," Brazier said. "Who are you?"

Those piercing eyes locked onto his. For a moment, he felt like a cadet under the scrutiny of a petty officer.

"Kathryn Stryker. Palatine Officer," she said.

"Palatine?" Switch blinked, pausing mid-cut. "They still have those?"

"Only when it suits the Ecclessius," Kathryn replied.

"Then you work for the Church?" Brazier asked, uncertain. The Palatine office sat in a grey area between Custodia officer and Ecclessiarchal agent. Created to wield powers usually reserved for the Church, it stood outside the Church's dominion—supposedly to keep the Church from using the office for its own ends.

"Not exactly," Kathryn said. "I operate with the Church's authority. But they don't know about my current mission."

"Which is what?" Brazier asked, unsure whether that was good or bad news.

"Capturing Isdria Laanorath and finding out how he and the Mirrovinjin are creating those things." She nodded at the hex's sculpted mass.

As if on cue, a volley skittered across the hull. The *Anchorite's* thrusters screamed under increased power and rocks pelted the ship. The deck shuddered as Matthias pulled a high-sprawl manoeuvre. Everyone grabbed the terminal again. Brazier tried not to think about the damage to his ship.

"How did you know Isdria would be here?" he asked.

"I followed him from Ilantia," Kathryn replied. "How did you know?"

Out of the corner of his eye, Brazier felt Freyen watching him.

"We didn't," he said. "We had information this might be where they're creating the ships."

Kathryn frowned, suspicion tightening her brow. "Information from who?"

Brazier glanced involuntarily at the hex, then back at her.

"Look," she said, before he could answer. "Seems like we're on the same side here. And the only way we can help each other is if we share what we know."

"Seems like it's more us helping you at the moment," Switch said, tightening the bandages around the Palatine's bicep. The woman winced slightly.

"You first, then," Brazier said. "If the Church didn't send you, then why are you here?"

"I was in that chair once," Kathryn said. "I captained the Gyre Star, Athelus. We were ambushed. The Mirrovinjin tortured me, same as they did that gnome."

"And now you're a Palatine?" Freyen asked.

"The torture left... side effects," Kathryn said, as the ship shifted direction and another tremor buzzed through their feet. "And the Navy doesn't like captains with side effects. They gave me an honourable discharge and the position of Palatine."

"Sounds like they were getting rid of you," Switch said, knotting the bandage, then fashioning a sling for Kathryn's arm.

"They were," Kathryn replied flatly. Then to Brazier: "How did you know they were making ships here?"

Brazier combed a hand through his beard, unsure what to make of her story. She was an independent agent, following a lead she thought resulted in the Mirrovinjin creating ships, which she believed were real. It seemed unlikely she was reporting to the Church. She was probably more ally than enemy.

He opted for the vague truth. Because it felt right, and because he was a terrible liar.

"A caster employed by a group of High Lords detected gyranic activity here," Brazier said. "They think the Church is creating illusions of Mirrovinjin ships. We came to investigate."

The woman blanked, then her expression shifted to disbelief. Switch moved around her, inspecting her wrist. Kathryn didn't seem to notice.

"You might want to report back that their intel's off," she said. "The Sorel Tan are making the ships. Not the Ecclessius. And that"—she nodded toward the hex display, where the pursuing Mirrovinjin vessel loomed—"is definitely not an illusion."

Another hail of needle-like projectiles struck the *Anchorite*. The ship banked hard to port, but several needles still found their mark. A whirring thrum sounded from their aft. On the hex, two needles jutted from a thruster disc before the gyranic blaze burned them away.

"Last time I checked, illusions couldn't do that," Kathryn said.

"These illusions are... different," Brazier said, but with the enemy ship pursuing them yet again, even he was beginning to doubt it. "Matthias, I thought we were losing them?"

"We're about to," the navigator growled. Brazier glanced toward him. Matthias' neck muscles were taut with strain.

On the hex, Brazier saw it: Matthias luring the larger ship into a narrow gulley. The cruiser would have to descend sharply to avoid being crushed by the rock walls, and the *Anchorite* could slip through, gaining precious distance.

It was a perfect getaway.

Except of course it didn't happen like that.

The *Anchorite* shot through the ravine, but the Mirrovinjin cruiser didn't descend. It accelerated, smashing through the narrowing rock walls, blasting aside colossal boulders in a spray of debris.

All four of them stared at the hex.

"At least it slowed them down," Switch said, still holding Kathryn's wrist. Brazier thought that was a generous assessment.

"If we can't lose them here," he said, "the northern tunnels are our only option. We can't outrun them in the void."

"Can we make it to Thela?" Kathryn asked.

"Kyor is closer," Freyen said.

"There's a secondary tunnel straight from the Maw to Thela," Kathryn said. "A Gyre Star was docked there earlier. I'm assuming it still is."

"I can get us there," Matthias called. "If you don't mind a few scratches along the way."

"We won't need to," Kathryn said. "We'll call for support the moment we clear the Maw. With luck, the Cauldron will send a ship or two."

"Matthias," Brazier said. "Once we're out of the drift, send a long-range hex cast to the Eclipse. Then make for the lower tunnel to the Cauldron."

"Yes, sir," Matthias growled.

"Find any secondary or tertiary tunnels along that passage," Brazier told Freyen. "If we can avoid the Rosantz capital, I want to."

The only evidence of the Church's role in this mess sat in their hold, and House Rosantz wasn't known for letting go of such leverage.

"There's a vertical passage halfway along," Kathryn said, wincing as Switch wrapped her wrist. "I passed it on the way here. But it's big enough for the Mirrovinjin ship. Our only real option is to call for aid."

Brazier met her gaze, then turned to Freyen. "Find any smaller shafts off the secondary tunnel."

Kathryn's brow creased. "Who's your friend down there? And why don't you want to hand him over to the Rosantz navy?"

Sharp, Brazier thought. Or maybe he was just terrible at hiding his thoughts.

"He's not really our friend," Switch said.

"But you know him," Kathryn pressed. "Who is he?"

"Gabriel. A witch hunter," Brazier said, choosing vague truth again. "And we have good reason to believe he works directly for the Grand Ecclessian."

"Then what in the black abyss is he doing with the Sorel Tan?" Kathryn asked.

"You said Isdria had an ally?" Brazier asked, fingers drifting to his beard again.

"I overheard them talking," Kathryn said. "Isdria called them their 'mutual friend.' Sounded like they were supplying the casters."

"The Church?" Switch said, looking up.

Brazier nodded.

"The Church may be using the Sorel Tan to create the ships, while keeping their own hands clean. Just supplying casters."

"That doesn't make a drop of sense," Kathryn said. "Why would the Church want to create Mirrovinjin ships? That's madness."

"It sounded mad to us too," Brazier said. "But Gabriel is the Grand Ecclessian's personal assassin. We know this first hand. If he's here, the Church is involved."

"A year ago I was captured by the Mirrovinjin and the Sorel Tan," Kathryn said. "I saw one of these ships while I was their prisoner. I saw Isdria Laanorath working with the Mirrovinjin."

"Maybe they're all in it together," Switch offered, shrugging. "One big party of darkness."

"The Ecclessius are happy to backstab and betray," Brazier said. "But I doubt they'd actually side with the Mirrovinjin."

"I hate to interrupt," Matthias said. "But we're about to exit the drift."

On the hex, the *Anchorite* surged through a narrowing gap between towering crags. Their pursuers were forced to veer portside, taking a wider route.

As the *Anchorite* cleared the final rock wall, the hex rescaled, shrinking the sculpt as the vast emptiness of the void opened ahead, stretching toward the tunnel north of the Maw.

Next to Brazier, one of the hex wells trembled as if a stone had been dropped into it.

"Whenever you're ready, Cap," Matthias said.

"Eclipse, this is the Anchorite," Brazier said, eyes locked on the Mirrovinjin ship steadily closing the gap. "We reached the target. The Sorel Tan were using sorcery to construct the ships, working with the witch hunter Gabriel, the same Ecclessiarchal agent who killed Eluthienn on the Grand Ecclessian's orders. We engaged and captured Gabriel. The Sorel Tan succeeded in creating a Mirrovinjin ship, and it is now pursuing us through the tunnels south of Thela. I say again: we have evidence of the Church's involvement and are fleeing toward Thela. End of hex cast."

The hex flattened.

"Message sent," Matthias said. "They won't receive it for four, maybe five hours."

"Eluthienn?" Kathryn said, eyes narrowing. "You mean Prince Eluthienn of Ravinica?"

"It's a long story," Brazier replied.

Kathryn's gaze sharpened. She looked ready to hurl questions at him, but before she could, Freyen cut in: "Got a route from the secondary passage."

"How long?" Brazier asked.

"Twenty minutes to the passage opening."

"We won't make it that far," Kathryn said. "We need to call for aid."

"Gabriel is the Grand Ecclessian's pet," Brazier said. "House Rosantz is more likely to use him as a bargaining chip than proof of the Church's involvement."

"The Church isn't creating Mirrovinjin ships," Kathryn said, her voice rising. "I saw the Sorel Tan working with the Mirrovinjin. With my own eyes."

"Then where were they earlier?" Brazier shot back.

"Here's an idea, let me question the one person on this ship who might know," Kathryn said, nearly shouting.

"At best, Gabriel will lie outright," Brazier said, trying to keep his voice level. "At worst, he'll fool you into making a choice that serves him. You can't trust a word that comes out of his mouth."

"This is a Vault-class Navarch frigate," Kathryn said. "If the Navy gave you this ship, there should be veritas on board."

"I doubt it," Brazier said, just as Freyen said, "Yes, there is."

His First Officer gave him a reproachful look.

"It's stocked," she said.

"You need to be trained to use it," Brazier said to Kathryn.

"Did you miss the part where I'm a Palatine?" Kathryn said.

Brazier exhaled, thinking fast. "That could actually work."

"And in the meantime," Kathryn pressed, locking her gaze on him, "we need to call for aid."

Brazier was about to argue but Freyen spoke first.

"Zee. I think she's right. The vertical passage isn't short enough. The Mirrovinjin will catch us before we reach any smaller shafts."

Brazier didn't answer right away. He stared at the hex sculpt, jaw tight, watching the distance between the ships shrink. House Rosantz might take Gabriel. They might imprison them, or they might not. They might render aid. He didn't know. Every institution he'd once trusted, the Navy, the Church, the Royal Houses, had blurred into the same grey silhouette of uncertainty.

He combed his beard.

He didn't know who to trust. But he did know that losing Gabriel to Thela was preferable to being shot out of the sky.

"So be it," he said. "Matthias—once we cross the relative horizon, open a channel to Thela command. Tell them we are pursued by an unknown enemy vessel and request immediate assistance."

Then, to Kathryn: "Come on."

Down in the vulnerum, Brazier requested veritas from the dispenser. The partition slid open, and he took the vial, uncorked it, and handed it to Kathryn.

Without hesitation, she tipped it back and swallowed.

"Not as bad as I remember," she said, handing back the vial.

"You may think differently later," Brazier said, returning it to the dispenser.

Out in the fuselage, Brazier hovered his hand over the hex terminal.

"No knees to the face this time," he said, giving her a look.

"Cross my heart and hope to fall into the abyss," she said.

Brazier almost dropped his hand into the filaments, then stopped.

"Or violence of any kind."

"Thought you didn't like this man," Kathryn said. Then, seeing his expression, added: "Alright, I promise not to touch a hair on his greasy little head. Can we do this before the serum wears off?"

Satisfied, Brazier opened the hold.

Gabriel sat slumped against the wall, cradling his punctured wrist between manacled hands. He looked up beneath a sweat-slick brow, face streaked with dried blood. His natural pallor had gone corpse-white.

For a fleeting moment, Brazier felt guilt for not giving him a numbing draught. Then he remembered Gabriel was a backstabbing murderer.

"And here I thought you'd forgotten about me," Gabriel rasped.

"You wish we had," Kathryn said.

"More beatings?" Gabriel smirked. "You know I'm trained to resist torture by witches. They're far scarier than you."

A shudder ran through the ship. Brazier and Kathryn steadied themselves. Then the Palatine crouched on her haunches, observing Gabriel with sharp, clasped hands.

"Why are the Sorel Tan working with the Mirrovinjin?" she asked.

"Well, they're not spoilt for choice in allies," Gabriel said. "Beggars can't be choosers."

"Are the Sorel Tan working with the Church?"

"That would make for interesting bedfellows," Gabriel said.

"You're the Church's agent. Do you report to the Grand Ecclessian?"

"Sometimes," Gabriel said, smiling faintly.

"How are the Sorel Tan creating the ships?"

"Didn't you watch?" Gabriel said. "They're formed, not built."

"How?"

"As I recall, you saw exactly how."

"Is the sorcery drawn from a source?"

"All sorcery is drawn from a source."

"Who is Isdria Laanorath's ally?"

Brazier stood back, watching. Kathryn's interrogation was precise and relentless. He decided he didn't mind handing her the reins, not when his own judgement was so clouded.

But whether Gabriel would answer that last question or not, Brazier never found out, because Matthias' voice pulsed through the terminal.

"Cap," the navigator said. "We're entering the northern tunnels. Thela's sent a squadron. And they're not messing around—seven ships: six destroyers and a cruiser."

"Overkill, but I'll take it," Brazier said.

"We've got a problem though," Matthias added. "They didn't ask about the enemy vessel."

It was then that Brazier caught Gabriel looking at him. There was no mockery now, no sly grin. The witch hunter's blue eyes locked calmly onto his, and Brazier felt cold stones drop into his stomach.

There was no smirk, no malice, just calm recognition.

It wasn't fear. It was understanding; as if all of this had unfolded exactly as Gabriel intended, as if Brazier had played his part to perfection.

What have I walked us into?

Kathryn was faster, already reading the same danger. She jumped to her feet, grabbed the terminal sides, and shouted into the filament: "Take the secondary shaft! Avoid that squadron at all costs."

"No can do," Matthias said. "They'll be on us before we reach it."

Kathryn whirled, fixing Gabriel with a glare.

"Is Isdria Laanorath's ally Varkoneth Rosantz?"

Gabriel smiled a bloody grin.

"Looks like you're about to find out."

Nineteen
Kathryn

Kathryn climbed the stairwell, her legs driving her upward, her free hand catching each rung with a precision impossible without the veritas. The pain in her arm and wrist was a distant memory, dulled by the cocktail of potions. She didn't need to look up or down, her hands and feet knew exactly where to go.

Just as she had known Gabriel had implied the Sorel Tan were allied with the Mirrovinjin to cover the fact they weren't. Just as she had known, even when the witch hunter said nothing at all, that the Sorel Tan were working with House Rosantz. And just as she had known, the moment the navigator told them they couldn't escape the Rosantz squadron, that they were out of options, and were about to be captured and imprisoned. Kathryn knew a lot of things right now.

She also knew she would pay dearly for all the things she knew. Her so-called training in interrogation had been little more than a brief secondment to Navarch Intelligence, cut short when she earned her captaincy. She had never really learned how to brace for the truth-telling serum's punishing aftereffects. But that was a problem for later. Right now, she was worrying about options, or more accurately, the lack thereof.

Her mind, seemingly of its own accord, ran through every detail of the past thirty minutes, searching for something she'd overlooked, anything that might open a path and get them out of this mess.

"The war casters," Kathryn shouted up to Brazier. "When they talked about supplying the war casters, I should have known!"

"Err, okay," Brazier said, glancing down at her over his shoulder. "What casters?"

"Isdria told Gabriel to thank his ally for providing the sorcerers," Kathryn said, reaching the top. She accepted Brazier's outstretched hand with her good arm and let him pull her onto the landing. "But Gabriel accused him of burning through them."

Brazier nodded slowly, clearly not understanding.

"Which house has casters in abundance?" Kathryn pressed. "Which house is rumoured to breed casters to keep their king alive?"

It would have been impossible to make that summation from Isdria's comments alone, but she was riding a wave of magically induced euphoria, making her excitable and chatty. She really needed to get a grip. The situation was bad.

Brazier's eyes widened, his mouth parting as realisation dawned across his features. "House Rosantz," he said. Then: "We need to warn the Eclipse."

On the nav deck, the navigator knelt in the hex pit, arms outstretched over its swirling currents. The gnome, Freyen, hunched over the command terminal, hands gripping the edges of the hex wells with white-knuckled intensity. Switch, the bronzite-armed enginator, was nowhere to be seen, and likely deep in the ship's guts, working frantically to repair the extensive damage the *Anchorite* had taken—was still taking.

"We're about to cross over," Freyen said, eyes locked on the display.

The hex showed a small shape darting toward an opening in the Maw's wall. Behind it, the larger ship loomed, unnatural in form, like a dire squid with needle volleys erupting from its head in steady, thirty-second intervals. Most missed their mark, vanishing into the darkness, thanks, Kathryn realised, to the navigator's ability to pre-empt their flight paths. Even with the enemy ship randomising its firing pattern, the *Anchorite* seemed to know exactly where the volleys would land, and evaded seconds before they struck.

She was about to ask where the navigator had learned to fly so well when Freyen shoved a vial of molten gold under her nose. "Here," she said.

"Thanks," Kathryn replied, taking the inertial mutagenis and tipping the potion into her mouth, swallowing it in several unpleasant gulps. The familiar knife-like pain broke out across her body, forcing her to grit her teeth as the ship crossed back over Maw Grindle's relative horizon.

Kathryn let out a relieved breath as the hex rescaled to the tunnel beyond. The *Anchorite* was now a discernible shape. So were the eight ships that had just appeared from the mouth leading out of Thela's cavern complex.

"Prep a long-range hex cast to the Eclipse," Brazier said.

"Ready to go," Matthias confirmed a moment later, as one of the wells next to Brazier trembled.

"Eclipse, this is the Anchorite. We now have reason to believe the Sorel Tan have allied with House Rosantz," he said, but stopped suddenly.

Following his gaze, Kathryn saw the hex had flattened.

"Matthias?" Brazier said.

The navigator's neck muscles bunched as his shoulders tensed, his head bowed. "They're jamming our hex casting," he growled.

Brazier pressed his hands into the command terminal, eyes roving the display, clearly searching for a solution Kathryn knew he wouldn't find. Then, his brow creased, confusion creeping across his face. "Where's the Mirrovinjin ship?" he said.

"Huh?" Freyen said.

"It should have crossed into the tunnel by now," Brazier said.

"You're right," Kathryn said. "It was right on top of us."

"Matthias, can you scope out to the Maw?" Brazier said.

The navigator's shoulders heaved with a deep breath. He shook his head. "That cruiser's war casters have the Anchorite locked down—I can't project anywhere," he said.

"You think the Mirrovinjin have withdrawn?" Freyen asked.

"Well, they didn't just disappear," Kathryn said.

"Maybe it did," Brazier said.

"Abyss save me," Kathryn muttered, pointing at the edge of Maw Grindle as annoyance cut through her good mood. "That ship is not an illusion."

"You heard Gabriel," Brazier said. "Those ships are formed from sorcery, not built."

"Formed or built, they're still real," Kathryn retorted. "Or did you miss the part where they nearly shot us out of the air?"

"I'll tell you what is real," Matthias said. "The incoming message from the Rosantz cruiser."

"On the hex," Brazier said.

"Shian Anchorite, this is Captain Orland Kranic of the Black Castellan. Power down your turrets and match our speed and course. We will escort you to Thela. Is that understood?"

"Understood," Brazier said, somewhat reluctantly, Kathryn thought. "Be advised, we have an enemy vessel in pursuit possessing multiple war casters."

There was a pause as the hex well flattened, the *Anchorite* and the Rosantz squadron speeding closer toward one another. Then the Rosantz captain's voice returned: "Negative, Anchorite. We are not detecting any additional gyranic signatures in this tunnel or a mile into the Maw. You are safe to power down your weapons and join our escort. Please comply."

"They're lying," Kathryn said. "No way they can't detect a ship that large."

"Same thing happened when we were picked up by the Eclipse," Freyen said.

"We can discuss this later," Brazier said, plunging his hand into a hex well. "Switch, get up here."

Thirty seconds later, the enginator stomped onto the nav deck, face flushed, damp patches under her armpits. She wiped perspiration from her brow with her real hand, smudging a line of dark grease across her forehead.

“Anchorite is not looking too pretty, Cap,” she said. “Three thrusters putting out less than fifty percent—” She cut herself off, mouth curling downward as she noticed the command display. “Where’s the Mirrovinjin ship? And who in the black hell are those guys?” she added, nodding at the Rosantz squadron.

“Mirrovinjin ship has disappeared, and that’s a Rosantz fighter squadron,” Brazier said. “They’re escorting us to Thela, where we’ll be taken prisoner.”

Switch looked from Brazier to Freyen, to Kathryn. “Maybe we don’t go with them to Thela, then?” she said.

“House Rosantz is supplying the Sorel Tan with sorcerers. They’re the ones helping create the illusions,” Brazier explained, tone grim.

“Then we definitely don’t go with them,” Switch said.

“We don’t have a choice,” Brazier said. “We can’t outrun them in our condition. But Sourant knows we’re heading for Thela.”

“He’ll know in a couple of hours,” Matthias corrected.

“And you think they’re going to come and rescue us?” Switch said.

“They know we have Gabriel, and to them, Gabriel is evidence of the Church’s hand in creating the ships. They still need our testimonies,” Brazier said, the last part confusing Kathryn. “They won’t risk Varkoneth handing us over to the Ecclessius. They will come for us.”

But Kathryn shook her head, her mind racing through the details and finding only bad outcomes.

“Your friends know we’re headed toward Thela,” she said. “They won’t know we’ve called for assistance, or that we’ve been taken prisoner by House Rosantz. For all they know, we’ve made for Kyor or found another escape.”

“Our friends are smart,” Brazier said. “They’ll make the same calculation we’ve made and know this is our only option.”

“Even if they do,” Freyen said, “will they attack Thela outright? Won’t they treat with Varkoneth and request our release? They don’t know he’s the one creating the ships. They have no reason to launch an immediate rescue.”

Brazier sighed, scratching his beard. "You're right. They won't risk an immediate assault, because they don't know House Rosantz are involved."

"Which gives Varkoneth time to hide Gabriel and get rid of us," Freyen said.

"Then how do we get a message to the fleet?" Switch asked.

"I can send a message to your friends once we're inside Thela," Kathryn said, the plan forming as she spoke. "They can relay it to their fleet, but you'll need to tell me who they are."

"Even if we told you," Switch said, "how in the deepest, darkest abyss are you going to pull that off?"

"If I can get a message to my superior in Ilantia, she might be able to get me out of whatever cell they put me in. And as a Palatine, I have a right to use epistolars. If I can get to Thela's, I might be able to send a message to your fleet."

"There are a lot of ifs, buts, and maybes in all that," Switch said, looking incredulous. "How do you plan on getting a message to your superior?"

Given I disobeyed her orders, refused purification, and escaped on a lander, she's likely to come to me, Kathryn thought, knowing odds were Demina would do exactly that. Instead, she said: "I'm a Palatine. I can pull a few strings, even from a prison cell."

"I'm getting a course correction and sprawl script from the Castellan," Matthias said.

Brazier held Kathryn's gaze, then said, "Comply and follow them in."

On the hex, three of the destroyers executed about-face manoeuvres, pivoting their bows toward the cavern complex entrance before beginning a braking sprawl. Moments later, the remaining ships mirrored the move, forming a loose perimeter around the *Anchorite*, guiding it into the formation's centre.

Like a shoal of fish, they moved together, gliding through the tunnel toward the vast expanse of Thela's cavern complex.

Matthias rescaled the hex as the *Anchorite* exited the

tunnel into the cavern. The filaments reformed, shifting into a detailed sculpt of the diamond-shaped Cauldron city, its vast surroundings, and the many ships hovering in its orbit. Just as it had hours earlier, the Gyre Star hung motionless, stationed just north of the city.

"It's now or never," Kathryn said, tearing her eyes away from the massive ship. "I'm going to need to know who I'm sending the message to."

Brazier scratched his beard again, his mouth bunching as he thought.

"Sephera will be the closest," he said. "Get them to relay a message to Aymeri La'Voline. They'll know where he is."

"And how many ships does Aymeri La'Voline have?" Kathryn asked, eyes darting back to the display. She tried to count the number of capital ships dotted around the cavern. She thought she spied five cruisers and countless smaller battleships.

"Enough to lay siege to Thela," Brazier said. "But he won't have enough soldiers to fight through the city."

"Which means we're going to need to find our own way out," Kathryn said.

"And go where?" Freyen asked.

"Back here, to the Anchorite," Kathryn said.

"You mean after you miraculously spring us from our prison cells?" Switch said, raising an eyebrow.

"No," Kathryn corrected her. "When my superior officer miraculously springs us from our prison cells. Then we make for the Anchorite."

The enginator shook her head. "I don't mean to drag your plan through the abyss, but I'll believe all of this when I see it happen," she said.

Kathryn would too, if she was being completely honest with herself. The veritas offered her a sharp and clinical mental assessment without the accompanying feeling of uncertainty or reservation. She knew the odds of her plan working were slim. She also knew it was the only option they had. But under the influence of the veritas, just having a plan made her feel good. She was finding the absence of any other emotions surprisingly refreshing.

“We’re coming in to land,” Matthias said.

On the display, the *Anchorite* and her escort floated up from the cavern floor toward the giant octagonal structure cutting through the city’s centre. The navigator flew them to an empty pier, slotting the ship into a berth. Two of the destroyers drifted into adjacent berths, while the rest hovered nearby, forming a semi-circular perimeter over them, well within range of their repeater turrets.

“We’re in your hands now,” Brazier said to Kathryn. Then, to the rest of them: “Let’s go.”

They followed him off the nav deck and down the stairwell.

“We’re leaving Gabriel here?” Freyen asked in the fuselage.

“The hold is locked to my command script,” Brazier said, reaching for the terminal. “No point making it easy for them.”

At the dwarf’s command, the boarding ramp descended, hissing as it lowered onto the polished grey tiles. The sounds of the dock and the city above surged up to greet them—a low rumble of activity punctuated by the hum of voices, the droning of ships, and the metallic clang of ongoing repairs. The noise grated on Kathryn, as if it were too loud.

Then, halfway down the ramp, she felt a dull thud in the centre of her temple, the dock’s lights making her wince, their intensity a stark contrast to the subdued blue glow aboard the *Anchorite*. But it wasn’t until they stepped out from beneath the ship, into the glare of the docks, that it truly hit her.

The truth-telling serum chose that exact moment to abandon her system, blossoming in her skull like a punch to the temple. A relentless *thump, thump, thump* pounded between her eyes, as if a tiny miner were chipping away at her forehead from the inside. She swallowed hard, fighting the rising wave of nausea clawing up her throat.

Black abyss, she thought, *that is a lot worse than I remember it being.* Along with the nausea, the dull ache was returning to her bicep and the cut along her wrist.

“You okay?” Switch asked, her augmented hand cupping

the back of Kathryn's arm.

"Fine," Kathryn lied, looking down at the grey Formarian tiling to shield her eyes from the light.

"They're coming," Brazier said.

Over the din, Kathryn heard it: *tromp, tromp, tromp*—marching boots and the clank of steel weapons and armour, merging painfully with the *thump, thump, thump* inside her head. Instinctively, she glanced up, searching for the soldiers coming to arrest them.

Her vision flooded with the white-blue glimmer of the dock's gyre channels, ships' thrusters, and Thela's many lights. Pain and nausea gushed through her, forcing her to recoil.

Shit in the abyss, she swore again, as her limbs, leaden and unresponsive, gave way beneath her.

She felt herself crumple, her mind anticipating the hard floor coming up to meet her.

She was falling, and falling, as if through the void itself.

Until she wasn't.

But there was no hard tiling beneath her.

Instead, she found herself in a chair, not on the docks or in the city, but in her childhood home.

The pain had vanished. The storm of piercing light was gone. She sat behind a wooden writing desk that seemed too small, as if someone had swapped it for a child's. Opposite her, her mother sat behind her own obsidian-black desk, Admiral's uniform razor-sharp as ever, quill in hand, scratching away at a piece of parchment.

The only other objects on the shining surface were two inkwells and a rolled parchment, its seal Navarch blue and unbroken. Just as it had been for the past fifteen minutes—fifteen, long, agonising minutes.

But Kathryn was older now. She knew the game being played and so sat in silence, staring at the edge of her mother's desk with every ounce of will she possessed.

The scratching stopped. Kathryn didn't need to look to know her mother's eyes were on her.

"This came for you two nights ago," her mother said.

Two nights? She'd held on to the letter for two nights?

Then, smothering the anger twisting in her gut, came a gnawing fear that the Navarch would demand an immediate response, that she was already too late, that her mother had reached new heights of cruelty, deliberately preventing her from accepting the offer in time.

When she looked up, the ghost of that sneering smile played across her mother's mouth.

"What is it?" Kathryn asked. But it didn't fool her mother.

"Your Navarch Academy admission letter," she said, her expression unchanged. "I suppose you want me to open it?"

Do what you like, Kathryn thought. *Whenever you're ready.*

Or she could shrug. She could say nothing at all.

But she didn't do any of those things. She couldn't risk her mother's wrath—her mother, the Admiral who could crush any chance she had of getting into the Navy with a single decision.

It was a new fear, one that had grown to eclipse even the fear of her mother's disappointment, a fear born of maturity and years of experiencing her mother's manipulations.

After all the time spent driving Kathryn's desperation to get into the Navy, her mother might give her exactly what she craved, only to tear it away the moment Kathryn thought it was hers.

And so Kathryn swallowed her pride. "You know I would," she said.

That seemed to displease her mother.

"It won't change anything," she spat. "You know that, don't you, Kathryn? It won't change who you are. It won't change *what* you are."

An orphan, Kathryn thought. *Not your real daughter.*

Even in her mind, the words cut through her, the pain like a rusted blade dragged down the inside of her chest, making her want to curl over, to clutch at her heart.

"Kathryn?" her mother said, an uncharacteristic shadow of concern flickering across her face. "Hey, Kathryn," she said again, in an even more unrecognisable tone. "Kathryn?"

She blinked, her vision skewed as if the world had tilted

at an odd angle.

Something cold and hard was clamped under her armpit, gripping her arm awkwardly to steady her. The dull thudding in her head returned, distracting her from the phantom ache in her chest.

Bracing herself, she managed to stand upright, finding she could just about see without the nausea threatening to overwhelm her.

"I'm alright," she said, pulling her arm from Switch's grasp.

Switch relaxed her grip but didn't let go.

"I'm fine. Get off me."

"Oh yeah," Switch said under her breath as she slowly released her. "Fainting is all part of the interrogator training, is it?"

Kathryn rubbed her chest, spared from replying by the ring of soldiers now encircling them. Each one was clad in the colours of House Rosantz, red tabards emblazoned with the black eagle sigil clutching a spear and worn over mail shirts. Some had swords drawn; others held crossbows levelled.

Their commanding officer, wearing a solid black tabard, the eagle rendered in blood red, pushed forward. Tall for a woman, with broad shoulders and an imposing stature, she carried herself with a striking, almost cruel beauty. Even through the glare, Kathryn could see the sharp angles of her jawline, high cheekbones, and lips curved with predatory elegance, all within a face possessed of the haunting pallor common to the Rosantz bloodline and its many offshoots. It was a striking contrast to her pitch-black hair, styled in a tousled topknot and tight bun.

"Shackle them," she spat over her shoulder. Two soldiers immediately produced black iron manacles. "Rayke—search the ship."

Three others marched up the boarding ramp at her order.

As their wrists were clamped in iron, the woman drew a short sword from her scabbard and let it hang at her hip.

"They want you in the cells," she said, looking at each of them in turn. "But they never said how they wanted you there. They never said they wanted you whole. So if any of you even think about resisting, I'll start taking pieces off."

Kathryn suspected the woman, who gripped her short sword like a butcher's cleaver, would really like it if one of them resisted.

"My name is Kathryn Stryker," she said, squinting at the woman and trying her best to form words without vomiting. "I'm a Palatine officer reporting to Lauren Demina, Captain of Ilantia's Custodia regiment. I'd like to request an audience with her."

The Rosantz captain shouldered Brazier and Freyen aside, coming nose to nose with Kathryn.

"My name is Rosalla Golfang," she said, her voice trembling with quiet anger. "I'm Captain of the Royal Household Guard, and I report to His Highness, Ramovand Rosantz. He'd like you to rot in a cell, so you could be Redcrosse reincarnated for all I cared, your request is denied."

Kathryn blinked hard, struggling to hold the woman's rage-filled stare, when suddenly she was staring into her mother's furious eyes.

It won't change who you are! her mother shouted in her face. *It won't change what you are!*

Kathryn shook her head, forcing the image from her mind, though the effort sent her headache ricocheting like a cast-iron ball around her skull.

The woman's glare burned into her for another tense moment before she barked: "Take them!"—spittle spraying into Kathryn's face.

Soldiers stepped forward, herding them onto the docks. Kathryn was pushed along, moving mechanically, sensing Switch at her side. Every time she glanced up, the glare brought on a renewed wave of hammering against her forehead.

She could only make out the bases of the repeater turrets, the leather-clad shins and boots of hundreds of people moving around her, and the relentless hum of gyre ships droning overhead.

"Tell me that was part of the plan?" Switch whispered.

"It was," Kathryn whispered back through tight lips. "Demina will come."

Her presence would soon be logged in Thela's hex network, activating the deserter script Demina had almost certainly placed upon her.

"Black abyss," Switch swore under her breath.

"She'll be here," Kathryn said.

"No," Switch said, nudging her arm. "Look."

Kathryn glanced at the enginator, then followed the direction of her nod. There, on their left, three piers over and plain as the midday sun on the surface, even with the omnipresent glare, was the *Orphan Guyan*. The miner sat in its berth, powered down, its thrusters a faint turquoise blue.

Kathryn's stomach coiled with sickness. All she could do was grunt her acknowledgement that she'd seen the ship and quickly look down again. If she'd harboured any doubts about the Sorel Tan's collusion with House Rosantz, they were now thoroughly laid to rest.

Apparently, Brazier had noticed it too, because Rosalla marched up to the dwarf, shouting: "Eyes forward, or I'll take one from you."

They continued toward the towering triangular slab that was Thela's southern facing. Kathryn risked another glance upward, seeing a geometric latticework of interwoven levels, balconies, and platforms, interspersed with the shimmering crystal-blue glow of gyre channels.

She swallowed dryly, tearing her eyes from the lines of light as they were herded past a dock command post, the square, two-tiered platform bristling with activity. Soldiers in black and red military doublets stood watch, overseeing the docks below. On its lower level, Rosantz troops lined the perimeter, their repeater crossbows held at the ready, their watchful eyes tracking every step they took.

Rosalla led the way to a towering chute, then called for a lift. Moments later, its double doors parted, and they were ushered onto the platform. With a shudder, the lift surged upward, carrying them toward the city above.

Kathryn closed her eyes against the disorienting shimmer of purple and grey light that rippled across the chute's interior walls, the colours shifting with each change in direction. She focused on her breathing, steadying her weak limbs as they slowed, moved horizontally with a faint lurch, then shot upward once more.

When the doors finally opened, they stepped into a low-ceilinged corridor. A single glowing vein of light stretched overhead, bathing the space in a dim, sterile glow. Cells lined either side of the corridor, their doors uniform grey.

They were separated and guided toward individual cells. But Kathryn, now battling with her roiling stomach, stopped in the middle of the corridor.

"Move!" Rosalla shouted in her ear. But Kathryn barely noticed. She pitched forward, heaving as vomit sprayed from her mouth and splattered across the floor.

"Disgusting bitch!" Rosalla spat, stepping back from her. "Get her in there."

Kathryn felt uncaring hands tighten around the back of her arm as she was dragged into a cell almost identical to the one where she'd left Erin Carmowright, with a small obsidian-black desk and two chairs facing one another.

The door slid shut behind her.

She collapsed into the chair opposite, wiped threads of saliva from her mouth, and pressed her throbbing temple against the desk's smooth surface. Its chill seeped into her skin, a balm against the relentless headache and the horrible, hollow feeling in her chest.

With her bandaged arm pressed to her chest, she wrapped the other over it. She deliberately didn't resist, letting the cold surface coax her into a slumber that eased the pounding in her head and calmed her churning stomach.

Half asleep, her mind began sailing across a sea of images. She stood on parade at the Navarch Academy's training concourse, clad in her white ceremonial doublet, surrounded by hundreds of other officers saluting in perfect unison. On the steps before the Academy's silver-grey façade, between two of the rectangular pillars, stood the blurred figures of the Navarch High Command, her mother among them, Kathryn sensed more than saw.

In the unreality of her dream, her fellow officers spoke as

they saluted, voices filled with hopes and visions of what could be, the dream a shimmering blur of expectation.

Then she was aboard the light cruiser *Valiant Rising*, standing at the head of the command terminal where the first officer, her commanding officer, should have been. Chaos erupted around her, reports of failed thrusters, empty repeater magazines, boarding parties flooding the ship.

The hex display flattened and turned to sludge as she thrust her hands into both wells, desperately trying to generate a clear picture of their surroundings, to locate the enemy, to find an escape.

Her heart pounded as she realised her hands were stuck, trapped as if the filaments had solidified, binding her to the wells. She couldn't see the battle. She couldn't issue orders.

Then the *Valiant* faded around her, flickering like a mirage, and she was on the *Athelus*.

She stood in the same position at the command terminal, surrounded by her crew. Their faces were stricken, their voices pleading with her not to give in to the Mirrovinjin's demands, that they wouldn't let the *Athelus* go in exchange for Kathryn, that they'd kill her and take the ship regardless.

Now, years later, Kathryn knew they were right, knew that she should have listened. Knowing the nightmare that was coming, she tried desperately to pull herself from the dream, to shake herself into wakefulness. But her hands were still clamped in the wells, her crew shouting, begging her not to go.

And now her hands were clamped at her sides instead of in the wells, her crew's voices turning into a cacophony, a storm of fiery blue columns and chanting voices. The Mirrovinjin emerged from the shadows, its pale hand tipped with long black nails reaching for her neck.

She cried out and threw herself backward, kicking and flailing to fend off the creature. Her limbs flung wildly, and her back slammed into something solid.

Gasping, she found herself staring up into a quartered gyre channel, her legs tangled around the chair now toppled onto its side, pain radiating from her shin in sharp, throbbing pulses.

It was soon matched by pain from her arm, which had come free of the sling and lay across her stomach, the bandages around her bicep staining red from the reopened wound.

Moaning, she pushed her arm back inside the sling, then pushed herself to her feet. She picked up the chair and dumped herself into it, her chest rising and falling with heavy, shaking breaths. A cold chill spread through her that had nothing to do with the cooling perspiration at her temples or the sweat running down her back.

In her desperation to catch Isdria, she'd gambled, convincing herself she'd capture him and have him in Ilantia's cells before she even needed to think about taking the daily dose that kept her from slipping into permanent psychosis.

It had been a gamble she'd been so certain of, she hadn't even considered it a gamble. So confident was she in her ability to catch the most wanted elf in all of Formaria, she'd embarked upon her mission, quite literally, without a second thought.

She barked a single, bitter laugh at her own stupidity and her own arrogance. The thought was followed by her mother, berating her for what Kathryn now knew to be a fact.

You were never good enough, she said, no longer angry, but imperious and vindicated. *No wonder I never accepted you as my own. I knew all along you would never be good enough, I knew you could only disappoint. I knew you would be an embarrassment to me and to all of those I trained before you.*

Her mother was right. She'd been right all along. She hadn't been good enough. She'd been ambushed and captured on one of her first missions as captain. She'd been tortured, her mind warped into becoming part of the creation of hideous Mirrovinjin ships. And she'd gone chasing after an elf who'd made a career of outsmarting every Intelligence branch in Formaria.

She'd been so arrogant, she'd believed with unfailing certainty she could achieve things that were so obviously beyond her capabilities.

She'd believed that Demina's treatment of her, the way the other officers acted around her, stemmed from pity for her condition. But in truth, they pitied her for fooling herself. They pitied her because she believed her own façade, that she kept clinging to the delusion she was anything other than a failure.

She slumped in the chair, the lingering acidity of vomit scratching at her throat, her bicep aching, and her mind numb. For several minutes, all she could manage was to listen to her ragged breathing and the quiet of the surrounding cells.

Then she remembered where she was: the cells in Thela, House Rosantz and the Sorel Tan, Brazier and his crew.

Black abyss, Stryker, get it together.

She pushed herself up in her chair, angry at her pathetic self-indulgence: *You do not have time to feel sorry for yourself!*

And with that anger came other thoughts. A voice spoke up, like an echo rising from the deep.

You weren't wrong.

The Sorel Tan were creating ships. They were working with Formaria's enemies, just like you told everyone, but those enemies just turned out to be traitors.

House Rosantz were supplying the Sorel Tan with war casters to conjure up warships—warships that looked like Mirrovinjin ships.

Illusions, that's what Brazier had said.

Maybe they were, after all. Maybe she'd been wrong. It wouldn't be the first time. But then she remembered what the witch hunter had said: "The source grows with every crop of harbingers we create."

Could the source be some form of Mirrovinjin sorcery they were drawing upon to create the ships? Which meant the Mirrovinjin could still be involved. Perhaps, like Switch had said, they were all working together.

House Rosantz, the Sorel Tan, and the Mirrovinjin—"one big party of darkness," she'd called it.

Maybe Brazier was wrong?

"Illusions can't create something real," she said aloud.

"This you know. They can't create something real enough to spit out bolts and shoot ships out of the air."

But nothing else in this theory made sense. She had no idea why these three disparate factions would ally with each other. She didn't know how the sorcery worked. She didn't know what the source was. And she didn't have her elixirs.

She almost laughed out loud again.

All of this, the theories and the plans of escape, could be meaningless. Either Demina would show up and break her free, or she'd be left to rot in this cell, out of options and her mind unravelling as the hallucinations clawed their way in.

She pressed her temple to the desk again, letting the cool wash over her. Somewhere far away, a door shunted open and closed again, followed by voices so muffled they were nothing more than a vibration.

Everything seemed to go quiet. Then another door shunted, close enough that she could hear it slide along the floor. Footsteps followed, turning into the marching step of boots. The muffled voices were a louder vibration now. Another door opened, and the voices turned into audible speech.

"This is Rosantz territory. You have no jurisdiction here," a stern male voice said.

"She's my officer. That's all the jurisdiction I need."

Who'd have thought I'd actually miss the sound of that voice.

"She's under arrest for violating a restricted zone," the male voice said.

"She's under arrest for a whole lot more than that," Demina retorted, ice running through her tone.

"And now she's in Rosantz custody," the man said.

"Over which I have authority," Demina said, without missing a beat. "As recognised by my command script, otherwise the hex network would prevent me from opening this door."

Roughly a second later, the door to Kathryn's cell slid open, and Captain Lauren Demina marched in. She wore a black leather cuirass over a crisp grey shirt, the yellow Custodia wyvern emblazoned over her heart. A crossbow hung in her arms, the strap draped across her shoulder, and a short sword sat at her hip.

For a moment, Kathryn was unable to reconcile the image in front of her. She'd only ever known Demina to wield power by cutting people down with words and influence. Seeing her like this, armed and armoured, was like watching a scalpel pretending to be an axe.

"Hi, boss," Kathryn said, sitting up and smiling weakly at Demina.

Kathryn caught a glimpse of the Rosantz guard behind her, his pale face a mix of frustration and fear, then the door slid closed.

The Custodia captain took her in, eyes roving over what must be her sorry-looking appearance. Then she dragged out the other chair and sat with the crossbow in her lap, eyes sharp as daggers, posture so tense it looked painful. Kathryn fought the absurd urge to smooth down her hair.

"You are so far down the abyss, daylight is a distant memory," Demina said. "So do not *boss* me."

"Got it, Cap," Kathryn said.

"You defied orders to undergo purification, as good as emptied the Custodia armoury, stole a lander, and sailed straight into a no-fly zone."

"It's not a good look," Kathryn admitted.

"And now the Navarch Liaison to Everaux is sitting in my office, spouting the same gibberish about ships and terrorist organisations," Demina said. "Given that you were the last person he spoke to, my immediate assumption was that you'd infected the man with the same madness that afflicts you."

Kathryn opened her mouth to explain, but Demina spoke over her.

"But then I received a report. Just as I was about to dismiss the man and have the officers take him back to his cell—"

Demina paused, as if preparing herself to say the words aloud.

"A report of a Mirrovinjin ship chasing down and destroying a transport vessel north of Ilantia, before mysteriously disappearing," she said.

That's why she's come armed, Kathryn thought. Not for her, but because of the ships. Something leaden dropped from Kathryn's ribcage to the pit of her stomach as realisation struck. *There's more than one ship.*

"The ships are real," Kathryn said. Then quickly: "The Sorel Tan are helping to create them, but so are House Rosantz."

Frustration flashed across Demina's face as her mouth thinned to a line.

"Hear me out," Kathryn said. "Just hear me out. I followed Isdria Laanorath into Maw Grindle, that's where they're creating the ships, using some kind of sorcery, conducted or powered by House Rosantz casters. But I wasn't the only one there. There's a group of High Lords who know about the ships. They sent a team to investigate the site who arrived when I did."

"A secret group of High Lords," Demina said, sounding doubtful. "And how did they know where the ships were being created?"

"They detected some kind of gyranic activity, or something," Kathryn said. The escape from the Maw was a blur to her, as was Brazier's explanation. "Look, that doesn't matter now. The crew they sent were arrested with me. Their captain is Brazier Veranquis, the others are Freyen, Switch, and Matthias—you can check."

Demina stood so abruptly Kathryn rocked back in her chair. The Custodia captain placed her hand in the cell terminal; her eyelids fluttered, then her brow furrowed. Disconnecting, she slid back into the chair, her posture no longer as statue-like as before.

"Brazier Veranquis and his crew have been taken to the throne room," Demina said.

"I need to get them out of there," Kathryn said.

"And do what with them, exactly?" Demina scoffed.

"There's a fleet led by those High Lords," Kathryn said. "Brazier got a message out to them before we were arrested. They know we're here. I need to get Brazier and his crew out of here and onto his ship so they can join that fleet."

"That would result in civil war," Demina said. "Even if these High Lords had the largest fleet in the underground, they would not send it here."

"They would if they believed we had evidence of another High Lord betraying Formaria," Kathryn said, her voice pleading. "You know the ships are real now. You know that wasn't a hallucination. You know that what I've been saying is true. This is true as well."

Demina stared at her so long Kathryn grew uncomfortable.

"I can't help you," Demina said. "They won't let me take you, and Brazier's crew are already being questioned. But my rank will let me overwrite the locking script in this cell."

"What about the guards outside?" Kathryn asked, her heart skipping with relief.

"I'll draw them away," Demina said. "As Palatine, you'll have access to the Cauldron's hex network but they'll shut you out the moment they know you're gone."

"Thank you," Kathryn said.

"I don't want your thanks," Demina said. "I want you to get this Brazier Veranquis off the installation. House Rosantz will see it's my command script that unlocked this door. If you don't stop them, they'll come for me."

She leaned back in her chair, then pushed her fingers beneath the breast of her cuirass. Kathryn was utterly at a loss as to what she was doing until she pulled out two small vials from an inner pocket Demina must have stashed them in.

"Found these in your chambers," Demina said, placing the vials on the table between them. "I guessed you'd probably forgotten to take them with you."

"Yeah," Kathryn said. "I was in a bit of a hurry when I left."

"You are by far the smartest officer I've got on the force," Demina said, shaking her head. "But you somehow still manage to make stupid mistakes."

"I'm working on it," Kathryn said.

"Work harder," Demina said, standing. She unstrapped the crossbow and placed it on the table next to the vials.

"I'll leave this here," she said, then placed her hand in the terminal. "It's done."

The cell door slid open, and Demina stepped through it, turning to the guard.

"I want this officer transferred into the custody of the Ilantia Custodia," she said as the door slid shut.

"That is not possible," Kathryn heard the guard say. "I have strict orders to keep her here until told otherwise."

"My rank supersedes those orders," Demina said. "Release this prisoner immediately."

"I'm sorry, Captain, but I do not believe you have jurisdiction here."

"That officer is a member of the Ilantia Custodia and is therefore under my jurisdiction," Demina said. "I am able to take her into custody in any territory across Formaria."

The guard was silent for several seconds. Then, in a voice with far less confidence: "I'll need to raise this with my superior."

"Then take me to them," Demina said. "I'm not going to stand around waiting for them to contact us over the hex."

"The prisoner—"

"Isn't going anywhere," Demina cut across him.

Several more seconds of silence followed. Then a door in the corridor shunted open and closed. Kathryn waited, barely letting herself breathe, the only sound her beating heart.

Then, confident they weren't coming back, she grabbed one of the vials so quickly she accidentally knocked the other, causing it to spin on the spot. She uncorked the vial in her free hand and downed its contents in a single gulp.

Wiping her mouth with her sleeve, she threw the empty vial onto the table, seized the other one, and placed it at the bottom of her breast pocket. Then she jumped to her feet, the chair skidding behind her. She threw her hand into the terminal, and even before the white-grey haze set in, she was requesting the cell door to open.

She disconnected, then, slowly and carefully, removed her arm from the sling. She could still keep it at an angle while holding the crossbow. She would just have to deal with the pain.

Gingerly, she picked up the weapon and stepped into the corridor, turning one way, then the other, as a realisation gripped her.

She had no idea where she was in the city, no clue how to reach the epistolar or the throne room.

Her eyes locked onto the nearest terminal. Without hesitation, she slammed her hand into it. The cool filaments flared to life as she requested a route to the city's epistolar.

The hex pulsed, and a map unfolded in her mind's eye. It traced a route through the labyrinthine city, highlighting lifts that would take her to where she needed to go.

Reaching the epistolar, she requested the next steps: a route to the throne room, then a location marker on the *Anchorite*.

The answer came swiftly. The ship was being detained on the same pier where they'd landed.

Let's hope they keep it there, Kathryn thought grimly.

She opened the door at the far end of the corridor and disconnected from the hex, pulling her hand free. Without breaking stride, she sprinted forward, veering right toward a set of lift doors. The nearby terminal flared to life at her command, unlocking the way.

Once inside, the platform surged into motion, the force pressing her into the floor. It shot upward at first, the walls a blur of muted light, before levelling out and hurtling horizontally through the city's core.

The lift slowed, its hum fading into silence before the doors slid open, revealing the expanse of a broad corridor. Rectangular pillars lined the passage, their gyre channels glowing with a rich lapis lazuli. The light spilled outward, drenching the space in an oceanic glow that rippled across the faces of hundreds of people streaming beneath it. Kathryn stepped out, unnoticed in the sea of movement.

Her boots tapped lightly against the floor as she crossed the corridor, her eyes fixed on a chute embedded in the opposite wall. At the terminal, she placed a route request and waited for the lift. A minute stretched into an eternity before the doors opened with a quiet hiss—

And five Rosantz soldiers stepped out

The sight of their red tabards sent her pulse racing, a jolt of cold fear tightening her chest. Her heart leapt into her throat, but they barely glanced her way, their gazes sliding past her as though she were invisible.

She slipped into the lift the instant they cleared the doors.

"Close," she whispered under her breath, willing the doors to obey. "Close."

The moment they slid shut and the platform jolted upward, she exhaled, a shaky breath escaping her lips as her heart continued to hammer in her chest.

The platform accelerated, the black and purple walls blurring into streaks, then dissolving into a haze as she shot skyward. The sound of rushing wind accompanied her ascent, soft at first, then swelling into a rhythmic *whum, whum, whum* that echoed through the chute.

Kathryn's brow furrowed. *Gyre platforms don't make noise*, she thought. *There's no wind in a sealed chute.*

A crackle broke through the rhythm, sharp and unnatural, followed by the unmistakable roar of flames. Her stomach twisted as a low, resonant hum joined the cacophony, rising slowly, a sound too familiar to ignore.

It wasn't a hum. It was chanting, an undercurrent of voices swelling until it filled her ears, drowning out everything else.

Oh no. Not now.

Blue flames licked at the edges of her vision, flickering against the chute's shimmering walls, their ghostly light dancing in time with the chanting that grew louder and louder, pressing in from all sides.

Her heart clenched, terror sinking icy claws into her chest, choking her breath as she gripped the crossbow tighter. Then, without warning, pain slammed into her knees, a brutal jolt that shot up through her thighs and left her gasping.

The impact forced the air from her lungs as the chanting fell silent. The flames winked out as though they had never existed, leaving only the quiet hum of the platform.

Kathryn groaned, forcing herself upright, her muscles trembling as she wiped sweat from her eyes with a shaking hand. At least she'd managed to keep hold of the crossbow, her arm still at a right angle.

The doors shunted open, revealing a walkway stretching across a short gulf of shadow. At the far end, a landing rose to meet a towering set of double doors, their polished grey surface faintly reflective despite the gloom.

To the left of the landing, three human priests sat motionless behind a dark, semi-hexagonal desk. The chamber's gyre channels glinted faintly with a fragile crystalline white that rose out of the darkness on either side of the walkway. Behind the desk, however, a column of channels climbed upward, their glow a deep blue glaze, casting jagged, shifting patterns onto the black desk.

Kathryn crossed the walkway, conscious of the sheer drop on either side of her. At the desk, all three priests had their hands in hex wells, eyelids fluttering erratically beneath their hooded amices.

She cleared her throat.

The priest in the centre snapped his eyes open so abruptly Kathryn recoiled, her grip tightening on the crossbow. He withdrew his hands from the wells in a slow, deliberate motion. His gaze settling on her, unwavering, dark eyes embedded in a pale, mask-like face devoid of emotion.

"Kathryn Stryker, Palatine officer," she said. "I require immediate access to the epistolar."

The priest's gaze slid over her, lingering on the weapon in her grip. His head inclined slightly as he spoke, his voice serene. "Please confirm your identity." He gestured to the nearest hex well, its surface shimmering beneath the gyre channel's glow.

Kathryn hesitated, her pulse quickening. By now, they likely knew she'd escaped, and if they'd locked her out of the hex system, this would end badly.

Trying not to think of what she'd need to do if that were the case, she sank her hand into the well and gave her Palatine script. The network registered her rank and identity yet remained maddeningly silent, offering no further confirmation. She disconnected, watching the priest sink his hand into one of the wells.

"Identity confirmed, Palatine Stryker," he said, and the tension bled from Kathryn's shoulders. "The epistolar is yours to use."

As quickly as she could without running, she strode up the steps. Reaching the double doors, she leaned her good arm against one and shoved it open. The door groaned on its hinges, and as it closed behind her with a resounding thud, the sound reverberated through the chamber, triggering a cascade of jagged silver light. The illumination leapt and scattered across the walls and vaulted ceiling, casting fleeting, fragmented patterns that dissolved as quickly as they formed.

For each of the chamber's hexagonal facings, slender pillars stood like silent sentinels, each crowned by a small bronze orb. Between two of the pillars, a set of narrow steps descended into a pool, the grains of black voidstone coiling and shifting like living threads.

Despite growing up around Formarian technology, Kathryn had always found epistolars unnatural, as if working despite the absence of gyranic power was something necromantic, like animating the dead. *I guess it's not called the Dead Network for nothing*, she thought, stepping up to the pool's edge.

There was the sound of air escaping mechanical joints. Then, from out of the spout hanging over the other side of the pool, a Constructii's sightless face appeared.

"Only tales are told," the face said, its metallic, almost feminine voice resounding around the chamber and sending the lines of silver light spinning into the ceiling.

"I understand the requirements," Kathryn said.

"Then step forward and tell your tale."

Kathryn placed the crossbow on the edge of the pool and descended the steps, the voidstone lapping at her breastplate like a sea of living ink. She held her wounded arm across her chest. She had no idea what would happen if the pure voidstone got into the wound. It probably wouldn't be anything good.

"A telling in Sephera," she said. "The teller is Palatine Kathryn Stryker. The witnesses are the Keepers of the Royal

Seal of House La'Voline. The tale is of Brazier Veranquis and the crew of the Anchorite, who have been imprisoned in Thela following their escape from Maw Grindle. Veranquis and his crew have evidence proving the Sorel Tan are conspiring with House Rosantz to help create the Mirrovinjin ships. They request immediate rescue from Thela by the King's fleet. The teller is Kathryn Stryker. The witnesses are the Keepers of the Royal Seal of House La'Voline and no others."

Kathryn stared into the bronzite face, listening to the voidstone shift around her, before climbing out of the pool.

She felt exhausted and hungover. But at least she no longer wanted to vomit everywhere, and the pain from her wounds had receded, a little.

She paced around the epistolar, throwing the door furtive glances and absentmindedly picking at the bandages wrapped around her bicep. Every few seconds she imagined she could hear the tramp of boots on stone as Rosantz soldiers came to arrest her. As long as the message was relayed to the fleet, it wouldn't matter, she told herself.

As long as—

"Your story is told, Palatine Kathryn Stryker," the face said, making her jump.

Kathryn practically threw herself back into the pool.

"A Telling at Thela," the face said. "The teller is Aaron De'Valois, Keeper of the Royal Seal of House La'Voline. The witness is Palatine Kathryn Stryker. The tale is of the Keeper's sadness at the message he must now relay. The fleet has been forced to disengage; their course is redirected to Sephera. No rescue will come. The Palatine and the crew of the Anchorite must devise their own escape, for rescue is impossible at this time. The teller is Aaron De'Valois, Keeper of the Royal Seal. The witness is Kathryn Stryker, Palatine, and no others."

Kathryn stood in shocked silence, the voidstone breaking against her like an evening tide.

Rescue is impossible at this time.

The words rang in her ears, dancing to the lines of light spiralling up the epistolar's dark walls. Brazier had been certain they'd come. And Kathryn had been certain her plan would work, that this time, she could really pull it off.

You were never good enough!

Her mother's scream echoed in her head, jolting her with its sudden appearance and reawakening vestiges of the veritas hangover. She felt cold and empty, all the weight of the past few hours rushing back to bludgeon her, to remind her that no matter what she did, she couldn't win. She just wasn't good enough.

But with that painful reminder, another memory surfaced, a lesson firmly ingrained over years of her childhood. It was one she clung to, had kept clinging to through everything, one she would keep clinging to because it was so etched in her mind by the woman who had carved it there.

"There's always options," she said. *That's what you taught me, mother.*

"Good officers create options."

She turned, picking up the repeater crossbow as she climbed out of the pool and headed for the epistolar's doors.

The pain in her bicep had receded to an uncomfortable ache. She could force movement into her unwilling muscles. She could grit her teeth against the exhaustion. She could create options.

Then let's go create some.

TWENTY BRAZIER

High above, a solitary gyre vein split the gloom, its pale, grey-blue light struggling to illuminate the seat of Rosantz power.

The throne, and the dais it dominated, was a low-backed monolith of dark obsidian built atop the silvery gleam of Formarian alloy. When silver-grey slabs and gyre-lined panels defined every chamber in the underground, Brazier thought so much black stone was an affront to the natural order.

He also thought it was unnaturally large. Brazier suspected a full-grown human male could stretch out and sleep upon just the throne. But from where Brazier knelt, its size was only a guess. Varkoneth Rosantz, King of Thela and High Lord of Thendergaarden, consumed the seat, leaving only the armrests visible, upon which he rested his thick, pale hands.

The rest of the King's flesh swelled against the confines of his high-collared black tunic, which merged into a tight-fitting robe, similar to the cassocks worn by select members of the Church. But for all his imposing appearance, it was the bronzite suspension belt encircling the King's waist that kept Brazier's attention.

A war caster, pale, hairless, and clad in robes as black as the dais he stood upon, leaned over the King, his spindly fingers slotting vials of shimmering blue liquid into ports along the belt. Working in complete silence, the caster tightened each vial, then pressed a button toward the back of the belt.

A whirlpool came to life and spiralled within one of the vials, the liquid draining into the belt in a series of controlled pulses. The King groaned, a deep, wet rumble that was somewhere between a burp and a death rattle.

Despite the fear clinging to Brazier like a second skin, the scene before him produced the absurd notion of a physician trying to keep a slug alive. That image wasn't helped by the smell Brazier suspected was emanating from Varkoneth. It was a combination of industrial cleaning fluids similar to those used to clean out engines, and the pungency of scorched metal. And beneath it, was something like mildew or stagnant water.

His task now complete, the war caster folded his hands in front of him and took his place next to the man Brazier assumed was Ramovand Rosantz. Tall and haughty, the prince and heir to the Rosantz throne sneered at them from beneath his mop of jet-black hair with an expression someone would typically reserve for overflowing sewage or piles of Mirrovinjin corpses.

The pale light swam across the prince's plate armour, giving its immaculate polish the illusion of liquid silver. It was identical to the armour worn by the guards lining the recesses of the chamber, who stood with unsettling stillness, like statues waiting to come to life.

Brazier, who had only glimpsed them while the crew were transported into the chamber, imagined them as faceless spectres in their full plate and helms, poised for the order to cut them down with the cold mercilessness of constructs.

He felt the invisible grip of the magical constraints tighten, and his eyes darted back to the caster. Raising just a single index finger, the caster forced Brazier and his crew further down onto their knees. The pressure wrenched their hands higher behind their backs, the strain biting into his shoulders and wrists.

If Brazier had been given a choice, he'd have taken manacles. There was something about the unyielding magical constraints that made him feel more helpless, unable to protect his crew, and galvanised the fear that he'd put their lives in the hands of a woman he'd known for all of five minutes.

She had seemed the very epitome of capability, confidence, and resourcefulness, right up until she'd vomited on herself and collapsed in a prison cell. All Brazier could do now was trust that Sourant would follow them to Thela, that they'd pick up the *Anchorite's* signature in the docks, and attempt a rescue. It was a long shot. But that's all he had.

All he could do now was buy time.

"Veranquis," Varkoneth said, his voice slippery and gargled. "Why do I recognise that name?"

"His father, Edmerin Veranquis, was executed as a traitor," Gabriel said distractedly.

Stood to Varkoneth's left, the witch hunter was busy retying the vambraces around his now-healed wrist. Like Isdria, who stood next to him, his wounds appeared to be completely healed.

"And his brother, Torquen Veranquis, lost his entire crew under suspicious circumstances and was forced from the Admiralty as a result."

"Like father, like son, like brother," Varkoneth oozed. "Traitors and conspirators."

The King nodded at his caster, and Brazier felt the magical constraints lessen. His hands and feet were still locked in place, but he felt the grip around his head and neck reduce.

Keep them talking. Buy yourself time.

"Looks like I'm in good company, then," he said. "A Royal House allying with terrorists."

"So high and mighty, Veranquis," Isdria crooned. "Just like your brother, until I cut him down to size."

The comment hit so abruptly that Brazier froze, his mind scrambling to process it.

"You've never met my brother," he said.

"Haven't I?" Isdria said, a smile that looked like it wanted to be a leer tugging at the corners of his mouth.

"It was your brother who captured an Ecclessiarchal ship and added it to the Sorel Tan's fleet. Your brother who sold one of the Church's greatest weapons in exchange for gold, of all things. Your brother who invited the Sorel Tan aboard the Luceron and asked me to slaughter his crew as part of the deal, just so he could escape with his treasure."

"If you think my brother would do something like that, you've clearly never met him," Brazier said. But even as the words left his mouth, the tale being spun reignited old doubts, the ones that had lingered like shadows over his family's final days as senior Navarch officers.

Torquen had sworn everything the Ecclessius claimed about them was a fabrication, and there was no reason to think Isdria's story was any different. But all thoughts of buying time were quickly being replaced with: Why would Isdria Laanorath lie about this?

"Twelve million gold Vidicks," the Sorel Tan captain said. "That's how much I gave him. That's how much his crew's lives were worth, all 172 of them. The Ecclessius stripped your family of everything, isn't that right? Your entire mining operation, and you never wondered how your brother managed to rebuild it so quickly?"

These are lies, Brazier told himself. *These are lies to weaken your resolve. Your only job is to keep them talking. That's all that matters. To get your crew out of here.*

But after all these years defending his brother's name, he couldn't help but think he might have been defending a traitor.

"It would seem your brother and I share something in common," Varkoneth said.

"And what's that?" Brazier said, trying not to spit the words.

"Pragmatism," Varkoneth replied. "Not all of us see the Sorel Tan's ideals as a threat to Formaria. Some of us see their necessity."

"And that's why you're supplying them with casters," Brazier said. "To create Mirrovinjin warships and weaken the other houses."

"To unite them!" Varkoneth growled.

The liquid in one of the vials formed into a tiny whirlpool, sloshing around the glass before it seemingly drained into the mechanical belt. Varkoneth groaned, leaning back in his seat, his eyes heavy with pain or fatigue, Brazier couldn't tell.

"For an age, we have hidden among the crevasses of this world," the King said. "Unable to gain the upper hand over our enemies, locked in perpetual stalemate, resigned to our fate, because we fear the power we once wielded."

"Once wielded," Brazier repeated, tone careful and probing, hoping Varkoneth would latch onto the topic. "Before the Sundering?"

Varkoneth's eyes glinted like onyx gemstones beneath dark grey brows.

"The same sorcery that creates the Mirrovinjin ships also rebuilds the Gyre Gates," he said. "The sorcery that was sundered from this world will return, along with those who wielded it. Our ancient cousins returned to help us reclaim Aetraya. To deliver us from the dark."

The part of Brazier's mind racing to keep the conversation alive nearly ground to a halt at the idea of a king, a High Lord of Thendergaarden, echoing the same dogma as the Sorel Tan.

"How?" he managed to say.

Varkoneth's gaze settled on him, cold and analytical, as though studying a peculiar specimen pinned under glass. Then, without shifting his neck at all, the King's face rotated toward Gabriel. The stillness of his body, juxtaposed with the slow, deliberate twist of his face, carried an absurdity that bordered on monstrous.

"Through a power you are already acquainted with," Gabriel said. "We have reawakened Duessa, the Queen of Dreams and third Lord of the Eternal Hunt. It is through her Aeturnic power that we now create fleets of Mirrovinjin ships to weaken Formaria's royal houses and rebuild the Gyre Gates."

The name split through Brazier's mind like a crossbow bolt. It was a name that until recently had been consigned to bedtime stories and children's tales. But she was a creature he now knew to be real, and one blamed for entire ages lost to darkness. And now they'd put her in service of a plan to tear Formaria apart.

One half of Brazier's mind reeled, stunned by revelations that made Isdria's earlier comments feel insignificant by comparison. The other half scrambled, frantically searching for the right words to keep Varkoneth talking.

"And while the other houses lose ships and soldiers, you grow stronger," Brazier said to Varkoneth.

It wasn't the Ecclessius attempting to seize power. It was House Rosantz.

"The Fromryr are fractured, led by an institution whose only goal is to maintain the status quo," Varkoneth said. "The Church is a rotting husk, clinging to the last vestiges of life while the rest of us fight for the underground's survival. Formaria needs to be united under a single banner. Under a single House. A single King."

"Under you," Brazier said, keeping his tone neutral.

"Who else has the strength?!" Varkoneth roared. "Who else is prepared to do what must be done? Time and again, I've implored the other High Lords to act. To infiltrate Nexoria and learn how the Mirrovinjin replenish their ranks! To send expeditions into the depths of Elliptica, where lost sorceries may yet linger! To journey east, to the Old World, and unearth the artefacts of our ancestors—anything to turn the tide, to pull us from the brink of annihilation! But they are weak!"

Keep him talking.

"And what about the Fenn?" Brazier asked abruptly. "When you reopen the gates, you reopen the door to another invasion."

"The Fenn haven't been seen in centuries," Varkoneth said, waving a pale, pig-fingered hand as if to swat away the idea. "The Celmyrians spend their days patrolling stinking forests and fighting off poisonous insects. It's been generations since one of their warriors fought a member of the Fennian races."

"How are you using Duessa's power?" Brazier asked, throwing the question out to all of them.

"Father," Ramovand said. "They know too much."

"It's all right, my sweet boy," Varkoneth said. "All of them will be dead before the day is done."

He turned his cold eyes on Brazier. "But the manner in which they die is up to them."

"Before you begin the messy business of relieving Veranquis and his friends of their knowledge," Gabriel said, unbuttoning one of the pouches on his bandoleer, "there's something I want from him."

The witch hunter drew a knife from a sheath behind his back and stepped off the dais toward Brazier. The folds around Varkoneth's eyes creased into lines of cold curiosity, but he said nothing.

Brazier's heart began a panicked rhythm against his ribcage as Gabriel knelt beside him. He gritted his teeth instead of squirming against his constraints. He didn't want to give any of them the satisfaction.

He felt Gabriel pull up his gambeson sleeve, then a sharp bite on his wrist. Brazier gritted his teeth harder as the knife dug deeper. Something cool pressed against the wound. He stared at the foot of the dais, not moving a muscle.

Then Gabriel stood and made his way back to his position on the dais, corking the vial of Brazier's blood and placing it back in the pouch. Brazier felt the sting of the wound and the blood trickling onto his palm as Varkoneth's eyes tracked Gabriel.

What in the black hell was that all about? Brazier thought.

"Just a little souvenir to remember him by," Gabriel said, smiling at Varkoneth.

The King released a faint gurgle, then turned to his war caster and nodded. Then, stone-still, the sorcerer raised his thumb and forefinger by half an inch from their position folded over his other hand.

Next to Brazier, Freyen grunted, her face flushed, eyes growing wide with pain. All thoughts of the pain in his wrist and what Gabriel would do with his blood vanished, replaced with fear.

"We'll talk!" Brazier shouted, his voice raw as he strained against the invisible force locking him in place.

"You already have, Brazier Veranquis. And from what you've said, it seems you know little and less about our plans," Varkoneth said. "But I am told you were aware of the ships. You knew where we were building them. How?"

"Release her, and I'll tell you everything you want to know," Brazier said, desperation bleeding into his voice.

Varkoneth raised a hand, gesturing to the war caster. Freyen's shoulders sagged as she let out a sharp, shuddering breath. Her face softened, but looking into Brazier's eyes her gaze was sharp as a combat knife: Don't tell him anything.

"Gyranic activity," Brazier said. "The sorcery shows unusual properties that can be detected. We followed the activity to Maw Grindle."

"You didn't say any of them were casters," Varkoneth said to Gabriel.

"That's because none of them are," Gabriel replied.

"We were attacked by one of the Mirrovinjin ships," Brazier said quickly. "We thought the Ecclessius were creating the ships to weaken the Royal Houses and entrench their power."

Varkoneth raised a thin eyebrow, but Gabriel said, as if the idea bored him: "He's deflecting."

The King's face creased into thick folds of anger as he waved an impatient hand at his caster.

To Brazier's horror, Freyen was lifted feet first into the air. Her curls brushed the floor as she writhed against whatever magical torment the sorcerer had cast upon her, a stifled scream straining through her locked jaw.

"Who detected our sorcery?" Varkoneth demanded. "Who sent you to spy on us?"

Freyen's scream became a wail, her writhing turning to spasms as the sorcery wreaked havoc on her nerves. Brazier's world collapsed inward, narrowing to a single, brutal choice: Hold out and give Sourant the element of surprise, or stop Freyen's torment by revealing they'd been sent by House Angelaux and House La'Voline, and in so doing, give Thela time to prepare her defences.

"A joint group of High Lords and Navarch commanders," Brazier said.

"Who?" Varkoneth spat, his suspension belt whirring as he leaned so far forward he almost stood.

"House—"

A deep boom reverberated through the chamber, like the sound of mountains colliding in the distance. Brazier's first, irrational thought was that the floating boulders of the Cawdora surface drift had somehow made it to Thela, crashing wildly into the Cauldron.

Another thunderous impact followed. It shook the chamber, causing the previously statuesque soldiers to become far more animate. They cast glances up to the ceiling where dust spiralled down in lazy, twisting patterns and spread through the air like a settling cloud.

Brazier's own eyes were on his First Officer. She had stopped writhing and now hung limp in the air, her head lolling, her body slack. But Brazier's heart steadied as his eyes locked onto the faint rise and fall of her chest, her breaths heavy.

"Thela is under attack, my King," the war caster said, his eyes fluttering under semi-closed lids.

From somewhere outside the chamber, Brazier could hear shouting, boots stomping on hard floors, the faint clatter of armoured soldiers rushing to stations.

"Central command has deployed the fleet," the caster continued.

"Against who?!" Varkoneth demanded.

"Inbound enemy fleet," the war caster said, then began to speak as if reeling off a list of ingredients. "Multiple Gyre Stars reported, significant presence from supporting cruisers, unflagged vessels. Two-thirds of the Rosantz defence force deployed. Rally-to-port orders issued."

With the war caster's report absorbing everyone's attention, no one seemed to hear the aching groan of a large door being opened behind them.

Suddenly, he turned to his King, eyes wide open and edged with fear. "My King, we're—"

The caster's next words were a garbled mess as blood spurted from his mouth, staining his lips a dark red. It took Brazier several seconds to notice the crossbow bolt protruding from the man's neck. The war caster tumbled backward, and Isdria roared: "Protect the King!"

The magical bonds holding Brazier dissolved in an instant, and he lunged forward on instinct. Freyen's body fell limp, her head an inch from the hard floor, but he caught her just in time, scooping her into his arms as another bolt hissed through the air, whistling past his ear before smashing into the dais and ricocheting into the shadows.

From the chamber's edges, the Rosantz guards poured in, their movements swift and coordinated. They formed a shield wall in front of the king and prince, as more bolts slammed into their shields, embedding themselves with dull, metallic thuds.

"Move!" Brazier heard Matthias shout in his ear, and suddenly the navigator's hands were under his armpits.

Even with Freyen in his arms, Matthias lifted Brazier to his feet as easily as if he were a child, forcing him in the direction of the throne room's large double doors.

"Switch?" Brazier said, turning back frantically to the dais.

"I'm here!" Switch shouted on his other side, and he felt her mechanical grip dragging his shoulder toward the doors.

"No!" he heard Varkoneth shout to someone. "Get the Storm to safety. We'll deal with this!"

If he said anything else, Brazier didn't hear. He was racing down the dark chamber toward the white light spilling in from behind a pale slab of a door easily five times his own height. Kathryn Stryker, the woman he'd assumed was lying unconscious in a pool of her own sick, stood next to it, her gaze trained down the sights of the crossbow. Every time she squeezed off a bolt, the gyre cartridge released a wisp of blue smoke that lit up her face and made her seem faintly ethereal.

"Go!" the Palatine shouted, without taking her eyes off the dais. "I'll cover our retreat."

They darted through the open door and Brazier squinted at the bright light in the T-section corridor stretching toward another set of large double doors. The bodies of four Rosantz soldiers lay strewn across it, bolts sticking from punctured plate mail or out of eye sockets, their blood pooling on the floor and running into the gyre channels.

"This way," Kathryn shouted, suddenly behind them and sprinting off to their left.

Brazier shifted Freyen into a position that would cradle her neck and followed, Matthias and Switch on either side of him. At the end of the corridor they piled into the open lift chute.

He heard Kathryn swear under her breath as she removed her hand from the corridor terminal. "I'm locked out," she said.

Switch dashed out of the lift, placing her real hand into the terminal's node. Brazier watched her eyes move under her lids, and a pulse ran down the terminal's channels to the floor channels in front of the chute. The platform bobbed under his feet, accepting the enginator's request.

"We're good," Switch said breathlessly, as both she and Kathryn clambered in after them. "And they still haven't moved the Anchorite."

Brazier caught a glimpse of Rosantz guards streaming into the corridor, just as the lift doors closed and the platform dropped them deeper into the Cauldron.

There was a second where all of them seemed to catch their breath. Then Kathryn turned to Switch and said, "So, you believing this yet?"

Switch's mouth broke into a wide grin. "I'm sorry I ever doubted you," she said.

This close, Brazier could smell the Palatine's sour odour and faintly rancid breath. He didn't mind, especially as he suspected he smelled little better. There was also a near-manic gleam to her eyes that made Brazier think whatever aftereffect the truth-telling serum caused, it wasn't entirely finished with her. Taking in her battle-worn appearance, he felt a sudden surge of admiration for the woman.

She looked like she was about to ask him something when, just after the platform shifted and began travelling horizontally, an echoing rumble ran through the chute.

Whatever shockwave hit that section of the Cauldron caused the platform to bump against the walls. Brazier felt his legs give way, and he had just enough time to ensure Freyen was cradled tightly in his arms before his knees hit the floor.

He heard a strangled "Ow" as Kathryn tumbled against Switch, and they both fell to their knees.

The platform automatically realigned itself and continued on. Matthias, who seemed to be the only one to keep his feet, helped Brazier stand.

"Sounds like the fleet got your message," the navigator said.

"I wouldn't be so sure it's your friends," Kathryn said, as Switch pulled her up with her augmented hand. "They didn't seem that interested in a rescue mission."

Brazier could make out the inside of the double doors at the end of the lift. As they began to decelerate, he could hear the sounds of battle beyond. The low-level drone of thrusters and the unmistakable repetition of tens, maybe even hundreds, of repeater turrets drifted toward them, becoming louder and louder.

The lift stopped. The doors parted.

And the roar of warfare hit Brazier like a punch. Two hundred feet of silver-grey tiling stretched out in front of them before separating into landing piers further beyond. The large repeater bolt throwers, which Brazier had only ever seen rotating lazily, were all aimed up into the cavern, spitting bolts into the air like angry scorpions defending a nest.

Such power fed through the gyre channels lining the floor that a knee-high turquoise glow had settled across the entire docks. Crystal-white pulses ran along them, feeding into the repeater turrets and the landing pads, creating short-lived silver shimmers atop the blue haze.

It would have been beautiful, if not for the sheer chaos unfolding around them. Turret crews carrying racks of bolts dove from cover to cover, desperately trying to reload the repeaters. Dock workers frantically attempted repairs on damaged turrets, while Rosantz sailors raced to their ships, all under the constant stream of enemy bolts crashing around them like spears hurled from an army of angry gods.

Speaking of the gods, overhead was a sight Brazier had never thought to see. Two Maw-class cruisers hovered out in the cavern, bolts pouring from them in streams that targeted the smaller attack craft rising up in the city's defence.

Brazier recognised the slim, tapering ventral hull and curved structural flanges of the *Sovereign Eclipse*. Beside it, was the thicker, deeper hull of one of the cruisers present at the rebel fleet's first meeting. And behind them, the Angelaux flagship, the Gyre Star *Pheradies*, loomed immense, its hull a beacon of bronze-gold pitted with gyranic blue. Turned broadside to face Thela, its port batteries unleashed streams of bolt fire, matching the relentless volleys from the cruisers below it.

When Brazier had imagined the rebel fleet coming to their rescue, it had been a nebulous idea in his mind. He'd not dwelled on the reality of what that would look like, or what it would mean. But now the reality stared him straight in the face, and it looked like Fromryr fighting Fromryr.

Despite the desperation to save his crew, despite the knowledge House Rosantz had allied itself with the Sorel Tan, despite their plot to restore ancient powers that could destroy the underground, a deep sense of despair gripped his heart like an iron hand. The Fromryr were now at war with one another, and it was at least partially his fault.

The last time this had happened, great houses had risen and fallen. The Fromryr, divided and isolated, had been easy prey for their enemies. They'd barely survived. The iron hand gripped a little tighter.

"Not to contradict you or anything," Matthias said, raising his voice, "but they seem pretty interested to me."

"Guess they changed their mind," Kathryn said. "We're going to have to make a run for it."

Brazier felt Freyen stir in his arms, and relief surged through him, cooling the sense of guilt and sadness. At least he was getting her to safety. At least his crew were getting to safety. Whatever came next, they'd be together. And for a moment, it didn't matter who she was. It didn't matter about her past. It only mattered that she would live.

He glanced up at the docks.

"Wait," he said. "They may have set a new security script on the Anchorite. We could be locked out."

He imagined them dashing for the ship, only to be forced to cower beneath its hull, unable to get off the docks.

"You think I didn't check that?" Switch said, throwing him a withering look. "They broke your command script, but the hex system still recognises us as the primary owners."

Brazier made a mental note to heap his First Officer with endless praise for her hex-writing skills.

"Okay," he said, adjusting Freyen into a more secure position. "We stick to the edge of the piers. Stay clear of the turrets."

They all nodded, their expressions grim. Then, without another word, they ran.

Twenty-One
Kathryn

Kathryn was riding a wave of euphoria and adrenaline she knew she would pay for later.

Convincing Demina to help her escape, sending the epistolar message, fighting her way to the throne room, then rescuing Brazier's crew and coming tantalisingly close to pulling off their escape, were all small victories her body rewarded with successive jolts of joy and self-belief.

Regular infantry called it battle frenzy. Redcrosse Knights called it the warrior's high. Others just called it bloodlust. Kathryn didn't care what it was called. All she knew was she'd never felt better.

That she'd accomplished something she'd set out to do was a rare enough sensation to savour these days. But she didn't think that was why she felt the way she did, though it certainly helped.

Staring into the faces of the four people in the lift, she finally felt as if she were part of a team. With their lack of uniforms and the casualness of their command structure, Kathryn might have mistaken them for free traders or miners. But they'd responded to each new threat like professional soldiers, and Kathryn suspected this wasn't their first catastrophe.

Fighting through it with them flooded her with enough adrenaline that she forgot about the exhaustion creeping into her muscles, her wounded arm, her wrist, and the accelerated dehydration from the veritas' aftereffects.

A part of her brain knew that becoming attached to a group of people after just an hour of knowing them spoke of something deeply unhealthy in her, something she really needed to address. But she didn't care. This was a rare feeling. And she was going to enjoy it while it lasted.

"We stick to the edge of the piers," Brazier said. "Stay clear of the turrets."

Then they were running across the silver tiles, their feet kicking through the knee-high haze of gyranic blue light.

Six-foot-long bolts crashed down around them, shattering the air with deafening bursts. Soldiers and dock workers shouted over one another, their voices lost in the chaos, while the roar of hundreds of ships taking off filled the air with a relentless, vibrating hum.

And no matter how hard she tried to breathe through her nose, every inhale brought with it the sickly-sweet smell of raw gyre ice burning. It clung to everything, churned up by the ships, the turrets, and the docks themselves, acrid and faintly chemical-like.

"Over there!" Kathryn shouted, pointing to a set of side steps that led down to the pier's lower level.

They sprinted toward them, boots hammering against the tiling as they descended. To their right, a repeater turret twanged and clicked in rapid succession. Three dock workers hurriedly fed fresh bolts into the magazine at its base.

On their left, they passed empty landing bays. Kathryn had just enough time to register their ghostly gyre channels, her brain telling her the power had been rerouted by demand from other parts of the network, when a crack resounded to their right.

Surprised shouts followed, then the loud clatter of metal.

The repeater turret had been hit just beneath its supporting mount, the impact sending the bow crashing to the floor in a tangle of warped bronzite.

For a fleeting moment that cut through her battle focus, Kathryn wondered what those crews thought about seeing their own kind firing on them. But the thought vanished the second her eyes fell on the ship behind the now repeater-less turret.

The *Orphan Guyan* sat on her landing pad, gyre thrusters devoid of light and seemingly no crew coming to start her up. She'd seen Isdria standing beside Varkoneth, and it had taken every ounce of her will to stop herself from fighting her way up to the throne in what would have been a heroic but utterly stupid attempt to capture the elf.

At least, she told herself, that problem might soon be solved. Glancing up into the cavern now teeming with ships, she knew she probably wouldn't be the only one searching for the Sorel Tan captain. Two cruisers blocked the Rosantz frigates and destroyers as they rose from the docks, preventing them from reaching the Gyre Star unleashing destruction upon Thela.

A part of Kathryn's mind registered the formation as the kind of posture deployed against drake battalions or mounted goblin riders, when Brazier's voice cut through to her: "Switch! Get her going!"

Kathryn only recognised the *Anchorite* when the enginator ran up to the landing pad terminal and threw her hand into the hex node. A crystal pulse ran down the terminal's side, split in two, then ran around the octagonal landing pad. The frigate's thruster discs began to spin up, just as the fuselage door dropped open.

They were on the ship in seconds.

"Make sure they know we're coming," Brazier said to the navigator as he made for the ship's medical bay. "At this point, getting shot out of the air by our rescuers would just be embarrassing."

"Aye, Captain," Matthias said, and pulled himself up the stairwell.

Kathryn manoeuvred around the open ramp and racked the crossbow on one of the wall mounts, before following Switch and the navigator up to the nav deck.

Even as the doors closed behind her, and the *Anchorite's* engines sent audible vibrations through the ship, she could still hear the muffled sounds of the battle raging around them. For a split second, panic gripped her, sending her already racing heart into overdrive. This close to salvation, they might yet be cut down by the dock turrets or take friendly fire from one of the fleet's ships. Or a war caster could lock onto them. Or they could simply collide with one of the Rosantz ships being shot out of the air.

Switch seemed to be thinking the same thing, because she immediately called up a display of their immediate surroundings. The hex filaments formed into a sculpt of the battle.

"Well fuck the black void," she said, real and augmented hands gripping the side of the command terminal as she leaned in, her eyes wide.

Kathryn thought that was a completely reasonable response to the chaos raging around them. With the hundreds of ships darting around the Cauldron's geometric angles, she felt like she was watching a swarm of insects kicked into a frenzy by an attack on their hive.

As the *Anchorite* sailed upward toward the cruisers, the hex rescaled and revealed the true scope of the battle. The rebel fleet had split into two attack groups, each one a single Gyre Star supported by two cruisers. One group attacked the Cauldron's docks, the other flew southward along the cavern's eastern border.

The southward group was conducting what looked like an extended strafing run against the Rosantz Gyre Star. Kathryn guessed they'd come from the tunnel leading to Ilantia and were deliberately drawing the larger ship's fire.

It seemed to be working.

Streams of needles poured from the Rosantz Gyre Star's hull-mounted turrets, while every few seconds filaments flew up from the hex display floor to produce explosive effects against the cruisers. They represented, Kathryn knew, gyranic attacks from the Gyre Star's war casters. What looked inconsequential on the hex would be wreaking havoc on the crew and their ship.

Watching it play out, Kathryn's mind began racing through attack vectors, breach points, and tactical egress routes. It took her a moment to recognise the restlessness as something she'd felt countless times before as a Captain. It was the frustration of being forced to wait, to coordinate the battle from a distance while her sailors fought in the thick of it. That she wasn't currently coordinating any of it made the feeling that much worse.

"They know we're coming," Matthias said, bringing her out of the memory.

Behind them, the nav deck doors parted, and Kathryn turned to see Brazier take one step onto the deck when a deafening *bang* came from somewhere on the hull. It rocked the ship so hard the dwarf was sent flying to the floor.

Kathryn felt as if someone had removed the decking from beneath her feet and brought it back again, but managed to hold onto the command terminal for support. She pulled herself up as the navigator produced the sort of sound Kathryn imagined a mountain lion might make at taking a wound from another predator.

"Rear aft thruster disc is gone," he growled.

Kathryn could feel it in her feet.

Losing an entire disc, along with the previous damage taken from the Mirrovinjin ship, the *Anchorite* was now at an angle, the decking pitching down to the left.

On the display, the tiny sculpt representing the frigate flew upward like an insect that had just lost a wing. Switch, who had dragged herself up off the floor, seemed to be taking it personally. The enginator let loose a string of curses, among which Kathryn just about caught, "hurt my baby." She was drowned out by Brazier joining them at the command terminal, shouting: "Get me a connection to the Eclipse!"

A second later, one of the wells pulsed.

"Eclipse, this is the Anchorite; we need immediate gyranic protection," Brazier said.

A man's voice, stern and gravelly, resonated from the hex: "You really should have thought about that before you ignored my order not to engage."

But then, as if the owner of the voice had stepped away from the hex: "Protective shielding on the Anchorite."

"There were unforeseen developments," Brazier said.

"I've noticed," the man said.

Then again, slightly further away: "Mr. Ormstar, we've

got what we came for. Bring us about and make full speed to rejoin the Pheradies under the withdrawal formation."

Now louder: "Anything else we can do for you, Captain?"

"Have every navigator in the fleet search for the Gloried Storm," Brazier said.

"The Storm is here?" the man replied, the easy confidence replaced with seriousness.

"That's where they're keeping the weapon," Brazier said.

"Mr. Ormstar," the man said, his voice further away again. "Relay orders to the fleet: The Sorel Tan flagship is in the vicinity and must be found. This is a priority one order."

Then, louder: "Good work, Captain. I'll see you and your crew very soon."

The connection dropped.

"The weapon?" Kathryn asked.

"I'll explain once we're on the Pheradies," Brazier said. "They're going to want you there as well."

The words sent another tiny thrill through her that she hid with a curt nod before returning to the hex display.

The two forward cruisers began a slow, ponderous about-turn. The engines of the second attack group flared to life, silver filaments streaking behind them as they flew southward into a defensive formation to shield the retreating cruisers while they turned their sterns to the enemy.

Watching the manoeuvre unfold on the command terminal, she found herself impressed. What must have been a hastily assembled rescue plan was being carried out with near-perfect results. By dividing into two attack formations, one could draw the Gyre Star's attention, then seamlessly shift into a defensive screen for the retreating cruisers. Then, as if rehearsed, the two groups merged back into a single, cohesive fleet for withdrawal. It was carried out with such skill Kathryn couldn't decide whether she was jealous or nostalgic.

"Hold on to something," the navigator said through clenched teeth.

"What do you think we've been doing," Switch replied.

"We're coming in to the Pheradies' hangar bay," the navigator said, and despite not seeing his face, Kathryn thought she detected a smile in his voice.

The *Anchorite's* sculpt turned sluggishly, as though its bulk were too unwieldy to bring its bow about with any real speed. The delay forced them into the *Pheradies'* portside hangar at an awkward angle, the decking tilting further downward as they descended.

A low whine echoed outside the ship, followed by a deep vibration that buzzed through Kathryn's boots as the thrusters overcompensated. Then came a jolt as the ship connected with one of the landing pads.

Kathryn's hands loosened their grip on the command terminal, tension bleeding from her shoulders as the relief of making it settled in. She glanced at Brazier and Switch, both looking exactly how she felt.

The red-headed dwarf smiled at her weakly, exhaustion creeping into the lines of his face.

"Let's go talk to some Kings," he said.

#

Brazier had offered Kathryn another sling, but she'd refused. Cautiously flexing her arm, she could extend it fully without the feeling of flesh ripping. After changing her bandages, it seemed the clotting potion had begun to work. Rather than a gaping wound across her bicep, she now had something resembling a nasty cut.

Kathryn and Brazier left Matthias tending to Freyen, and Switch tending to a very sorry-looking *Anchorite*. The enginator had stopped swearing and descended into a sort of angry brooding. But despite the impressive scowl, Kathryn could sense that she and the rest of the crew were grateful to be alive.

The mood on the *Pheradies* couldn't have been more different. As they walked through the corridors, Brazier quickly updated her on the rebel fleet: an alliance between House La'Voline, House Angelaux, and a group of Navarch Admirals who believed the Church was responsible for the ships.

That a faction had deliberately formed in opposition to the Church was almost impossible to reconcile with her worldview of the Fromryr, a disparate people held together by centuries of politics and bureaucracy so firmly entrenched it couldn't possibly be undone. That it had now descended into civil war was something Kathryn's mind simply struggled to accept.

Apparently, the same was true for the soldiers around her. As Kathryn and Brazier moved through the Gyre Star, it was impossible to ignore the looks etched across the crew's faces. It was a quiet disbelief mixed with something not unlike fear.

Gyre Star crews were handpicked: best-in-class graduates from the Navarch Academy or hardened veterans pulled from cruisers and battle frigates. They were chosen for their resilience under pressure, their ability to adapt, and their unshakable resolve. But that resolve looked like it was fraying at the edges.

The knowledge they were fighting their own kind clung to them, visible in every grim expression and flicker of manic, feverish energy. *Rebel*, she imagined them saying to themselves. *I'm a rebel now.*

Or maybe that was what she was saying to herself. Kathryn turned the thought over in her mind: the idea she was no longer part of the country she'd spent most of her life training to serve; the country she'd fought to protect. She was on the other side now, whatever side that even was.

The realisation should have cut deep. It should have made her ache with loss. It should have conjured her mother's voice. Would the Admiral who had trained some of the Navarch's greatest officers think even less of her now? If she'd still been alive, would she have disowned and disavowed Kathryn, as she'd always threatened to do? Would rescuing her fellow soldiers and joining a rebel fleet be good enough?

Kathryn found her conscience unusually silent on the matter. Maybe that was because of the lingering euphoria of escaping death. Or maybe it was because her exile to Palatine wasn't too far removed from being a rebel. Kathryn was just one more step down a path her mother had always expected her to end up on.

And then it crept in.

Like a shadow looming up behind her, her mother's smile rose behind her eyes. It was that hawkish face, that glint, not of disappointment, but satisfaction and the pleasure of seeing Kathryn fall exactly as she'd predicted. But even her mother, with all her cruelty, couldn't have imagined this particular mess she'd found herself in.

Kathryn shook her head, cutting off her mother before she could speak. The triumph flowing through her had already dissolved; she didn't need it put into words.

Their escort, a young officer who looked barely out of the Academy and had the same quietly shocked look as everyone else, stopped beside a terminal and pressed his hand into its node. The door slid open, revealing the commanding officer's personal quarters.

The space was painfully familiar: an elongated octagon, similar to others she'd been in, including her own once upon a time. It rose to a shallow peak, the gyre channels set to a bruising azure that somehow managed to convey calm and quiet authority. A set of dark green couches lined the far wall, a knee-high bronzite table standing in front of them, spotless and unused, as if its owner valued appearances over comfort.

At the far end, a door likely led to a bedchamber and head. To the left stood a personal command terminal, smaller than the ones on nav decks but large enough for four people to gather around. Four people were gathered around it now: a man in Angelaux colours, a man and a female dwarf in Navarch doublets, and a war caster in a green robe.

Kathryn suddenly felt self-conscious.

The room was immaculate, its air carrying the aniseed smell of Charok tea, the supple tang of leather, and the faintly wood-oil scent of recently polished surfaces. It was neat and clean. She, on the other hand, carried the unwashed odour of several battles and wore only half her armour. The entire sleeve of her tactical plate had been removed so

Switch could bandage her bicep. She suddenly felt lopsided, ridiculous, and smelly.

"So," said the man at the far end of the terminal. Standing half a foot taller than the others, his brown hair fell messily to his shoulders, and his green and gold plate armour barely contained his barrelled chest. His gambeson beneath was an intricate layering of beige and cloth-of-gold, the fabric slashed into thin panes. Combined with the close-cut beard, Kathryn thought he looked like a well-groomed bear.

"We send one famous captain off to complete a mission, and he decides to come back with another."

It took Kathryn a moment to realise he was referring to her. She supposed there weren't many Gyre Star Captains who had been captured, suffered from incurable hallucinations, and ended up as Palatines. *Captains who have fallen as far as you!* her mother spat from the back of her mind. Kathryn clenched her fists at her sides to stop herself from flinching at the unexpected intrusion.

"I'm not a captain anymore," she said. Then added, because she was fairly certain she was talking to Marcus Angelaux: "Your Highness."

"You're a Palatine. We received your message," the King said. Somehow he managed to inflect every word with annoyance. It was the sort of ability that could only be developed if you grew up born to rule. "That's why we're here, starting the sort of war that hasn't been seen in half a millennium."

"We were unable to confirm our intentions over epistolar," the man to the King's left said. He wore a captain's doublet and stood with the sort of straight-backed implacability even her mother would have been proud of. She recognised his voice as that of the Captain of the *Sovereign Eclipse*. This was Sourant.

"We couldn't know if Varkoneth was using you to bring us to Thela. We had to assume your message was a trap."

Kathryn suddenly felt very stupid. Of course her request for rescue would have been interpreted as a trap. That's the first thing she would have assumed if she'd been in their shoes.

"And yet you came anyway?" she said.

"We had to," Marcus said, though he didn't sound happy about it. "Your message stated Brazier had evidence the Sorel Tan were working with House Rosantz?"

Kathryn coughed awkwardly instead of looking at Brazier. To his credit, Brazier didn't show any sign of surprise.

"That would be Gabriel, the witch hunter we captured," Brazier said. "Who was then freed from our ship when we were captured."

The King's expression soured. He released an annoyed sigh through his nose.

"Even so," he said. "Your little detour hasn't been for nought. At the very least your capture has brought to light House Rosantz's involvement in all of this. And we can have a message sent to the Conclave, letting them know one of their own has turned traitor and is collaborating with the Sorel Tan."

He looked down at the dwarf on his left. "What did I tell you? A creature like Varkoneth wouldn't be too far from all this rot."

The dwarf nodded, but her expression remained unreadable. Kathryn noticed a scar running down her left eye, leaving her at least partially blind. Taking in the rest of her, Kathryn recognised the heavy brow and the nose that had been broken more than once. Kathryn had seen Admiral Benera Korst before, at a naval parade, and only from a distance. But she knew the woman's reputation well.

Korst had served in Navarch Intelligence, running operations both as an intelligence officer and Admiral. Two camps existed within the Navarch, those more and those less inclined toward the Ecclessius. Korst was well known to belong to the latter.

"Did you discover any evidence of the Church's involvement?" Korst asked.

"None," Brazier said. "It's Varkoneth who is attempting to weaken the other houses so he can rule as Formaria's only king. I don't think the Ecclessius is involved."

Kathryn wouldn't have thought Marcus Angelaux could

look any more annoyed, but the bear-like man's features darkened so much she thought he might start beating his hands on the terminal.

But if he was about to say something, it was interrupted by the door hissing open, revealing a man who also looked every inch a king. Tall, with combed dark hair and handsome despite his age, he wore polished leather boots and plain leather armour beneath a steel breastplate, the insignia of House La'Voline engraved just above his heart.

A long sword hung at his side, its gold hilt swimming beneath the gyre light as he moved. Kathryn didn't need to see the honour guard he'd left in the corridor to know this was Aymeri La'Voline. He stepped up to the command terminal as if he owned it and all the air it occupied.

"Your Highness," Sourant, Korst, and the war caster said almost in unison.

Aymeri gave Kathryn and Brazier little more than a cursory glance.

"We've got a lock on the Storm. She's heading eastward at maximum sprawl," he said, his voice deep, commanding, and filled with self-assurance. "But the Storm's fast. Only the Crucible, the Tempest, and the Vanguard will be able to maintain pursuit. Our Gyre Stars will have fallen behind in an hour. But my casters are also telling me there's an unusually high amount of gyranic energy surrounding the ship. They should be able to track her for several leagues."

"That's if we want them to," Korst said. "With the Gloried Storm comes Isdria Laanorath and the weapon he's using to create the Mirrovinjin ships. But that costs us a full withdrawal from Thela, where we know Varkoneth is at his most vulnerable. Half his fleet is abroad, and we've crippled most of the Cauldron's defences. If we wanted to apprehend the traitor, now would be the time to do it."

Kathryn had to stop herself from voicing her support for the first option. Pursuing Isdria Laanorath with several cruisers sounded like exactly the sort of thing they should be doing. She was almost annoyed when Brazier interrupted.

"There's more," the dwarf said.

He seemed to hesitate for a moment, as if what he was

about to say might be too unbelievable.

"The weapon they're using is a Lord of the Eternal Hunt, and it's being used to rebuild the Gyre Gates."

Kathryn turned, very slowly, to face Brazier. Everyone else in the room seemed to be waiting for the dwarf to deliver the punchline. Kathryn had the sudden and horrible feeling Brazier might be mad.

"You must be mistaken," Aymeri said.

That's one way of putting it, Kathryn thought. The dwarf had just claimed mythical beings were real and responsible for rebuilding ancient portals that had lain in ruins for hundreds of years. It was a staggering, ludicrous notion.

"No sorcery in this world can rebuild the Gyre Gates. The magic that sundered us from the other worlds was of the other worlds. It would require that sorcery to rebuild them."

Kathryn frowned at the King. What he said was true, but he hadn't contradicted Brazier's claim the Lords of the Eternal Hunt were real.

"I don't know how they're achieving it," Brazier said, shrugging.

"Which Lord?" the man to Marcus' right asked. The war caster was draped in green robes, his face hidden behind a bronzite mask, the kind often worn by casters who had endured severe disfigurements. His voice, strained and breathless from the two words he'd spoken, sounded as though he'd run the length of a ship. He also sounded like he was taking Brazier's statement seriously.

"They said they'd reawakened Duessa," Brazier replied.

"The Queen of Dreams," the caster said. Kathryn thought she detected fear in that breathless voice. He was definitely taking Brazier's statement seriously.

"How did you discover this?" Korst asked.

"Varkoneth told us while he interrogated us," Brazier replied. "Given he planned to execute us, he didn't think revealing the information a problem."

Korst placed her hand into one of the terminal's wells and closed her eyes.

"Get a message to Admiral Adremar in Thendergaarden. Tell him I need a report on the current state of the Gyre

Gates. Tell him it's a high priority order."

"You know you won't receive that report," Sourant said, once Korst had disconnected. "They'll know you're with us."

"You're right," Korst said. "But it'll make him look."

Kathryn was about to interrupt. She wanted to ask if they were all seriously considering the existence of mythical beings and the idea they could rebuild the Gyre Gates. But a memory resurfaced, and Kathryn suddenly felt a heavy feeling in the pit of her stomach. She was in Demina's chambers overlooking Ilantia. She was asking someone else to kidnap Ariadne. The Cradle was low on manpower. All available troops had been reassigned from the Gyre Gate south of Calanthis Major. It had felt like a passing comment at the time. Now it felt critically important.

"Tell him to look into the Gyre Gate south of Calanthis Major," Kathryn said, not meaning to blurt the words out. All eyes turned to her, and she had to stop herself from clutching her naked arm to her waist. "There were troop transfers from the gate to Ilantia and Kyor several days ago."

Admiral Korst's head snapped to Kathryn.

"How many?" she asked.

"The entire squadron," Kathryn said.

"So any activity around it wouldn't be reported," Korst said, then placed her hand in the hex well again. "Updated message for Admiral Adremar. Investigate the Gyre Gate south of Calanthis Major as a high priority request."

"This might still be a lie," Sourant said. "To convince us to pursue the Storm."

"And yet my casters detected the Storm because of its gyranic and Aeturnic output," Aymeri said. He turned to the caster. "Could they be detecting this being?"

"It's possible," the caster said.

His masked face bent to the terminal, as if he were thinking.

"The Queen of Dreams would explain why I have detected so much Obliquency. She's the Lord of falsehood and deceit. But I don't know how she could rebuild the Gyre Gates, her sorcery is of another realm entirely."

Kathryn was still trying to be openly shocked that admirals and kings were giving serious consideration to the existence of beings most people considered allegorical. Yet something was starting to fall into place for her. It was only when Brazier spoke that she realised what it was.

"They said the same sorcery that creates the ships is rebuilding the gates," he said. "But they didn't say how."

"Duessa is the source," Kathryn said, as if the words were a revelation to her. She was only now putting two and two together. Brazier no longer seemed completely out of his mind. "Isdria said the source grows with the more harbingers they create. But they lost the first harbinger. They escaped."

"Harbingers?" Sourant asked.

Brazier turned to her, a look of realisation in his eyes.

"In the Cawdora surface drift they were torturing a captive with Aeturnic sorcery," he said. "Shortly afterward, a Mirrovinjin ship appeared. I think he was a harbinger."

Ice-cold dread crawled down her spine with such force it was all she could do not to shake. The iron chair, the sorcery, the torture, all meant that *she* was a harbinger.

But you survived. You didn't end up dead like the gnome, or completely losing your mind like the Navarch liaison.

Then suddenly, columns of blue fire lit up in her mind's eye, and the Mirrovinjin leaned over her, reaching for her with pale, claw-like fingers. Her heart hammered against her ribcage. She shook the image from her mind.

Everyone turned to her.

"Palatine?" Sourant said, his brow furrowing.

"My apologies," Kathryn said, trying to ignore the looks from everyone else. "It's been a long day."

"It has for all of us," Sourant said, an eyebrow raised.

He turned to the others.

"We've received five separate reports of Mirrovinjin ship attacks," he said. "Which means they're creating more of these harbingers."

Five more ships.

The cold dread resurfaced. She felt both helplessness and the need to act, combined with something resembling anger. Isdria Laanorath was torturing other Fromryr for his own gains, just like he'd done to her. She felt an odd sense of kinship to these victims, and a drive to deliver revenge on their behalf.

"And Duessa grows stronger," the caster added, bringing her mind back to the room. "As does the potential for rebuilding the Gyre Gates."

"Then our decision has been made for us," Marcus said. "We chase down and intercept the Storm, capture the damned elf, and kill this Lord of the Eternal Hunt."

You're damn right we will, Kathryn thought. She almost said it out loud.

"The Storm is our priority, My King," the caster said. "But we don't know how to destroy Duessa. She's a being of another world, we don't know if we can."

"Eluthienn killed Lokul because he's a descendant of a Scion of Redcrosse," Marcus said, stabbing a thumb into his plated chest. "And so am I. I'll breach the Storm with every soldier here and kill the bitch myself."

Kathryn glanced from face to face, searching for the same shock that gripped her, but no one else seemed surprised by the King's claim that the Prince of Ravinica had slain a Lord of the Eternal Hunt. The last she'd heard, Eluthienn was still in exile, a fugitive in hiding. She felt as if she'd joined a briefing on a battle with only half the information she needed, and no one was willing to bring her up to speed.

"While I applaud your enthusiasm," the caster said. "That's not entirely accurate."

The King's eyes flashed with anger, and for a second, Kathryn half expected him to throttle the war caster.

"If that throne-less upstart, Eluthienn Leonette, can kill a vampire king, I think I can handle the thing's little sister," Marcus growled. He cast his look upon them all as if daring one of them to say otherwise.

"I wasn't referring to your capabilities on the field," the caster said. "But the link between the descendants of Redcrosse and the Lords of the Eternal Hunt."

"Guilfier is right," Aymeri said. "Eluthienn claimed only he could slay Lokul because his forebear, Leoncoure Leonette, did the same thing a thousand years prior. We don't know if our lineage holds the same magical connection."

"It doesn't," Brazier said. "On the way to Lokul's lair, Lyander and Gabriel crossed into the Immuratum at Acheron to find information that would corroborate Eluthienn's claim—which they found. And I saw with my own eyes Eluthienn kill Lokul."

"You're referring to the Library of the Nine," Korst said.

"That's real?" Sourant asked, raising an eyebrow.

"The library is real," Korst said. "What we've never been able to ascertain is whether a breach existed in Acheron, and if the Ecclessius had access to it."

Kathryn resolved to stop reeling at each new revelation and simply get on board. The Lords were real. A foreign prince had killed one. And there was talk of a library buried deep within the demon realm. She had the sudden notion that this might be far bigger than just Isdria Laanorath and the Mirrovinjin ships.

"Acheron is in the hands of Orpheus Velgar," Sourant said, "who by all accounts is just as likely to break bread with you as to throw you over one of his balconies and into the abyss. How did Lyander and Gabriel gain access?"

"We didn't really get round to having that conversation," Brazier said.

"There's long been speculation the Ecclessius granted Orpheus free rein over his little operation in the east," Aymeri said. "Sponsoring a criminal to guard a breach gives the Church access to the Immuratum while keeping their hands clean. I'd wager the crossing was arranged."

"Then the question is," Marcus said, "how do we gain access to the breach and find this demon library?"

If anyone was surprised at the King's suggestion of flying off to a criminal stronghold and crossing into the demon realm, they hid it well. For Kathryn, the whole conversation was beginning to put her own reckless behaviour into a new perspective, and one she felt a lot better about.

"Acheron is over three days away," Aymeri said. "And none of us, as far as I know, have the sort of relationship with Orpheus Velgar that would mean we could use its breach."

"I wasn't planning on asking for permission," Marcus growled. "And unless you know of any other magic portals into the demon realm, this is our only option."

"We do know of other breaches," Korst said.

This didn't seem to surprise anyone either. Though Sourant said, "Sounds like our new intelligence branch has as many secrets as the Ecclessius."

"This is a new secret," Korst replied. "The officer we sent to investigate the Aeturnic being on the surface has discovered that it rules over a breach into the Immuratum."

"It's all go in Yeggardania," Sourant muttered.

"What entity?" Aymeri asked.

"We're not sure," Korst said. "But our officer has made contact. He believes the entity has access to the breach, along with a retinue she has gathered about her."

"She?" Aymeri said.

"It's female, whatever it is," Korst said. "Our officer refers to it as the Handmaid."

"And where is this breach?" Aymeri asked.

"Several miles east of Calaxis, by the surface," the Admiral said. "Considerably closer than Acheron."

"Even so," Sourant said, "we don't know where this breach leads. Or how to get from it to the library. Unless you happen to have a map of the Immuratum?"

"Our officer informs us the breach is a type of junction," Korst said. "It will take whoever uses it to wherever they need to go."

"This officer appears to be incredibly well informed," Sourant said.

"Our officers tend to be. That's why we choose them," Korst replied.

"Then our last remaining issue is getting to the surface," Aymeri said. "All our ships' signatures have been flagged," he said. "Right down to the landers. We won't get within a mile of Calaxis, or any other installation, for that matter."

"There are other routes to the surface," Sourant said.

"There are," Korst agreed. "But we can't risk them, especially as most surface clearing teams have been reassigned to the front. And our contact is in Calaxis."

"We'll go," Brazier said.

Kathryn's head snapped round to the dwarf. She very nearly blurted out what a stupid idea that was, before she saw his face.

Brazier stood with his arms crossed, staring into the hex display with a strange look scrunching up his brow. He looked as if he'd made a particularly hard decision, as if this had been something he'd been thinking about for weeks and had finally reached a resolution.

"We have a contact on the Calaxis docks who can get us into the Spire," he said, then shrugged. "Well, technically my navigator has the contact."

"How do you know they can get you into Calaxis?" Korst asked.

"Because this'll be the fourth time she's done it," Brazier said. "The Anchorite is registered as a pirated ship, but our contact has created an alternate signature in the local network. Calaxis is one of the few places we can actually dock."

"This could work," Korst said.

"Smuggle yourself into Calaxis, then across Yeggardania to treat with an unknown being, then into the Immuratum," Sourant said. "That is fraught with potential failure at every turn."

Kathryn thought that was a severe understatement. Every part of that journey offered its own flavour of certain death. But she was also, Kathryn realised, considering how she could ask Brazier if she could go with him. Which was absurd. Certain death aside, she wanted to be here, with this rebel fleet, to ensure they captured Isdria. Still, the thought tugged at her.

"If you've got a better suggestion, Captain," Korst said. "I think we'd all like to hear it."

Sourant shook his head. "Just setting out the risk here," he said.

"It's noted," Korst said. "Everything we've done so far has had the potential for failure. We're making highly risky moves because we have no other option. This is the same."

"Yes sir," Sourant said.

The matter apparently settled, Korst turned to Brazier.

"To be clear, Captain Veranquis," she said, "you are volunteering you and your crew to enter the Immuratum, seek out the Library of the Nine, and retrieve the knowledge we need to destroy Duessa?"

Brazier didn't hesitate.

"I am."

Kathryn felt that tugging sensation again, somewhere around her chest. It was just the ghost of a feeling, nothing too obvious, and something she could ignore if she wanted to. But she knew what it meant. For a very brief moment, she'd been part of a crew, fighting to protect each other, to escape together, working toward a shared purpose. She reminded herself it was a ridiculous thing to feel, given how long she'd known Brazier's crew.

You need to stop being so pathetic, Stryker.

"We'll send a unit with you," Aymeri said. "Including a second navigator."

"Thank you, Your Highness," Brazier said. "We'll depart as soon as we've made the required repairs to our ship."

Kathryn felt a little sad, and very stupid. She smiled at Brazier to hide her feelings. He gave her a confused smile back.

"Miss Stryker," Sourant said. "We thought we might make use of your experience."

Kathryn turned to Sourant, cautious of what he was about to ask. She wanted to stay aboard the *Pheradies* in the hopes of influencing their decision to pursue and capture Isdria. If they needed to use her experience as Palatine, she might be sent elsewhere.

"You previously commanded a Gyre Star, correct?"

The question caught her so completely off guard, her mind blanked. She said nothing for several seconds. Then she gathered herself.

"Not for very long," she managed.

Sourant continued, unfazed.

"Prior to that, six years' service on a Vault-class cruiser. Top of your class at the Academy. Recipient of the Distinguished Cross."

He paused, then added, "And more importantly, you were one of Admiral Thrace's."

Kathryn stiffened. Even after all these years, hearing the phrase *one of* struck something deep inside her, something she spent a good deal of energy trying not to unearth.

"Yes sir," she said curtly. "But this—"

"The Vanguard of Winter lost its captain," Sourant interrupted. "Along with six deck officers."

Kathryn blinked.

"Our numbers were stretched thin even before all this started," Sourant went on. "Now, they're at the limit on every ship in the fleet. You're one of the most experienced officers here, so—"

He met her gaze.

"We need you to captain her."

Kathryn opened her mouth, then closed it again.

She had the oddest sensation. It was like being winded without actually being winded. Her thoughts scrambled, acting purely on reflex. *I was honourably discharged. I'm not allowed to pilot a ship.*

Her internal voice slipped into her mother's so seamlessly Kathryn found it hard to tell one from the other. *You were never good enough*, she said with quiet intensity.

But another thought broke through her consciousness: She would captain a ship. The thing she'd been fighting so hard for had now been handed to her, simply dropped in her lap. And it would mean she might be the one to capture Isdria Laanorath. She might be the one to bring him to justice, to prove to everyone she'd been right all along. The revelations about Lords of the Eternal Hunt, foreign princes, and breaches into the Immuratum suddenly seemed utterly inconsequential, because she would be a captain again.

"Miss Stryker?"

Sourant's tone suggested this was the second time he'd said her name.

"Do you accept the offer?"

Kathryn licked her lips, just to make sure she didn't mess up the next words out of her mouth. "I'd be honoured to," she said.

Sourant nodded.

"Congratulations on your new command," Korst said. "We'll send over all fleet information once you're aboard the Vanguard. You'll need to get up to speed quickly."

"Understood, sir."

Marcus smiled at her. "Welcome to the fleet."

Aymeri tipped his head slightly.

"You're one of us now," Sourant said.

A thrill cascaded through her. She felt it in every nerve, every inch of her body. It lit her up, and she smiled. No, she grinned. She grinned so hard that she was vaguely worried she looked like a fool.

Beneath it, a small, rational part of her whispered a warning: that she might be making a mistake, that at any moment she could end up on the floor, frothing at the mouth, that she might not be good enough, that like every other time, she would fail. But that fear, that dark river of doubt flowing with her mother's venom, was nothing compared to the ocean of headiness surging through her veins.

She was going to captain a ship, and not just any ship. It was a ship in pursuit of Isdria Laanorath. After so long fighting for the things she wanted, only for them to be handed to her, she almost doubted it was true.

She could hear her mother's laughter again. But it had become further away now. It had become easier to ignore. Kathryn straightened her back and lifted her chin, meeting the eyes of everyone there.

She wouldn't fail this time.

EPISTOLAR MESSAGE FION TO VALLORANDYL

A telling in Vallorandyl.

The teller is Emries von Cadst, Duke of Ylstgaar, Adjutant to the Fion Throne, and Marshal of the Western Front.

The witness is Vermillies Sidtch, Lord Regent of Ravinica and Absolver General.

The telling is of the mixed tidings which the Lord Regent brings before me. Your victory at Alstgaar and successful repositioning of sympathetic Ravinican lords has granted the empire strategic advantage, and earned you imperial favour. Moreover, Isdria Laanorath's intelligence regarding the underground weapon corroborates our suspicions and provides leverage against the Fromryr's designs. We knew the Fromryr would not so lightly allow Fiondagaard to consolidate its power on their borders and that they would seek a means to destroy us.

This power, this Duessa, another Lord of the Eternal Hunt—they dare meddle with forces beyond their comprehension. Within Fiondagaard, of all these Lords, she remains the most inscrutable, veiled in deepest mystery. To us, she bears a darker epithet: The Priestess of Lies. Our ancient legends speak of her power as rooted in a religious belief, its potency nourished by faith. An unholy communion between deception and devotion. Soon, perhaps, the truth behind these tales will be laid bare through Brazier

Veranquis, the dwarf who once more finds himself entangled within our plans.

And thus, from one malcontent we move inexorably toward another. Varkoneth Rosantz, power-mad and unscrupulous as ever, foolishly courts disaster by aligning with the Sorel Tan and daring to rebuild the Gyre Gates. That much of this tale I am certaint of, beyond any doubt; for I know Varkoneth, and I know such a creature would risk all for personal gain.

Such reckless ambition weakens Formaria and renders it vulnerable, ripe for conquest by our forces. Yet, peril shadows fortune. The Gyre Gates' reconstruction heralds not merely war but existential catastrophe. A gateway reopened could unleash Fey legions, augmenting the Fromryr and flooding our world with primal, heretical magic—magic we have painstakingly purged from our own empire. This possibility fills me with dread and revulsion. It threatens everything we have built and demands immediate imperial attention. Vermillies, wring every scrap of truth from the elf. Spare no severity in your interrogation. Discover the means to halt or reverse this sorcery, and the emperor will elevate us beyond our greatest ambitions. Beware deceit, for the elf will lie even in agony. Your vigilance is our last shield against disaster. The teller is Emries von Cadst, Duke of Ylstgaar. The witness is Vermillies Sidtch, Lord Regent, and no others.

Epistolar message Vallorandyl to Fion

A telling in Fion.

The teller is Vermillies Sidtch, Lord Regent of Ravinica and Absolver General.

The witness is Emries von Cadst, Duke of Ylstgaar, Adjutant to the Fion Throne, and Marshal of the Western Front.

The telling is of the dark tidings I must now recount. The elf we believed to be Isdria Laanorath has proven a monstrous fraud. After another night of exhaustive interrogation and severe torment to extract the second half of his tale, methods I believed thorough enough to break any creature, I left him to my guards' custody. Within mere moments, reports emerged of his transformation into a goblin. I will say this again to avoid misunderstanding. Isdria Laanorath turned into a goblin. I know not how, or by what sorcery, but his wasted form slipped from the manacles and escaped through bars unfit to hold such a diminutive horror. Vallorandyl is now in lockdown; every resource is committed to recapturing this fiend.

Yet graver still is the message he left behind, a story woven with malevolence, implicating us directly in the Gyre Gates' reawakening. A story that I fear we were meant to hear. Almost immediately following my prior message, confirmation arrived of gyranic disturbances in western Formaria, exactly where the goblin's tale implied a gate had been rebuilt. Our war casters tremble at sorcery so ancient and potent it defies comprehension. My Duke, we stand ensnared in machinations beyond my understanding. I now recount to you, the remainder of the creature's tale. I implore your wisdom and swift counsel, as the weight of these developments crushes my will and burdens my conscience. I await your guidance and commands; I remain ever a loyal servant of the empire.

Twenty-Two
Brazier

Brazier had gathered the crew in the fuselage. Matthias sat on the opposite bench, the back of his head pressed against the wall behind him, his eyes half-closed but still alert. With his fingers laced and resting in his lap, he looked like he was in communion with the ship.

Freyen leaned against one of the bulkheads separating the fuselage from the armoury, her arms wrapped around herself. Dark rings shadowed her eyes, her pale skin tinged with shades of grey.

Seeing her there so fragile, yet so full of secrets, Brazier was caught between the urge to scoop her into his arms and the burning need to demand answers. He didn't know why, but now, of all times, the sense of betrayal flared to life. Every time his eyes flicked to her, it was like a fire roaring at the back of his mind, forcing him to clench his jaw just to contain it.

Instead, he turned his focus on Switch, who stood in the centre of the armoury with one foot planted atop a toolbox. In her augmented hand, she brandished a complex bronzite gear wheel system that, Brazier could only assume, was part of the engine.

The sight triggered a sudden flashback: *The Chalice*, its armoury, and the moments before they'd headed out to the *Solace*. He clenched his jaw harder, forcing the memory back into the void where it belonged.

This wasn't like before. This was different.

“Let me get this straight,” Switch said. “You volunteered for us to go to the surface, meet an Aeturnic entity, and cross over into the Immuratum?”

“I did,” Brazier said.

“When I think of all the many places to die in this world, Yeggardania, the Aeturnum, and the Immuratum come top of the list,” Switch said. “And we’re going to do all three?”

“We are,” Brazier said.

“One small question, Cap,” Switch said. “Why?”

“Because we’re the only ones who can get into Calaxis,” Brazier said. “Karenna is only going to arrange passage if we’re there.”

He glanced at Matthias, who gave him a non-committal shrug. Brazier clenched his jaw again, then stopped when it started to hurt.

“Got it,” Switch said. “Fully agree. But why are we carrying this out? Why can’t we just escort Aymeri’s people up to the surface and give them a fond farewell as *they* go off into Yeggardania?”

“Because I stood in front of a group of people who are risking their lives to do the right thing, and I said we’d do it,” Brazier said. “Because those people are trying to stop Formaria from descending into complete anarchy, and they need our help. And because I am tired of playing escort and scout and blades for hire, tired of sitting idly by while others shape events. I am going to make a difference. This is the mission. None of you have to take part if you don’t want to.”

Brazier only realised he’d stood up after the fact. The others seemed momentarily frozen, their reactions suspended in the air.

Switch and Matthias wore nearly identical expressions, a blend of surprise and carefully guarded neutrality. Freyen, however, stared at him with something else entirely. From within the tired shadows of her eyes, her gaze was sharp and focused, as if trying to decipher a particularly intricate hex script.

Matthias leaned forward, resting his forearms on his thighs, pearl-grey eyes dancing with mischief.

"Well, why didn't you just say so," the navigator said, chuckling. "You know I could use a change of scenery. And you really think any of us are walking away? After that little speech?"

"Yeah Cap," Switch said, scratching her nose. "You should have just said you wanted to go save the world—would have made more sense."

"I'm being serious," Brazier said.

"So are we," Switch said. "You want to go to hell and back, literally, we're your crew."

Brazier felt a little of the tension drain out of him, like a pressure valve had just released. He turned to his First Officer, trying not to fidget with his gambeson's rock locks.

"Freyen?" he said.

Freyen still hadn't stopped giving him that look. Brazier was fairly sure she hadn't broken her gaze since the moment he'd started talking.

"I don't remember being very idle over the past few months," she said, sounding exhausted.

"You can say that again," Switch grumbled.

"But Switch is right," Freyen said, finally breaking her gaze and glancing at the enginator. "We're your crew. If this mission is what you think we should be doing, then we're with you."

That didn't sound like the resounding yes he'd hoped for but he'd take it. At the very least, it seemed to have quenched the flames at the back of his mind.

"Alright," he said, glancing down at his hands, then back up at them all. "I'll be more upfront about my feelings in the future."

"Best to get these things out in the open," Switch said.

"Never a good idea to keep them bottled up," Matthias added.

"Yeah, alright," Brazier said. "How are we looking?"

"Well she's definitely taken a beating," Switch said, creating a metallic tap-tap as she patted a bulkhead. "Three thruster discs need replacing, including one of the rotating mounts."

"We're down a repeater, another needs a new torsion spring, and another needs a new flight chamber," Freyen said.

"Replace the spring and flight chamber; a whole new repeater will take too much time to install," Brazier said, grateful to be talking about repairs instead of feelings. "Same with the rotating mount. Can we do without one thruster?"

"As long as we don't need to make too many high-sprawl manoeuvres, we should be okay," Matthias said.

"Okay," Brazier said again. "I don't know when this unit is arriving, but let's assume it's soon. So let's get to it."

He let the others drift off to their various duties and headed for the galley. He wasn't sure if he was actually hungry, but he didn't know when he'd get another chance to eat. The last time he'd had anything was back on the *Eclipse*, and he figured that once he started cooking, the hunger would catch up with him.

During the months they'd owned the ship, he'd done his best to replace the bland, mushroom-based ration cakes with something, anything, more varied. But underground, *variety* was a relative term. It meant lichen- or moss-based foods, especially with supplies of real food dwindling thanks to Fiondagaard's invasion of Ravinica.

Now, instead of just mushrooms, they had thin algae strands mixed with lichen flakes that were supposed to mimic the "spices" found in Syracuta and Zymifar. There were root blends packed with chunks of purple carrot, onion, and, if you were lucky, potato. And larvae blocks coated in real honey, which Matthias assured him was a particular delicacy, and Brazier had decided he'd be taking his word for it. Everything was dehydrated, pressed into neat rectangular blocks, and stored among gyre ice refined to a degree that would help preserve it. And, of course, there was Charok tea.

He rummaged through the wall compartments, pulling out two pots before grabbing a pair of algae strand blocks. Dropping them into the pots, he set them under the wall spout above the sink. He was reaching for the palm-sized wheel to pump the water through when he heard the galley door slide open behind him.

"Are we fighting to save Formaria?" Freyen asked, as the door slid shut behind her.

"What?" Brazier said, taken completely off guard. He blinked, completely thrown. Of all the questions she could've asked, he wasn't expecting that. He opened his mouth, then closed it.

"Tell me we're fighting to save Formaria and not for Brazier Veranquis' personal campaign."

Brazier stood there, momentarily stunned. Then, before he could stop himself, he said: "What if my personal campaign is saving Formaria?"

He regretted the words the moment they left his mouth. Even to his own ears, they sounded childish and petulant in a way that made him wince internally.

"Right now, saving Formaria looks a lot like righting whatever wrongs you think have been done to, or by, your family," Freyen said. "And it's making you reckless."

"Then why didn't you say so below?" Brazier said.

"Because this is all we have, this ship, this little family, and I'm not prepared to break it apart. And I still believe you're the one to keep it together," she said, then nodded at the door. "They do too."

His own words came rushing back to him like a wave rolling through a gorge: *none of you have to take part if you don't want to.* Guilt and regret curled into a tight knot in his stomach, moving in right next to the ball of childishness and petulance.

"The Brazier I knew wouldn't storm off into the Immuratum," Freyen said. "He wouldn't believe a word that came out of Isdria Laanorath's mouth. And he wouldn't let it risk his crew's lives."

Brazier felt his shoulders droop as his exhale turned into a sigh. He stared at his feet, then looked up at Freyen

"Isdria Laanorath isn't lying," he said. Saying it out loud felt like driving home a knife that had been hovering over his heart. The pain he'd been holding off finally sank in.

“You don’t know that,” Freyen said, her face creasing into a mask of disbelief. Several curls fell over her eyes as she shook her head. “Why let this torture you?”

“Torquen made it clear to me the Ecclessius had lied about my father, that they’d executed him for secrets he wasn’t supposed to know. But it wasn’t the same with the Luceron. He barely spoke about it. Whatever he did on that ship haunted him.”

He paused, then, as if he had to force the words out: “And he came back with a lot of gold. Isdria didn’t make that part up.”

“Torquen Veranquis was one of the best dwarves I knew,” Freyen said. “If he did any of what Isdria claimed, it wouldn’t have been for himself.”

“Doesn’t make what he did right,” Brazier said.

“Right and wrong aren’t always as clear-cut as you want them to be,” Freyen said.

“So I’ve discovered,” he snapped, the flame sparking back to life.

She shot him a look, half wounded, half inquisitive. He let out another sigh. He’d timed this badly, and it certainly wasn’t how he’d imagined starting this conversation. But would there ever really be a good time to question the person he loved about her involvement in a terrorist organisation?

Probably not.

And with Isdria’s words churning like a poisoned bog at the depths of his conscience, he needed to know. One way or another, he needed the certainty of the truth.

“Why didn’t you tell me you were a former member of the Donnie Shied?”

If Freyen was shocked that he knew about her past, she didn’t show it. But the intensity burning behind her eyes seemed to dim, transforming into something like sadness.

“Because that isn’t my life anymore,” she said, eventually. “That was a long time ago. The person you see now, the one who joined the Chalice, isn’t the same gnome who became a member of the Donnie Shied.”

"I'm willing to accept that," Brazier said, carefully, as if one wrong word might break something between them. "But I need to know why my first officer joined in the first place."

"I didn't," Freyen said. "I was born into it."

That gave Brazier pause. Freyen took a breath, as if to prepare herself.

"All I know of my family, my real family, is they died in the war," she said. "I was placed into the Foundry, what the rest of Formaria calls the Covenant of Praetoria."

Nearly three hundred years ago, Lord Marshal Alena Praetoria had introduced a law ensuring war orphans would be raised by some of Formaria's best and brightest. Recognising the toll the Eternal War was taking on the Fromryr's social fabric, Thendergaarden had signed the Covenant of Praetoria.

Under its terms, any high-ranking military officer or administrative leader who retired was required to adopt war orphans. The legislation was hailed as one of the most impactful in the Fromryr's long history. Everyone from former generals to bishops took it up.

But it still wasn't enough.

The war produced too many orphans. And in a nation locked in perpetual conflict, too many senior officers died in their posts. Still, those who made it into the system almost always became some of Formaria's most capable officers. They in turn raised war orphans, handing down the Fromryr's martial and administrative knowledge from generation to generation. Suddenly, Freyen's seemingly inexplicable skill set began to make a lot more sense.

"The officer who raised me and my adopted brothers and sisters, was a retired infantry officer," she said. "But he really worked for the Donnie Shied.

Most of his charges ended up in the Knelderian military. But a handful, those of us who demonstrated an interest in the cause's ideology, were selected as recruits for the Donnie Shied."

"He indoctrinated you?" Brazier said.

"It didn't feel like that at the time," Freyen said, shrugging. "The idea that Formaria should be restored to its former glory. The anti-Ecclessius stance. The belief that the Kneldier deserved greater independence, like the elves. That we shouldn't be subject to the Church's tithes. That our people shouldn't be sacrificed by the hundreds of thousands for a war that never ends. It was irresistible to someone whose entire family had already been lost to that war."

Something in Freyen's words struck uncomfortably close to home. He'd been raised to believe in the Eternal War, that serving, and even dying, in Formaria's defence was the highest calling. But what if the narrative he'd grown up on had been different? What if he'd been raised on tales of Formaria's former strength, on the promise that rebuilding the gates could deliver a swift and lasting victory? A new era of hope? What choices would he have made instead?

"I spent three years in the Donnie Shied," Freyen continued. "At first, it was just hex work, breaking networks and rewriting scripts, rerouting supplies, helping spies get into installations or smuggling them onto ships. But then I saw a side of the Donnie Shied I didn't think existed, not at the time, anyway. A side that looked a lot more like the Sorel Tan."

She sighed, running a hand through her curls. Brazier saw pain reflected in her brown eyes.

"My first field mission was part of a unit sent to break into a hex network and plant a relay-signalling script in an outpost north of Kronos," she said. "But our unit was ambushed by the Mirrovinjin. We kept calling for evacuation, but the response was the same: the area was too risky to land in. Omega picked up the activity, and its Praefector sent a company, assuming allied Fromryr were under attack. But as soon as they arrived, more Mirrovinjin war parties showed up. The Praefector had no choice but to send reinforcements to support the reinforcements he'd already deployed. Most of the spire's forces were drawn into the fight, leaving it wide open for the Donnie Shied raiding force. Their target was a rear admiral's granddaughter they meant to ransom."

"You were set up?" Brazier said.

"We were nothing more than well-timed bait," Freyen said. "I was the only one who made it out. Omega's detachment picked me up, not realising who I was. And in the chaos the Spire was thrown into, thanks to my former colleagues, I got off the installation before they could question me."

The Freyen he knew seemed to have disappeared in front of his eyes, replaced with the hollow shell of her former self. The quiet, almost mysterious confidence he found so attractive had given way to someone more fragile, as if she'd been stripped of all her armour.

"They think you're dead," Brazier said, making it more a statement than a question.

She looked up at him, a sudden fire smouldering among the shadows of exhaustion.

"The Sorel Tan. The Donnie Shied. The Church. They're all the same," she said. "They're all willing to sacrifice their own for a supposedly higher purpose. I found out the hard way. Switch and Matthias, they found out their own way too. That's why they'll follow you into the Immuratum, because they know you're not willing to sacrifice any of us."

"You're damn right I'm not," Brazier said.

He glanced around the galley, not wanting to meet her eyes. He suddenly felt both foolish and guilty but wasn't sure why.

"You think I'm an idiot for wanting to fight for Formaria?" Brazier said. "For thinking we should try and make a difference?"

Freyen shook her head, the fire in her gaze expunged, her eyes glistening with so much caring that Brazier felt it in his chest.

"Wanting to keep fighting, despite everything the Church has done to your family—to us," she said. "That's why I love you."

She took a tentative step toward him, cupping his wrist in her hand. "Just promise me you won't go running off into battle because you think you need to make up for something you had no say in. Because I can't follow you down that road."

She was inches from him now. He could smell lilac, and the more indescribable scent of softness, of home.

"Seems fair to me," he said. "No more rash decisions."

She shook her head, one way, then the other, her curls bobbing playfully in front of her face.

"I love you too," he said.

"Even though I'm a runaway terrorist?" she asked, a hint of genuine fear flickering in her eyes as they searched his own.

"No," he said. "You're Freyen Fortigris, First Officer of the Shian Anchorite."

Then, because suddenly it felt like they'd fixed something deep and painful between them: "Defender of Teuron."

That carefree laughter tumbled out of her.

"Master of hex cloaks," he added, secretly hoping to make her laugh again. But she only smiled and took another step toward him.

"I like that one," she said softly, then kissed him on the lips.

For all he knew, minutes or seconds could have passed before he felt her fingers unbuttoning the front of his gambeson. He pulled back, giving her a questioning look.

"We're about to go to hell," she said. "And your cabin is too far away."

Brazier needed no other explanation than that.

#

Afterward, he tossed two more algae blocks into the pan, and they ate, half-naked in the galley, their clothes scattered across the benches and floor.

Brazier had a feeling Switch and Matthias knew exactly what they'd been up to, and were giving them space on purpose. He was grateful for it.

Something inside him felt looser, like a knot that had finally come undone. Isdria's words still lingered, like the scar tissue of an old wound that, now and then, pulled tight. But knowing Freyen was no longer part of the Donnie Shied, and had never subscribed to its more violent tendencies, made the ache that much easier to bear.

They left the galley together and headed for the nav deck, when the sound of strangers' voices drifted up from the fuselage.

"Our new friends," Brazier said. "I'd better say hello."

He started down the stairwell, when Freyen appeared in front of him. She reached out, fingers threading gently through his beard as she cupped his jaw, then kissed him.

"I'll see you later," she said, before turning toward the nav deck.

Brazier watched her go, right up until the doors slid shut behind her. He found Matthias at the bottom of the fuselage, arms crossed over his chest and leaning against a bulkhead. The navigator was watching the group of soldiers at the far end of the fuselage, an amused smile creeping up his face.

"Vandemir Vonclaire," Matthias said, so only Brazier could hear.

"Who?" Brazier asked, confused.

"Lanky one," Matthias said.

The soldiers all wore the quartered leather armour of House La'Voline, burnished red in two quarters, deep forest green in the others, layered over chainmail vests and skirts. Their boots and gloves matched, all burnished red.

Among them stood a man in similar armour, though on him it seemed to cling rather than fit. Strands of grey hair poked out from beneath his skullcap, curling against his beard. His leggings were striped red and green, and with the skullcap and the way he had just delivered a joke to roaring laughter, Brazier thought he looked less like a soldier and more like a court jester.

To Brazier's surprise, the man Matthias had called Vandemir held a Gorefelder in one hand. The long, two-handed sword came up to his chin. Its scabbard, made of orange and green reptilian skin, only covered the blade to the ricasso, the unsharpened section near the hilt where Vandemir gripped the weapon.

Seeing the Fromryr's heaviest sword in the hands of a man who looked like he belonged to a group of travelling performers was almost comical.

Vandemir snapped his head around, and the moment he spotted Brazier, he hushed his crew with a single glance.

"Rumour swirls aboard the Pheradies," Vandemir said, his Harothellian accent so thick and lilting every r rolled effortlessly into the vowels. He propped the sword against a bulkhead and took a loping step toward Brazier.

Although he wasn't quite tall enough for his head to graze the ceiling, he stooped anyway, one hand trailing along its surface, making him look awkward and gangly.

"Like a Ravinican thrush, it flits from one end of the ship to the other, singing its pretty little song. And it says there be a dwarf in need."

He took another stride forward.

"And I said to the thrush, 'In need of what now?'"

Another step, but then casting his gaze behind him, so he could address his squad as well.

"The thrush says to me, in hushed tones, 'In need of killers, he is. And not just any killers, mind. The meanest, most wretched, bloodthirsty, murdering children of the abyss he can find!'"

Hoots and jeers went up from his squad. Brazier gave Matthias a questioning look, but the navigator was smiling like he'd never seen anything so entertaining.

"And I asked the bird," Vandemir continued, "'Why would he need individuals of this particular temperament and disposition?' And you know what the bird says to me? He says, 'He intends to cross into the Immuratum. To find, none other, than a book.'"

The man smiled, flashing his teeth like a goblin at a blood feast.

"'Well now,' I said to the bird, it's a good job your song reached my discerning ears. For I know of such nefarious, wicked creatures fit for such a task as this.'"

He took another step forward, his voice dropping to a theatrical whisper.

"Thrice-damned and abyssal reprobates. Sinners so vile that demons, casting one look upon their visage, are overcome with envy of their wickedness. Killers of the blackest sort, even the abyss, that takes all in the end, spat them back out, unwilling to stain its halls with their corruption."

The man gestured grandly, his grin widening.

"Brazier Veranquis, I present to you: the Rex Populaire."

More hoots and jeers followed, along with stamping boots and the butts of weapons. Brazier, who had been tutored in multiple Old World languages, recognised the name as roughly *The King's People*. Although most translations would lean toward The King's low-born people.

"Pretty name," Matthias said. "You come up with that all by yourself?"

"I did," the man said, feigning a modest bow. "Although the King in question seemed not to like it. Alas, like many names, it seems to have a will of its own—etched into our minds and refusing to leave."

"Bet he's thrilled about that," Brazier said.

"If you bet on that, my good captain, you would surely lose," the man replied with a smirk.

"Captain Vandemir Vonclaire, at your service," Vandemir said. He straightened, sweeping his arm toward his squad.

"And now, allow me to introduce the members of our most famed unit."

He pointed to one of the two women in the unit. Slim and wiry, she was cruelly beautiful in the way only some human women could be. Her long dark hair framed a pale face of striking angles, her merciless brown eyes set beneath arched brows. Even her lips, full but unforgiving, seemed carved into sharp curves.

She held a longbow and a quiver of black-feathered arrows between her knees, causing Brazier to blink. Given the effectiveness of the Formarian repeating crossbow, few Fromryr ever used a bow, and it had been years since he'd seen one wielded by anyone other than a Sorel Tan.

"Loraine de'Arney," Vandemir said. "Prefers a bow to a crossbow, and women to men. Believe me, there are many a dead fool who've tested the latter fact."

He gestured to the man beside her. Bald and burly, he wore his La'Voline leathers trimmed and polished to perfection. A heavy gold chain hung around his neck, a large cross resting against his chest. His hands sat atop the gilded pommel of a great hammer, its surface etched with intricate carvings of small animals, while his green eyes studied Brazier from within heavy lids.

"Bertrand Cosar," the man said. "A warrior who thinks he's a priest. He refused the Knights Redcrosse, for, as he says, lesser men need the Saviour's sword as well. We try not to take it as an insult."

He pointed to the man sitting next to Bertrand. Where Bertrand was burly, his companion was outright brutish. His cropped hair jutted out at odd angles, pockmarks roughened his cheeks, and his nose and lips seemed too large for his face, throwing his features off balance. Even his posture felt uneven, his broad frame leaning slightly to one side, as if he might walk with a limp.

"Godenforte," Vandemir said. "Tells everyone his mother was a half-blood giant whom his human father wooed into his tent before taking her maidenhood. I would strongly advise you not to question the veracity of that tale."

He nodded to the other woman, sitting on the opposite side of the bench. Her short ginger hair was cut to her jawline, framing a soft, almost girlish face. But her eyes, magically deadened and unfocused, stared straight at Brazier, their pale emptiness betraying at least partial blindness. He found the contrast between her youthful features and the clear weight of battle experience strangely unsettling.

"Atlas Hayl, our sometimes navigator. She can do the sort of things to ships that would have most other navigators clamped in irons," Vandemir said, causing Matthias to raise an eyebrow. It was hard to tell with Matthias, but Brazier thought he looked impressed.

"Atlas is also one of the only navigators who can stand to be around us," Vandemir continued. "Only Redcrosse knows why."

"The man next to her is Solon Cray. We believe he hails from Celmyr, but as the only two words he seems to know are his own name, we cannot know for certain. He is rather handy in a fight, though."

Solon's long, dark hair hung in unwashed strands around his sun-darkened face. He sat slumped on the bench, the only one not wearing chain mail, his bare arms visible beneath a worn La'Voline jerkin. His gaze was fixed on the hammer head between Bertrand's feet, vacant and unreadable.

"And last, the boy next to him," Vandemir said.

Limp curls of foppish brown hair were draped over half a face that seemed gifted with protracted youth. Of all the Fromryr, Brazier found a human's age the easiest to guess, but the boy in his fuselage could've been anywhere between eighteen and twenty-eight.

"Olivier Kant. A thief and professional miscreant, if ever there was one. He could steal the sight from your eyes, the breath from your lungs, and the words from your mouth—and you'd be none the wiser. If anything goes missing from your ship, I would simply consider it a fee, as you'll never get it back."

Olivier spun a Gold Vidick through his fingers, rolling it from one to the next in a practiced rhythm. With a quick flick of his hand, it vanished, gone as if into thin air. He looked up and winked at them.

Matthias mimed a silent applause, and the boy, still seated, offered an exaggerated, theatrical bow.

"Desperate for attention, aren't you," Loraine said.

"Not all of us are born with eyes trailing after us," Olivier said. "The rest of us have to earn it."

Loraine scoffed. "You've not earned a single thing in your life."

"Such is the burden of thieves," Olivier said, feigning hurt.

Brazier nodded in their general direction.

"This is all of you?" he asked Vandemir. When Aymeri had said a unit would escort them, he'd been expecting at least double the number sitting in his fuselage.

"The rest are dead," Vandemir said. "Which is a stroke of luck, for I am told it's likely only a handful will be permitted across the unholy barrier into the realm of chaos."

Brazier was also thinking about the trip through Yeggardania, but decided not to say anything. Seven more swords were still better than just the four members of the *Anchorite*.

"Well, we're glad to have you," he said. "It's two hours to Calaxis. Your people are welcome in any communal areas of the ship, but I'd avoid the engines. My enginator doesn't take too kindly to distraction."

Vandemir leaned in, flashing a grin of yellowing teeth, some already succumbing to rot. In a world where even basic magic could fix something as simple as poor dental hygiene, Brazier wondered just how bad the man's diet had to be to get teeth like that. Then he caught the sweet tang of rum on Vandemir's breath, and it made sense.

The Captain lowered his voice. "Best if they stay here," he murmured. "Wherever this lot goes, carnage tends to follow. And I'd hate to see a fine ship like this so sullied."

"Just the fuselage, then," Brazier said.

"Sensible choice," Vandemir said. "Now, you'll be needing these."

He unstrapped a small leather bag from his belt and loosened the strings. Digging inside, he produced a tangle of wooden crosses and leather thongs. There were four of them.

"Never been much of a believer myself," Vandemir said. "But I'm told they work wonders against demons and others of their ilk."

Brazier pulled one of the crosses free from the tangle, holding it up in front of his face. He'd never been much of a believer, either in the human saviour-god of the Fromryr, nor in any of the Dwen'hiema religions built around the abyss.

He turned the plain wooden piece between his fingers and, unexpectedly, found himself missing Lyander. There was no doubt the Rex Populaire looked every bit as capable as their eccentric captain claimed. But Brazier would have traded all of them for the sullen exorcist in a heartbeat.

There had been something solid and implacable about Lyander, and it hadn't just been his size or the reach of his sword arm. It was about who he was, and who he'd chosen to become, despite what had happened to him.

"We should discuss the plan, such as it is," Vandemir said, watching Brazier.

"Nav deck," Brazier said, pulling the leather thong over his head. He took the other crosses and handed one to Matthias. "This way."

"After you," Vandemir said, gesturing dramatically at the stairwell, before spinning round to his crew.

"Remain in the fuselage, and only the fuselage," he said. "Try not to kill each other while I'm gone."

Twenty-Three Kathryn

One of the Vanguard's nav deck doors wouldn't close properly. It kept sliding toward the wall, jamming against something unseen, making a feeble attempt to seal before giving up and opening again.

In its defence, it was doing better than its counterpart. The other lay discarded in the corridor, a slab of bronzite, blackened with char, one jagged edge smudged with soot. Translucent shards of gyre ice were scattered around it, catching the dim light and shimmering faintly against the wreckage.

Kathryn followed the path of destruction upward.

The channels that should have fed power through the nav deck ceiling were not just empty, they were gone. Somewhere deeper in the hallway, a dripping noise echoed. A steady, rhythmic trickle against metal.

Drip. Drip. Drip.

She hoped the water system hadn't taken too much damage. She'd been offered a fresh Angelaux doublet and her wounds had been treated in the *Pheradies'* vulnerum. But she still needed to wash.

She stepped over the debris and through the nav deck doorway, scanning the damage. The walls were a mess of twisted metal, bronzite panels torn open, exposing a darker layer beneath, embedded with tangled pipe channels. Dark stains, thick and congealed like old soup, streaked across one side of the command terminal, pooling into the decking. A lot of people had died because she'd sent that epistolar message. A lot of people had died getting her and Brazier's crew off Thela.

The old Kathryn, Captain Kathryn Stryker of the Gyre Star *Athelus*, would have catalogued that. She would have filed it into a mental compartment and closed the door, to be viewed only through the clinical lens of rationality.

The current Kathryn struggled to do that.

Her chest tightened, guilt rising like a dark wave. It was an emotion captains couldn't afford: a luxury. Any thought or information that wasn't useful at the time was to be suppressed for the sake of the mission.

I always knew you'd be too weak!

Her mother's voice made her wince. She ground her teeth, breathing deeply to steady her heart. But the shadow didn't linger like it used to. She could focus on the mission instead, and the outcome: the anticipation of capturing Isdria Laanorath, of righting the wrong that had been done to her, of having the opportunity to command a ship again, no matter how risky that might be.

She surveyed the rest of the nav deck, *her* nav deck.

Of the five support terminals surrounding the command terminal, only three remained intact. One had been reduced to a charred bronzite stump. Another was scorched, its hex node burned out, and was now just oily black sludge. The channels running through walls and floor glowed faintly blue. Some had turned completely translucent, hollowed out by the damage.

The crew looked worse than the ship.

There were just three of them and a navigator, all human, all looking like they'd been dragged through the abyss and back. And from their rank insignia, not all of them were even officers.

One woman, mid-twenties, wearing an Angclaux officer's green doublet, her brown hair scraped into a bun, sweat-sheened and frantic, clutched the edge of her terminal like it was the only thing keeping her upright. She was relaying a damage report to the repair crews, but Kathryn recognised the signs. She was still bracing as if in battle, expecting the next impact, the next jolt.

A man in a white gambeson with forest-green trim stood behind another terminal, dark hair matted with sweat, a short curling beard slick with grime. He was a sergeant, judging by his shoulder emblem. His hand rested in the hex, eyes fluttering as he relayed personnel locations throughout the ship. A deep gash split his left brow, blood smeared across his temple despite repeated attempts to clear his vision.

The last man, leaning over his terminal, wore an Angelaux officer's doublet. His dark olive skin and bookish features made him look more like an academic than a naval officer. His head and right wrist were bandaged, and his shin splinted, the bindings tight but uneven. Either he'd refused the vulnerum, or the ship's Anomancer hadn't had time to heal him fully. Right now, he was speaking into the hex, his voice steady despite the situation, assessing the damage to the engines. From what she could hear, they were about the only part of the ship still operational.

The navigator knelt in the pit. Facing the wall, he had short blond hair and wore a black shirt and loose trousers. Both arms were held out at his sides, fingers splayed. The hex beneath them formed two whirlpools.

The ship was a beaten-up mess. The people flying it were a beaten-up mess. But she didn't care. At this point, she'd have commanded a rusted bucket and thanked whoever gave it to her. At the back of her mind, her mother seethed with contempt for her lack of pride. Kathryn ignored it as she stepped onto the deck.

She stood for a second, hands clasped behind her back, trying to settle into command. It was easier than she thought it would be.

"It's customary to acknowledge the commanding officer when on deck," she said.

The sergeant froze mid-report, pulling his hand from the terminal.

"Or has that changed since I was last in the navy?"

The bookish officer turned toward her.

"Captain Stryker?" he asked.

"The very same."

The navigator remained in his trance, flying the ship. But the others stared. The only sound was the background chatter filtering from the hex terminals. Then came a visible shift, as if they'd all woken up. The lieutenant straightened, drew a sharp breath, and bellowed: "Captain on deck!"

Everyone snapped to attention, saluting as one.

"At ease," Kathryn said. "Names."

"Lieutenant Gideon Du'Voire, Officer of the Watch." The bookish one.

"Sergeant Karland Agathor, First Repel Team." The man in the gambeson.

"Second Lieutenant Elvie Pontifore, Gunnery." The woman gripping the terminal.

She'd been told en route that the officers had no idea she was among those they'd rescued. All they knew was that their mission had been to extract a vital asset from the traitor Varkoneth Rosantz. In carrying out that mission, a significant number of the *Vanguard of Winter's* crew, including many of their fellow officers, had died.

Sourant had suggested she keep the truth to herself, at least for now, to prevent resentment from the start. Kathryn had grunted her agreement at the time, but thought lying to her crew from the outset a poor way to begin command. And now, standing before them, she decided she wouldn't.

You do not owe them honesty or compassion! Her mother's voice raked at her consciousness with such unexpected force she felt faint. *You owe them your resolve, your guile, your relentlessness. You do not owe them your friendship!*

Kathryn only realised her hand was brushing her temple when she felt a day's worth of sweat come away on her fingers. The others exchanged quick, uncertain glances.

Kathryn swallowed. *So much for getting that under control.*

"I want to take this opportunity to thank you," she said, straightening. "Without you, my friends and I would never have made it off Thela. I owe you my life."

Gideon blinked. "We weren't aware—"

"I know," Kathryn said. "I'll bring you up to speed soon. But first, bring me up to speed. How bad is it?"

"We've got thirty percent casualties," Gideon said, voice tired but clipped. "Structural damage runs throughout the ship, concentrated in the bow and along the inner bulkheads."

As he spoke, Kathryn mapped the damage in her mind.

"Multiple hex systems are down," he continued. "Parts of the ship are completely cut off, including secondary crew quarters, main engineering, and secondary engineering. We're using runners until we can get the system back online."

"Hull repeaters?"

Elvie answered. "A quarter destroyed. Another quarter inoperable."

"Most of the damage is gyranic," Gideon added grimly.

Kathryn exhaled through her nose. That meant melted or blasted apart, and impossible to repair without docking at an installation.

"The good news," Gideon said, "is that most of the damage hit the bow."

"And the engines?"

"Fully operational. Output holding at over ninety percent."

Kathryn nodded. That was good. It meant they were still in the pursuit, that they *could* still pursue.

"War casters?"

"One remaining," Karland said, his voice deep and resonant, like it came from his chest. "In the vulnerum."

That was less good. A ship this size needed at least two war casters, one to protect the ship, the other to perform anomancy on the crew. She suspected she would have to choose between the two, a decision she wasn't looking forward to.

She stepped up to the command terminal, scanning the sculpt displayed across the surface. Three ships flew down the primary tunnel in tight formation, another three positioned further ahead. At the front, two ships ran side by side, the third trailing slightly behind.

And beyond them all, pulling ahead, was a single ship.

Kathryn's stomach tightened. She recognised the *Gloried Storm*, even on the hex. Behind it, the entire rebel fleet moved as one, driving hard toward their target, *her* target.

From the vast spear-shaped expanse to the south, Kathryn assumed they were just north of Maw Veraxies.

"Current mission status?" she asked.

"All ships still in pursuit," Gideon said. "Gloried Storm is pulling ahead. Only the Tempest, the Crucible, and ourselves can keep up."

He came limping down to the command terminal, standing less than a foot from her.

"But, sir—" he said, a desperate whine undercutting his voice. "We need to pull back to the main fleet. We can't make these repairs ourselves. If we take any more hull damage, we'll crack like an egg."

There was a quiet pleading in his eyes that, to Kathryn's shame, annoyed her. The man had been through the abyss, had probably lost friends to save her. He didn't deserve her contempt.

"That is not our mission," she said, her voice soft but firm.

"One more hit—" Gideon started.

"This is an ongoing operation," Kathryn cut in, firmer now. "If we pull back for repairs, we slow the fleet. We don't have that luxury."

She pointed at the hex display, jabbing a finger toward it.

"We are rebels in the eyes of the Ecclessius. The only real proof that House Rosantz are traitors is aboard the Gloried Storm. If we don't capture it, we lose everything."

She took a breath, forcing her voice level again.

"We'll remain within the defensive perimeter of the Tempest and Crucible."

Gideon's face shifted from disbelief, to frustration, then reluctant acceptance.

Kathryn recognised his type: the good soldier, the one who cared about doing the right thing. But he could also be dangerous, because he trusted his emotions too much. He was the sort who made a good ally and a terrible enemy.

Her mother would have relieved him of duty on the spot. But she wasn't her mother. Which meant if she wasn't going to do what her mother would have done, she needed to bring him onto her side. That meant she needed to gamble.

"I need a first officer," she said. "You're it."

Gideon blanked, mouth slightly open.

"Congratulations, Mr. Du'Voire," she said, extending a hand. He took it slowly.

"When I have time, I'll find you the proper insignia."

"Thank you, Captain," he said, still sounding as if he didn't quite believe it.

Kathryn pressed her palm into the hex well, giving the command out loud: "Gideon Du'Voire is hereby promoted to First Officer of the Vanguard of Winter."

The system registered the change, flashing through her mind's eye. It flagged requests, additional security accesses, new chambers, pay increase, scheduled meetings between Captain and First Officer. She could deal with them later.

Somewhere in the background, she heard clapping. She pulled her hand free, looking up. It came from Karland and Elvie, and between just the two of them, it sounded diminished. But at least it seemed to have snapped Elvie out of her post-battle haze. Kathryn let the moment stretch, then moved on.

"Our mission is to capture the Gloried Storm, take Isdria Laanorath, and destroy the weapon he and Varkoneth Rosantz are using against Formaria."

She turned to Gideon.

"To do that, we need this ship operational. Find me two more officers capable of running a nav deck. If you can't find officers, take sailors. Once that's done, get enginator teams on minimal repairs to the inner bulkheads."

"Yes, sir," Gideon said.

Kathryn turned to Elvie.

"Ms. Pontifore, reroute all hull repair teams to internal maintenance. We'll make do with the repeaters we have. Structural integrity is priority."

"Yes, sir."

She turned to Karland.

"Sergeant, you're now a deck officer. Coordinate triage across the ship, then reallocate personnel into battlegroups. I want teams organised for boarding actions."

Karland gave her a hesitant look, but nodded.

"Yes, sir."

Gideon glanced up from the terminal.

"Sir—"

Kathryn felt her jaw clench at the tone of his voice. The muscle memory of her time as a commander told her Gideon was about to question something.

"I thought we agreed the Vanguard couldn't engage directly—"

We agreed.

The phrase lit a flicker of anger in her chest. Maybe he was going to be a problem after all.

She turned to him slowly, trying to shut out the intrusive voice clawing up from the depths of her mind. The words *weak* and *pathetic* broke through her consciousness in her mother's voice. Kathryn ground her teeth again.

"We can't win a shooting match with the Storm," she said. Her tone was measured.

"If we engage, and we will, we'll have to get inside their firing arcs and board under covering fire from the Tempest and Crucible."

Gideon's brow furrowed, frustration creeping into his expression. He opened his mouth—

"This is the mission," Kathryn said sharply, cutting him off. "You will follow these orders, First Officer—"

But she never finished the sentence.

A boom tore through the ship. The deck shuddered violently and Kathryn lurched forward.

She had no time to brace. Her knees buckled, and with her hands clasped behind her back, she couldn't catch herself. Her head cracked against the terminal's edge. A white-hot blossom of pain erupted in her temple. The world spun.

Blue columns of fire flared up around her, blurred and shifting through the haze overlaying her vision. Kathryn tried to move, to push herself up, but her arms wouldn't respond. Something heavy pinned her wrists at her sides. But not the floor.

Iron clamps.

And then a face appeared: pallid grey, with sunken eyes, hollow cheeks, and a split black ravine running down the middle of a white skull.

No.

Some part of her mind said the word. But she registered it weakly, like a half-formed thought in a dream. *Not now.*

Then fear took over, cold and suffocating. She tried to shrink away, but the iron chair held her in place. The Mirrovinjin leaned closer, then shifted, pulling away. Someone else took its place.

Isdria Laanorath.

Kathryn froze in a moment of pure, paralysing terror. Then rage burned through her like wildfire, rage at the fear he'd caused her, rage at what he'd done to her mind. She snarled, lunging, trying to tear free. She screamed. She didn't even know what she was shouting.

Isdria barely acknowledged her. His blurred silhouette turned away, looking past her.

At first, she thought it was the Mirrovinjin again, but the pale, sunken face was someone else. It was another elf, she realised. They were talking. She couldn't hear the words but she understood: something had gone wrong. It was taking too long. It wasn't working.

Then she heard shouting. A crossbow bolt sliced through the air.

Another bolt followed, then more.

And Isdria and the other elf were gone. The blue flames guttered out. She heard voices, dwarven and human voices. A man stepped into her blurred vision, short hair, deep voice, and wearing the unmistakable blue military doublet. They were getting her out. They were saving her.

No.

"No!" Kathryn cried out, her voice ragged. They couldn't, not now.

"Get Isdria! Get Isdria!"

Her heart pounded with frustration. She was so close. They could end this. The Navarch would know she wasn't insane. They'd know the ships were real. She wouldn't lose her captaincy.

"Get Isdria!"

But the man was gone. A woman loomed over her now, hair pulled into a severe bun. She had a sharp jawline, and beneath it, an admiral's doublet. Kathryn's chest seized with dread.

You were never good enough!

Her mother's words slammed into her like a physical blow. And for the first time, her hallucination collapsed into something worse. Somewhere far away, her mind registered that the two unstable parts of her psyche had merged, and that it meant she was in a bad way.

You were never good enough to be one of mine!

The pain of those words resulted in a deep sense of failure, a weight on her chest. She tried to squirm away from her mother's face, from her judgment, and realised her back was against something hard, but smoother than the iron chair.

There were crystal blue, almost white lights coming from somewhere around her. The woman standing over her was no longer her mother. Her hair was brown instead of blonde, and the curves of her face were softer. There was concern in those features.

She wasn't on the nav deck. She was somewhere else. Which meant she wasn't in command.

The realisation hit her like cold water. A jolt of alarm flooded her system. She'd failed again. Just when she'd been given the one thing she wanted, when she'd been so close to capturing Isdria, she had lost it all.

She tried to rise, to push herself up, but her arms wouldn't move. They wouldn't obey. Her body didn't feel like it belonged to her anymore.

She heard a voice, somewhere above her, soft and concerned.

"Not yet."

A hand pressed against her shoulder, holding her down.

No, no, no.

She fought against it, but they were too strong and she was too weak. She collapsed back with a dull thud. The darkness crept in at the edges of her vision, curling inward, closing over her like a shroud.

Her last thought, as her consciousness slipped into the ether, was of her mother's voice and her own failure. In the dreamlike haze of her fractured mind, they blurred into one.

Twenty-Four
Brazier

On the hex display, the *Anchorite* crept toward Spire Calaxis, just as the doubt crept up from the pit of Brazier's stomach. The closer the ship drew to the Spire, the closer the doubt reached for his heart, like a steel hand tightening its grip. He glanced up at Switch, and Freyen standing next to her, both of them armed and armoured. Was he rolling the dice with his crew's loyalty? With their lives?

They had accepted this mission because they believed in him, believed he was the one who could hold their crew, their family, together. That trust came with a weight he hadn't fully grasped until now, an entirely new layer of responsibility atop the burden of command. Yet, for all its gravity, it couldn't quite smother the undeniable thrill of being part of something bigger, of being needed.

The gnawing awareness that any choice he made could lead to disaster, could lead to death, was simply part of command. Torquen and his father had told him as much more than once. And while he'd been Captain since the moment his brother had died, the decisions he'd made before had always been out of necessity.

They'd been split-second calls to keep his crew alive, or choices where no good option existed—like running protection for illicit mining operations because it was the least bad choice at the time, or agreeing to spy on secret magical rituals because agreeing meant their freedom, disagreeing meant their imprisonment.

But this, crossing into the Immuratum, was different. It wasn't survival. It wasn't necessity. It was a choice, and a deliberate one. He could feel that difference pressing down on him, like a mantle he couldn't shrug off.

So he latched onto the thrill instead: the idea that they could save Formaria, that they were fighting back against the ever-encroaching darkness, because the alternative was standing by while someone else did it for him. And, Brazier realised, he was becoming sick of others doing it for him.

"Signature received, Dauntless Pretender," Amelia's high-pitched, girlish voice crackled over the hex. The gnome was one of Karenna's, one of many she had slipped into positions around the spire. Officially, Amelia worked in dock command. Unofficially, she answered to Karenna.

It wasn't the only thing she had a hand in. Brazier had no idea how she'd pulled it off, but the spire's hex network recognised the *Anchorite* as the *Dauntless Pretender*, a name he suspected Karenna had chosen as a joke.

"Docking schedule's a mess, we're packed to the brim. I'm slotting you straight into the maintenance bay. Looks like you could use it."

Brazier exchanged a look with Switch and Freyen. 'We're packed to the brim' was code for security is tighter than usual. Given the civil war underway less than two leagues from the spire, he shouldn't have been surprised. Calaxis was probably on high alert for any unscheduled arrivals like them. But by dropping them straight into maintenance they could bypass the dock inspectors. Or that was the idea. They'd never actually had to do it before.

"We appreciate that, dock command," Brazier said.

"Maintenance crews are all tied up, so you'll have to wait your turn," Amelia said. Meaning, stay in the ship until someone comes and gets you.

"Sit tight while I find you a slot."

"Understood," Brazier said, and the connection dropped.

"How accommodating of her," Vandemir said. Towering over the crew like an emaciated giant, he looked out of place even among the *Anchorite's* eclectic members. "Although, if you were to ask me, none of what she said is what it truly means."

"Oh really, what gave it away?" Switch asked.

"It was the name of the ship," Vandemir said, deadly serious. "That was my first clue."

"Inspectors will be crawling the docks," Brazier said. "So we're going straight into maintenance, where we'll wait for someone to meet us."

The *Anchorite* glided into the Spire's cavern complex, drifting down toward the east-facing docks. Half the Spire was embedded in the cavern's western wall, its docks and landings jutting outward like shards of unearthed quartz. On the hex display, the structure's western face was hidden by dense rock, but Brazier knew what lay beyond, tunnels stretching into the depths, most of which led to Maw Grindle.

Matthias set them down on a large landing pad, the thrusters fading to a low, imperceptible vibration. Then a heavy shunt as the platform sank into the floor. The *Anchorite* descended with it, slipping beneath the docks into the maintenance bay below.

"Powering down," Matthias said. "We're on auxiliaries."

The hex display flattened, the nav deck lights dimmed, and the thrusters' vibrating hum faded into silence. They were in. This was happening. They were heading to Yeggardania and crossing into the Immuratum. Brazier had the sudden urge to move with purpose, to not think, but to act.

"Let's go," he said, picking up the repeater crossbow he'd leaned against the command terminal and throwing the strap over his shoulder.

In the fuselage, Vandemir's unit stood ready. The lanky captain pushed past them, making his way to the armoury, where he grabbed his Gorefelder, resting the unsharpened length of the blade on his shoulder.

Brazier stood by the terminal, eyes fixed on the black and silver filaments, his thumb absently tracing the foregrip of his crossbow. After a minute of silence, the hex pulsed, then trembled.

"Open her up," came an aged female voice, surprising Brazier—Karenna had come herself.

He sunk his hand into the node and opened the fuselage ramp. They marched off, his crew first, followed by the Rex Populaire.

The maintenance bay was an octagonal pit, each facing quartered by glowing gyre channels. A bronzite frame, along with racks and hoists, circled the pit, surrounded by piles of thruster discs, arm extensions, and random parts, gear wheels, pistons, pipe-like channel systems, and what looked like half an engine core, its segments broken open like an egg. The air was warm, sharp with the sweetness of burnt gyre ice, mingled with cleaning oils and old sweat.

Karenna stood next to one of the bay's terminals. Short even for a gnome, the node and its silver filaments almost reached her chin. The bat-like ears of her race poked out either side of long grey-streaked hair, framing a broad, weathered face that crinkled like a dried rag when she smiled. Now, as always, she wore brown coveralls over a white buttoned shirt, the fabric lined with pockets overflowing with quills, measuring instruments, and scraps of parchment. She looked like someone's grandmother, and Brazier had to remind himself, and not for the first time, not to be fooled by her appearance.

Thanks to the swirling currents of magical energy spilling into the open wound that was Maw Grindle, rogue casters and free traders could find new and powerful substances to bottle and sell, if they were willing to risk the goblin rider swarms, fledger ghouls, phractii, and whatever else dropped out of Yeggardania. According to Matthias, Karenna, the aged-looking grandmother, was almost solely responsible for moving those substances throughout Formaria.

"You four really know how to choose your timing," she said, her voice a wet croak. She pulled Matthias into a rough embrace, thumping his bicep affectionately before moving to Freyen, cupping her cheeks like a mother fussing over a child.

"The Praefector's got his britches in a twist over the reports from the north. He's sending orders up and down the spire, each one contradicting the last."

She shook her head and hugged Brazier next, then Switch. He breathed in the faintly alchemic smell of base spirits and something a lot like home-cooked stew.

"Which suits me fine, of course. That puffed-up idiot doesn't know one end of command from the other."

She gave Switch's real arm a firm squeeze before turning to the Rex Populaire, eyeing them with clear disapproval.

"Still," Karenna continued. "He's got just enough sense rattling around in that skull to sniff you lot out. You couldn't be more obvious if you tried."

Vandemir raised an eyebrow. "Begging your pardon, but more obvious about what, exactly?"

Karenna snorted. "Who you belong to."

She jerked her chin toward their armour. "Reports coming in say ships belonging to House La'Voline attacked Thela, and you lot are wearing La'Voline colours."

Vandemir glanced down at his chest, as if only just noticing the green-and-red quartered leather.

"Yes, those colours," Karenna said. "Come on. We do this quickly, or we don't do it at all."

They followed her over to one of the lift chutes, where she placed her hand into its terminal.

"Jaynus," she said, eyes closed. "I need a straight run to the surface. No stops. Yes, eastern docks, maintenance bay three, level four."

The lift doors parted and Karenna pulled her hand from the node.

"Get in."

They piled onto the platform. With barely enough space for all of them, Brazier was forced to hug his repeater to his chest. The lift doors closed, the platform shunted into action, and began rising through the spire.

"Anchorite has seen better days," Karenna said, glancing at Brazier.

From the corner of his eye, he saw Switch scowl.

"Tell me about it," she said.

“We were in a rush,” Brazier said.

“We’ll have her fixed up by the time you’re back,” Karenna said. “I suppose I don’t want to know where you’ll be back from?”

“You don’t,” Brazier and Freyen said at the same time.

Karenna humphed disapprovingly.

“You’re going with Folgar, at least. He’ll look after you. But no matter what he says, do not drink his Banshee Black. The Hexenbrew Bitter and the Honeywood Pale are fine. But the Banshee? That’ll have you behind a tree and dropping your britches before you can say the squirts.”

Brazier frowned. When Korst had told them they’d be meeting a dwarf named Folgar, she hadn’t mentioned anything about ale.

Karenna must have caught his expression.

“Folgar has many talents,” she said. “Brewing is sometimes one of them.”

“And where, might I ask, does this resourceful individual conduct his brewing?” Vandemir said.

“The surface,” Karenna said.

“And he doesn’t consider that a little risky?” Vandemir said. “What with it being in a poisoned forest?”

“And all the poisoned creatures,” Loraine said.

“Poisoned air in some parts,” Olivier added.

“I heard the rivers are poisoned as well,” Godenforte said.

“I think our host gets the point,” Vandemir said.

“Folgar has a knack for survival,” Karenna said. “It’s one of his talents.”

The lift slowed, and the walls around them began to brighten. Brazier craned his neck, staring up at the octagonal dot of yellow light far above, no larger than his thumbnail. It expanded as they ascended, until the walls shifted from dark iolite to lavender spinel, then to a softer blend of purple and grey as light flooded the chute.

The lift slowed again, and they all lifted their hands to shield their eyes as the brightness washed over them.

They had arrived on a large, square platform, roofed but open to the elements. It led onto even larger balconies bordered by chest-high walls.

Beyond them, the forest stretched out into a vast expanse of thick, spiralling brown trees, their canopy a shifting mosaic of greens. The air was heavy with the scent of rich, loamy earth, the sharp tang of bark, and the crispness of the open sky.

As his eyes adjusted, Brazier couldn't decide what unsettled him more, the overwhelming flood of colour, or the raw, unfiltered smell of it all.

"Well, brothers, would you look at who has chosen to grace us with her presence, it's the Queen of Calaxis herself," said a dwarf in a maroon gambeson, with a Harothellian accent similar to Vandemir's but lighter and more sing-song. He sported a long black beard, a shaven head, and walked toward them with his arms outstretched in a welcoming gesture.

"Don't you forget it, Folgar," Karenna said, stepping off the platform.

"Oh, I never shall," the dwarf, apparently Folgar, said, taking Karenna's hand. He half-bowed and planted a kiss on her fingers. Turning to the rest of them, he hooked his thumbs in his belt and sniffed.

"And what have we here," he said. "These must be the mad bastards who volunteered to cross into the Immuratum. Now I have to say, I was sceptical when I received the message, but some of you look like you belong there."

"As some of the vilest, most despicable killers in all Formaria," Vandemir said, stepping off the platform. "We'll be taking that as a compliment."

"Certainly, certainly," the dwarf said. "Now, which one of you is Brazier Veranquis?"

"That would be me," Brazier said.

"Folgar Fortinbrow of Helmharothell," the dwarf said, holding his hand out for Brazier to shake. "Captain of the Rendarian Fifth, Surface Liaison Officer to the Admiralty, and most importantly, brewer of the finest ales above and below the surface."

He turned to the rest of them. "And if there were more time, I'd be sharing many a vintage with you fine people," he said. "But we leave right now, while the sun is up and Yeggardania is at her least deadly."

Folgar wagged a finger at them, eyeing them all with creased brows. "But make no mistake, *least deadly* is a relative term, as everything in this forsaken place desperately, desperately wants to kill you."

Brazier stopped himself from pointing out that was a fact they all already knew.

"Come on," Folgar said, waving an arm toward the steps down the spire. "We'll do names and introductions on the way." He turned to Karenna. "Until our next meeting, Your Highness."

The gnome rolled her eyes. "Immuratum, huh," she said, raising an eyebrow, her mouth bunching into a disapproving line. "I swear, I can't tell if trouble follows you four around or you go looking for it."

"Usually it comes to us," Switch said. "But occasionally we can't help ourselves."

"Well, you watch yourselves out there," she said, nodding to the dwarf behind the terminal.

The platform hummed to life and began sinking back into the spire. Karenna waved once, then disappeared from view.

Folgar led them down a short flight of steps onto one of the balconies. The rest of his unit were already there, scattered across the open space, either leaning against the walls or sitting around talking. Like Folgar, they wore maroon gambesons beneath steel half-plate. Some carried spears, but most carried long-range repeating crossbows. None of them seemed particularly concerned about the forest that "desperately" wanted to kill them, which stretched out around the Spire's walls. Brazier wondered how long he'd have to spend above ground before the people-eating forest no longer unsettled him. *Too long*, he decided.

"Lorfimir, Dregan, Nondrick—you're bringing up the rear," Folgar shouted. Three dwarves all barked "ye'sir!" in response, gathered their weapons, and fell in behind the Rex Populaire.

“Open her up,” Folgar called to a dwarf stationed by a terminal.

Another member of his unit handed him a large hand-axe, which Folgar rested on his shoulder as they followed him down a longer flight of steps. They led to a courtyard surrounding the Spire, ending at a gatehouse.

Its thick, pale grey double doors were inlaid with geometric patterns, their surface shimmering like polished stone beneath the midday sun. With a deep mechanical hum, they parted, sliding into the gatehouse walls. Beyond them, a muddied track stretched outward, winding into a dense forest swallowed in murkiness.

“Two rules if you want to live,” Folgar said. “First rule is, do what I say. Second rule is, follow rule one. Is that understood?”

“I think we’re clear on that,” Brazier said, tucking his repeater stock into his shoulder.

They followed Folgar into the forest. With the sun swallowed by the dense canopy, Yeggardania was steeped in a perpetual green gloom, a shifting blend of light and shadow. The air was thick, saturated with damp, musky richness, the scent of fungus mingling with the sweeter rot of decaying wood.

Brazier had made more than a few surface missions as a miner, but every time, the smell reminded him of one thing. He definitely didn’t like it.

Beside him, Switch sniffed and scowled, her expression dark with a deep dislike she seemed to be trying to convey to the forest around her.

“It’s not that bad,” Freyen said.

“It’s bad enough,” Switch grumbled.

Brazier caught the looks on the faces of the Rex Populaire, most of them seemed to share Switch’s sentiment. Loraine had already nocked an arrow, her bow half-drawn. Vandemir had unsheathed his massive sword, resting the flat of the blade against his shoulder, while Solon, the brooding Celmyrian, had drawn a pair of short swords so polished they glinted even in the forest’s half-light.

As they moved deeper into the forest, they ran through introductions, first the Rex Populaire, then Brazier's crew. Folgar nodded at each name, offering little more than a grunt in acknowledgment.

The path twisted ahead, winding through shifting pockets of warmth and cool. Now and then, something rustled in the underbrush, a fleeting disturbance in the dense foliage. Brazier's eyes darted from tree to tree, but no matter how fast he looked, he saw nothing.

The third time it happened, Folgar halted so abruptly Brazier nearly walked into him. The dwarf raised a hand, signalling them to stop. Brazier froze, eyes scanning the forest, blood pumping between his ears. Seconds passed, but whatever had caught Folgar's attention remained unseen, until two moths the size of shields flitted out from behind a tree and across the path ahead of them.

They drifted through the air, their bodies ice-white, their wings glowing with shades of blue gyre light and curling silver patterns. They fluttered in a wandering, dreamlike zigzag, trailing silver dust that shimmered in their wake. Looking directly through it, Brazier's heart almost stopped.

For a moment, he thought he saw a figure up ahead on the path, a soldier, standing far off in the gloom. He carried a spear and was clad entirely in bronzite armour, down to an ancient-looking scale skirt. Then, without warning, the soldier turned and bolted, sprinting down the path as if something were chasing him. Brazier blinked hard, rubbing his eyes. When he looked again, the path was empty.

"Kikkora," Folgar said, his voice a rumbling whisper. "Strange creatures. Wings produce a gyranic chemical to attract mates. Makes the rest of us see into the past. No real trouble unless you're caught beneath them."

"What happens then?" Switch asked.

"Insanity," Folgar said.

"You see a man who looked like a lizard?" Brazier heard Olivier ask behind him. "Standing upright, like a man, but had lizard's feet and a lizard's head, with rows of teeth."

"I was busy watching the forest," Loraine said. "While the rest of you gawked at the pretty butterflies."

"Cut the chatter and keep your eyes peeled," Vandemir said, his voice devoid of its usual melodrama. Brazier took some comfort in knowing he wasn't the only one on edge.

The moths drifted off the track and vanished into the forest. Despite their size, the trees swallowed them instantly.

"On we go," Folgar said.

Five minutes later, as they reached a fork in the path, Brazier's heart had finally returned to its normal rhythm.

Folgar veered right, and the path twisted into an S-curve before opening onto a muddy clearing, where a single massive tree stood at its centre. Tarps had been roped to its thick trunk, stretched taut between wooden poles planted around the clearing.

Beneath the makeshift canopy, heavy iron cauldrons sat in neat rows over stone fire pits. Wooden barrels stood beside a large mash tun, alongside what looked like a copper trench and a small mill. Wooden tables overflowed with glass bottles and jugs, their contents ranging from pale amber to pitch black. Brazier could just make out a stream running along the far end of the clearing, babbling quietly.

"Welcome to the Fortinbrow brewery," Folgar said, turning to face them as he walked backward, an arm spread wide in invitation.

A wave of scents drifted toward them, a combination of yeast and ripe fruit, along with hints of roasted chestnuts and honey. In spite of the location, Brazier found himself regretting the lack of time. A Honeywood Pale suddenly sounded damn inviting.

Folgar rested his axe against the nearest table, stooped, and picked up one of the barrels as if it were filled with feathers.

"Right," Folgar said, carrying the barrel to Solon. "You look like you can manage this."

The Celmyrian squinted at Folgar through his messy curtain of hair, then, slowly, sheathed his swords.

"Atta boy," Folgar said, pushing the barrel into Solon's stomach. The Celmyrian grabbed it by either side, grunted as he took the weight, then shifted it onto his shoulder.

"You do too," Folgar said, picking up another barrel and handing it to Godenforte. The man took it and tucked it under his arm.

"And you," Folgar said, pointing at Bertrand. He handed the man a barrel, and like Solon, he shifted it onto his shoulder, carrying his hammer in the other hand.

"Not that we'd have any complaints, but I thought you said we wouldn't be drinking any of the ale?" Vandemir said.

"We're not," Folgar replied. "This is what you might call tax."

"And who might we be paying this tax to?" Vandemir said.

"A delightful new resident of the Yeggardanian forest known as the Handmaid," Folgar said.

"The entity who controls the breach?" Switch asked. "The one we're meeting?"

"The Handmaid doesn't just control the breach," Folgar said. "She holds sway over this part of the forest. It's thanks to her I'm able to brew in peace, and Calaxis is, shall we say, *less affected* by the other residents of Yeggardania."

"You pay some forest spirit in ale and she tells all the big bad monsters not to eat you?" Switch asked.

"Right you are," Folgar said, picking up his axe and setting off back the way they had come.

They set off after him, and where the path forked, they took a left.

"Oh, and if I were you," Folgar said over his shoulder, "I wouldn't be calling her a forest spirit. She won't be taking too kindly to that."

"Noted," Switch said.

"What is she then?" Freyen asked.

"I'm no expert," Folgar said. "But as far as I can tell, she's of the Aeturnum."

A sudden chill washed over Brazier, like stepping past a river's edge or walking too close to a waterfall's spray. Both Switch and Freyen glanced at him, their own unease mirroring his.

"What makes you think she's a being of the Aeturnum?" Brazier asked.

"Darkness," Folgar said. "Clings to her like a shadow just before sundown."

Brazier walked in silence, his mind suddenly working at double speed. Aeturnic creatures were well outside his wheelhouse, but he'd wager one of them wouldn't be too eager to let them cross into the Immuratum to find a book that would help destroy *another* Aeturnic being.

"How did you come across this entity?" Brazier asked.

"She found me," Folgar said, eyes fixed on the forest ahead. His tone was calm, but Brazier noticed that, like him, he never stopped scanning the trees. "Or more precisely, her toad found me."

Brazier nearly stumbled. Assuming he'd misheard, he said, "Her toad?"

"Leopine," Folgar said. "Likes the ale. Well, actually, it's really the only thing he likes to drink in this forest. I can't say I blame him."

"And what does she want?" Brazier asked. "Other than ale for her toad."

"Who can tell the minds of Aeturnic beings," Folgar said. "They're as foreign to us as fish are to the mountains. But I know this, however she came into this world, she came recently. And like all beings of darkness, she does not like those of chaos."

"And so I suppose," Vandemir said from just behind them, "she plays gatekeeper to the Immuratum so she can exact a toll from all the mischievous demons who try to cross? Just to get one over on them—is that it?"

"Well damn," Olivier said. "Even demons have to pay tax."

"It's a toll," Bertrand said, shifting the keg onto his other shoulder. "Not a tax."

"Trust a thief not to know the difference," Loraine said.

"She neither taxes nor tolls them," Folgar said. "Far as I know, she captures and imprisons them. What she does with them then, I cannot say."

"And your arrangement with her," Brazier said. "It means she'll let us cross?"

"Well, she won't kill you outright," Folgar said. "Whether she lets you cross or not is another question. But that's why we've brought the ale." He winked at Brazier. "Sweeten her up a little."

Brazier didn't know how he felt about putting their chances in three barrels of ale for a toad that wouldn't drink anything else. But right now, that was his only plan and it wasn't a very good one.

"Folgar," he said. "You were told why we need to cross into the Immuratum?"

The dwarf shook his head without looking at Brazier. "Get you there, get you across, and get you back. That's all I know," he said. "In my experience, spies aren't privy to what they spy on."

Brazier placed a hand on Folgar's arm, bringing him to a stop.

"In the Immuratum, we need to find a book that will tell us how to destroy an Aeturnic being."

Folgar nodded slowly, then ran a hand over his bald head. "Might've been an idea to bring a few more barrels of beer."

"Do we have a problem?" Vandemir asked.

"Might do, might not," Folgar said, the corners of his eyes creasing into deep crow's feet as he scratched his beard. "One thing Aeturni hate more than Immurati—that's other Aeturni."

"Seems to me we'd be doing our Handmaid a favour, no?" Vandemir said.

"All Aeturni want a slice of our world," Folgar said. "Sometimes they work together to get it. Sometimes they work against each other."

"Then let's hope she's not feeling too cooperative with her own kind," Vandemir said.

"And what if she is?" Freyen asked.

Vandemir grinned, a wolfish smile of yellowing teeth. "That's what you brought us for."

"Well wait just a minute now," Folgar said, waving a finger at Vandemir. "The Fortinbrow brewery relies on the protection of the Handmaid. I've got a good thing going here."

Vandemir dipped his chin, the smile turning into a thin line.

"This is what we'll do," Brazier said, hoping to head off an argument before it began. "We'll put forward our case to the Handmaid, and explain that it's in her interest to let us cross. We'll tell her another Aeturnic being is gaining power in Formaria, and we intend to destroy it before it consumes all of the underground. But if she refuses, the Rex Populaire will need to intervene."

Folgar opened his mouth to argue, but Brazier cut him off.

"Formaria's survival relies on us getting that book," he said. "You'll be compensated for the brewery. You have my word."

Folgar grunted. "Korst did mention something about it being pretty important you crossing," he said. "Think the word she used was *paramount*."

Folgar swept a critical gaze over the group, exhaling sharply. "Should've brought more fighters, too."

Shaking his head, he turned away. "Let's get this over with," he muttered, striding into Yeggardania.

They walked for what Brazier guessed was another two hours, the conversation sparse. He kept stealing glances at his crew. He was searching for a reaction to his makeshift plan, to the idea he was going to convince a possibly ancient and unpredictable being of another world to let them kill one of its own kin. But if they doubted him, they kept it well hidden. He turned his attention to the darkening forest, doing his best to hide his own.

The dim light faded further, thickening the shadows and draping the trees in a deeper gloom tinged with shades of blue. Once, they heard a continuous clacking, followed by the strangled scream of some unknown creature.

They all stopped dead in their tracks at the sound, peering into the trees, but nothing made itself known to them. The forest remained eerily quiet, until, out of nowhere, Loraine said, "What in the deepest darkness am I looking at?"

Brazier followed the archer's gaze off to their left. A bank sloped gently upward, a stream flowing down through the trees.

Except it wasn't flowing down through the trees. It was flowing up.

"Yep," Folgar said. "Sometimes it does that. I tend to avoid using the water when it's going the wrong way. Not that I've had any side effects, mind, but you can never be too cautious."

Everyone stood and watched the stream, as if they were transfixed by a spell.

"Won't make any more sense the longer you stare at it," Folgar said. "Come on."

"You reckon it's safe to drink from?" Olivier murmured, his voice barely above a whisper.

"Why don't you do us all a favour and find out," Loraine shot back, though the usual barbed edge in her tone was dulled.

Brazier wasn't the only one the river had unsettled. But he couldn't shake the feeling that it wasn't just the river. A stillness had settled over the forest, thick and unnatural, as if the entire place were trapped, somehow frozen in time.

The soft blue haze of the lowering sun thickened, darkening into something that belonged to midnight, not the trailing edge of afternoon. And the air had cooled, sharp and sudden, accompanied by a strange silence.

Brazier became increasingly aware of every step on the leaf-carpeted earth, every boot scuffing a wayward tree root, or Bertrand or Solon shifting the barrels into a more comfortable grip.

The path began to veer alongside a narrow river, flowing in what, much to Brazier's relief, seemed like the right direction. They followed it for another hour as the forest began to thin, the trees peeling away until the path finally broke from the river and opened onto a vast clearing.

Beyond it lay a city of Formarian ruins, framed in the midnight blue hue of evening.

Towering trees, some as large as primary chutes, their trunks thicker than the *Anchorite* was wide, had grown all over the ruins. Their roots cracked through the tiling, swallowed staircases, and coiled through courtyards, their limbs weaving through the city like an army of snakes.

What remained of the city's geometric design was fragmented. In front of them, steps led up to an open gatehouse, the walls on either side long since collapsed, revealing the ruins beyond.

Only three structures could really claim they still stood: a stepped pyramid broken into two levels, a courtyard centred around what looked like an octagonal well, and a semi-octagonal amphitheatre, its tiered seating split by three massive cracks.

The exposed Formarian alloy tiling, dark grey beneath the trees' twisting limbs, barely resembled the pristine, unyielding material Brazier knew. What hadn't been swallowed by the Yeggardanian forest had been shattered and blasted apart, its remnants lying in scattered heaps, rubble choking the streets.

Brazier, who had always found comfort in the ageless and near-indestructible Formarian cities, suddenly felt exposed. It was as if he'd stepped into a world where he didn't belong, where the Fromryr weren't the dominant peoples.

"This way," Folgar said, his voice tight, clipped. He moved through the gatehouse without looking back, cutting a path through the rubble toward the pyramid.

Inside the city walls it was a maze of decay and ruin. A canal cut through the city's heart, running parallel to the pyramid's flank, its waters sluggish and murky.

Off the pyramid's side, a collapsed stairway jutted into the canal, its broken steps forming a crumbling dock now tangled in roots and overgrown with trees. Brazier scanned the wreckage, spying several terminals, shattered and crumbling, their frames hollowed to ruin. The few still intact stood dead and empty of hex. There was no gyre light anywhere. The place felt forgotten, lost to time.

That notion died at the foot of the pyramid, just as the smell hit them. It was a rancid, putrid sweetness, and beneath it, the metallic tang of blood. It brought bile rising up the back of Brazier's throat, forcing him to swallow dryly and breathe through his nose. Behind him, someone coughed and spat.

"Best you get used to it," Folgar said. "It only gets worse from here."

"She hiding a dead troll up there?" Switch said.

"Wouldn't be the worst thing I've seen in this place," Folgar said, eyes sweeping the ruins before turning to face them. "The Handmaid has gathered about her the denizens of the forest. We enter her lair now."

The dwarf held Vandemir's gaze, but the Captain merely flashed him a yellow-toothed grin.

"Fair warning, Mr. Fortinbrow," he said, his theatrical voice laced with a gambler's bravado. "But I'd wager we've seen worse still. Lead on."

Folgar's jaw tightened, the muscles bunching and loosening, then without another word he began climbing the steps. Brazier, still disgusted by the smell, resisted the urge to spit and fell in behind him. His crew followed, the Rex Populaire and Folgar's squad bringing up the rear.

When they reached the middle level, they stepped onto a wide landing. An open gateway loomed ahead, its massive doors shattered, the jagged chunks of alloy strewn everywhere.

Above them, the pyramid's upper half gaped open, like a raw, broken wound. The structure was a ruin, its shell cracked and crumbling, as if something had blown it open from the inside.

Beyond the shattered gateway, faint lights flickered with the spectral hue of gyre ice. They moved forward, every step tightening the air around him, thick with the cloying rot of damp and decay. Brazier's pulse quickened, and despite Folgar's presence, his fingers curled tighter around the repeater's grip, his finger hovering over the trigger.

Inside, the stench hit harder, a wall of foul, rotting musk that clung to his throat as his eyes adjusted to semi-darkness.

A hall stretched out before them. It was flanked by octagonal pillars that rose like silent sentinels. Their path led toward a short flight of steps, up to a cracked landing and a great doorway, its alloy façade fractured and crumbling, as if the ruin had seeped into its bones.

Gyre ice burned in alcoves in the walls, smoking gently and casting blue light into the darkness.

And down to the source of the rot.

Carcasses were piled and left to fester. Ribcages splayed wide, jagged and empty, their meat blackened and sloughing from the bone. The creatures, whatever they had been, were twisted into obscene shapes, their decay frozen in the blue light.

Folgar crept through the rubble, his steps soft and careful, picking a path around mounds of moss and rotting detritus. They moved with him, boots whispering over cracked alloy and decay. And then he saw it.

The toad.

At first, Brazier mistook it for rubble, a chunk of the shattered door flung across the hall, or a slab of ceiling collapsed from above. But then it blinked. Wide, yellow eyes gleamed like lanterns in the gloom. It sat, hunched and squat, a mass of slick, warty hide and bulbous, mottled growths, its skin a canvas of disease-coloured patches. It was massive, the size of an adolescent bear. And yet, he found himself grimly reminded that in Yeggardania, this was probably considered small.

Then Brazier saw the others.

Something scuttled along the wall to his left, a blur, quick and low. His head snapped around, just in time for a shape to dart past on the right. His heart pounded as he caught a glimpse of leathery skin stretched tight over wiry limbs, a maw crammed with jagged yellow fangs. Its face was a nightmare: a stubby grey snout and six ridged holes where eyes should have been, raw and red-rimmed. Then it was gone, swallowed by the shadows.

Switch and Matthias reacted in sync, crossbows raised, bodies taut. Their sights flicked from one movement to the next, and for a moment Brazier thought they were going to open fire.

"Easy," Folgar said, his voice low but firm. He raised a hand, palm out. "They answer to the Handmaid. They know to do you no harm."

And then it stepped out.

From behind the pillar closest to the landing, a figure emerged, a shape Brazier knew only from legend, and which caught the breath in his throat.

Half reptile, half man, and towering over six feet tall, its body was wrapped in dark green scales, thick and ridged like living armour. The head, long and lizard-like, ended in a cruel snout, rows of serrated teeth glinting beneath nostrils that flared as it took a breath. Bony crests jutted from its skull, jagged spines crowning its face, framing yellow eyes, slitted and cold as shattered amber.

It wore a leather harness, strapping dull bronzite plating to its thighs and shoulders. In its clawed hands, it gripped a bronzite spear, the edge darkened with age and use.

As it stepped up to the left of the doorway, the hall's gyre light carved details from its ancient hide. Its scales were worn to a leathery, almost petrified texture, the green faded to something like stone. Dozens of scars latticed its body in crisscrossed trenches. One in particular, wide and deep, cut from the crest of its snout down through its maw in a permanent ravine.

Brazier stared at the Fenn, his pulse a tight drumbeat in his ears. He couldn't decide what shocked him more, the fact that he stood face-to-face with one of the Fromryr's ancient enemies, or that one still existed in Yeggardania at all.

And he wasn't alone. He could almost feel the tension rolling off the others, all eyes on the creature that had nearly destroyed their race, on the creature Varkoneth Rosantz no longer believed existed.

"The rest of you see that?" Olivier said, his voice thin with disbelief. "Tell me the rest of you see that."

"We're seeing it," Bertrand replied, his voice low and tight.

"Others," Godenforte said. "On our flanks."

To his credit, the man's deep voice was professional and calm, but Brazier's head snapped around anyway. Instinct drove his gaze left and right. His eyes cut between the pillars, scanning the shadows where the gyre light pooled and broke against the ruins. But what crept there wasn't Fenn.

The shape moved, fluid and silent, with a predator's grace, gliding from pillar to pillar. Humanoid, its body was lean, sinuous, moving with the poise of a great cat. But where paws should have been, Brazier saw four human hands, long-fingered, the tips thick and padded.

Its skin was slate-purple and smooth, with a pale stomach that shifted and flexed as it prowled. Its face was broad, with a flat nose. Dumpy cheeks, too round, too soft, and almost dwarven, were framed in the unmistakable angles of a feline brow and pointed, twitching ears.

From its head, thick, rope-like strands spilled, forming mane-like hair. But each lock was as thick as one of Brazier's fingers, and they swayed with its movements, heavy and sinuous as living cords.

Watching the creature watch them with uncanny, predatory eyes, Brazier realised he had absolutely no idea what he was looking at.

Above the doorway, something else caught his attention. It clung to the wall with hooked claws, tearing into the shattered alloy tiles, causing dust and debris to spill down and patter the landing in a dry cascade.

It looked like a bat, except it was the size of a man. Its body was draped in pale, wiry fur that clung in tangled strands to its leathery skin. The creature's head twisted, a full, unnatural rotation, and cartilage cracked wetly as it brought them into view with its small beady eyes.

They were set either side of a pair of wing-like nostrils folded into the front of its face, which shuddered as it sniffed.

Below them, its maw gaped into a V-shaped grin bristling with layered rows of needle-thin fangs. The skin around its mouth was tight, stretched thin and leathery, twitching with something almost like anticipation. Brazier got the distinct impression the thing was hungry.

"Such a mess you make, Olander," came a voice from the darkness beyond the doorway. Human and female, it possessed the polished, crisp enunciation of Fromryian high society. It was the kind of voice that belonged at court, wrapped in perfumed silk.

But what emerged from the shadows was anything but.

The woman was draped in what had once been a white gown but was now stained and ruined, its fabric turned a mottled grey with filth. The hem dragged, blackened with clinging grime.

Her face was hidden behind a gauzy veil, moth-eaten and stained, concealing what lay beneath. But it was her body that turned Brazier's blood cold.

She was wrong, all wrong.

Her arms, stick-thin, almost skeletal, ended in wrist-length gloves, torn and frayed at the cuffs. From the shredded fabric, long, blackened fingers emerged, fingers that looked scorched, charred to the bone. They clutched the doorframe with a scrape of nail on stone.

She didn't walk. Instead, she pulled herself forward, her body lurching, joints popping in sudden, broken motions, like a marionette. Her legs unfolded, far too long, stretching beyond any human proportion, twisting and bending with every unnatural step. She moved with a tortured rhythm, like a skeleton trying to remember what it was like to walk.

Every jarring twitch made Brazier's stomach knot tighter, yet the voice never lost its elegance.

"Whatever shall I do with you," she said, her head tilting sharply, the veil shifting as she regarded the bat-creature above. Her tone was amused and familiar, as though scolding a pet. "And just as we have guests. Naughty boy."

The creature stilled beneath her gaze.

Just then the toad released a thunderous, bellowing croak that rolled through the hall and rattled in Brazier's chest.

"Yes, I know, my love," the Handmaid purred, her voice dripping with affection. She reached out, her skeletal fingers brushing over the toad's warty crown in a slow, tender stroke.

"There are so very many of them," she cooed, as though soothing a fretful pet. "They're making all our new friends so terribly nervous."

Then her head snapped toward them, too fast, too sharp, the motion predatory and jarring beneath the delicate veneer of her voice.

"You're not here to make my friends nervous, are you, Folgar?"

The question hung in the air.

"Nay, my lady, nay," Folgar said, his voice smooth and careful. "Never would I seek to upset your court."

He dipped his head slightly, though his eyes never left hers.

"I come in need of a favour," he continued, "and with gifts for the prince."

With a wave of his hand, he signalled to Solon, Bertrand, and Godenforte. The trio moved without a word. Solon hefted his barrel forward, placing it with a heavy thump before the steps leading to the landing. Bertrand and Godenforte followed suit, their barrels settling into place next to Solon's. Folgar spread his hands wide, presenting the offering.

"Three barrels of Banshee Black," he announced, his voice carrying through the hall. "The prince's favourite."

The air felt thick with a tense, expectant pause. Then the toad moved. Its belly swelled, ballooning wide as it drew in a deep breath. And then—

Snap.

A blur of wet, pink muscle. Brazier barely registered the lash of the toad's tongue before it struck. *Whap.* The tongue hit the nearest barrel with a slick, meaty slap, curling tight around the wood. With terrifying speed, it reeled the barrel back, straight into the yawning cavern of its mouth.

Then came a crunch, a sickening crackle of splintering wood and crushed iron bands, as the barrel folded like a child's toy between the toad's jaws. Banshee Black burst free, a thick, dark cascade, its frothy, brown-gold crown spilling down the creature's throat and into the stagnant pool beneath it. The heavy aroma of black ale, spiced and rich, drifted through the air, mingling with the rot and decay.

The creature gave a deep, wet croak of satisfaction.

"Oh, Leopine," the Handmaid sighed, her voice laced with indulgence, like a mother humouring a spoiled child. She turned her veiled face back to Folgar.

"How generous of you, Folgar," she said, her voice honeyed. "I trust all goes well under my patronage?"

"Never better," Folgar replied. "Your influence over the forest never ceases to amaze me."

The Handmaid tittered softly, the sound muffled behind her veil and blackened fingers.

Behind her, Leopine released a low, throaty croak. Brazier, who was starting to pick up the subtleties in the creature's tone, thought he sounded annoyed.

The Handmaid's head turned slightly, the veil shifting as though she were smiling beneath it. She reached down and ran her blackened fingers along the toad's mottled crown once more.

"Now, now," she purred, her voice teasing, "jealousy is unbecoming of a prince."

Leopine's throat vibrated, but he stilled under her touch. Folgar shifted his weight a fraction, then cleared his throat.

"Which brings me," he said carefully, "to the favour I need to ask."

The Handmaid tilted her head, slow and birdlike, her veil shifting with the motion. She said nothing.

"The crossing over which you rule," Folgar said, his arm sweeping out to gesture to the others, their stillness a collective tension. "We humbly request the use of it, so my friends here might reach the Immuratum."

The Handmaid's titter returned, her fingers brushing her lips once more.

"Oh, Folgar," she said.

Folgar let out a nervous laugh, the sound thin, brittle.

"It wasn't a jest, my lady," he said carefully. "We seek to use your crossing."

The shift was instant.

"What need has anyone of the Infernal realms!"

The Handmaid's scream shattered the air, her girlish voice twisting mid-cry, warping into something wet and guttural, a sound that rattled deep in her throat like something drowned trying to speak.

Brazier's heart pounded, his skin prickling with raw, instinctive heat. This was not a good start.

He forced himself to step in.

"Knowledge," he said, steady but cautious. "Knowledge hidden in the demon world."

Out of the corner of his eye there was movement. The cat-like creature prowled low, creeping on all fours, edging toward the landing's steps. The bat-thing clinging to the wall above twisted its head, rotating too far, its fanged maw parting slightly as it fixed its gaze on him.

Then the Handmaid's head snapped round toward Brazier.

"The Infernal realm hides knowledge beyond reckoning," she said, her voice slipping back into its delicate, girlish lilt. Her fingers toyed with the edge of her veil.

"Much of which is… forbidden."

The veil twitched again. Her head snapped to Folgar.

"You seek the library!" she screamed. "What trickery is this? What betrayal?"

The Handmaid moved.

She jolted across the landing, her motions sharp and jagged. Halfway down the steps, her body lurched in erratic bursts. Then, far too fast for something that moved like that, she was towering over Folgar, her presence a shadow swallowing him whole.

And she was growing. Before Brazier's eyes, she stretched. Her limbs lengthened, her hunched frame unfolded a half foot taller, maybe more.

Brazier only realised he'd raised his crossbow when he found himself staring down its sights. Out of the corner of his eye, he saw the others had done the same, their weapons levelled.

Folgar lifted a hand, patting the air with an urgency that screamed: *Don't.*

Then the Handmaid shrieked.

"Do you seek my demise!"

The sound shattered through the hall, her voice splitting, no longer entirely human. It echoed as though spoken in a dozen voices at once, layered and seething.

"Do you seek the knowledge of my ruin? After everything I have done!"

Her arm lashed out, a gloved hand snapping around Folgar's throat. Brazier barely had time to process what he was seeing before Folgar cried out.

His body jerked, his hands clawing at the fingers locked around his neck, but he couldn't pull them away. The Handmaid's grip was absolute.

And then—

Brazier watched in horror as Folgar's flesh blackened beneath her touch. Veins swelled beneath his skin, something black twisted beneath the surface, like worms burrowing into rotted fruit.

Folgar's feet lifted from the ground, his body hanging limp as if he weighed nothing at all.

"It's another Aeturni!" Brazier shouted. The urge to act clawed at him, to pull her wrist away, to free Folgar. But the thought of touching her was enough to make his stomach churn.

"We need to know how to destroy another Aeturni," he continued, forcing the words through the thick knot of dread in his chest.

The Handmaid's head tilted, her veil fluttering as she turned to him.

"Who?" she demanded, her voice a scratching bite, sharp as broken glass.

Folgar's face was changing. His jaw had begun to turn black, the sickening colour spreading like rot beneath his skin. His breath came out in desperate wheezes, each one a rasp, and he clung to her wrist, his fingers trembling with the last ounce of his strength.

Brazier's heart hammered in his chest. "Duessa!" he shouted, the name escaping before he could stop it, panic flooding his voice.

The change was instant. The Handmaid's grip loosened, dropping Folgar like a broken doll. He crumbled to his knees, his breath heavy and laboured, each inhale a tortured rasp.

Brazier had to fight the urge to check if the dwarf was still alive. Because if there was going to be a fight, it would be now.

The Handmaid took a crooked step back, her movements still jagged, as if her body resisted the retreat. Across the landing, the Fenn had stepped forward, its massive, scaled frame now standing at the very edge.

Out of the corner of Brazier's eye, he saw more movement, the Morletts, slithering from behind the pillars, their leathery skin catching the gyre light as they edged closer. And beyond them, the red-haired cat-thing had circled wide, stalking low, its gaze locked onto Matthias like a predator choosing its moment.

Then the Handmaid spoke, her voice a whisper that barely carried across the heavy air.

"You seek the destruction of my Queen."

A shiver crawled up Brazier's spine. He had thought things couldn't get worse. He had clearly lacked imagination.

"Say the word," Vandemir murmured somewhere behind him, his voice cold. "And we'll end this farce right now."

Beside Brazier, Folgar let out another dry, rasping wheeze, then spat onto the stone. He was alive. But Brazier barely registered it. His focus was locked on the Handmaid.

But she wasn't looking at them anymore.

Her head tilted, her veil shifting slightly as though she were lost in thought, her whole frame caught in a moment of eerie stillness.

"You seek the destruction of my Queen," she repeated, softer this time, almost distant.

Then her voice dropped, darker and heavier.

"Know you not what blessing you bring before me, Folgar."

"My lady?" Folgar rasped, pushing himself unsteadily to his feet. His fingers rubbed at his throat, which, to Brazier's relief, was fading back to its normal colour.

"The tale she wove is what you see before you now," the Handmaid murmured, her voice laced with something almost tender. She turned her veiled face toward Leopine.

"My Queen of Dreams and her jealousy. Even with all she had, and my loyalty as her handmaid, her jealousy was absolute—of our love and the happiness we found."

The toad croaked, low and mournful, the sound vibrating through the hall. The Handmaid let out a slow, shuddering sigh.

"And so she sang her spiteful song, spun the tale that made it real. My prince, my Leopine, my love, twisted into what you see now," she said. "For so very long, we have been trapped in this prison she spun... the Handmaid and her Toad Prince."

The silence stretched, until the cat-thing, its gaze never having left Matthias, rose onto its hind legs. It stepped closer to the Handmaid, its thick, human fingers cupping to whisper something into her ear.

She stilled, then her head jerked from Matthias to the others.

"In the Library of the Nine, you will find instructions for the Queen's demise," she said, the softness gone, replaced by something edged and final. "You will bring an end to our suffering."

Then, slowly, she raised a long, blackened finger and pointed it at Matthias.

"But the Lucidian must remain."

Matthias regarded the Handmaid with his moon-grey eyes, unblinking and unreadable.

"No deal," Brazier said.

He had no idea what she meant by Lucidian, but he didn't need to. There was no way he'd leave Matthias in the hands of an Aeturnic being, in the heart of the Yeggardanian forest, surrounded by monsters.

With two crooked snaps, the Handmaid moved. One moment she was across the landing, the next she was there, her veiled face mere inches from his own.

The scent engulfed him. The sickly rotting sweetness of the hall intensified so much he had to clench his jaw to avoid gagging.

"I seek no hostages, little dwarf," she rasped. "I seek the Lucidian's skills."

Matthias tilted his head slightly, utterly unfazed.

"You're going to have to be a little more specific," he said. "I'm not short on talents."

Brazier could almost hear Switch rolling her eyes.

The Handmaid lingered on Brazier for a beat longer, then slowly turned to Matthias, her veiled gaze settling on him. She smiled. Or at least, Brazier felt that she did.

"Three Handmaids there were," she said, her voice singsong. "Three Handmaids to serve the Queen in her every need. But now they are lost, and there is only me." Her tone shifted, light and lilting, but beneath it, something brittle. "Alone, with my Leopine and my court of darlings. But sorely do I miss my sisters."

Matthias looked bored.

"Never had much to do with your kind," he said, arms crossed. "Not sure how I can help."

The Handmaid's veil twitched.

"The mind of a Lucidian transcends the limits of what your kind calls the Navigoria," she said.

The Morletts closed in. Their leathery limbs clung to the stone, circling like carrion birds. One crawled up the pillar to Brazier's right, another settled unnervingly close to Matthias.

Brazier felt the air tightening, pressing in. He swallowed hard, the mantle of responsibility reappearing, pressing down on his shoulders. The crew had trusted him. He had brought them here. He couldn't lose one of them.

"Seeing beyond the veil of the maelstrom to the hallowed places of this world," the Handmaid continued. "You can see where others cannot."

"Matthias," Brazier said, steady despite the unease curling in his gut. "We do not have to agree to this."

The Handmaid tittered, turning to him.

“Little dwarf,” she purred, almost indulgently. “You are in my court. And my new friends are so very hungry. And they are so very many.”

Brazier glanced over his shoulder. Where before there had been only five or six Morletts skulking in the shadows, now the hall crawled with dozens of them.

Thirty, maybe forty of the black and grey-skinned creatures, their wiry bodies slinking over stone, scaling pillars, clinging to the walls with clawed fingers that scraped against the crumbling alloy. Their red-rimmed, eyeless faces twitched, drawn in closer, encircling them.

“Say the word,” Vandemir murmured, low and cold behind him. “And we’ll show her what hunger looks like.”

Brazier’s heart pounded, hammering against his ribs, each pulse a reminder of what little control he had over the situation. His fingers clenched tighter around the grip of his weapon. The rush of blood in his ears drowned out everything else, a sickening mix of helplessness and guilt.

Because no matter how sharp Vandemir’s bravado, even he must know they stood no chance against numbers like these.

“I’ll do it,” Matthias said.

Brazier turned to him, ready to argue. “Matthias—”

But the navigator only shook his head, his expression calm. Brazier could see the resolve in the navigator’s eyes. And that somehow made it worse.

Brazier was their captain. He was supposed to carry the weight, not pass it to someone else.

“I’ll stay,” Matthias said, turning to the Handmaid. “I’ll find your sisters.”

Then, as if it were nothing—“Keep an eye on things from this side of the crossing.”

For the briefest instant Brazier considered giving the order and letting all hell break loose, even if it was only for the satisfaction of not handing over one of his own. His fingers itched. His heart thundered.

But he knew the thought was nothing more than self-indulgence, a hollow act of defiance.

Somewhere deep in his mind, beyond the anger and the helplessness, rationality sat like a stone in his gut. There was nothing he could do.

The Handmaid clasped her hands together, her fingers locking tight.

"How wonderful," she said, her voice sweet.

And the Morletts, every single one of them, retreated into the gloom, vanishing like mist burned away by sunlight.

The Handmaid turned, her veiled face shifting toward the cat-thing.

"Inform the ferryman," she murmured. "He has passengers to take upriver... to the Library."

The thing moved immediately, darting up the steps, its tail flicking lazily behind it. Its human hands made no sound as it slipped through the doorway and disappeared.

The Handmaid spread her arms wide, her silhouette stark against the dim light.

"And now we are all such good friends," she cooed.

Brazier knew he should feel relieved. He should feel immense gratitude for their sheer good fortune, for the fact the Handmaid wanted her old master dead as much as they did.

But the mantle on his shoulders was too heavy.

All Brazier could think about was the roll of the dice, the gamble he had taken. They had won the crossing. They would reach the Immuratum. But the dice had yet to tell him Matthias' fate. And deep in his gut, Brazier had a horrible feeling he wouldn't be as lucky with his navigator.

TWENTY-FIVE
KATHRYN

Kathryn felt warm, uncomfortably warm. Her clothes stuck to her skin, damp with sweat, and her head pounded with a dull, throbbing ache. It was like she'd spent the night drinking and woken up too soon.

She tried to move her legs—

But was trapped.

She shifted her arms, feeling soft sheets beneath her fingers, but like her legs, she could barely move them. A pulse of unease shot through her as she opened her eyes and saw a deep blue channel of azure above her. For a split second, her brain told her she was back in Ilantia.

A flood of panic surged through her. She kicked frantically at the sheets, twisting to free herself. She tried to roll out of bed, only to tangle her legs further, sending herself half over the side and crashing onto the floor like a fish out of water.

A wave of nausea curled in her gut like something rotten. She swallowed it down, ripping the sheets off herself at the same time as rolling onto her back. Kicking away the last of the fabric, she took a deep breath. Someone had removed her doublet and boots, and she wore a cream shirt, now stained with sweat.

Kathryn took in the rest of the chamber. It was small and rectangular, a bronzite washbasin to her left, the cot to her right. The wardrobe and drawers were inset into the bronzite walls at the foot of the bed, next to her boots and folded doublet.

Opposite—

A portal slid open, and a woman stepped into the room. She wore a green officer's doublet with white trim. Her curled ginger hair was pinned up in a messy bun, framing a round, youthful face with large bright eyes. They looked down at her with the anxious earnestness of a junior officer. The woman, the girl, really, clutched a mug in her left hand.

"Oh, abyss," she gasped, scrambling forward. "I've already messed this up!"

Kathryn blinked.

"Excuse me?" she said, letting the woman help her up.

She stood unsteadily, one hand on her stomach, waiting for the headache to pass. It didn't.

"Sorry, sir," the woman corrected herself quickly. "I meant I've already messed this up, sir."

Kathryn resisted the urge to roll her eyes.

"No," she said. "What have you messed up?"

The woman straightened.

"I was assigned to look after you, sir," she said in a rapid, breathless ramble. "I went to get you some water, I thought you might want some when you woke up, I was only away for a second, but you woke up, and I didn't know—"

The more she spoke, the more agitated she became. Kathryn held up a hand, cutting her off.

"I'm fine."

She patted herself down, more for show than necessity.

"Look at me, I'm fine. What's your name?"

The woman blinked, then straightened further.

"Ensenya Kilburn," she said. "But everyone calls me Sen or Senya. Which you can, too. If you want. I mean, of course you can—you're the captain."

She gave a nervous little laugh, turning a shade of red. Then, as if catching herself, she took a steadying breath, her eyes shifting from Kathryn to somewhere over her shoulder.

"Okay, Senya," Kathryn said, and the girl smiled, clearly pleased Kathryn had used her name.

"What's your rank?"

"Second lieutenant," Senya said, standing straighter. "Second Lieutenant Ensenya Kilburn."

"And you were assigned to me from where?"

"Well… I was reassigned to the vulnerum to help with the wounded, but before that I was in engineering, and before that I was in maintenance."

She shrugged sheepishly.

"They move me around a lot."

Kathryn nodded. She knew exactly why Senya would be moved around a lot.

"You're adaptable," she said, trying to sound encouraging. "That's good in an officer."

Senya beamed at her.

"Thank you, sir! I am!"

Kathryn gestured at the mug.

"And thoughtful."

"Oh! No problem, sir!" she said, handing her the mug.

Kathryn turned to the washbasin, pouring herself some water. She drank slowly, gauging her stomach's reaction. The nausea eased slightly. Given how little she had eaten in the past day, she was probably just hungry.

"Why am I not in the vulnerum?" she asked.

"Oh, yes!" Senya said quickly.

"Our anomancer said there was nothing physically wrong with you, aside from the bump to your head. We needed the beds for the critically wounded, so they moved you here instead."

Makes sense, Kathryn thought, taking another sip and bracing herself.

"What's the current status of the mission?"

Senya shrugged.

"They don't really tell me stuff like that, sir."

Why am I not surprised?

"That's okay," Kathryn said, moving to get her boots and doublet.

Senya made a startled sound, quickly stepping out of the way. Kathryn slipped her feet into her boots and threw on her doublet, leaving it unbuttoned. She still needed to cool down.

Moving to the portal, it slid open for her, revealing a chamber not unlike the captain's quarters aboard the *Pheradies*, just smaller.

Two green couches faced each other over a low bronzite table, set within a semi-hexagonal alcove. A writing desk stood against the far wall, parchment neatly stacked, ink bottle and quills lined in a row. A bronzite chest and an intricately carved wooden box stood at its foot. Whoever had commanded the *Vanguard* before her had been tidy.

And behind the desk was a command terminal. Kathryn strode to it, ignoring the pounding between her eyes, sank her hand into the hex well, and requested the ship's status.

The damage report reeled off in her mind's eye with everything she already knew. Then, a new line: a primary support bulkhead had buckled from damage sustained in battle. The spatial anchor hadn't kicked in fast enough. But there were no casualties and no cascading damage. That must have been what rocked the nav deck.

She checked their position. The *Vanguard* was still in formation with the *Tempest* and *Crucible*, the three ships pulling further ahead of the fleet.

She scanned the nav deck logs, and felt a flash of annoyance that made her clutch at the hex filaments. Gideon had already reported her injury to the *Pheradies*—the word 'incapacitated' jumped out at her as she read his message.

Her irritation boiled into outright anger when she saw he'd also requested withdrawal to the main fleet. Kathryn exhaled sharply, her grip on the filaments relaxing when she saw the response denying repairs and ordering the pursuit to continue.

Ten minutes later, another message had come through, this one directly from Admiral Korst. The fleet had reached out to the other Royal Houses and the Navarch. They'd received no response, and so all other Fromryian vessels were to be considered hostile. They were on their own.

Kathryn closed the logs and checked the *Storm's* trajectory.

If she had to guess, it was heading to the Hyralian Gulf—it's what she would do. The Mad Soup, as sailors called it, would be a perfect place to lose pursuing ships. But this far out from the Gulf, anything could happen.

There was still time to catch up with the *Storm*, plenty of time. But right now, she had other problems. Namely, Gideon Du'Voire, her newly appointed First Officer who had gone behind her back the moment she wasn't there.

Thinking about it made her head pound harder, and an image of her storming onto the nav deck and punching his face in flashed across her imagination.

She took a breath, pressing the mug to her temple, letting the metal cool her headache. Her First Officer was just another problem to solve.

A problem of your own making.

It was her mother's voice.

Kathryn froze, causing the mug to slip from her fingers. It hit the command terminal and clattered to the floor.

The Admiral stood across the command terminal, hands clasped behind her back so tightly Kathryn could hear the wooden ruler splintering. Her blonde hair was wound into a bun so severe it hurt to look at, while her hawkish, angular brow and cheekbones sat above a sharp nose and thin, bloodless lips.

Her eyes bored into her. The colour of hard-packed gyre shards, they were filled with an ice-cold hatred that shocked Kathryn into silence. All she could do was stare back.

Until a cough behind her made her spin.

Senya waved awkwardly, seemed to think better of it, then pulled her hand behind her back. She straightened, then pretended to be interested in a spot just over Kathryn's shoulder. If Kathryn's heart hadn't jumped into her throat, she might have found it endearing.

She turned back to the command terminal, but her mother was gone.

"Here."

Senya's voice startled her. The girl stood at her side, holding the mug out for her. Kathryn stared down at it.

"Are you okay, Captain?"

Kathryn forced herself to smile.

"Just a headache."

She glanced back once more. There was nothing.

She cleared her throat. "Just a headache," she repeated, more forcefully. She exhaled slowly, willing her pulse to settle.

Senya, oblivious to the storm in her mind, placed the mug carefully on the writing table, then turned back to her, still wearing that eager smile.

Kathryn acknowledged her with a nod, then sank her hand into the hex well, gave her command script, and requested a tether to the ship's navigator.

"Receiving, Captain."

The *Vanguard's* navigator sounded calm and focused. If he was struggling to maintain pursuit while also handling incoming communication, he didn't let it show. Kathryn found his steadiness mildly soothing.

"Inform the Pheradies that Captain Stryker has returned to duty with only a minor head injury," she said in her mind, thankful the two ships were far enough from each other they couldn't tether directly. If she'd had to speak out loud, she didn't think she could have kept the tremor from her voice. "The Vanguard is fully operational and in full pursuit of the Storm as ordered. Associate the message with my command script."

"Understood, Captain."

There was a brief pause, then: "Sending communication now."

Kathryn disconnected, pulling her hand from the hex. At least someone was following her orders. The thought made her think of Gideon again. She needed to be on the nav deck. She needed to move.

Glancing back at the bedchamber and the washroom beyond it, she thought of the warm water that would strip away the day's sweat and grime. It was a luxury she didn't have time for. She would just have to smell.

She started for the door, then hesitated.

Senya still stood there, hands clasped behind her back, stuck between staying put and trailing after her. Half at-ease, half at-attention; if hesitation had a posture, the girl was pulling it off. Kathryn suppressed the urge to shake her head.

"Come with me," she said.

"Yes, sir," Senya said, catching herself just short of saluting. She turned the reflex into a clipped, marching step instead.

Kathryn placed her hand into the chamber terminal, and the portal hissed open. She stepped out into the corridor, Senya falling in beside her. The ship's dimmed gyre channels cast long shadows ahead of them.

"Listen," Kathryn said, deciding she needed to put this poor girl at ease. "I'm just filling in for your last captain. Temporary. I won't be here long, so you can relax."

Senya glanced at her. "Absolutely, sir. Totally relaxed, sir."

But she wasn't. If anything, she straightened, as if she'd just been given an order.

Kathryn stopped at the next junction and turned.

"I mean it. After this mission, you'll probably never see me again. So don't treat me like a permanent fixture."

Senya nodded, gaze dropping to Kathryn's boots. She almost looked disappointed.

Under any other circumstances, Kathryn would have welcomed the possibility of friendship. She would have seriously welcomed it, even from an awkward junior officer suffering from minor hierarchy worship.

But her head was pounding, her First Officer was directly undermining her orders, and her mother had made a brief but terrifying appearance outside of the usual confines of her brain. Kathryn didn't have time for incompetence, no matter how endearing.

"Just do your job and stay out of the way," she said. It came out harsher than she'd intended.

She thought about apologising, but just kept walking instead. She'd figure out how to say sorry later.

At the end of the corridor, they reached a chute, and Kathryn called for a lift. As they waited, the ship groaned from somewhere deep in its bones, a low, mournful sound like some ancient leviathan calling out one last time before sinking into the black.

She tried not to see it as an omen.

The lift arrived. They stepped in, the silence stretching between them. Kathryn focused on what she'd say to Gideon, using it as a shield against the things she didn't want to think about: her mother's apparition and the way the recently taken elixir didn't seem to be working.

Just get through this, she told herself. *Catch up with the Storm and find Isdria. You can worry about your poor mental state once it's all over.*

The lift deposited them outside the nav deck.

Someone had cleared away the shattered door panel and the shards of gyre ice, but the other half of the door had been jammed open. Not great for security, but at least she didn't have to step over debris every time she walked in. The leak, however, hadn't been fixed. Somewhere inside the walls, water still dripped.

Not like you were getting a shower anyway, she thought, stepping onto the deck.

"Captain on deck!" Elvie snapped, standing at attention.

Karland straightened behind the terminal. Two others Kathryn didn't recognise, both standing around the command terminal, did the same.

But her new First Officer was nowhere to be seen. She noted the missing terminal but kept her expression neutral. She tried not to see it as another bad omen.

"At ease," she said.

They relaxed.

The newcomer to the left of the command terminal was a man in his early thirties, with neatly cut dark brown hair, blue eyes, and a well-defined jaw. He had the sort of thoughtful face that looked contemplative even when it wasn't trying. His white undershirt was ruined, a deep stain of blood soaking into the fabric, spreading down to the green officer's trousers he wore. His doublet was missing; Kathryn assumed it had been just as bloodied and had been discarded somewhere else.

Opposite him stood a woman with dark brown hair pulled into a combed-over bun. Sharp jaw, sharper cheekbones, and deep brown eyes that looked like they missed nothing.

Unlike her counterpart, she wore a full officer's uniform, untouched by blood.

"Names and ranks," Kathryn said.

The woman spoke first. "Second Lieutenant Rayne Carter, Hull Defence."

The man followed. "Lieutenant Avery Hurst, Forward Battery Officer."

"Admiral Hera Laine Thrace, Gyre Star Commander."

Her mother's apparition stood at the far end of the command terminal, as solid and real as the two officers flanking it.

Kathryn's breath caught. Her pulse slammed against her ribs. The headache returned in full force.

"You'll never be good enough!" her mother spat, her lips peeling back, flecks of spittle flying. Even in real life, Kathryn had never seen her look this angry.

"Why, Kathryn? Tell me why you will never be good enough!"

Her mother stalked around the terminal like she used to circle her writing desk, each step like a prowling animal.

Kathryn felt herself shrink, muscles coiling, bracing. Her mother loomed, feet away now, voice rising to a raw, jagged edge.

"Why, Kathryn?" she screamed.

Kathryn flinched, her body acting on instinct, expecting the ruler.

"Captain?"

Senya's voice sounded muffled and distant, as if she were speaking through a dense fog. Kathryn snapped her head around.

"Are you alright, Captain?" This time clearer, louder, leaving a faint ringing in Kathryn's ears.

She turned back. The spot where her mother had been was empty. But the weight of her presence remained, pressing against her skull, her thundered pulse worsening the ache in her head. A droplet of sweat crawled down her temple, yet she felt ice-cold.

The others stared, concern plain on their faces.

"Just the headache," she said, forcing a smile, and stepping up to the command terminal. She pretended to take an interest in it while her heart returned to its normal rhythm. It showed a moving sculpt of the *Crucible*, *Tempest*, and *Vanguard* in pursuit of the Sorel Tan ship. Their formation had pulled so far ahead of the rest of the fleet that the hex couldn't track them at this magnification.

Her gaze jumped to the empty terminal where her First Officer should have been.

"Where's Mr. Du'Voire?" she asked, letting it hang for anyone to answer.

"Said he was feeling faint from the head wound, sir," Karland said. "Took himself to the vulnerum."

She glanced up at him. Karland didn't look like he was trying to hide anything. But it didn't stop the sharp pang of dread.

She didn't like Gideon being out of her sight, but resisted the urge to tether to the vulnerum and check. Kathryn was already coming across as unstable. She didn't want to appear paranoid as well.

"Very well," she said, then louder, for the navigator. "Mr. Pervaine, give me shipwide."

The navigator lifted his palm, the flat of his index finger facing the ceiling. "Tethered," he said, voice calm as ever.

Kathryn exhaled and spoke.

"This is the Captain speaking," she said, raising her voice. "I wish I had been appointed your Captain under better circumstances. I wish you hadn't been forced into assaulting Thela. I wish House Rosantz had never betrayed Formaria. And I wish you hadn't lost so many friends and colleagues because of that betrayal. But we are here, and it has fallen to us to right those wrongs. My name is Captain Kathryn Stryker, and together, we will take the Gloried Storm, bring the terrorist Isdria Laanorath to heel, and deliver justice for our fallen."

She paused, just long enough for it to settle.

"Stryker out."

Merrin dropped the tether. The hex flattened.

Next to her, Senya started clapping, a broad grin splitting her face.

"That was really great," she said, shaking her head the way people do when they're genuinely impressed. "I loved it."

The others exchanged hesitant glances. Then, one by one, they joined in, the applause awkward at first, before settling into something almost genuine.

"Thank you, Ms. Kilburn," she said, keeping her expression neutral, hiding the flicker of embarrassment at Senya's enthusiasm. She could only hope the rest of the crew had felt what Senya did.

Deliver brutal honesty when the occasion calls for it. Emphasise shared responsibility. Show assertion. That's what makes a crew loyal to their Captain.

They were her mother's words, her mother's voice.

Kathryn's heart fluttered at their appearance, and she forced the thoughts from her mind before it could conjure the apparition again.

You know what you're doing, she told herself, pressing her palms against the command terminal, grounding herself in its solidity. She had been the youngest Captain appointed a Gyre Star Commander. She'd done this before.

I do not need my mother haunting my every move.

The thought wasn't just an assertion. It was a command.

Kathryn waited for the last of the applause to fade before speaking. "Mr. Pervaine, prep a message to the Pheradies."

One of the wells beside her pulsed.

"Ready when you are, Captain," Merrin said.

She took a breath. "Pheradies, if the Storm reaches Maw Klioxies, she's gone. She'll have a clear run—either to eastern Formaria or into a surface drift, and we'll lose her. If we push her toward the Hyralian Gulf, she'll be forced to slow. That buys the fleet time to catch up. I recommend sending messages to Reantha and Theselan with her current trajectory. Have them move to intercept, force her to change course or box her into the Gulf. End message."

"Hex cast sent, sir," Merrin confirmed.

Rayne tilted her head. "You think that'll work, sir? That they'll actually send ships to intercept?"

"Every Captain and Admiral dreams of being the one to retake the Gloried Storm," Kathryn said, including herself in the statement. "Don't underestimate the ego tied up in that."

"Could end up putting a bunch of ships in our way," Avery said, frowning. "We might have a fight on our hands, sir. With other Fromryr."

The Fromryian military ran on strict hierarchy, but junior officers were encouraged to be inquisitive, to make suggestions, to take the initiative. In the vastness of the underground, whole battalions could be cut off for days, even weeks on end. Survival depended on officers who could act without waiting for orders.

But this wasn't just about tactics. Avery and Rayne were testing her, probing to see what kind of Captain she was. Did she shut down debate or welcome it? Did she put faith in her officers or keep her cards close to her chest? Could they trust her?

"You're right," Kathryn said. "But that's a risk worth taking. The Storm makes it to the Maw, and we lose. We have a better chance in the Gulf, even if we have to fight through our own to get there."

Avery's brow smoothed. His posture eased, just slightly. "Yes, sir."

It was a small victory, tiny, really. But she savoured it. She'd forgotten how much she enjoyed the push and pull of command: the way relationships had to be navigated like battlefields, a messiness other captains often struggled with or chose to ignore altogether. It made her guiltier about how she'd treated Senya.

She glanced at the girl, about to ask what her specialism was to see if she could find something useful for her to do. But Karland spoke first. "Incoming tether from a runner in engineering, sir. Requested for the Captain."

Kathryn nodded. "Transfer it to the command terminal."

She placed her hand in the hex and gave her command script, then disconnected so the message could be played out loud.

A woman's voice burst from the hex, rushed and frantic, the words tumbling over each other. She sounded like she'd sprinted the length of the ship.

"Sir, Gideon Du'Voire is heading for engineering," she panted. "He's rounded up junior officers and sailors—sir, it's a mutiny, he's saying the ship's too damaged, that we'll be destroyed if we engage again. He's taken weapons from the armoury. He's going to take the main engineering deck and shut down the thrusters."

Anger and panic twisted into the same emotion. Her fists clenched on the edge of the command terminal. Her imagination produced another scene of her punching her First Officer hard enough to break his nose.

She took a breath, forcing the anger to turn to pragmatism, forcing her mind to move through her options with objectivity. She could give her First Officer a beating later. First, she needed to stop him.

"How many?" she asked.

"Six, maybe seven," the woman said.

Gideon had enough for a surprise attack on engineering, but not enough to take the ship. That gave her time.

Avery placed his hand in a well, and the hex display flattened. A cross-section of the *Vanguard* unfolded in front of them.

Kathryn turned back to the hex well. "What's your name, sailor?"

"Urilla Gosse, sir," she said. "Enginator Technician, sir."

"Follow Du'Voire's group. Keep eyes on them. Report any changes directly to command."

"Yes sir, understood, sir."

The connection dropped.

"Mr. Agathor," Kathryn said. "Do you have soldiers you can trust?"

"Yes, sir. Sergeant Royer and Sergeant Faber. Their teams would be more than happy to take back engineering."

The anger lacing his voice was reassuring. Apparently, she wasn't the only one who had a problem with Gideon.

"But they're supporting repairs at the bow, sir."

She didn't need to check the hex sculpt to know they were on the wrong side of the ship.

"They'll never get there in time," Kathryn said.

She turned to the officers on deck.

"Mr. Hurst, Ms. Carter, Ms. Pontifore—select your weapons of choice and come with me to engineering."

"Yes, sir," Avery said, a flicker of excitement in his voice.

"Right away, sir," Rayne added.

Kathryn turned back to Agathor. "Make sure Royer and Faber are aware of the situation. Have their teams meet us in engineering on the double. Advise them they'll most likely be entering a live situation."

Avery moved fast, sinking his hand into a single terminal. A wall panel slid open behind him, revealing the nav deck's compartment. He grabbed short-range repeating crossbows, handing one to Rayne, another to Elvie.

"I should come with you, sir," Karland said.

"I need you here, coordinating." She also wanted someone here who disliked Gideon as much as she did.

A muscle in Karland's jaw twitched, but he nodded. "Yes, sir."

Avery passed Kathryn a repeater crossbow, two magazines, and a short sword with belt. She tied the belt around her waist, clipped the magazines to it, then swung the crossbow strap over her shoulder.

"Let's move."

"Erm, sir…" Senya started.

"I need you to stay here as well," Kathryn cut in, before she had to let the girl down more gently. Senya was the last person she'd want in a fight. "Support Mr. Agathor. Coordinate incoming updates from teams around the ship."

"Yes, it's just that…" Senya shifted on her feet, turning one way, then the other, her arms swaying slightly.

"You'll be fine," Kathryn said. Under different circumstances, she might have given her more reassurance, but time was against them.

She turned to the others. "On me."

They fell in behind her as she strode toward the corridor. The last she saw of the nav deck was Karland relaying orders, his voice sharp and steady, and Senya standing awkwardly at the command terminal, clearly uncertain what to do with herself.

Kathryn wondered if she'd ever been like that: innocent and unsure, a little clumsy. She decided, probably not. Clumsy and unsure were two things her mother had never stood for. They'd gone straight away, if they'd ever existed in the first place.

And innocent? Trying to stay one step ahead of her mother's cruel games had driven that from her long ago.

It had been a long time since she'd wondered what her life would be like if Admiral Hera Laine Thrace hadn't been her mother. But the thought was as useless now as it had ever been. Her life was what it was. And right now, her life meant relieving her First Officer from duty.

As the lift doors sealed shut and the chamber dropped, Kathryn spoke. "You understand that you may need to engage against fellow sailors." She made it a statement, not a question.

Avery activated his crossbow's gyre cartridge. The cylinder hissed as it began to smoke faintly. "Mutineers, sir."

Rayne nodded, her jaw set. "Lieutenant Hurst is right. They stopped being fellow sailors the moment they turned against the ship."

Kathryn glanced between them. "Some of them may be friends of yours."

Avery didn't hesitate. "Not anymore they're not."

The lift slowed, pivoted into a right-angle section, then shot forward horizontally, carrying them deeper into the ship.

Kathryn turned to Elvie. There was a nervousness in the woman's eyes, maybe lingering battle shock, or the idea of fighting her own crew.

"Gideon was always a piece of work," Elvie said, lifting her chin a notch higher, as if she could will away the hesitation in her voice.

The others chuckled.

"Ain't that the truth," Rayne muttered.

Kathryn kept her tone even. "Follow my lead. Open fire only if I do. But until the other teams arrive, they outnumber us. We might not get the luxury of offering them a way out."

A chorus of yes, sirs. The lift slowed.

"Here we go," Kathryn said, tucking the repeater into her shoulder, ready to bring it to her eye line.

"We've got a straight corridor ahead," Avery said. "Then a doorway into an antechamber. Another set of doors beyond that. Engineering's past them."

"Fan out the moment we hit the corridor," Kathryn said. "Use bulkheads for cover."

Another round of yes, sirs.

The lift doors slid open, and Kathryn was already moving. She rushed out, pressing against the nearest bulkhead before the doors had even finished retracting. Her heart pounded as she swept the corridor.

It was empty.

She pushed forward, repeater raised, eyes locked on the door ahead. The others followed, steps tight, controlled.

"Elvie, get the door," Kathryn ordered.

Elvie moved to the terminal. Avery and Rayne fell in behind her, forming a stacked line, Avery's hand firm on her shoulder. Kathryn's pulse kicked up a notch.

She wished they'd had time to stop at the ship's armoury. Advancing with a shield would've been a hell of a lot better than going in exposed.

"Opening," Elvie said.

The door slid aside, and Kathryn was moving before it was even two-thirds open. They entered a large antechamber, easily the size of two Vault-class landers. Overhead, a vaulted ceiling split down the centre by a gyre channel bathed the space in dim blue light.

Two side doors led to different engineering halls. The double doors ahead led to main engineering.

Kathryn didn't like how quiet it was. She didn't like how open it was. If she was being honest, there wasn't much about the situation she did like.

She moved fast, crossing the chamber as the others fanned out. Elvie stepped up to the terminal again.

Kathryn wanted to tell her to check in with Karland, to get an update on the other two teams, to find out if Urilla had eyes on Gideon. But they were too exposed, too vulnerable. They needed cover, and now.

The thoughts raised the hairs on the back of her neck. Every instinct screamed at her not to glance at the doorways flanking the chamber.

Change position. Keep moving. Never let the enemy back you into a corner. Never let them pin you down.

Her pulse hammered now. Her mind honed in on the present. She wasn't sure if those were her mother's words or her own.

She nodded at Elvie. The doors parted, and they rushed forward.

The *Vanguard's* main engineering deck was vast, an octagonal chamber easily twice the size of an epistolar hall. Eight towering bronzite pillars formed an open ring in the centre, framing the heart of the room: a massive bronzite sphere, floating mid-air, five feet across. It spun in place, a low whir vibrating through the deck. Gyre channels split its surface and cast a rippling blue shimmer across the floor and walls.

Terminals lined the perimeter, some built for single users, others wide enough for multiple operators. A staircase ran along two of the chamber's faces, leading to an upper landing that overlooked the lower level. Directly opposite was another set of double doors.

And no one was there.

Kathryn moved on instinct, darting left toward the cover of the terminals. The others followed, fanning out, crossbows trained upward, sweeping the landing for movement.

Her mind worked fast. *They're gone. They knew we were coming. They're hitting another part of the ship.*

Then her knee buckled.

There was a wet sound, slick and sudden, like she'd stepped in something. Her shin slammed into the edge of a terminal. Pain exploded up her leg, sharp and sickening. She clenched her jaw, forcing down the instinct to hiss through her teeth.

"Captain," Avery said, catching her under the arm and hauling her upright.

Kathryn looked down. A boot-sized skid cut through a pool of blood. Across the wall ahead, red splatter fanned outward in sharp, chaotic arcs. More of it coated a nearby terminal, pooling thick at the base of one of the bronzite pillars.

"We're too late," Elvie said.

She stood between Avery and Rayne, watching as Avery steadied Kathryn, but Elvie's eyes kept drifting, to the blood, to the pillar, to the floor.

She didn't see the bolt come crashing down from above.

A *twang, click*, and a split second later it punched clean through her temple. The force snapped her sideways.

Seeing her head twisted, eyes still wide with shock, hit Kathryn like a body blow. Then guilt surged up, hot and bitter. She'd brought Elvie here. She'd given the order. And Elvie had died because Kathryn had been stupid enough to give Gideon the benefit of the doubt, because Kathryn hadn't wanted to be like her mother. The senselessness of it made her vision blur with rage. The emotion lasted a fraction of a second.

"Down!" she shouted, even before Elvie's body hit the floor.

She dropped to her knees, shins landing in the blood. Avery and Rayne hit the deck behind their terminals, Rayne cursing under her breath.

"There's only two up there," Avery said.

Then the doors behind them slid open. At the same time, the doors to the right also shot open.

Five officers stepped through, crossbows raised, led by Gideon. Another five emerged from the opposite chamber door. Above them, the two on the landing moved in, weapons trained down at them. They were surrounded and outnumbered.

"Drop them!" Gideon barked. "Do it now!"

"Captain?" Rayne's voice was tight with anger.

Kathryn exhaled, a flash of shame burning her chest. Every fibre of her being wanted to fight, to punish Gideon for his betrayal. But she couldn't risk losing more lives. She couldn't risk making more mistakes.

"Drop your weapons," she said bitterly. "There's too many."

A second of silence was followed by crossbows hitting the deck.

"Come out," Gideon said. "Slowly."

Kathryn stepped from behind the terminal, moving onto the open decking in front of the pillars and the whirring engine core. The vibrations from the bronzite sphere hummed beneath her boots in a steady, mechanical pulse.

She stopped in front of Gideon, chin high, shoulders squared. Her First Officer studied them with quiet scrutiny, not gloating, not pleased, just calculating. He looked at them the way an enginator might look at a hex schematic, weighing inputs and outputs, checking for flaws. It was as if they were nothing more than an equation in the grand plan of Gideon Du'Voire. It made Kathryn want to drive her fist into his jaw.

"You traitorous little bitch," Rayne spat.

For a fraction of a second, Kathryn assumed she meant Gideon. Then she saw where Rayne's glare was aimed. It wasn't at Gideon, but at the young woman standing just behind him.

"Urilla?" Avery said, his voice dry with disbelief.

Urilla Gosse had mousy brown hair, soft brown eyes, and a face that barely looked twenty. Kathryn had been outsmarted by a girl who couldn't be six months out of Navarch training. The sneering laughter echoing around her skull could have been Kathryn's, or it could have been her mother's.

"What have you done with the rest of engineering?" Kathryn asked.

Gideon's bookish features twisted into something almost pained.

"Those who didn't resist are unharmed," he said.

Kathryn felt a sharp spike of anger. He couldn't even say it outright, couldn't bring himself to admit he'd killed his own crew. He just danced around it, dressing it up in polite phrasing.

"What in the abyss were you thinking?" Rayne snapped, her glare still locked on Urilla. "You think the King's going to let you off when he finds out you killed your own? Mutineers are put to the sword."

Something flickered in Urilla's eyes, real fear, cutting through the bravado. She went from looking twenty to looking fifteen in the space of a breath. And like most children, she covered the mistake with anger.

"We're going to Thendergaarden," Urilla said, her voice high with defiance. She sounded like a spoiled child. "They'll pardon us. They'll put you to the sword."

That was too much for Rayne. She lunged for Urilla, fist drawn back, ready to drive it straight through her smug little face. But Gideon moved faster than Kathryn would have given him credit for, stepping in to block the blow.

Then—

Three sharp twangs and clicks.

Three soft thuds.

Rayne grunted, her momentum vanishing as she staggered into Gideon's arms. Three bolts jutted from her back, two in the shoulder blades, one buried deep in the base of her neck.

"No!"

Kathryn wasn't sure if she shouted or just roared some half-formed battle cry tearing from her throat.

Instinct took over. Her hand found the hilt of her sword, yanking it free in a smooth, vicious motion.

She had known Elvie and Rayne for less than an hour. It didn't matter. In that time, they had accepted her as their Captain, followed her into battle, and trusted her. And Gideon Du'Voire, the bookish little shit who looked like he belonged scolding people in a library, had taken that from her. That it was her fault for not relieving him of duty earlier only turned her anger into something sharp and blinding.

Animal instinct took over, and she was only faintly aware she intended to kill her First Officer.

Whether she did or not, she didn't know.

White-hot pain exploded at the back of her skull. Her vision cracked, distorted, then went completely black.

Her last thought was of losing her balance, anticipating the way her knees would slam into the deck, and the sharp jolt of pain she should have felt when she hit the floor.

But the pain never came.

Twenty-Six
Brazier

They stood on the crumbling pier, its surface a patchwork of cracked, greying alloy, half-consumed by a web of tree roots that had forced their way through the ruin. The ground beneath Brazier's boots felt unsteady, worn thin by time and neglect.

Above them, midnight reigned, but behind the canopy of trees that strangled the city, the sky stretched empty and starless.

The canal ran straight through more ruins, vanishing into a dense fog that curled over the broken landscape. It thickened into an opaque wall of white, swallowing what remained of the Formarian city beyond. Clinging to the rubble and licking at the surface of the water in slow, shifting motions, Brazier thought the fog looked like a wall of wraiths waiting at death's threshold.

He wasn't a spell caster but he knew sorcery when he saw it, and this was sorcery. If he had to guess, whatever power had obliterated this place had also torn a hole through reality itself, creating the breach into the Immuratum.

And from within that sorcerous fog, a shape moved.

The ferry emerged, its outline materialising from the white expanse like a memory bleeding into the present. It was large, wooden, and capable of holding around twenty people. Brazier didn't know much about ocean vessels, but it looked like the kind of ship that needed a mast and sails

Yet it had neither.

Instead, a single figure moved it forward. The ferryman was a humanoid thing, at least seven feet tall and draped in a black, tattered shirt and trousers. It rowed with a single oar, the motion slow, methodical. The fabric of its clothes hung loose, revealing glimpses of pink flesh.

And as the boat drew closer, Brazier saw the ferryman's face, or rather, the lack of one.

Where eyes and a nose should have been, there was nothing but a flap of stitched skin, ragged and uneven. The crude sutures ran in a bloody rim from its forehead, across its temples, and down to where its lips should have met. But the stitches had pulled too tight, distorting its face, forcing its mouth into a ghastly half-snarl. Beneath the torn lip, its gums were exposed, raw and toothless.

Cold sweat prickled at the back of Brazier's neck. His fingers twitched on the repeater's trigger.

But the ferryman wasn't the only thing sending a chill down his spine. He glanced up at the Handmaid and her 'court,' standing along the pier's edge, motionless and watching.

Matthias was gone, left behind in her chambers with Folgar and his squad. And for the first time in a long time, Brazier felt as if he were unanchored.

The four members of the *Anchorite* had always been together. But now, there were only three, and it felt like going into battle with half his armour missing, like he'd forgotten to strap on his greaves.

And while he hated to admit it, of all of them, he had wanted Matthias with him the most.

Freyen and Switch were capable, more than capable. But no matter how bad things got, Matthias had a way of making light of a situation. Even when his suggestions were questionable and often reckless, somehow, they made the weight bearable. And without him, that weight pressed just a little heavier on Brazier's shoulders.

"Folgar will look after him," Freyen said, offering Brazier a reassuring smile.

Switch grunted in agreement. "And if there's anyone who

can be left alone with an Aeturni and come out the other side, it's Matthias Phaser," she said. Then, with a raised eyebrow, added, "The Lucidian."

"Anyone want to explain what one of those is?" Loraine asked, looking between them.

"Someone with extreme sensitivity to hex reduction," Atlas said. She was looking at the space between them. Her clouded eyes were vacant, but her voice was sharp. "Gives them abilities to command hex in ways most of us can't. Rare in a dwarf."

Switch blinked. "Huh," she said. "Explains why he can do things to the engines even I struggle with."

Vandemir arched a brow at Brazier. "You didn't know about this?"

Brazier shook his head. "Matthias isn't really the sharing type."

The conversation died as the ferry cut through the dark waters, drawing closer. The surface swished softly as the boat slid forward, breaking the canal's stillness. A dull thunk sounded as the hull kissed the pier.

The ferryman stood near the stern, his faceless head turning slowly, stitched skin pulled taut as he faced the Handmaid. She inclined her head toward him, then turned to the group.

"Three suns shine down upon a field of war, a watchtower, and a mountain pass," she intoned. "Through these, you will find the Library. But beware the crippled king, do not steal from the dead, and give no names to infernal kin."

Switch muttered, so only they could hear, "You don't think she could have given us a map instead?"

The ferryman bent over, moving like someone with ancient joints, and lifted a heavy wooden boarding plank. With a dull thud, he dropped it onto the pier and secured it in place.

Brazier placed a foot on the plank, testing its weight. With a deep breath, he stepped forward, crossing onto the ship. The moment his boots touched the deck, the boat shifted beneath him, rocking with the motion. He threw an arm out, steadying himself against the railing. Unlike the underground ships of Formaria, this felt as if it could keel over at any moment.

"You all good there, Cap?" Switch asked.

"Think so," Brazier said, knowing he sounded entirely uncertain. He glanced up at the ferryman, but the faceless figure remained still, unconcerned.

One by one, he helped the others aboard, each of them struggling against the ferry's instability. Some half-sat, half-fell into their seats, eager to be done with the crossing.

"What in the blackest abyss—" Vandemir grunted as he all but collapsed into his seat, arms thrown wide for balance.

Godenforte landed beside him with even less grace, sending the boat lurching. Brazier gripped the side of the vessel as it rocked violently. The ferryman turned on them with a sudden snarl, a wet, guttural sound that raised Brazier's hackles.

"Well, maybe if this thing had been built like a proper ship…" Vandemir muttered.

Once the last of them were aboard, the ferryman yanked in the boarding plank and, without a word, pressed his oar into the water. The boat shuddered as it pushed away from the pier, cutting through the canal's blackened surface. Like Brazier, most of them were gripping something, anything, to steady themselves on the rocking ship.

The ferryman turned the vessel, angling it toward the wall of fog ahead. Brazier cast one final glance over his shoulder. The Handmaid and her court stood motionless on the pier. A gallery of monsters, watching them set sail for hell. Maybe there was irony in that. Brazier wasn't sure. He was too busy holding onto the side of the ship.

They were quickly swallowed by the fog. The only sounds were the rhythmic dip of the oar slicing into the water and the ferryman's ragged, uneven breathing. Brazier sat just in front of him, doing his best not to imagine it breathing down his neck.

If Matthias had been sat next to him, the navigator would've said something right about now. Some joke to break the dread. Something wildly inappropriate and poorly timed that made Switch roll her eyes. But it would've cut through this silence. Without him, sitting beneath the ferryman felt like sitting beneath an executioner and waiting for the axe to swing.

Around them, the fog was so thick he could barely make out the other side of the boat. Shadows of figures shifted in the gloom. Vandemir was too large for the cramped seats, his knees pressing up against his chest, his greatsword sheathed and resting against the hull. Godenforte, Solon, and Bertrand were squeezed beside him.

In front of them, Atlas, Loraine, and Olivier sat rigid, while Switch and Freyen shared the space next to Brazier.

He peered over the side of the boat. The water was barely visible, just three feet of black, inky surface before disappearing into the fog. Then, just as he started to think the mist was thickening, a hazy glow broke through the whiteness.

Brazier looked up.

Three orbs of faint yellow hung in the sky, forming a loose triangle. At first, Brazier thought the fog impaired their light, turning it into a weak, sickly glow. But as the fog thinned, their light remained the same. Eventually, it revealed the canal's edges.

Only it wasn't a canal anymore.

They drifted through a vast river, its waters no longer deep blue but thick and black, moving in a slow current. The ferryman lifted his oar, and when he did, slick droplets slipped from its edge like oil.

The last of the fog peeled away and the Immuratum sprawled before them. The riverbanks stretched outward, leading to a wasteland of barren rock. Jagged hills and craggy outcroppings punctuated the landscape, their surfaces a dead, sickly palette of deep brown and washed-out grey-green.

And overhead, the three suns burned weakly, their orbs different sizes, their light off, as if shining from too far away. They cast a vomit-tinged pallor across the barren wasteland.

Brazier's first thought was nothing could possibly live here.

His gaze moved to Godenforte. The man gripped the cross around his neck. Beside him, Bertrand had lowered his head, his own cross clutched tightly in his grasp, lips moving in a silent prayer. Brazier resisted the urge to do the same.

The boat slowed, the ferryman guiding them toward a short pier of black stone. Unnatural and unfamiliar, its edges were unnervingly sharp, its surface curved and twisted into a distinct wavy pattern. The ferry nudged against it with a dull knock, and the ferryman looked at them. Or at least, he tilted his faceless head down at them.

"Think this would be our stop," Vandemir said, nudging Godenforte.

Along with Bertrand, he gripped the heavy wooden plank at their feet, and slowly, they lifted it and set it over the side of the boat, bridging the gap to the pier.

One by one, they clambered off the ferry, each as unsteady on their feet as they had been getting on.

Brazier went last, his boots landing on the strange black stone with a thud. The moment he stepped onto the pier, the cold realisation they were in another world hit him with a bone-deep fear. What if they never left? He turned to the ferryman, doing his best to inflect his voice with authority.

"You'll wait here for our return," he said.

Rationally, he knew the Handmaid needed them to come back and destroy her former master, making their passage back part of the deal. That did nothing to make him any less anxious though. For a long, agonising moment, the ferryman simply stood there, still as death. Then, slowly, he nodded, his stitched lips pulling into something that might have been a grin. Brazier convinced himself that was a good sign, nodded back, and followed the rest of them off the pier.

Loraine and Olivier had already moved ahead, climbing the short bank leading away from the pier. They followed them up onto the rise. Reaching the top, Switch gave a long, low whistle.

The plain stretched wide before them, endless, barren, and to Brazier's surprise, littered with white stones and shards of bronzite.

Then he looked closer.

They weren't stones or bronzite shards. They were skeletons, sun-bleached and half-buried in the red-brown dirt. The bronzite shards were armour and weapons. It was a battlefield, the scope of which hit him like a blow to the chest.

He looked to his right. The battlefield stretched as far as the eye could see. He turned left, and it still didn't end. The war that had raged here was now a sea of armour and broken bones. And it reached far ahead of them, to a structure built over what looked like a deep, jagged gorge. Reminiscent of the castles of Ravinica and Celmyr, its dark towers loomed over a curved passageway. It was a gatehouse, Brazier realised. But it looked more like some monstrous maw.

This was the watchtower.

To Brazier, who had only fought in the confines of the underground, where strength of numbers could often work against an attacking force, the sheer size of the battlefield before him was breathtaking. This was war on a scale he had only ever read about. It was a war without end. For some reason, he imagined what Matthias would've said about it: probably something clever about dying above ground being overrated. Maybe he still would, if they made it back.

Beyond the fortress, another plain stretched toward a wall of jagged mountains, their peaks sharp and cruel against the dim, sickly sky. Brazier could just make out a pass in the centre of those mountains.

"A field of war, a watchtower, and a mountain pass," Freyen said, a note of awe inflecting her voice. "Just like the Handmaid said."

"And the Library just beyond," Vandemir added. "Let's hope."

"Guess we didn't need that map after all," Switch muttered.

Brazier tightened his grip on his crossbow.

"Stay sharp and move quickly," he warned. "Just because the Handmaid didn't mention fighting any Inferni doesn't mean we won't have to."

With that, he started down the bank, boots crunching against the loose earth.

On the plains there was no wind, no movement, no sound beyond their own footfalls. It was neither hot nor cold. Everything felt lifeless in a way that had little to do with the actual dead strewn around them.

Nearly half an hour into the plains, and after the third time he'd glanced at the horizon, he forced himself to stop. Seeing so much sky meet so much land was disconcerting to a Fromryr. And he knew he wasn't the only one feeling that way. Every now and then, he saw one of them throw a distrustful look into the distance before glancing down, as if what they saw caused a pain behind the eyes. Given the armour and weapons jutting out of the ground, it was probably best to concentrate on what was in front of them. And even that was distracting enough. There was enough bronzite here to rival the wealth of a king.

They pushed deeper into the battlefield, and the remains began forming into mounds, some arrayed in eerie, perfect lines, as if entire ranks had fallen at once.

Among the bones, something caught Brazier's eye, a skeleton still clad in full bronzite armour. For a moment, he thought he recognised it, not the person but the style. It was the same as the soldier he had seen through the Kikkora's time-warping magic.

"All the remains are human," Freyen observed, walking beside him.

"This must've been before the Fromryr came together," Brazier said, his voice quiet. "These are soldiers of the human Old World."

Freyen nodded. "Yes... but there are no remains of whatever they were fighting."

Brazier tried not to think about what she was implying with that statement.

"Maybe demons collect their dead," he muttered, trying to sound offhanded. But Freyen cast him a look that told him she didn't buy that one bit.

Regardless of who, or what, had done the killing, those who had fought here had almost certainly been trying to reach the watchtower, and the Library. Had the humans' ancient ancestors been seeking the same knowledge they were? The same means of destroying a being that had plagued their world? It would mean a feud spanning millennia. And one that had not yet ended. And one they were now playing a part in. For some reason that made him feel hollow and insignificant, like a grain of sand on a beach that could be blown away at any moment. Had this story played out before? Would it play out countless times after he'd died? Brazier was so lost in thought, he barely heard Vandemir call out. Freyen nudged his arm, and he turned to see the Captain lingering at the rear, naked steel resting on his shoulder.

"My eyes aren't what they used to be," Vandemir called to him. He gestured ahead. "But that looks like a dead man walking."

Brazier followed his gaze.

At first, he saw nothing, just piles of bones and bronzite scattered across red-brown dirt. But then there was movement. A vague shape appeared in the distance, a man, or something shaped like one. Brazier caught the bronzite armour. A sword dangled from its grip, dragging through the dirt as it shambled forward.

"We've got another one on this side," Atlas called.

Brazier turned. He saw another, and closer. This one's armour was different, a pleated bronzite skirt and cuirass, its shoulders adorned with turquoise-carved pauldrons.

Brazier's heart began taking additional beats. This one was close enough that he could make out the white bones beneath the bronzite armour. He could see the shins and wrists, the grinning skull and its empty sockets.

"There's two," Switch said, pointing off to the right.

Brazier saw it, a third figure moving in staggered, unnatural steps, as if it were dragging itself forward.

"A fourth," Bertrand called from behind.

Brazier didn't bother looking. His mind had already jumped ahead, his imagination screaming that the whole battlefield was about to rise. His heart had forgotten about rhythm and simply hammered against his chest.

"To the watchtower! Now!" he shouted, waving them forward. "Move!"

"You heard the dwarf!" Vandemir bellowed. "Run!"

They ran, the battlefield a blur as they cut a path through ribcages and shattered skulls.

The only sound was their breathing, their clanking armour, and the scrape of boots on shifting earth.

The watchtower loomed, far in the distance, and Brazier had never wanted to be somewhere as badly as he wanted to be in that eerie, haunting structure.

A yelp rang out behind them.

Brazier spun. Olivier struggled, his foot caught, no, held. A skeletal hand clamped around his ankle, its bony fingers dug into his boot. He hacked at it with his blade, breaking apart its wrist, its hand falling loose, and yet still it crawled toward him.

Coming to his aid, Bertrand raised his war hammer and swung. The hammer struck the skeleton with a sickening crunch, scattering bones into the air.

Next to Brazier, Switch loosed a volley, bolts thudding into another armoured skeleton, slamming into its chest, its limbs, then its skull, before it crumbled into pieces.

"Keep moving!" Brazier shouted, forcing himself to ignore the clouds of dust rising around them.

They ran again, the watchtower's gatehouse rising ahead of them, one hundred feet, seventy-five, fifty, and hope flared in Brazier's chest. The gatehouse was open. They were going to make it.

But he could see the dust clouds in the corners of his eyes now. A low rumble rose, merging with the blood pumping in his ears. He thought something might have screamed in anger, something animal, something that lacked vocal cords.

Freyen and Brazier reached the towers first and spun, crossbows levelled.

The sight was horrifying. The battlefield had awoken. A skeletal horde, armed and armoured in bronzite, rose in waves, the clatter of their emergence kicking up so much dust a brown haze had settled beneath the skyline. It created a thick, musty smell, like old parchment.

They fired, bolt after bolt, smashing through skulls, blasting apart limbs, but where one skeleton fell, another stepped into its place.

"Inside!" Brazier yelled between shots.

Loraine, Atlas, Olivier darted beneath the gatehouse. Solon and Bertrand were right behind.

Vandemir shouted something as he ran, but Brazier couldn't hear him over the clack of his crossbow and the roar of the horde.

He shouted again, pointing inside the passageway. But Brazier was too busy firing at the skeletons throwing themselves at the two men.

"The terminal, damn you!" Vandemir shouted, as they both reached the gatehouse.

Brazier and Freyen dashed in after them, firing as they moved. Then came a wet suction sound, something like joints popping and gears shifting into place, and a grate came crashing down. Its teeth slammed into the earth, sealing them inside. A second later, the skeletal horde collided with it. The impact sent bone fragments flying, dirt and dust exploding through the gaps. Brazier and Freyen threw up their arms, shielding their faces as jagged bits of skeletons clattered through the grating.

Brazier tried to shout for Freyen but inhaled a lungful of dust. It hit the back of his throat like hot ash, burning as he collapsed into a fit of coughing. He reached out blindly, his fingers scraping against Freyen's cuirass. He latched on and pulled her close, dragging her into the passage with him, both of them hacking and choking.

His eyes burned, his vision blurred with tears. Snot dripped into his beard, and he wiped it away with a grimy sleeve, blinking hard to clear his sight. He turned, tried to find Vandemir and Godenforte, but his eyes streamed. He tried to call Vandemir's name, but all that came out was a dry, rattling wheeze, sending him into another coughing fit.

Then a firm grip latched onto his arm, pulling him upright.

"We've got you," Vandemir said, his rolling Harothellian accent steady and grounding.

Through the haze, he saw Freyen being helped to her feet, Godenforte bracing her with an arm. To Brazier's dust-blurred vision, the man just looked like a solid slab of maroon.

They were half-guided, half-dragged up a set of steps, the world shifting around them as their boots scuffed stone. Then he saw flat ground, air and open sky. The hand released him, and he heard a wet heave. Then came another, and something splattered against the floor beside Brazier.

"You all good, Captain?" Bertrand asked.

Vandemir wiped his mouth and spat. "Don't think their terminals agree with the Fromryian constitution."

"You don't say," Loraine muttered.

Brazier's vision began to sharpen little by little. He blinked rapidly, taking in his surroundings. Battlements stretched ahead, a tower loomed to one side, and two smaller ones rose nearby. In the distance, the silhouette of mountains rose, dark and distant.

"Here," Atlas said, her voice close.

The navigator tipped a flask over Brazier's face, water pouring over his burning eyes. Brazier forced himself to keep them open, letting the cool liquid wash away the dust. Beside him, Switch did the same for Freyen.

Brazier wiped at his face, blinking rapidly. His vision cleared, revealing the space around them. An oval courtyard, perched high above the battlefield, overlooking the endless plains, the skeletal horde, and the dark winding river beyond. But it was the structure itself that drew Brazier's attention.

The entire watchtower was forged from the same dark alloy as the pier, its design a strange, shifting blend of architecture and anatomy. The walls curved unnaturally, their edges merging into the floor with the eerie likeness of ribcages fused together.

The buttresses stretched out in exoskeletal formations, their spines arching like the segmented legs of some long-dead creature. Above them, the arches twisted, curling into petrified tendrils, as if frozen mid-motion. It was all vaguely Formarian in style, but fluid, too fluid. And Brazier had the sudden notion they were standing on something that was still alive.

"Making your skin crawl too, Cap?" Switch asked, taking

a slow swig from her flask.

"Not exactly my style," Brazier muttered.

He wanted to get through this place as fast as possible, and it wasn't just the architecture. The sound of the horde outside had risen to a dull, grinding cacophony. Sooner or later, they'd find a way in.

"Have we found a way through?"

"This way," Loraine called. "There's a bridge on the other side."

A set of steps led downward through an open gatehouse, vanishing into another courtyard. Brazier didn't question. He didn't ask for more details. He just moved.

"Let's go," he said, and the group followed Loraine down the steps and into the unknown.

The second courtyard was larger than the first. An oval expanse, surrounded by towering walls of the same dark alloy. Three massive double portals lined the space, one on either side, another straight ahead.

The whole courtyard was lined with statues.

They stood scattered and poised, warriors locked in combat stances, many frozen mid-strike. The figures were clad in the same dark-green, organic alloy as the watchtower, their armour moulded into sleek, unnatural curves. There was no pattern to their positioning, no symmetry. They were warriors locked in place, as if they had been stopped mid-battle and left to stand for eternity. Only when Brazier passed within two feet of one did cold realisation dawn.

These weren't statues.

They were people fused or embalmed somehow; Brazier didn't know. But every single one of them wore the same armour as the skeletons outside. Every single one had been caught in some kind of martial strike. A chill crawled up his spine.

"Their faces," Freyen whispered.

Something in her tone made Brazier look up. His stomach turned. The warrior closest to him had a mask of horror etched into its face. Its eye sockets were too large. Its mouth gaped open far too wide, stretched beyond what the human jaw should have allowed. It was a scream, trapped in time.

Then it moved.

The thing turned, its twisted, frozen face locking onto Brazier. The horror, disgust, and revulsion lasted only a second and instinct took over. Brazier's arms worked automatically, lifting his repeater, his fingers squeezing the trigger. A single bolt left the crossbow and ended straight in the not-statue's gaping maw. The impact snapped its head backward. It dropped its sword, hands clawing at the bolt buried in its throat. Then it wailed, a wet, ragged shriek, and exploded.

Grey-green gore and dark red blood sprayed across the courtyard. And chaos erupted. Every not-statue in the courtyard moved at once.

"Back-to-back!" Vandemir roared.

They whirled, forming a tight circle in the centre of the courtyard. The things moved inhumanly fast, lunging toward them in erratic, jerking movements.

Brazier didn't bother to aim. He fired, reloaded, fired again. Each bolt slammed into armour, tearing through limbs. An explosion of gore splattered his face. He wiped at his eyes, turned, and saw Vandemir cleave one from shoulder to hip, its body splitting apart in a geyser of dark brown blood.

Solon drove a sword into one's ribs, then buried his second blade through its screaming mouth.

Bertrand swung his war hammer up, catching one mid-lunge, its body exploded against the nearest door in a burst of shattered bone and metal.

And for a moment, a single moment, Brazier thought they were winning. The Rex Populaire tore through them, cutting down two, three, four of the not-statues.

Then he saw Olivier.

The boy was surrounded by two before a third appeared. All of them closed in, forcing him back, blades hacking, cutting him off from the others. He swung his sword desperately, barely deflecting their strikes.

"Vandemir!" Brazier shouted. "Olivier!"

They were converging, drawn to him like scavengers to

a dying animal. But in shifting toward Olivier, they exposed their backs to the Rex Populaire. Steel flashed and crossbows fired. One by one, the not-statues were torn apart, their bodies exploding into thick, black-red gore.

Vandemir and Godenforte reached Olivier in seconds, cutting down the last of his attackers. When the final one fell, crumpling into steaming viscera, a silence hung over the courtyard, broken only by ragged breathing.

Bertrand turned to Olivier.

"They seemed to like you," he said between breaths.

Olivier let out a nervous laugh, plucking a particularly thick piece of gore from his shoulder.

Vandemir exhaled deeply, then paused. His hand lifted to wipe his face, then froze mid-air. A look of dawning realisation spread across his features.

Brazier barely registered it before Vandemir grabbed Olivier by the neckline of his leather armour and yanked him forward until they were nose-to-nose.

"How much did you steal, boy?" Vandemir growled.

Olivier blinked, his voice a note higher. "Steal?"

Vandemir lifted him off his toes. "How. Much?"

Olivier let out another nervous laugh. "Oh, you know… a bit here, a bit there… nothing they'd miss—"

Vandemir's voice rose like a crescendo. "Perhaps it's escaped your notice—" he shook the boy, hard "—but they miss it! You good-for-nothing, abyss-damned fool!"

"Oh, you idiot," Loraine groaned.

Bertrand crossed his arms, scowling.

"Don't steal from the dead."

Vandemir dropped Olivier.

"Give it here."

Chagrined, the boy reached beneath his leather armour and pulled out a sackcloth bundle, handing it over without meeting Vandemir's gaze. The captain peered inside.

"Coins?"

"Pre-Migration bronzite," Olivier muttered. "Worth a fortune, those."

Vandemir shook the bag in Olivier's face. "Is this all?" he demanded. "Is it?"

"Yes, sir," Olivier said quickly. "I swear."

Nearby, Atlas nudged a length of what looked suspiciously like ancient intestine from her boot with the tip of her sword. She grimaced.

"You thinking we give them back, sir?" she asked.

"Not like we've got anything else to try," Vandemir said.

Brazier should've known the Handmaid's words were more than metaphor. In the Immuratum, riddles were rules. He was leading this mission; he should have made sure the rest of them understood that.

"We'll throw them over the battlements," Brazier said, already turning toward the courtyard. He wanted to rectify the mistake as quickly as possible. But before he'd taken three steps, a deep, wet grinding sound rang out. The portal doors on either side of the courtyard shuddered open.

And the not-statues came crashing out.

The first wave dashed into the courtyard without hesitation. Brazier's crossbow was already up and firing before he could think. One exploded, then another, and another. But there were too many.

He instinctively fell back, Switch, Freyen, and Loraine closing in beside him. Their bows and crossbows snapped off shots, each impact sending fragments of metal and gore flying. But the tide kept coming.

More than half veered toward Vandemir's group, cutting them off and dividing them in two. Bertrand, Solon, Olivier, Atlas, and Vandemir fought in a tight retreat toward the steps, blades flashing, boots kicking up dust.

"Go!" Vandemir bellowed, cutting a statue in half at the waist. "Get to the Library!"

Brazier didn't hesitate. "Move!"

He turned, pulling back toward the far doors.

"Loraine!" he cried.

The archer had stopped. She swore, loosed another arrow, her shot punching through a thing's oversized eye socket.

"You can't get to them!" Brazier shouted.

Loraine swore again, but this time she spun and ran after them. They sprinted through the open doorway, down a dimly lit passage, then down another flight of ribcage-like steps. Brazier's breath burned at the back of his throat, but he didn't slow.

The passage opened onto a short walkway, another curved gatehouse, open, leading onto a bridge. A deep, jagged gorge yawned beneath it, as if a god had carved a wound into the land with a colossal blade. And beyond the bridge, the plains, the mountains, and the library.

They ran. The bridge's low walls blurred at their sides as their boots thundered over the stone. And the battle still raged behind them, the distant sounds of metal clashing and bodies breaking.

"Idiot boy," Loraine said as they reached the other side.

No one argued. They were all too out of breath. Freyen's dust-coated hair had matted to her face, and black strands stuck to Switch's forehead where she'd wiped her brow. Brazier ran a hand through his own, breaking through tangled knots and coming away grimy. He nodded at the plain and the mountain pass beyond.

"That's a half-hour run," he said.

"And then some," Loraine muttered.

Brazier exhaled. "Then we'd better get started."

He caught Switch's and Freyen's eyes. *In case giving back the bronzite doesn't work.* The words hung between them, unspoken. What they would do if it didn't work, Brazier didn't know. He'd have to cross that bridge if they came to it.

"Come on," he said, breaking into a jog.

They ran in silence.

Sweat soaked through Brazier's gambeson, the heat trapped beneath layers of plate and cloth. Every few minutes, he glanced over his shoulder, checking the bridge, the battlements, watching for the first sign of pursuit. But no shapes crossed the bridge. No shadows moved on the walls. Whatever had happened to the Rex Populaire, it seemed the skeletal horde wasn't chasing them, yet.

The mountains loomed ahead, jagged faces rising sharply from the plains, sheer rock cutting against the sky. Flatland vanished in an instant, replaced by sheer cliffs and a passage.

Initially wide enough for thirty soldiers to march shoulder to shoulder, it soon narrowed into a thin ravine flanked by craggy walls.

Brazier slowed as they neared the entrance, glancing back at the watchtower one last time, shielding his eyes from the pale, weak suns. Nothing moved. But they were too far now to see clearly.

They took a moment, just enough to catch their breath, passing around water from their skins. Then they pressed on. The ravine narrowed fast, twisting through sharp rock formations, jagged crags jutting from the walls, the path barely wide enough for a small lander to squeeze through. They wound through several sharp turns, the walls closing in, forcing them into single file.

Then the passage opened onto a wide expanse. Towering cliffs and shattered crags surrounded them, a natural fortress of stone. And in the centre of it all, the Library of the Nine.

Like the watchtower, it was all wrong. Forged from the same dark, organic-metal alloy, the structure was massive, built into a perfect circle, its body formed from nine distinct towers. Each one was flat-topped, oval-shaped, and lined with exoskeletal protrusions that made them seem alive.

At its base, the Library's entrance comprised two double doors seamlessly fused into the walls. And at their centre, there was a node.

It was placed just as it would be in a Formarian installation. But instead of hex reduction, the node seemed to contain a pit of raw flesh. It was red and slick, like the exposed muscle of a limb stripped of its skin.

They approached the doors, two massive, curved slabs of dark, organic metal.

"Anyone else notice everything here looks like something the Formarians made, only twisted into the demonic version?" Switch said.

"Fairly sure we've all noticed," Freyen said.

"Who cares who made the damn place," Loraine said. "Let's get this done."

She stepped forward, exhaled sharply, then pressed her palm into the fleshy pit. Her face contorted instantly, lips curling in revulsion. Her eyelids fluttered as if giving a hex command. Then, just as suddenly, she pulled away.

Brazier heard a *thunk*. The doors split apart, grinding as they slid into the walls.

Loraine shook her head, flexing her fingers. "You'd think they'd have better defences for all this ancient knowledge."

"Because the legion of skeletons wasn't enough?" Switch said.

"I meant for in—"

Loraine's words cut off. She jerked forward, clutching her stomach, then vomited. It splattered across the threshold.

Freyen stepped forward, a hand on her shoulder, but Loraine shoved her off, spitting. She wiped a string of saliva from her chin.

"I'm fine," she said hoarsely. "Guess I spoke too soon."

She swallowed, took a deep breath. "I'm good."

Brazier wasn't convinced, but she straightened and stepped into the library.

Inside, the air changed almost immediately. Gone was the arid stillness of the wasteland. The air here was moist and clammy.

The floor beneath them was solid but forged into vine-like patterns spiralling outward from the centre. Brazier's mind kept trying to equate it to something living, his imagination comparing it to splayed-out tendons. He ground his teeth and focused on looking straight ahead instead.

They moved cautiously as they followed the corridor's curve. The walls were exoskeletal, rib-like, and arched overhead, seamlessly merging into the ceiling. And a dull grey-green pallor filled the space, a low glow with no apparent source, as if the walls themselves leaked light.

Then came a bend in the corridor, and the light changed, becoming whiter, stronger. And with it came a low and continuous moaning.

The sound wasn't loud. It wasn't frantic. It was continuous, and devoid of life. Then the smell hit them: rot and decay, and something like prolonged death, mixing sweat and damp mould.

Weapons raised, they stepped forward.

The corridor opened into an oval-shaped chamber. At either end, a large circular portal gaped, leading into unseen passages. Around the chamber's perimeter, pillars lined the space, each holding an orb that emitted the strange, unnatural white light. And beneath them, Brazier saw what was making the moaning.

It came from alcoves, each lined with a person. The figures were pressed against the walls, arms outstretched, wrists locked in shackles above their heads. Their skin was wrong, grey, blackened, and decayed. But still they moved, twitching and shivering as if still alive. The stench thickened, heavy and cloying. But it wasn't the smell that made Brazier's stomach churn. It was their backs.

Their ribcages had been split open, their lungs removed. But they weren't discarded. They were flayed, sliced into thin, even sections, and laid across their exposed spines, spread out like the pages of a book. Brazier's breath locked in his throat, and anger boiled somewhere beneath his sternum.

Then he caught movement from the ceiling: a limb, long and pale grey-green, its surface rippling like tendons beneath skin. It was an elongated arm, bent at the elbow, a hand at the end.

It drifted downward, spindly fingers brushing across one of the prisoners' backs, turning the layers of lung like someone leafing through parchment. The person twitched, a full-body spasm. Their moan hitched, and Brazier gripped his crossbow so hard his fingers were going numb.

Then he saw another figure, standing in front of one of the prisoners. It was a man, or something shaped like one. He was draped in tattered red robes, the fabric frayed at the edges, black grime crusting the hem. Bent at the waist, he appeared to be studying the flayed lungs, his head moving in slow, deliberate nods.

Stories of the hell that was the Immuratum were told throughout Formaria. But none of them came close to capturing the pain, humiliation, and torment that Brazier saw before him.

For one brief moment, he forgot about the mission. He

forgot about Duessa and the Rex Populaire, and imagined burning everything here to the ground.

"What in the starless black void are we looking at?" Loraine whispered.

The figure heard her.

It didn't turn or shift its stance. Only its head rotated toward them.

Staring at its face, Brazier almost forgot to breathe. Pasty white skin clung too tightly to its skull, stretching thin around a mouth that was too wide. The lips were grey-green, the colour of rotting flesh. Its eyes were sunken, hollow, and nearly all white, save for the tiny pinprick pupils that twitched between them.

And hanging over its tattered robes was a cross turned upside-down. Brazier didn't know why, but that detail horrified him most of all.

You're here to do a job, he told himself. *You're here to destroy Duessa. Formaria is counting on you.*

Then the thing smiled.

"Welcome, friends," the demon said. Its voice was high-pitched, like a child's. But the words stretched, the tone unnatural, as if a child's body were inhabited by something much older.

"The Library requires names," it said. "What are yours?"

"No names," Brazier said quickly, his voice sharp and meant for the others. "Under any circumstances."

The demon's head twitched. Its empty gaze darted between them, lips pulling back, stretching its too-wide grin.

"The Library knows my name, and so I may use it," it said. "It is Belboran Ha'Korvar. What are yours?"

"I am itching to kill this thing," Loraine muttered.

"Me too," Switch said.

Brazier felt the same. Every muscle in his body screamed to act, to erase the thing standing before them. But he forced himself to focus.

"We aren't attacking unless it attacks us," he said, keeping his crossbow lowered. "We need to find the book."

The demon's smile stretched further, splitting the corners of its mouth.

"All these books can be yours," the demon crooned. "If you tell me your names."

"We're not here to share names," Brazier said. "We're here to find the book that tells us how to kill a Lord of the Eternal Hunt."

The demon grinned. Its lips parted, curling too far up its face, revealing row upon row of yellowed, needle-thin fangs sprouting from blackened gums.

"To take, you must give," it said. "Only answers can provide answers."

Brazier felt his jaw tighten.

"Give what?"

"Answers," the demon said. "To the riddle."

Out of the corner of his eye, Brazier saw Switch shift her stance, an almost imperceptible movement that brought her crossbow snug into her shoulder.

"Say the word, Cap," she murmured. "And I will pin this thing to the nearest wall."

She had no idea how much Brazier wanted to give that order. But they needed the book.

"If we answer your riddle," Brazier said slowly, "you'll give us the book?"

"If you answer correctly," the demon purred.

"And if we get it wrong?"

The thing giggled a high, wet, child's laugh.

"You become a book."

A cold weight settled in Brazier's chest. Stories of the Immuratum said demons could bind a person to their will through verbal contracts. He had no idea if it was true, mainly because he'd never paid attention, because he never expected to need to. He suddenly wished he had asked the Handmaid a lot more questions about the Library.

"You know what they say about demons," Freyen said to him. Her eyes were wide with concern. "That they can trap you with words."

"That is what I've heard," Brazier said, with a casualness he didn't feel.

He turned to the demon.

"Can we discuss the riddle among ourselves before

giving you the answer?"

The demon twitched. Its mouth drooped, a flash of irritation crossing its grotesque face.

"Discussion is allowed," it said, voice dropping.

Brazier glanced at the others. Severity painted their faces. Tight grips held their weapons. Switch was shaking her head.

"This is a trap," she said.

"Lyander must have managed to outsmart this thing," Brazier said.

"Lyander was an exorcist," Switch snapped back. "It was his job to outsmart things like this."

She wasn't wrong. But short of searching through what could be an endless library, it was the only choice they had. And as much as he'd like to pin this thing to a wall, as Switch had said, he had a feeling it wouldn't be the only defence the Library had.

He turned back to the demon.

"Give us the riddle."

The demon inhaled, long and deep, as if savouring the moment. Then it spoke.

"In the time before our sundered past, there lived a weaver. Not of cloth or precious silks, but of whispers, wonders, and wild things."

It giggled.

"By the glow of hearth and starry night, she spun her threads to dance upon the tongues of those who listened. Each night, she gave life to heroes and villains, love and betrayal. Kingdoms rose and fell at the whims of poems and rhymes. And to those who believed, her tales became as real as the ground beneath their feet."

Its voice shifted, growing deeper and becoming unnatural and guttural.

"But for false gods like her, doubt was her undoing."

Then it snapped back into its childlike tone, light and teasing.

"A single skeptic's gaze could unravel her work. A non-believer could cause her towers to crumble into dust and her legends to fade. Like a mist at dawn."

There was a pause, then the question: "Who was she, this mistress of illusion, this conjurer of dreams? Who was she?"

Brazier turned the lines over in his mind, repeating them like a chant, trying to recall if he'd heard them before. *A weaver, but not of cloth. A maker of wonders and wild things. Kingdoms rose and fell at the whims of poems and rhymes…*

He'd done well enough in his studies. But history had never been his focus. He'd cared more for strategy, warfare, the things that kept people alive. He glanced at the others. Switch shrugged, expression blank. Loraine hadn't taken her eyes off the demon. She looked like she was debating whether to shoot it now or later. But Freyen's brow had furrowed. She absently tucked a dust-covered curl behind her ear.

"Any of you remember your history lessons?" Brazier asked.

Switch gave a dry, mirthless laugh. "Didn't have history lessons."

"Me neither," Loraine said.

"I don't think this is about a specific person," Freyen said, her voice quiet, thoughtful. "Or even a being."

Brazier frowned. "Kingdoms rose and fell at the whims of poems…" He exhaled. "Sounds like something magical to me."

Switch snapped her fingers. "Wait. You're right. Mistress of illusion. Conjurer of dreams… Doesn't this sound like someone we know?"

Brazier blinked. "Err… is this someone we've met?"

Switch rolled her eyes, shook her head, and stepped in close.

"The Queen of Dreams," she whispered.

Brazier felt his stomach tighten.

"That's… worryingly coincidental," he muttered.

Freyen twirled a strand of hair around her finger, her gaze distant.

"Maybe too coincidental," she said.

"It called her a false god," Switch pointed out. "Immurati, Aeturni, they don't like each other, right? Makes sense to call it a false god."

"A single skeptic's gaze could unravel her work," Freyen murmured. "Doesn't sound very god-like to me."

Loraine snapped her fingers. "Wait. What did you say? Just before."

Brazier frowned. "That it's worryingly coincidental?"

"No, no. Before that, the line from the riddle. About kingdoms."

Brazier repeated it. "Kingdoms rose and fell at the whims of poems and rhymes."

Loraine's eyes narrowed.

"Poems and rhymes."

She let the words linger for a moment.

"Those are stories."

Freyen froze, her fingers still mid-curl.

"A storyteller," she said, her voice lighting up with realisation.

"She gives life to heroes and villains."

Brazier scratched at his beard, only to grimace as his fingers came away coated in sticky dust. He wiped them on his gambeson.

"What about the part where the stories become real to believers?"

Freyen shook her head.

"Stories do become real to those who believe them. Not in a literal sense. But this is a riddle."

Brazier felt the pieces slotting into place.

"By the glow of hearth and starry night," Freyen continued. "That's where stories are told. Maybe not for us, underground, but for everyone else."

He found himself nodding. He wasn't sure if it was confidence or desperation, but he was convinced. And more importantly, he trusted Freyen's instincts over his own when it came to something like a riddle.

"Are we in agreement?" he asked.

"It's got my vote," Loraine said.

Switch shrugged. "Sure."

Brazier turned to the demon. His palms were sweaty. His heart fluttered. His eyes flicked to the people in the alcoves, trying not to imagine life as one of them.

"Our answer is storyteller," he said.

The demon twitched.

"Are you sure?" it asked, voice sharp.

There was something petulant about it, like a child denied something it wanted. Then its voice dropped, thick and unnatural. A deeper tone bled into the high-pitched whine.

"What about your other answer? Are you sure you wouldn't like to give that?"

Brazier had to stop himself from physically recoiling at that voice. He was very sure. He was definitely very sure.

"It's storyteller. That's our answer."

The demon snarled. Then it glided toward the terminal. Brazier froze. Its hem barely touched the ground as it moved. There were no steps, no motion of feet, just a smooth drift, like it had never been walking to begin with.

It reached the terminal, touched something Brazier couldn't see, and the portal ahead of them opened. Like a whirlpool, the strange material twisted from the centre, spinning open to reveal another corridor beyond.

The demon didn't turn. It twisted its head, turning without moving its body in another gut-wrenching movement.

"Follow it. To your right," it rasped, voice wet, all pretence of innocence gone. "Into the Chamber of the Six."

Brazier swallowed. Now that the opportunity was here, he wanted out. He wanted through. He wanted gone from the Library as quickly as possible.

"Come on," he said.

Giving the demon a wide berth, one eye on the limb still hanging above them, he moved quickly to the other side of the chamber.

The others followed close behind. Brazier led them as instructed, moving through the oval corridor until they reached a junction.

As directed, they veered right. The dim grey-green glow that suffused the halls shifted. The air grew thicker, heavier, as the hue deepened to pallid amber. Thin, coiling channels ran along the floor, their grooves leading them toward an open expanse, a walkway stretching across a vast oval chamber like a bridge.

A yellow-brown light illuminated the space with no discernible source. It simply was, seeping from the air itself, casting an unnatural glow over what lay beneath them.

Brazier stopped, peering over the edge. Then his stomach turned. Below, embedded in the ground, were pods. They weren't natural or technological, but something in-between. Their walls were formed of a hardened brown sludge, the tops covered in a misty film, as if moisture clung to their surface. And inside them were human forms, face down and motionless. The air reeked: a musky, stagnant stench, layered with urine and something faintly chemical, like cleaning oil masking decay.

Brazier's skin itched. He couldn't decide which was worse, the smell of rotting human, or the unmistakable stench of *growing* human.

Switch eyed the pods, stepping close but not too close, to the railing.

"You think these things…" she started, but she didn't need to finish. They all knew what she meant. These things were grown for books.

"I do," Brazier said, and for the second time in less than ten minutes, he had the overwhelming urge to burn the entire Library to the ground. One glance at Freyen and Loraine told him they felt exactly the same.

At the far end of the walkway, another orifice-like portal loomed.

"Come on," Brazier said, moving toward it.

Then—

A loud thump came from above them.

Brazier's head snapped up. The ceiling, like the rest of the building, was formed from that almost organic exoskeletal material. He swore he had imagined it. Then it happened again. *Thump.*

Freyen tensed. "Captain?"

Thump.

They all turned their eyes upward as a deep, wailing cry rang out somewhere outside the Library. Brazier felt his pulse tick up.

"Skeletons?" Switch asked.

"Or something else," he muttered.

Another thump sounded, this one louder. It was followed by a sound that made his skin crawl: a *crack*.

Not wanting to waste any more time, he crossed the walkway, the others just behind him. The portal split open as they came close, its surface slithering apart. Inside was a smaller chamber, rounded and lit from above by a white-green light that seemed to bleed down the walls. And at the centre were six figures standing in a circle, arms outstretched and completely still.

Their skin was black with rot. Their lungs, carved open and flayed, spread into thin layers along their backs, bound and stacked like the others in the Library. The smell here was so thick and heavy that Brazier, who had been trying not to notice it, felt the urge to retch.

Another *crack* came from above the walkway. Then a sound like something clawing against rock. Something was trying to get inside. Brazier turned sharply to the others.

"Switch, take those two," he ordered, pointing to the leftmost bodies. "Freyen, take those. I'll take these. Loraine, watch the entrance."

Loraine gave a sharp nod, knocking an arrow in her bow and turning toward the walkway behind them.

"Tell me they're dead," Switch muttered.

Brazier didn't even pause.

"They're dead."

He had no idea if that was true. He decided he wasn't going to think about it.

"They're very dead."

They moved quickly. The pages, or skin, rather, were covered in text. Words had been carved into the flesh, forming a script he hadn't seen in years. It was an obscure Old World tongue. He felt himself frown. Growing up, Brazier had a tutor, an aging gnome with a severe crook in his back and hair so white that Brazier's ten-year-old brain had imagined it would one day turn completely translucent. The gnome had also been endlessly patient, which was lucky, because Brazier had been a terrible student. But for children of high-ranking officials, learning Old World languages was a completely useless and absolutely necessary status symbol. He'd scraped by in his tests. And now, leaning over the lung-page, he could make out just enough words to make sense of it all. Switch, however, wasn't so lucky.

"It's in some kind of demon language," she said, making a sound of disgust. "I can't read a word."

Freyen wasn't faring much better.

"I think it's Old World… but I can't read it either."

Brazier kept his eyes scanning the text.

"Look for the word Regina. It means Queen."

More thumps sounded from above, followed by scrabbling and scratching. Brazier did his best to ignore them. He scanned the lung-page in front of him. Words leapt out: Dominus Immortalis, Pater Magnificus. They were useless. He flicked the page over.

"Here," Freyen said, motioning him over.

She pointed at a line of text. It read: Regina Insaniae. Brazier translated it to The Mad Queen. Freyen pinched the edge of the leathery skin, peeling it back carefully. On the opposite page there was a drawing of a woman in flowing green silk robes, trimmed with gold thread. Her skin was alabaster-smooth and her lips painted red. She was beautiful except for her eyes, which were pools of fire. Beneath her name was the inscription: Duessa.

A crack split the air behind them, louder than before. They whirled as a grey-green shape fell from the ceiling, crashing onto the walkway below. The half-skeleton, half-statue sprung to its feet, snapped its head toward them and screamed.

Loraine's arrow punched through its mouth, cutting off the shriek, and the creature exploded, raining down shards of blackened bone and gore.

"Switch," Brazier said.

"On it, Cap."

She moved, stepping to Loraine's side, repeater raised. Brazier and Freyen turned back to the lung-pages. There was another thud, more screams, something else crashed onto the walkway behind them. Brazier forced himself to focus. His finger dragged down the text, his mind filtering words as quickly as he could process them: hypocrisy, falsehood, jealousy. He flicked to another page.

"The Mad Queen leads those astray…" he read aloud, part of his mind surprised at how easily the translation came to him. Then another: "She disguised herself as a princess in distress to lead the false idol into imprisonment…"

There were more shrieks and explosions of gore. Switch's repeater fired nonstop now. Brazier ignored it. He read faster.

"Disguises herself as a beautiful elf of nobility, but hides her true hideous form. And that of her handmaids."

The next page, half-smudged with black rot—

"…weaves illusions to manipulate perception…"

Another crash rang behind them, followed by another guttural scream. Brazier wiped the sweat from his brow, ignored the stench, and flipped another page. And then, a single line stopped him cold: her tales come true.

"Her tales come true," he muttered, scanning lower. "…woven through belief and deception…"

His heart kicked harder.

"The Queen of Dreams rises and falls upon her listeners' hearts…"

He read it again. He wasn't misreading it.

"Rises and falls upon her listeners' hearts," he repeated aloud. It was correct.

A word jumped out at him: Harbingers. Then a few lines down: "Messengers of her deception… she grows stronger with the spread of their lies… her power accumulates…"

"That's exactly what Kathryn said…" Freyen whispered. "About the source growing stronger with the harbingers."

Brazier turned another page, half-aware of the battle behind them, half-aware of the growing urgency curling through his gut.

As one lie is believed, another is created... Her tale built upon a web of lies... With belief, illusions become reality... Once fully believed by all, the tale is true. The sorcery cannot be undone... it is permanent...

Then he read a line that sent hot excitement shooting up from his belly: belief is her making, doubt is her undoing.

Loraine cursed.

"There's more getting through!" she shouted.

Brazier flipped to the next page, and found it: her destruction woven through her followers' doubt. A paragraph below, he read: Praenuntia Primus. *The First Harbinger. The Herald. Through their unbelief, her destruction is assured. But not all threads may be unspun, only those borne of the entwined harbinger crop may be undone.*

Brazier read it aloud: "The First Harbinger. It is through the unbelief of the First Harbinger that her destruction is assured."

He continued reading, translating aloud: "If the First Harbinger is slain, the sorcery remains until the second can be found, and made to disbelieve the lie."

Freyen's eyes widened.

"Kathryn," she said, voice half a whisper, as if she couldn't believe it.

Brazier frowned.

"She knows where the First Harbinger is?"

Freyen grabbed his gambeson, yanked him to face her.

"It is Kathryn."

He stared.

"What?"

She raked her fingers through her hair, speaking fast.

"It's Kathryn," she repeated. "She's the First Harbinger."

And suddenly it clicked. A horrible sense of realisation settled into his bones. Freyen pressed forward, voice urgent.

"She was captured a year ago by the Sorel Tan. Before all of this began. She told everyone about the ships, that's why she lost her position. But no one believed her at the time."

"Which is why the ships didn't appear then," Brazier said.

"And the First Harbinger escaped," Freyen said quickly.

Her eyes were sharp now. He could see her thoughts racing.

"That's what Kathryn overheard Isdria say to Gabriel," she said. "But she didn't know they were talking about her."

Brazier's mouth parted in disbelief.

"If Kathryn stops believing the Mirrovinjin ships are real…"

"Then she destroys Duessa."

His thoughts spiralled, every piece of the puzzle falling into place.

"But we told her the ships aren't real," Brazier said, mind working through it even as the urgency pressed down on him. "She knows the Sorel Tan are working with Varkoneth—"

"But she still believes the Mirrovinjin are involved," Freyen interrupted. "That the ships are real. She still believes the lie."

Brazier inhaled sharply. He remembered the fire in Kathryn's voice, the conviction, and her absolute certainty that the ships were real. Having been chased by them twice now, Brazier couldn't blame her. They certainly felt real. But she hadn't been in the throne room. She hadn't heard Varkoneth and Isdria reveal their plans. She had no reason not to believe in the lie. The realisation hit him like a hammer. A sudden clarity of purpose cut through the fear and doubt of the last few hours. The need to move overcame him. His thoughts raced ahead, back through the horrors of the Immuratum and back to the Handmaid and Matthias, and finally to Kathryn. He needed to make her believe the ships weren't real. He needed to break her faith in the lie she'd built for herself.

"We don't know who the second harbinger is, do we?" Brazier said. He'd framed it as a question. But he already knew the answer. Freyen shook her head, expression grim.

"We need to get to Kathryn," he said, his heart pounding. "And quickly."

Twenty-Seven
Kathryn

Kathryn stood behind the command terminal of the Gyre Star *Athelus*, seven members of her deck crew staring at her. They were silent, waiting, and not daring to speak.

The air was thick and charged with the kind of tension that built before a surface storm. And it wasn't just the last three hours of hit-and-run assaults weighing them down.

The hex display showed the *Athelus* holding position several leagues west of Maw Heiron and nearly six leagues north of Xeron Spire. But it didn't matter. Neither landmark appeared on the map. They were too deep, too far down the abyss.

The Gyre Star floated in the heart of a vast cavern complex, buried ten leagues beneath the surface. It was a junction of four secondary tunnels stretching outward, north, south, east, west. A quarter mile below them, tertiary tunnels webbed into the primary passages. A quarter mile above, the same was true. If the hex sculpt had displayed a vertical cross-section instead of an overhead map, it might have looked like the tangled root system of some vast, buried weed. Kathryn knew her brain was just making irrelevant pattern recognitions, trying to distract her, because in all those tunnels, those roots and stems, waited thousands of Mirrovinjin.

And there weren't just warriors.

The enemy possessed drake squadrons, fast enough to

swarm the *Athelus* in seconds. Whole broods of tunnel brawlers had burrowed into the rock and waited to drop from the ceiling onto the ship—just one of them could punch straight through their hull.

And at least fifteen witches hid among the mass: blood maidens, bone seers, and necropolic warlocks. Between them, they had enough magic to shatter the ship's defences, enough raw power to kill every caster aboard the *Athelus* several times over.

Kathryn pulled her gaze from the hex display and met her war caster's eyes. Jeneries Laravmore stood across from her, brown-blond hair damp, flopping over his forehead. His storm-blue caster's robes, identical in shade to their officers' doublets, were dark with sweat. They'd gone through the academy together. He was her age and from a minor house with ties to House Guildain. He had never held it against her that she wasn't highborn. They had become friends in spite of their different upbringings, perhaps even because of them.

Right now, her friend looked afraid. Maybe he saw the same fear in her, the same confusion. They both knew none of this made sense.

They had already fought off two Mirrovinjin war hosts. There had been hundreds of warriors, an ambush that should have been their breaking point. Yet they'd survived. They'd thrown the enemy back. And yet here it was, a third war host, larger than any she had seen before. It was the kind of force deployed to take installations, to storm cities, to break battalions. It wasn't meant to ambush a single Gyre Star.

And yet they were here, surrounding them.

"Incoming communication," Askel said.

Kneeling in the nav pit, his arms were held at sharp right angles in front of him, fingers poised over the hex. His white shirt hung loose over his thin frame, damp with sweat. "It's them."

"On the hex," Kathryn said. Her voice was steady. She hadn't given in to fear yet. She wouldn't give in to fear.

"Translator protocol activated," Askel confirmed.

A voice erupted from one of the hex wells, wet, raking, and filled with clipped vowels and a guttural sharpness that sent a pulse of hatred burning through her. It was instinctive and primal, a thousand years of war between their species baked into their nature, a hatred refined through centuries of bloodshed.

"I am T'lak Shan-Kar," the voice rasped through the hex. "Lictor General of the war host Ban-Al-Karvoc. You are surrounded. Your weapons are depleted. Your gyre reserves are spent. We know this. Our war casters sense it. You cannot win. We will destroy you."

Kathryn's fingers curled against the command terminal. "Then why don't you just get on with it?"

There was a pause, then: "To whom am I speaking?"

"Kathryn Stryker," she said. "Captain of the Gyre Star Athelus. And we will kill thousands of you before you kill us."

The Mirrovinjin made a sound, somewhere between a click and a hiss.

"That will not be necessary," T'lak said. "Further death can be avoided. We propose an exchange. Your life. For theirs."

There was half a heartbeat of silence, then: "Submit yourself to us. Here. Now. And your people leave unharmed."

Kathryn stared at the hex.

The Mirrovinjin didn't bargain with the Fromryr. She couldn't even remember the last time one of their race had spoken to one of the Fromryr. There was no doctrine for this, no precedent, no lesson drilled into her skull from years of training.

Harvore's expression soured, deep lines creasing the bridge of his nose and forehead.

"This is a trap," he murmured, low enough that it wouldn't carry over the hex.

The dwarf stood to the right of the command terminal, arms crossed, the end of his blond-braided beard curling against his wrist. He'd been growing it for a decade and it was still nowhere near his belly button. His daughters teased him for it. They were both eight and twelve. Kathryn had met them, along with Harvore's wife, the first time their mission had taken them back to Thendergaarden. They'd invited her for dinner.

She was thinking about that now because she already missed it, because she knew she'd never have it again.

"We have no choice," Kathryn said, matching his quiet tone. The silence on the nav deck was suffocating. If someone dropped an insignia pin, she'd have heard it hit the deck. Every crew member was holding their breath.

"We can fight," Harvore said.

"And we will die," Kathryn replied.

"The abyss takes us all in the end." His voice was steady, but his eyes pleaded with her. "I say today's as good a day as any."

She almost gave in then, almost. But she had already made her choice.

"I will not throw away the lives of this crew if there's a chance they can be saved," she said. "And I will not be responsible for the loss of a Gyre Star."

The words sounded cold and unfeeling, but they hit home. The Fromryr couldn't build new ships. They couldn't replace what was lost. Their martial strength lived in the preservation of the bronzite behemoths, not in their sacrifice. It was a truth hammered into every Fromryian from birth, a fact of life. And right now, that fact was the only thing keeping her upright, making sure she did the right thing.

"T'lak Shan-Kar, I accept your offer," Kathryn said. "My life for that of my crew. I will take a lander and fly down to any location you request. Your forces will retreat from the southern passages, allowing my ship to leave."

"One-fifth mile north of your location," the Mirrovinjin responded.

On the hex sculpt a cluster of filaments pulsed, marking the rendezvous. It was a ledge overhanging one of the secondary tunnels.

"It is agreed."

The connection dropped.

"Kathryn…" Jeneries' voice was quiet, strained.

She turned. The war caster looked like he wanted to vault the command terminal and physically stop her.

"It's done," she said.

She felt calm. She wasn't numb or resigned, just quiet. It was as if the decision had already been made somewhere beyond her, and she was simply following its path.

"Mr. Krask, send a message to the hangar bay. Have a lander prepped and ready to go."

"Yes, sir," Askel said. He didn't even try to hide the sadness in his voice.

Kathryn turned to Harvore. "Mr. Desriden."

Harvore straightened, hands snapping to his sides.

"I hereby relieve myself of command. As second in command of the Athelus, you are now its Captain."

Silence pressed against her. There were things she should say to her crew, things that should have been meaningful, something final. But if she met their eyes, if she opened her mouth, she wasn't sure she'd be able to hold steady. So she didn't. She just nodded once.

"See it home safe," she said. That was all she could manage.

She turned and walked off the nav deck, keeping her eyes forward and trying not to think about what was to come or what she was leaving behind. She focused on the present, on one foot in front of the other, the mission.

In the hangar bay, she passed maintenance and flight crews in navy-blue coveralls. They saluted as she walked by. She saluted back. She didn't meet their eyes.

Chief Petty Officer Galen March jogged up beside her. He had a shaved forehead, a week's worth of beard, and a belly pushing out against the faded maroon coveralls he swore were his lucky uniform. Kathryn would miss the late nights drinking homebrew mushroom whiskey with him and the officers, playing taroti until they were too drunk to hold their cards straight. He wasn't a senior officer, but he'd been in the group for a year. Kathryn was pretty sure it was because he was sleeping with one of them.

"Lander's ready to go, Cap," Galen said.

"Good," she said.

"I didn't get a request for weapons or additional ice reserves."

They passed four landers, each one under repair, and then moved beneath a bronzite repair frame, its mechanical arms idle.

"Won't need any," Kathryn replied.

Galen frowned. "And it's just you, Cap?"

They reached the lander. It hovered above the landing pad, blue gyre light pulsing in rhythmic waves through the octagonal channel. Its hatch door stood open.

"Just me," Kathryn said.

Galen hesitated. "We don't get much information down here, but the word is… we're surrounded."

"Several war bands strong," Kathryn confirmed. "And we're in the middle of it."

Something shifted in Galen's face. It was a quiet, sad acceptance, the kind of look people got when they heard a friend hadn't made it back from battle.

"And now you're going out there on your own?" he asked.

"I am," Kathryn said. Nothing else needed saying. He understood.

Galen exhaled. "Guess I won't have to pay you back for that last game, then."

Kathryn let out a short, surprised laugh. Galen grinned back, but there were tears in his eyes. He straightened and snapped a salute.

"It's been an honour, sir."

She returned it, held it, then let it go. She didn't say anything else. She didn't need to. She turned and climbed into the lander.

Kathryn placed her hands in the hex wells, guiding the lander out of the hangar bay and into the yawning darkness of the tunnel—the stem, as her mind saw it. The location tracker pulsed in the display, a cold beacon pulling her forward.

She felt a soft tap at the base of her skull: a tether request from the *Athelus*. She accepted it as the lander slipped into a secondary tunnel—one of the branching offshoots.

On the tunnel floor below, the Mirrovinjin swarmed. There were so many that, in her mind's eye, they blurred into a single mass. It was an army of shifting grey and white wraiths, rippling like fog across the rock.

The overhang came into view after another hundred feet. It jutted from the tunnel wall, maybe a hundred and fifty feet above the ground. She brought the lander up, easing it into position at the ledge's edge.

"I've reached the agreed location," she said in her mind.

"Acknowledged, Captain," Askel's voice came through. "We're seeing movement in the tunnels behind us."

"The Mirrovinjin are sticking to the deal?" she asked.

"Seems so," Askel said.

"Then so will I."

The silence stretched. Then, finally, Askel said: "Goodbye, Captain. And good luck."

Kathryn didn't answer. She couldn't. Her heart had begun to hammer against her ribs, a deep, heavy beat. The animal in her knew what was coming, knew what pain felt like, knew what death smelled like. It was all she could do to keep it at bay.

She disconnected.

Out on the lip of rock overhanging the tunnel, the world was black. The only light came from the lander's thruster discs, casting long shadows against the stone.

Ahead, a narrow passage wound off to the right. A faint blue glow pulsed from deep within. Behind her, out in the abyss, floated the *Athelus*.

From this distance, it was nothing more than a bronze-gold oval ending in a soft blue glow. It was like the fireflies that dotted the surface, their golden bodies trailing lazy, luminescent light.

It was her first command. She was the youngest officer to captain a Gyre Star in nearly two centuries, a feat that had eclipsed even her mother's early accolades. More than that, it was a feat that had pulled her out from beneath the shadow of Admiral Hera Laine Thrace, so that she was no longer just *one of hers*, but Captain Kathryn Stryker.

And now, as she watched it slowly pivot south, heading for the safety of Formaria proper, it felt deeply cruel to have it taken away. That feeling of unfairness cut through the rising panic tightening in her chest, but it lasted only for a moment.

She took a deep breath and focused on the tunnel below her and the primary shaft where the *Athelus* was now slipping away. Everything was silent.

It should have been alive with the sounds of thousands of Mirrovinjin: the clatter of their weapons, the guttural rasp of their voices, the low, monstrous calls of their beasts. Instead, all she could hear was the distant hum of the *Athelus'* gyre thrusters.

It was too dark to see below, even if she wanted to. But she should have heard something.

And she didn't.

Maybe they'd already retreated, holding up their end of the deal. But they couldn't have moved this fast. And even from up here, she should have heard them. She should have heard hundreds of Mirrovinjin warriors, heavy footfalls, the scrape of armour, the guttural hiss of their voices. Instead, she heard nothing. It was like they had vanished, or had never been there at all.

The wrongness of it pressed against her, reigniting the panic she had barely managed to keep at bay. She couldn't stand here. She had to move.

Kathryn turned and followed the passage.

The farther she got from the lander, the darker it became. The darker it became, the more the sharp edges of the tunnel walls warped into looming figures, jagged and shifting in her mind's eye. The more they loomed, the harder her pulse pounded. She could hear it hammering in her ribs, could hear her own breath, thin and shaking.

Her boots crunched against dust and dirt that had settled undisturbed for thousands of years.

Then she saw a light.

She stepped into it, and it was like crossing a threshold into another world. One moment, there was nothing but blackness. The next, there was a wave of fiery blue light. She flinched, shielding her eyes.

When her eyes adjusted, she saw six columns of blue fire burning from piles of gyre ice. They blazed in a perfect circle, their glow cutting into the cavern's darkness. At their centre was an iron chair.

Kathryn moved toward it slowly, her body screaming at her to turn and run.

Then movement came. Not from the chair or the fire, but from another passage leading into the cavern. Then another, this time to her left. Figures emerged: two, three, four Sorel Tan elves. Their ochre gambesons whipped around their shins. Their swords were unsheathed, gleaming in the firelight.

Her mind blanked. They weren't Mirrovinjin. They were elves.

No.

She didn't know why they scared her so much, or why she should be more afraid of them than the Mirrovinjin. But the panic hit like a shockwave, overriding thought. She tried to move, to turn, to run. Her legs didn't work. Her boots dragged through the dirt, refusing to obey. She stumbled, trying to get back to the passage. Then she fell. The cavern vanished. The fire vanished. Only blackness remained. The panic clawed at her ribs, tore through her mind, ripped at her insides.

She jolted awake.

Bright lights shone overhead, a crosshatch of crystal white that turned the bronzite walls a pale gold.

Kathryn squinted against the glare, instinct clamping her eyelids shut. But she forced them open. If she closed them, she might slip back into the dream.

Something wet dribbled down her chin. It tasted of salt and stomach bile. She'd been frothing at the mouth.

The air was thick with noise, urgent voices talking over one another. She heard the sound of someone groaning, then a sharp gasp. It was all distant and scattered, blending together. She could smell copper, the faintly acetic scent of sorcery, and sweat. She didn't know where she was.

Until it all came flooding back.

She thought of engineering, of Gideon, of Elvie and Rayne, and of the blow to her head. The moment it all crashed back into focus, a hollow ache bloomed in her chest.

I failed them. The thought twisted, growing sharper, angrier. She thought of Gideon—what he'd done, and what she had allowed to happen.

You never were good enough.

The words cut through her like a blade. Kathryn flinched. She tried to move, tried to push herself up. She couldn't. Her hands were locked in place, invisible magical constraints binding her down. All she could do was move her head. She forced her chin against her chest, straining to see.

Out of the corner of her vision, a war caster in a beige gambeson stood next to a bronzite bed, one hand pressed to a young man's chest, the other hovering above, fingers shifting, something akin to a heat haze warping the air around them.

But that wasn't what made Kathryn's pulse spike.

At the foot of her own bed, standing as solid as the bronzite walls around her, was her mother.

She wore a full Admiral's uniform. Her blonde hair was pulled into that severe bun. Her sharp, predatory features gave her the look of a bird of prey sizing up a wounded animal.

Her hands were clasped behind her back, but they weren't holding the ruler. Her upper arms weren't tense enough for that. Kathryn could tell; she had been able to tell since she was eight years old. She had learned to read her mother's moods in the way she held herself, in the look in her eye, in the slightest variance of her voice's pitch.

Right now, she wasn't angry. She wasn't here to punish.

She was here to gloat.

It was in the glint behind her eyes, and the almost-smile, so slight most people wouldn't notice. But Kathryn knew. It was in the barest curl at the edge of her mouth, as sharp and merciless as the rest of her.

"Too soft. Too weak," her mother said, her voice so clear Kathryn could believe she was real. She *did* believe she was real. "You lacked the edge. You were too preoccupied with others."

She stepped closer to the bed, voice cutting like honed steel.

"You needed, Kathryn. That was your flaw. You needed others the way a newborn needs its mother's breast. You never learned to stand alone. Never accepted the loneliness of command. You couldn't even stand to be without me. The woman who hated you."

Kathryn couldn't look away. Her muscles were locked so tight that pain knifed down her ribs, cramping the side of her stomach. Her nails bit into her palms, stinging, burning.

Something wrapped around her arm.

She jerked so violently that pain lanced through her shoulder, nearly wrenching it from its socket. She tore her eyes away from her mother and found herself staring into the uncertain face of Ensenya Kilburn.

"Oh no," Senya muttered, eyes flicking over Kathryn's face. "Oh, err, I can sort that. No problem."

She reached for something behind Kathryn's head, then dabbed at the corners of her mouth with a cloth. The coolness of it made Kathryn realise how clammy her skin was.

The war caster stepped up beside Senya. A bun of brown hair surrounded her tired face, bags forming beneath her brown eyes. Her gambeson was stained with blood around the sleeves, and where she'd wiped her hands. It made her look more like a surgeon than a war caster.

"What are you doing?" the war caster asked, too tired to be angry.

"Gideon Du'Voire sent me," Senya said quickly. "The First Officer. He wants the Captain brought to the nav deck as soon as she's awake. And, err—she's awake."

The war caster's brow creased. "I was told to keep her here. Under no circumstances was I to let her leave."

"Well, now she's wanted on the nav deck," Senya countered, trying to square her shoulders, make herself look taller. "It's on the hex, with First Officer Du'Voire's command script."

The war caster's frown deepened, making her look even more exhausted. Then, after a pause, she stepped out of Kathryn's line of sight.

Senya glanced down, squeezing her forearm in quiet reassurance. Kathryn took the moment to check the foot of her bed. Her mother was gone.

Relief flooded through her like cold air.

"So it is," the war caster muttered, reappearing. She moved her hand somewhere out of sight, and Kathryn felt the constraints release.

Senya helped her sit up.

"You've got a minor concussion from multiple impacts to the head—easy to fix," the war caster said. "But there's something else in your system. Something I don't recognise. Almost like a witch hunter's anti-Aeturnic elixir. Or an anti-mutagen. It's fighting something off, but I don't know what."

"Most people don't," Kathryn murmured, more to herself than to the war caster. The woman gave her a questioning look.

"Thanks for your help," Kathryn said, swinging her legs off the bed, letting Senya take some of her weight as she stood. She was steadier than expected.

Gingerly, Kathryn probed the back of her skull. There was no bump, no pain, and the crushing headache from before was gone.

"Thanks again," she said, nodding once to the war caster before turning for the door, Senya moving close at her side. As they passed the bed with the unconscious young man, Kathryn leaned in, keeping her voice low.

"Don't run," she murmured. "Just walk."

"Cool and casual," Senya said. "That's what I'm known for."

Kathryn suppressed a smile, mostly because she didn't think Senya was trying to make a joke.

The vulnerum was a series of hexagonal chambers linked together, each with four or five beds arranged in a loose circle. They passed along the walkway that separated the chambers, heading for the exit.

Senya stepped up to a nearby terminal and opened the door. They didn't look back. They just stepped out into the corridor.

As the door slid shut behind them, something hard pressed into Kathryn's chest, and for a panicked moment she thought she'd been seriously wounded.

She patted at her chest frantically, almost tore open her doublet, then her hand found the lump in her breast pocket. She breathed out a relieved sigh as her fingers closed around the vial she'd forgotten was there.

"Err, everything okay, sir?" Senya asked. "You look like you're having a fit."

Kathryn took the vial from her pocket and held it up to her face. It was still intact and uncorked. She could probably get away without drinking it for another day, but given anything could happen during the next day, now was probably the best time. She uncorked the vial and knocked the contents to the back of her throat.

"I'll explain later," Kathryn said in answer to Senya's questioning look, before placing the empty vial back in her breast pocket.

"How did you manage to break Gideon's hex script?" Kathryn asked, wanting to avoid Senya asking about what she'd just swallowed, and genuinely curious.

Senya hesitated. "Err... well, you never actually confirmed Gideon's new role in the hex network." She gave Kathryn a guilty glance. "So it kind of left him in between Officer of the Watch and First Officer, meaning there was a... sort of backdoor I could mess with. Adjust some of his protocols."

Kathryn stared at that soft, innocent face. She looked into the bright hazel eyes caught between youthful uncertainty and the thrill of having gotten away with something.

"You know how to do that?" Kathryn said. "Why aren't you working in Intelligence?"

"Yeah, no," Senya said, rubbing the tips of her fingers together like she didn't quite know what to do with her hands. She shook her head. "They don't let me do that sort of thing."

"They should," Kathryn said, pulling her to a stop.

Senya beamed, bouncing slightly on her toes. "Well, thank you, Captain."

They kept moving, heading for the lift.

"Gideon's taken the nav deck, then?" Kathryn asked, her

mind jumping to Karland and Jacob.

Senya gave her another guilty look.

"I guess so? But I don't really know," she admitted. "I'm sorry, Captain, I should have told you before you left. But I'm pretty sure Urilla and Gideon are friends. They might even, you know..." She made a vague hand gesture. "Be together."

Kathryn felt something cold settle in her chest.

"When I told Karland, he said you'd be walking into a trap," Senya continued. "He told me to leave the nav deck and try to find you if they sent you to the brig. I locked Gideon out of the hex system before I left." She hesitated. "I'm really sorry, Captain. I should have said something, but you looked like you were in a rush, and I might have been wrong."

Elvie and Rayne's faces flickered across Kathryn's mind, but she was too angry at herself to be angry at Senya. The rational part of her knew this was her fault; she should have sent Gideon to the brig the moment she took command.

"It's okay. I was in a rush," Kathryn said. "Did Karland get a message to Sergeant Royer and Sergeant Faber?"

"Oh, yeah, he did," Senya said. "Told them to reroute to the nav deck. Either defend it against Gideon or retake it if necessary. Really hoping they just have to defend it."

Kathryn stopped in front of the lift terminal and called for it to take them to the armoury.

"Let's assume they've been forced to retake it," she said. "And need our help."

Senya perked up, a mix of excitement and nervousness dancing in her eyes. "Oh! Well, that's good, because I took extra combat lessons during the academy." They stepped into the lift. "Because I wasn't very good at first, but then I passed."

Kathryn was about to tell her that, at most, she'd just need to hold a tower shield—

—then her breath caught. Her stomach clenched.

At the end of the corridor, just beyond the closing lift doors, was her mother, standing still as death.

She looked like a living nightmare, her face contorted in

anger, her shoulders rigid, the ruler twisting behind her back. Kathryn's heart slammed against her ribs. The doors were too slow, far too slow.

And then they closed. The moment they did, Kathryn exhaled.

"Captain?" Senya asked, brow furrowed.

Kathryn snapped her head toward her.

"That's good to hear," she said, voice even.

She turned back to the doors, half-expecting her mother to be on the other side, prying them open with her bare hands.

"Do you know if we've changed course?" Kathryn asked.

"I checked the nav logs," Senya said. "We're still in formation with the Crucible and the Tempest."

Which meant Jacob had ignored any orders given to him by Gideon. And Gideon couldn't even relieve the navigator and plot a basic emergency course to Thendergaarden himself, because Senya had locked him out of the hex.

At some point, though, he'd stop trying to get back in and just have one of his officers do it. Kathryn could only hope Sergeant Royer and Sergeant Faber were keeping him busy trying to retake the nav deck.

The lift doors slid open, revealing a large chamber with a reinforced bronzite counter running down one side.

Like most armouries, the gap between the counter and the ceiling was narrow and designed to shield the armoury sergeant or master-at-arms from any incidents outside the counter. At the far end, another door led into the weapons hold.

Kathryn crossed the chamber in quick strides and stepped up to the counter. The man behind it was thick-set, balding, and dressed in a green gambeson. He looked up at her with small, distrustful brown eyes.

"Captain Kathryn Stryker," she said.

His gaze jumped to Senya.

"Hi, Lieutenant," he said.

"Hey, Anthor," Senya replied, smiling.

Anthor's eyes returned to Kathryn.

"Going to need you to confirm that, Captain," he said.

"It's just that we've never met before."

Kathryn placed her hand in the terminal. Anthor did the same on his end. The hex pulsed as she connected. She gave her command script.

A moment later, Anthor nodded.

"Captain Kathryn Stryker," he said. "Nice to meet you."

"Likewise, Sergeant."

The armoury door unlocked, sliding open. Inside, a short corridor led into the weapons hold. Racks lined the walls, filled with crossbows, combat weapons, and mail armour. And the thing Kathryn was most hoping to find—shields.

She moved toward the nearest row, her hands going straight to a five-foot steel tower shield.

"What's Anthor's relationship with Gideon like?" she asked Senya, keeping her voice low.

She hefted the shield off the rack and handed it to Senya. The girl took it, grunting as she tested its weight.

"So I'm pretty sure they hate each other," Senya said. "Or maybe just Anthor hates Gideon. Gideon kind of talks down to anyone who isn't an officer, so yeah, anyone who isn't an officer kind of hates him. So that's... most of the crew."

"That is not hard to believe," Kathryn muttered, pulling a crossbow from the wall and slinging it over her shoulder. And it was exactly what she wanted to hear.

She grabbed a magazine strap from its mount and looped it over Senya's shoulders. The girl adjusted it, still balancing the tower shield with some effort. Then Kathryn turned, looking through the open doorway toward the counter.

"Sergeant."

Anthor snapped his head up.

"Get in here."

He hesitated for half a second before pushing himself up from his chair and stepping into the corridor.

"Yes, sir?"

Kathryn met his eyes. "Grab a crossbow and one of those tower shields. We're retaking the nav deck."

Anthor's mouth dropped open slightly. He blinked, then collected himself.

"Yes, sir."

He reached for one of the crossbows, yanked a spare magazine off the rack, then grabbed a shield. Kathryn pulled extra magazines for herself, checking their weight.

"All right," she said. "Let's move."

She would have liked to round up a half-dozen others, but there wasn't time. And in the tight corridors around a nav deck, too many people could be just as dangerous as too few.

The professors at the Navarch Academy claimed the Formarians had designed them to be fortresses, where a small, entrenched force could cut down a much larger attacking one. Maybe they had, maybe they hadn't. Either way, storming one always came with a high casualty rate.

The mounting costs of your weakness!

It was her mother's voice again. She was standing outside the armoury corridor. Kathryn froze. Her mother's face was twisted with fury. Her posture was predatory, like she was about to lunge forward and rip her apart.

"Can I ask who we're taking the nav deck from, sir?" Anthor said.

Kathryn forced her gaze to him, locking onto his brown eyes, willing herself not to look back. *If I don't look, she'll disappear.*

"Gideon Du'Voire," she said.

Kathryn saw Anthor's grip tighten around his crossbow. "Sir, yes sir," he said, and there was a hint of enthusiasm there, maybe even anger.

Kathryn risked a glance toward the corridor exit. There was nothing. Her mother was gone. She let out a slow, controlled breath. *Just don't look at her. That's all I have to do. Just don't look.*

"Err..." Senya shifted her weight. "So maybe I should have a repeater? You know. In case I need to shoot someone?"

Kathryn did not want Senya shooting anyone, no matter how much extra combat training she'd taken.

"You hold the shield. I shoot," Kathryn said. "You remember the training for that?"

Senya hesitated, then nodded, seeming pleased by the idea of working together.

Keeping her eyes on the floor—*do not look, do not look*—Kathryn led them out of the armoury and toward the lift. At the terminal, she made a request for a route to the nav deck. The doors slid open, and they shuffled inside, shields scraping against the platform as Senya and Anthor adjusted for space.

As the lift sealed shut, Kathryn deliberately cast her eyes downward, focusing on her weapon. She activated the gyre cartridge, removed the magazine, reloaded it. She checked, then rechecked. If her mother's apparition wanted to materialise again, she refused to see it.

"Gideon has mutinied," she said as the lift doors closed. "Along with roughly fifteen other officers."

"I always thought he was the type," Anthor muttered. He leaned his shield against his shoulder and activated his crossbow's gyre cartridge.

"Sergeant Royer and Sergeant Faber know about the mutiny. They may already be storming the nav deck."

Anthor let out a low chuckle as the lift shot horizontally through the ship. "I know both of them, sir," he said. "If they know Gideon's a mutineer, they'll be competing to see who gets their hands on him first."

"That's good to hear," Kathryn said, and meant it. She needed some good news.

"We'll be coming in through the main corridor," she continued. "I need you identifying friendlies before we move through. Assuming they haven't already taken the nav deck."

"Got it, sir," Anthor said.

The lift slowed. She felt the shift in pressure beneath her boots as they began to rise through the ship.

"We should be coming up on the nav deck soon," Anthor said.

Kathryn stepped back, giving room for Senya and Anthor to form a two-person shield wall in front of her. The sound of repeaters firing drifted toward them, along with muffled shouts and distant cries.

"Here we go," she murmured.

The lift jolted to a stop. The doors slid open, and chaos crashed into them.

Two crossbow bolts slammed into Senya's shield the instant the corridor came into view. The impact made her flinch, but she didn't break. Her face was a mask of determination. Anthor risked a glance over his shield before ducking back down.

"They're ours, sir," he said. "I can see Royer."

Kathryn peered over the top of the shield. The corridor stretched ahead, leading straight to the nav deck's open doorway.

Men and women in green gambesons or officers' doublets crouched behind bulkheads, spaced every seven or eight feet. They leaned out, fired off several shots, then snapped back into cover.

Inside the nav deck, returning fire lashed out from behind the doorway.

Two bodies were propped against the wall behind the second-nearest bulkhead—one with a bolt buried in their shoulder, another with a bolt through their neck. Two more lay sprawled outside the nav deck itself, both wearing officers' doublets. Gideon's people? Or Royer's? Kathryn couldn't tell.

She ducked down again.

"Forward march! Step as one!" she ordered.

Senya and Anthor hefted their shields and pushed forward, shuffling five steps into the corridor.

"Stop and absorb fire!" Kathryn called, pressing in behind them. Another round of bolts slammed into the shields, rattling through the corridor. She kept her head low.

"Friendlies approaching from behind!" she shouted.

A voice from ahead called back: "Confirm friendly identification!"

"Captain Kathryn Stryker!" she bellowed over the crash of impacts.

"Ben, it's Anthor with the Captain!" Anthor shouted.

"Anthor!" the voice shouted back. "Get up here!"

That was all Kathryn needed to hear.

"Forward march! Step as one!" she commanded. "Move!"

Senya and Anthor surged forward.

Kathryn risked a glance over the shield, just long enough to take in the shifting skirmish, then ducked back down.

"Forward ten feet!"

Senya was panting with the effort, her arms trembling, but she held. Anthor, on the other hand, hadn't even broken a sweat.

The rain of bolts was relentless now. A *ping-ping-ping* of metal against metal, coming in successions of threes and fours.

They passed two bulkheads. A figure ducked out as they moved past, pressing in just behind Kathryn.

"Sergeant Alistair Faber, sir," the man said.

"Good to meet you, Sergeant," Kathryn replied, keeping her eyes ahead.

"Likewise, sir," he said.

"Five feet," Kathryn ordered.

Senya and Anthor pushed forward, shields raised, step by measured step.

They reached the last bulkhead. Ahead, the corridor split into the semi-octagon surrounding the nav deck.

"Halt!" Kathryn barked.

Senya and Anthor planted their shields. On either side, four soldiers in green gambesons huddled behind bulkheads.

Bolts crashed against the shields, ricocheting off in sharp metallic shrieks. Some found the gap between the shield wall and the cover behind them, hissing through the air before crashing into walls, the deck, or bulkheads.

"Status update," Kathryn said.

"Six left in the nav deck, sir," one of the men responded. He had messy blond hair and a nose broken and reset at an angle. Bolts whipped past the gap between them, but he didn't so much as flinch. She assumed this was Royer.

"Five confirmed kills. We've lost three of our own."

Kathryn gave him a nod, then grabbed Faber's arm to get his attention before turning back to Royer. She made the hand signal for fire as one, on my mark. Royer and Faber both nodded. She turned to the soldiers on her right, giving the same instruction. The woman directly behind the bulkhead caught her eye and nodded in understanding.

Faber shuffled up beside her. Then they rose as one.

She squeezed the trigger, firing into the corners of the doorway. Royer and the woman did the same from their bulkhead positions, bolts hammering into cover, cutting off any chance of return fire.

Kathryn emptied half a magazine before dropping back down behind the shield wall. She heard a sharp *oomph* and a strangled cry from inside the nav deck, followed by a low, pained moan. It was someone trying not to scream.

"Confirmed hit!" Royer barked.

"Confirmed hit!" the woman on the left echoed.

Beside her, Faber muttered, "No clue if I hit anything."

Kathryn held back a smile.

"Mr. Du'Voire!" Kathryn shouted. "You are outnumbered and unable to form an effective defence against an attacking shield wall. Put down your weapons and surrender the nav deck."

There was only silence.

Then came a heavy thud, followed by someone crying out and the sharp sounds of a struggle. There was fighting inside the nav deck. Kathryn's mind jumped to Karland and Jacob.

"Forward march! Step as one!" she ordered.

Royer and the woman fell in behind Faber as they advanced toward the nav deck.

"Maintain formation. Stop two feet inside."

They pushed forward, shields tight, Faber and Royer sweeping their crossbows left and right as they breached the nav deck entrance.

Two bolts hissed through the air, skimming inches over Kathryn's head. Faber fired back instantly. Something clattered to the deck on their left.

She peered over the shields.

Three officers knelt beside single terminals, hands raised, weapons tossed aside.

"We surrender!" one of them called out.

Behind the command terminal, two pairs of boots flailed wildly, kicking out in a desperate struggle.

"We accept your surrender," Kathryn called back.

Then, to Faber and Royer: "Get their weapons."

The sergeants, along with several others, moved fast, rushing out from behind the shield wall to disarm them.

Kathryn pushed past Senya and Anthor, stepping down onto the lower deck. Crossbow levelled, she rounded the command terminal and found the source of the scuffle.

Gideon lay sprawled atop Karland.

His face was frozen in shock, mouth slack, eyes wide with a fear that would never leave him. Blood trickled from the corner of his lips. A lot more seeped from the puncture wounds riddling his chest and stomach, pooling beneath his doublet and spreading across the decking. Karland lay beneath him, panting, a knife gripped in one hand. His other was still clenched around Gideon's throat.

"Went for Jacob, sir," he rasped, meeting Kathryn's gaze. "Had to take him out."

Kathryn nodded. "Good work, Mr. Agathor."

The navigator was kneeling in the hex pit. Arms outstretched, head bowed, chest rising and falling in a steady rhythm, like he was half-asleep, like there hadn't just been a skirmish around him or that he'd almost been killed by one of his own crew. *Typical navigator*, Kathryn thought as the rest of Royer and Faber's teams spilled into the nav deck.

The three remaining mutineers stood in silence, hands on their heads, faces grim. Others, now dead, had been propped up against the nav deck walls or were lying behind the terminals.

It was a hollow victory.

These men and women should have been her crew, not her enemies. And there were precious few of them after the attack on Thela. Thinning their ranks further with internal fighting was the last thing they'd needed. And it was all her fault.

The last of the adrenaline bled out of her, leaving only exhaustion. Her legs felt too heavy, her arms like they didn't quite belong to her. This could have been prevented.

Do not think about that. You know what happens when you think about that. Think of the mission. Think only of capturing Isdria Laanorath.

Kathryn turned to the command terminal.

The hex sculpt played out on top of it, showing their fleet's position. They were pushing southeast, past Karagon, now equidistant between Reantha and Theselan.

The Storm had pulled further ahead.

"Message from the Tempest, sir," Jacob said from the hex pit. "Confirmation that Reantha and Theselan have deployed their fleets. The Storm is making for the Gulf."

Kathryn exhaled, letting her shoulders relax.

"And so are we."

TWENTY-EIGHT
BRAZIER

Fighting off the last of the not-statues had cost them more than they could afford. Loraine had emptied her quiver. Brazier had handed off his final spare magazine to Switch and was down to half a mag. Freyen had long since drawn her twin blades, the polished steel smeared with streaks of sickly brown-green gore.

By the time they crossed the walkway, the floor was so slick with the viscous remains of their attackers that Switch lost her footing entirely. She went down hard, chain armour clattering as she landed on her back. The gore coated her from head to toe. It smeared across the back of her head, plastered to her gambeson, and dripped down her neck in a nauseating sludge. Her scowl was so fierce that Brazier didn't dare ask if she was all right. He could guess well enough—not that he had much room for concern. His mind was fixed on one thing, and one thing only: getting them out of the Immuratum.

Now that they had the means to destroy Duessa, everything else faded into background noise. There was no space left for fear, or fatigue, or even the sour taste of regret that kept creeping up his throat. Still, it was there, unmistakably gnawing at the edges of his focus.

I should have convinced her.

If he'd been better, clearer, if he'd made Kathryn see that the Mirrovinjin ships were a projection, an illusion, this entire ordeal could have been avoided. They could have ended it at Thela. There would have been no retreat or desperate scramble for rescue. There would have been no reckless plunge into a realm that had been sundered from reality a thousand years ago precisely because it threatened the very existence of the Fromryr.

Now, as they sprinted down the warped corridors toward the librarian's chamber, every step felt heavier than the last. The library's strange yellow light crept into his bones, sapping his spirit. He realised with a sharp sense of guilt that crossing into this place hadn't just been a risk. It had been a wild, senseless gamble with the lives of people who had followed him without question, people who trusted him. And they were running out of time to make it worth the cost.

The portal to the librarian's chamber peeled open as they approached. It slid back into the walls with a sick, wet slickness that Brazier's mind interpreted as a deliberate perversion of the Formarian architecture this place seemed built in the likeness of.

There, standing dead centre beneath the twisted lattice of hybrid organic and metal arches, as if it had been waiting for them this whole time, was the demon librarian. It tilted its head, studying them with its predatory, almost childlike curiosity. Then it gave that smile, wide and eager, like a child spotting a table full of sugared treats.

"Would you like another riddle?"

The voice had the sing-song lilt of innocent invitation. Come play, it seemed to say.

"I'd like you to rot in the void," Switch snapped.

Without hesitation, she levelled her crossbow and fired. Before Brazier could even think to stop her, the bolt slammed into the demon's eye with a meaty slap, burying itself to the fletching and snapping the thing's head back on its thin, unnatural neck.

"Cease fire!" Brazier barked, throwing out an arm, palm down, patting the air to rein her in. "Abyss damn it, Switch!"

"It had it coming," Switch shot back, her crossbow still raised, eyes narrow.

Brazier started to reply, but the words dried up in his

mouth as the semi-mechanical hand, the one that had been turning the pages of the human-books, twitched, then lashed toward them with impossible speed.

It was too fast to dodge, too fast to counter. Brazier braced himself, chest tightening, and prayed his breastplate and gambeson would take enough of the force to keep his ribs intact.

But the blow never landed. The metal hand froze, knuckles cocked into a fist, trembling in the air not three feet from his chest. Brazier's breath caught. His eyes darted sideways.

The demon's head still hung limp, snapped back at a grotesque angle, the crossbow bolt jutting from its ruined eye. But its arm was outstretched and rigid, fingers splayed wide and clawing toward the mechanical limb, as if holding it back. It was as if, in its final spasm of will, the demon librarian had stopped the blow itself.

Slowly, its head sagged forward. It lolled to the side like a drunk clawing back toward consciousness, swaying once, twice, before a twitching hand groped for the bolt protruding from its ruined eye.

The first grasp missed entirely, clawing at empty air. The second brushed along its cheek, smearing black ichor in a greasy smear. The third time, its fingers found the shaft. With an awful, patient slowness, it pulled.

The bolt slid free with a sucking pop and came slick with thick black gore, strands of viscera clinging to the fletching. Brazier's stomach turned as he saw what could only be the remnants of the demon's eye dangling from the bolt's tip.

The demon let the bolt fall to the floor with a heavy clatter, black ichor leaking down its cheek in steady rivulets. Its one remaining eye fixed on them, cold, livid, and calculating.

Without breaking its stare, it rotated its outstretched wrist, fingers still splayed in that clawed shape. The mechanical limb shuddered, then withdrew, folding back into its alcoves like a predator slinking away into its den.

When the demon finally spoke, its childlike lilt was gone. Its voice had deepened to a rasping gurgle, like stones grinding in a flooded throat.

"Your friends," it growled, "die beneath the blades of captured souls. But I can make them stop. All you need do is answer my riddle."

Loraine muttered under her breath, "What is it with this thing and riddles?"

"Who knows," Freyen replied tightly. Her twin blades were held tight at her sides. "But I don't think we've got a choice."

Brazier felt the war raging inside him. It was the sharp, desperate need to get out of this place now, pulling hard against the colder, clearer understanding that surviving the Immuratum meant playing by its rules.

It only took a heartbeat. Survival won out.

"We'll do it," he said. "Give it to us."

The demon slipped straight into the riddle, its voice once more light, sing-song, and gleeful.

"Once, in a hall of echoes and painted stars, there lived a man. Not bound by script nor name, but free to become whatever the moment demanded."

It giggled, high and sharp, as a slick rope of gore slithered down its ruined face and splattered wetly on the floor. It didn't seem to notice.

"With each rise of his curtain, the man was reborn, wearing a face that was not his own. A villain with bloodied hands. A lover whispering oaths beneath a moonless sky. A fool, a king, a god, a ghost. His voice spun stories so finely stitched that even truth forgot where it ended."

The demon's chin dropped, eyes narrowing beneath its brow, the grin splitting its face until its lips curled into something sharp and feral. Its voice gutted down into a rasp.

"But when the lanterns dim and the stage grows cold... when the crowd has gone and silence returns... who remains? Who is this man whose face is not his own?"

A heavy silence settled over them. Brazier's mind buckled under the weight of the riddle, the pressure of urgency making his thoughts churn instead of flow. He forced himself to breathe, to think.

"Do you think it's a Lord of the Eternal Hunt?" Loraine

asked, uncertain.

"Your guess is as good as mine," Switch replied, her crossbow still levelled.

"Free to become whatever the moment demands," Loraine mused. "Sounds godlike to me."

Brazier frowned. It didn't feel right. The pieces were there, but they weren't fitting.

He shook his head. "I don't think so."

"Spun stories so finely stitched even truth forgot where it ended," Switch added. "That's got to be magic, right?"

His lips pressed into a tight line. No, something about it was still off.

"What lives in a hall of echoes and painted stars?" Freyen asked.

"A god of the Aeturnum?" Switch offered, though she didn't sound convinced.

Freyen shot her a look of flat disbelief. But Brazier's thoughts snagged on what Freyen had said.

"There was a curtain," he said, not yet knowing why it felt important.

"There's lanterns, too. And a stage," Freyen added.

The demon's guttural snarl raked through the chamber. "Your time to answer grows close."

"You never gave us a time limit," Brazier shot back, holding the thing's gaze. "We have as long as we need."

The demon tilted its head and smiled that terrible child's smile. "You do," it said sweetly. "But your friends don't."

Brazier's gut twisted as he turned back to Freyen, but his eye caught a flicker of movement at the hem of the demon's robe. The dark gloop that had pooled beneath it was crawling and slithering over its foot, up its leg, drawing itself back into the demon's torn flesh. *Self-healing*, Brazier realised, his stomach lurching. If they failed this riddle, he had no idea if they could kill the thing.

"He wears a face that is not his own," Freyen pressed, pulling his attention back. "He can be a fool, a king, or a lover, and he lives in a hall of echoes with painted stars."

And then it clicked.

"He wears a mask," Brazier said, the realisation

blooming in his chest. "Actors wear masks."

"And he can play different roles," Freyen added quickly, turning to Switch for support.

"Do actors live in halls of echoes?" Switch asked, still sceptical, but softening.

"That's a theatre," Brazier said, his certainty building.

"Never seen one," Switch said, giving a half-shrug.

"I have," Loraine said. "In Ravinica, they have curtains and a stage."

"When the crowd goes silent," Freyen continued, her voice low and thoughtful, "the answer is actor. It must be."

The demon snarled, the sound scraping through the chamber like rusted blades grinding together. Brazier exhaled, more a grim laugh than relief.

"I sincerely hope that was right," he said, eyeing the demon warily, "because I think you just gave it the answer."

The demon's remaining eye rolled back beneath its lid as it closed, and it lifted its hands, palms up, as though presenting some dark offering to the void. It held them there, as if frozen mid-ritual. Then its eye snapped open. It lowered its hands to its sides.

"It's done," the demon rasped. Its voice thick and rough.

"The guards. The statues. The skeletons. They've been called off?" Brazier asked, his tone sharp, leaving no room for games. The demon gave a slow nod.

"That's good enough for me," Brazier said. And it was. He didn't need to say it twice.

They didn't walk. They ran. The demon's head swivelled with them as they bolted from the chamber, its neck rotating a full one-eighty degrees as they fled down the corridor.

Brazier didn't spare it a glance. He drove himself forward, pounding toward the exit, heart slamming in his chest. The door to the Immuratum yawned open ahead, still mercifully unsealed. They ran through it, then out into the clearing. And they didn't stop there.

Brazier set the pace, hard and fast, spurred by too many reasons to count: the gnawing fear the demon had lied, the memory of its gore knitting itself back together, the certainty that something, somewhere in this abyssal place still wanted their lives. The others kept pace. They gave no complaints. By the time they staggered to a stop at the ravine mouth, they were soaked in sweat and gasping for breath.

Brazier unclipped his flask and drank deeply, though the liquid did little to wash away the grit in his throat. Switch let her crossbow clatter to the ground and bent over, bracing herself on her knees, chest heaving. Freyen drained her own flask in long, desperate gulps. Loraine squinted out across the horizon, shielding her eyes against the glare of the three unmoving suns.

"I don't see any movement," she said, voice rough from the run.

The watchtower loomed in the distance, silent and still. From this far, it might have been a painting, if not for the dust clouds billowing faintly behind it. They were the only sign that a battle had raged outside its battlements just an hour before.

"It's too far to tell," Brazier said.

"These suns haven't moved," Freyen said, still catching her breath.

"So?" Loraine shot back.

"We've been here for hours," Freyen replied. "But the suns haven't shifted. Not even a little. Either time doesn't pass here, or it's moving so slowly we can't see it."

On any other day, Brazier might have let that chew at his thoughts. He might have wondered at the implications of a place where time itself came unstitched. But here, in this nightmare, it was just another rotten layer on top of everything else, the immortal demon, the army of the dead, and the books made from human lungs.

The Immuratum had proven worse than Yeggardania, and that was saying something. At least in Yeggardania, you had a chance of killing what tried to kill you.

"Don't think we can make any safe guesses about this place," Brazier said grimly, clipping his flask back into place. He motioned them forward with a jerk of his chin. "Let's move."

They set off at a run, not the blind sprint they'd used to flee the library, but a steady, grinding pace that still burned in the lungs. Brazier pushed them hard, keeping their speed just shy of collapse. They followed their own trail, boot print for boot print in the churned earth, breath coming in heavy, raw pulls that left no room for talk. Sweat crawled down Brazier's spine. His leathers clung to his legs like wet parchment, chafing with every stride.

By the time they pulled up at the gatehouse fronting the bridge, his breath rasped in his throat, and a bitter trickle slid from his brow and into his mouth. It was acrid resin with an undercurrent of something musty and wrong. He gagged, the bile rising sharp in his throat.

Realisation came a half-beat later, and it almost made him heave again: it was the blood of the not-statues. He bent double and spat it out. Instinctively, he raised his sleeve to wipe his mouth, only to find it slick with the same foul gore. He let his arm fall and spat again.

"I have never wanted the Anchorite's head as badly as I want it now," Switch panted between breaths.

Brazier glanced at her. Her face was flushed, streaked with grime and blood and sweat, her hair soaked through with the same clotted mess that coated them all.

"You should see yourself," she said, catching him staring.

Beside him, Freyen upended her flask, draining the last drop. Brazier unclipped his own and offered it over, but she shook her head.

"Thanks," she rasped.

"Imagine doing this for every battle," Loraine said, her voice tight as she dragged herself up the steps to the gatehouse.

"Why would we want to imagine that?" Switch shot back.

"It's what they do in Ravinica," Loraine said, still panting. "March all day and night. Then run at each other across an open plain."

It was the most the archer had said since they'd met her, and Brazier caught the thread beneath her words. She was talking to fill the space, to fend off the creeping dread none of them wanted to name. She didn't know what they were about to find in the watchtower, and she didn't want to dwell on it. Neither did he.

He followed her up the steps, forcing himself not to think about what it would feel like to crest the ridge and see his own crew lying dead beneath it.

"We get flown into battle in ships," she went on, her voice lighter, like she could joke her way out of fear. It seemed wildly uncharacteristic of the brooding woman she'd presented herself as. "Or the Mirrovinjin bring the battle to us."

"Almost sounds luxurious when you put it like that," Freyen said, her lips pulling into a grim smile.

"Makes you wonder how they do it," Loraine added, still climbing. "Maybe they're feeding them something different."

"Anything but mushrooms," Switch grumbled.

"They train for it," Brazier said, his father's words surfacing from memory of his long-ago trips to Vallorandyl. "Build it up like your sword arm. Hard miles make strong legs, or something like that."

And then he broke into a light run.

"Come on," Brazier said over his shoulder, and they ran with him across the bridge.

Toward the other side, he slowed to a fast walk, not because they were safe but because they needed to listen. The sounds of fighting had gone. If there was still battle ahead, it had moved on from the ramparts.

The watchtower loomed above them, quiet as the grave. They pushed under the gatehouse and up the steps, toward the spiralling corridor they'd come from.

"I can't hear anything," Loraine said, hope creeping into her voice like light under a locked door.

"Me neither," Brazier replied. "Doesn't mean something here doesn't want us dead."

They climbed the steps cautiously, weapons at the ready. Brazier and Switch kept their crossbows tight to their shoulders, tracking every shadow. Loraine had drawn her scimitar, Freyen her long knives, the blades gleaming even in the dim light.

At the open double doors to the courtyard, Brazier froze. The first thing he saw was the blood. It ran in thin rivulets down the top steps, pooling against the threshold.

He climbed two more steps, slow and careful, keeping his aim steady as his eyes caught the way the light played off the streaks. It wasn't red. It was grey-green. He let out a breath as the knot in his chest eased a fraction.

They stepped into the courtyard, threading paths through the sticky carnage. The flagstones were slick with gore and ruptured husks. Brazier led them around the worst of it, each step heavy with the stench of rot, tomb air and old violence. Everything was silent.

Loraine nodded toward the steps leading to the upper courtyard. Brazier followed her gaze. There was more blood and more wreckage smeared along the steps. They moved carefully toward it, and Brazier's eyes caught a dark smear along the inner wall of the gatehouse. It was thick, wet, and red—Fromryian.

Someone had tried to pull themselves up the incline but hadn't made it far. Then he heard it. It was a *shunt, click*, pause, then *shunt, click*, pause. The sound filtered down from the upper level, hollow and rhythmic.

Brazier's pulse kicked up, and he climbed the steps, crossbow tight to his shoulder. He kept low, scanning right, past the doorway to the watchtower's main gatehouse, then left. There were more splintered bodies, more bones and slick gore. It led in a grim trail straight to the base of the tower, to the heavy double doors of the inner keep.

Someone sat slumped in the doorway, back pressed against the frame, keeping the doors from closing fully. They tried, groaned against his weight, nudged him gently like they wanted to shut but couldn't, then slid back into their recesses.

Loraine let out a curse. She broke into a run, sprinting across the gore-streaked landing. Brazier moved to follow and saw it all too clearly: Bertrand.

The man sat hunched like a discarded doll, thick hands resting in his lap. His war hammer lay abandoned at his side, covered in grey-green muck. Loraine dropped to her knees in front of him. She sighed, head falling to her chest as the weight of it sank in.

"I'm sorry, big man," she whispered.

A deep gash split half of Bertrand's face, carving through his right eye, shattering his cheekbone, and tearing his jaw apart. Blood soaked his left side, a dark stain running from under his arm. Brazier guessed a blade had found its way beneath the armoured gap and punched clean through the armpit. That was the wound that had finished him. It would have come fast, he hoped, for Bertrand's sake.

Brazier's gaze slid to the dark corridor beyond the body. A circular chamber waited at the end, shadowed steps spiralling away to the right, curling upward.

"The others may need our help," Brazier said, moving toward the corridor.

Loraine stayed frozen, still kneeling.

"Cap's right," Freyen said softly, stepping up beside her. "You can't help him now. But the others might still have a chance."

"Damn the black abyss," Loraine spat, and pushed to her feet.

She strode past them, fast and hard enough that Brazier had to quicken his pace to keep up. Inside, signs of the battle were everywhere: slick smears across the floor, splintered bone and half-crushed fragments of the enemy.

A set of sealed double doors sat to their left. To their right, the spiral staircase climbed the tower wall, streaked with blood and gore.

They found Solon halfway up. His body sprawled across the steps, one arm splayed wide, the other clutching a sword in his lifeless grip. Grey-green gore soaked him from head to boot. So much of it had burst across the walls, the landing, the balustrade, it looked like he'd drowned in the blood of his enemies. His leather jerkin was punctured over and over, but of his own blood, Brazier saw none. His dark mane draped across his face, but from what Brazier could see beneath it, Solon looked almost peaceful, as if this was exactly the way he would have chosen to die.

"That one's hard as bronzite," Switch said, her voice tight

with admiration.

Loraine's mouth pulled into a grim line, eyes heavy with loss.

"Not anymore he's not," she said.

She started up the next set of stairs, but a cough rasped out from above, low and wet. It was followed by a groan and muffled voices. Loraine broke into a run. The rest of them charged after her, boots thudding against stone, Brazier cursing the weight in his legs and the fire in his thighs. He pushed through it, forced himself to keep going, just in time to see Godenforte blocking the top of the stairs.

The man was a mountain, gripping his blood-slick long axe crosswise like a gate bar. He claimed his mother was half-giant, and staring up at him now, Brazier didn't doubt it for a second. Behind him, Olivier knelt, supporting Vandemir's shoulders. Atlas crouched over the Captain, working a knot into the bandages around his waist. Vandemir's leathers were unfastened, his chest bare, grey curls of hair matted with blood. His gut wound leaked fresh crimson, soaking the cloth in dark red. Loraine and Brazier dropped to their knees beside him.

"They got you good, Cap," Loraine said, trying for levity, but her voice was too tight to pull it off.

"Gut wound," Vandemir growled, his face a twisted grimace as he winced through the pain.

"We'll get you to a war caster in Calaxis," Brazier said, but the words hung hollow in the air.

Vandemir met his gaze, steady and grim. No need to say: *If we make it.*

"Lucky for me," Vandemir rasped, "this'll kill me good and slow."

"And painfully too," Olivier added, unhelpfully. "Heard that's how gut wounds go."

"You don't say," Vandemir snapped, his voice tight with pain. "Now get me up!"

They moved fast, Atlas and Olivier slinging his arms over their shoulders and hauling him to his feet. Vandemir grunted through clenched teeth, his breath sharp and shallow. As they started guiding him toward the stairs, he grunted again.

"My sword," he rasped. "Back there."

Brazier followed Vandemir's nod. The landing curved away to an open oval doorway, black as pitch inside. He stepped in slow, crossbow up. The chamber beyond was bare, except for a broad embrasure at the far end. A single not-statue knelt in the centre. Vandemir's sword jutted from its chest like a flag planted in conquered ground. Unlike the others, this one wore the corroded ruins of what must have once been a crown, and the suggestion of intricate armour, though time and decay had gnawed most of it away. It leaked grey-green sludge from its gut and thighs, but it hadn't burst apart like the others.

Cautious, Brazier crept forward. He nudged the not-statue's knee with the tip of his boot. Sticky ichor smeared the leather, but the thing didn't move. He checked for any twitch of latent life, then slung his crossbow across his chest and grabbed the hilt. Bracing a foot on the thing's chest, he yanked the sword free with a wet slither. The skeleton sagged, caving in under his boot and crumpling like parchment.

Disgust crawled across his skin as the ichor soaked into the treads of his boot. He scraped it off on the nearest wall and stepped back onto the landing.

"Looks like you found the Crippled King," Brazier said, holding up the sword.

"Not so much of a cripple, as it turns out," Vandemir rasped, as they moved for the stairwell.

"You'd think they'd be out of practice after all these years," Vandemir went on, breath coming shallow now.

Brazier thought of the unmoving suns.

"I don't think it works like that here," he said.

"Aye," Vandemir agreed, voice hoarse. "There's truth to that."

"No book," Olivier noted, eyes flicking to Brazier as they cleared the landing.

"Not one we could carry out," Brazier said. "But we got what we came for."

"At least this wasn't all for nothing," Vandemir growled,

but the effort put a grimace on his face as they came to the landing where Solon lay sprawled.

Sweat beaded on Vandemir's brow. He looked down at the corpse of his man, and there was iron in his eyes, but not surprise.

"I assume you had something to do with stopping these things?" he asked Brazier, gaze locked on Solon's quiet form. "Didn't seem like giving the gold back slowed them much."

"I think we did," Brazier said, but the words felt thin.

Olivier stared at Solon like the sight might hollow him out from the inside. His face twisted in raw, unspent grief.

"He doesn't need your guilt," Vandemir barked, shaking the boy hard enough to snap him from the trance. "He'd have ended like this one way or another, on some battlefield or another. That's the price of being Fromryr. Endless war means when, not if."

"Still my fault," Olivier said, low.

"Aye, boy!" Vandemir snapped, his voice rough as gravel. He shook Olivier again, harder. "It was. But that won't change a black-damned thing. So be done with it."

"Ferry's still there," Loraine called.

She stood at the arrow slit, one arm braced against the wall as she peered outside.

"Then we don't keep it waiting," Vandemir said.

He turned back to Olivier, pinning him with his eyes.

"You want to make this right, boy? Get me the abyss out of this place."

Then to Brazier, voice harder than iron: "Take his body. We're not leaving him here to rot in this damned tower."

Brazier nodded. He handed Vandemir's sword off to Loraine, then crouched beside Solon's body.

"I'll take the legs," Switch said, already moving in beside him.

Together they lifted Solon, who was heavy as stone. When they reached the exit, Vandemir gave a single grunt: "Godenforte."

The big man answered with a nod, slinging Bertrand's corpse over his shoulder like a sack of grain. Without another word, they turned and carried their dead out of the tower.

#

Brazier's arms were dead weights by the time they reached the river. His mouth felt as if it was lined with grit, and a sharp ache in his groin told him he'd pulled something. Sweat had baked layers of gore into his skin, and he caught himself daydreaming about standing in the *Anchorite's* head, beaneath its hot water jets and scrubbing his face raw. But more than anything, he just wanted his crew back on the ship. He wanted his crew safe inside its bronzite hull, with its full spread of repeaters trained on anything stupid enough to pick a fight.

Olivier's tight, haunted expression jumped out from his memory. It reminded him of Matthias—of the space where his navigator should be. Somewhere across that endless plain of broken skeletons, slogging under Solon's weight, Brazier had made a quiet promise to himself. He'd do better by Matthias.

Maybe that wasn't fair. Somewhere along the way, they'd shifted from allies of convenience, to crew, to maybe, perhaps, something that looked like friendship. But Brazier had never tried to build that friendship. He'd never asked a thing about his past. And Matthias, for all his ease and dry wit, never volunteered. Perhaps that was because he knew Brazier still clung to some ideal of the Fromryr, and what they should all live their lives for, and Matthias' life was in direct contrast to that ideal. He wasn't entirely sure why, but Brazier suddenly felt a little foolish.

Freyen caught his eye, nodded at him. "You good?"

"I think a trip through hell puts some things in perspective," Brazier said.

Ahead, Switch snorted and threw a glance over her shoulder.

"You can say that again," she said. "I am never taking the Anchorite's hot water for granted ever again."

They picked their way down the riverbank and onto the

pier where the ferry waited, bobbing gently in the thick, black water that passed for a river in this place. The ferryman sat like a carving at the stern, paddle resting across his knees.

As they climbed aboard, his head creaked toward them. But that was all. No words came from its jagged mouth. They laid Solon and Bertrand down between the benches, folding their arms across their chests. Vandemir, pale as ash, slumped between the benches too, braced against the side of the ferry. His hands were clamped over his belly wound, his breath tight and shallow. Brazier eased himself down across from them, legs shaking from the run.

The ferryman stood and drove the oar into the black water. They drifted away from the pier and were carried back down the river.

“We should change those dressings, Cap,” Atlas said.

Vandemir shook his head, a flicker of stubborn fire in his sunken eyes.

“Won’t make a lick of difference,” he rasped. “Only a war caster’s keeping me from the abyss now. And I plan on making it to a war caster.”

“You’re black-damn right you will, sir,” Loraine said.

Vandemir gave her a thin smile, then turned his tired gaze to Brazier.

“Tell me what you found in that demon library,” he said. “Tell me what the book said.”

Brazier wiped at the grey sludge caked behind his ear, feeling it smear cold and slick across his fingers. He flicked it into the water.

“To kill Duessa,” Brazier said, his voice heavy, “the first harbinger has to stop believing the tale she’s been told.”

Blank stares met him from Vandemir, Loraine, Olivier, and Atlas. Only the towering form of Godenforte didn’t look up. He was staring down at Bertrand’s still body.

“And who and what, may I ask, is a harbinger?” Vandemir growled.

“It’s a long story,” Brazier said, feeling another crust of gore in his hair and grimacing.

“Good,” Vandemir barked, then grimaced hard, his hand clutching the soaked bandage at his side. “Maybe it’ll distract me from the hole in my gut."

"The Sorel Tan used Duessa to create the illusion of Mirrovinjin ships," Brazier explained. "But to make those illusions work, they needed people to believe in them. To carry the lie. Those people are the harbingers."

"So you've got to find the first harbinger," Atlas said, brow furrowed.

"We already know where she is," Brazier said. He scratched at his beard, then cursed himself for working the grime deeper into it. "The hard part's getting to her. Last time I saw her, she'd been made commander of the Vanguard of Winter."

"That's the ship leading the hunt for the Gloried Storm," Vandemir said.

"I know," Brazier replied.

"What if she dies?" Olivier asked.

"Then the sorcery stays in place until we find the second harbinger. And if they're dead, we hunt the third."

"It's never easy," Switch muttered, staring out into the mist curling around them. She shook her head. "Why is it never easy?"

Nobody answered. Instead, they let the silence settle over them, heavy as the mist creeping in around the boat. The only sounds were the steady dip and splash of the ferryman's oar, Vandemir's tight, ragged breathing, and the occasional grunt of someone peeling crusted gore from a patch of skin they hadn't expected it to reach.

The air cooled, the soft heat of the Immuratum fading into something sharper, crisper. Brazier, still damp with sweat and ancient blood, felt the chill kiss his skin and welcomed it. For a moment, he could pretend he felt clean.

"We're here," Loraine said, nodding past Brazier's shoulder.

He turned, spotting the jagged silhouette of the Handmaid's broken pyramid rising out of the shadows and the pier descending down from it to the waterline. Above them, the sky was a soft black, tinged with a faint turquoise haze. The stars were bright and sharp like pinpricks through the veil. Their light filtered through the canopy in pale shafts, draping the ruins in a ghostly, bone-white glow. It made the place feel ancient and abandoned, like the surface world had long since forgotten the Formarian race that built it.

Three figures stood waiting at the edge of the pier—Folgar and his two soldiers, arms folded across their maroon gambesons, faces carved from stone. Folgar's mouth was a flat line. His brow was creased.

The ferry drifted in, and the ferryman slowed them with a single pull of the oar before they bumped gently against the Formarian alloy pier. Folgar's gaze lingered on Solon and Bertrand, and a shadow deepened in his expression. But he didn't say anything. *Something's wrong*, Brazier thought. *More wrong than what we're carrying off this boat.*

The ferryman moved, laying the plank across to the pier with a clunk.

"Give them a hand," Folgar said to his soldiers.

The dwarves clambered aboard without a word, lifting Solon and Bertrand between them, careful to protect their burden.

Brazier stepped over the bench to Vandemir, who sagged into himself, his skin pale white now, dark rings beneath his eyes like bruises from too many sleepless nights. Brazier bent down to lift him under the arms and caught the stench rising from his wounds.

"I know," Vandemir rasped, a bitter crack of a smile on his blood-flecked lips. His eyes were heavy, fighting sleep with sheer stubborn will.

"If there's one thing we Fromryr are good at, it's holding out for a war caster," Brazier said.

Vandemir's voice dropped to a raspy whisper.

"Maybe when I was younger. But you won't be getting me to a war caster now."

"Doesn't mean we're not going to try," Brazier said.

He hauled him up. Vandemir's face twisted with pain, and a wet sound escaped his mouth. When he opened it, Brazier caught the dark stain of blood on his teeth. Godenforte moved in, bracing Vandemir's other side, and together they got him off the ferry.

"Did you find it?" Folgar asked.

"We did," Brazier said. "How fast can you get us back to Calaxis?"

Folgar's eyes went to Vandemir's soaked bandages, reading the situation like a field report.

"If we can rig a stretcher, maybe," he said. "One of the lads can run ahead. Get the war caster topside."

His hand ran over his scalp, scratching at the stubble as his frown deepened.

"But there's something you need to deal with first," Folgar said, and Brazier's gut went cold.

"Matthias?" Brazier snapped.

"He's fine," Folgar said, raising his hands as if to settle a restless crowd. Switch and Freyen had closed in at the name.

"Though the Handmaid seems to think she needs him a little longer," Folgar added.

Brazier felt his chest tighten, going hot and cold all at once.

"We'll see about that," he said.

Folgar's jaw tightened, but he didn't push back against Brazier's growl. His eyes flicked back to Vandemir.

"Best get you up there," Folgar said. Then, to his soldiers: "Take the bodies round the outside. Meet us outside the gates. Morletts catch their scent, they'll be on us like rats."

Atlas, Olivier, and Folgar's soldiers hefted Solon and Bertrand and carried them off along the pier, toward a set of stairs that curved around the pyramid's flanks and led into the city. The rest of them climbed the main steps, with Brazier bracing Vandemir between his shoulder and hip. His gut itched to draw steel and storm the place outright. One glance at Switch and Freyen told him they were thinking the same thing.

"I'm sorry for your losses," Folgar said quietly.

Vandemir gave a grunt that might have been a nod but even that small effort seemed to drain him. His breath came shallow and ragged. It was another reason to move faster.

They passed through a long-ago opened doorway and into the gloom of the pyramid. Brazier could already smell the rot clawing at them from inside as they turned right and began the climb to the main chamber. By the halfway mark,

Vandemir was almost deadweight as he leaned into Godenforte's shoulder. The Captain ground out weak protests between clenched teeth.

At the top, shadows peeled away from the walls. The Handmaid's court watched them from the edges of the gloom, slipping behind pillars and darting along the floor. The Fenn warrior stood like a statue, its reptilian eyes fixed on their every move. Leopine, the giant toad, lolled in its shallow pool by the chamber door, unmoving except for its black, glassy eyes, which tracked them lazily.

As they reached the last step, the cat-thing slipped from the shadows of the inner doorway. Silent, smooth, its dwarven face blank and monstrous, it padded a slow circle around them. Brazier felt every hair along his arms rise.

"Of all the things here," Loraine muttered under her breath, "it's that one that makes my skin crawl the most."

"I hear that," Switch added, her voice low.

Then a child's giggle shivered out of the Handmaid's chamber. Moments later, she appeared in the doorway, her limbs jerking with unnatural stiffness as she dragged herself forward, clawing at the walls for balance.

"I take that back," Switch murmured. "That's worse."

"Don't mind Lopatis," the Handmaid cooed sweetly from behind her veil, her voice as brittle as ice underfoot.

"He doesn't understand why others find him so distressing. Poor thing, last of his kind."

Her head snapped toward Switch with a predator's speed, voice hardening to steel.

"After your kind hunted his to all but extinction!"

Folgar gave Switch a dark look. The enginator shrugged, unbothered.

"We didn't mean any offense, my lady," Folgar said, tone cautious.

"You never do, my sweet Folgar," the Handmaid replied Her voice lilted like a blade through silk.

"Did your friends find what they sought? Many enter the accursed realm, but few return."

"We found the means to destroy Duessa," Brazier said, forcing steel into his voice. "We can break her sorcery once we return to Calaxis. But I need my navigator first."

The Handmaid clicked her tongue, sharp as the snap of a trap.

"Telling tales, Folgar?" she teased, with a hint of venom. "How unlike you."

Beside him, Godenforte jostled Vandemir harder.

"Stay with us," he growled. "Keep those eyes open."

Vandemir's lids fluttered. His grip weakened. Brazier felt it in the slackening weight against his side.

"Not long now," the Handmaid crooned, tilting her veiled face toward Vandemir.

"I feel him slipping. But his flesh need not go to waste. My court still has use for it."

Godenforte snarled low, raising his axe in warning. Out of the corner of his eye, Brazier caught Loraine shifting her weight, her hand falling to her scimitar. In response, the tension in the room snapped tight as rigging before a surface storm. The gyre light dimmed, shadows tightening around them like coils.

"Or," the Handmaid said, her voice turning smooth and cold, "I can save him. Snatch him back from the void that claws so desperately for him."

Her veiled face pinned Brazier in place.

"All you need do," she purred, "is let the Lucidian remain in my keeping."

Brazier's hand froze on Vandemir's back, inches from his repeater's grip. He could feel Switch and Freyen watching him. He could feel their unspoken question tightening in the air between them.

This was just another choice with no clear answer, another black-damned decision with nothing but uncertainty for an outcome. The Handmaid's bargain was a question wrapped in sorcery: do you believe I'll honour my word? Or do you let Vandemir die?

"Now is not the time to dawdle," the Handmaid said softly. "His time grows short."

Vandemir's breath slipped to a rasp. His head sagged. Brazier felt the weight of a dying man gone slack in his arms.

"When do we get Matthias back?" Brazier asked. His

voice sounded far away to his own ears.

"When his task is done," the Handmaid answered, smooth as polished bone.

Which could mean never. He might be trapped here. He might be trapped here forever.

"Quickly now," the Handmaid pressed.

She turned to Vandemir, then back.

"My ability to save him is almost gone."

Vandemir's hand slid free, his body slumping. For a heartbeat, Brazier stood frozen, holding Vandemir's dead weight in his arms, but feeling only the weight of the decision. He thought of Matthias' grin, the reckless, sarcastic wit, the confidence with which he could put them all at ease, no matter the circumstances. He'd trusted Brazier. He'd trusted him to lead. He'd trusted him to protect the crew. And Brazier was about to betray that.

"We'll do it," Brazier said, the words tumbling out before he could taste their poison. "Matthias stays. Save him."

The Handmaid moved like lightning, her jerking gait devouring the space between them in three strides. She thrust her hand over Vandemir's wound, and the air around them warped.

Brazier felt it in his skin, like a thousand pins prickling his flesh. He tasted copper in his mouth. Vandemir gasped, his body convulsing as the Handmaid's sorcery seared through him. His eyes snapped open, wide with pain and wild confusion. And just like that, it was done. The Handmaid staggered back, her limbs bending the wrong way as she retreated up the steps, her grotesque form twisted, jagged, disjointed.

Vandemir writhed in Brazier's grip, tearing away the blood-soaked bandages to reveal nothing but a pale, angry scar across his belly. He touched it, eyes wide, breathing deeply.

"What have you done?" he rasped, staring at Brazier.

I've given up my navigator. I've given up one of my crew. Brazier's throat felt like it had been scraped raw.

"How long will it take?" he asked the Handmaid, his voice hoarse. "How long until Matthias is done with your task?"

She lifted a gloved hand to her mouth and giggled like a child.

"How many are the stars? How deep is the void? How old is the gyre?" she whispered. "Questions without end."

Around them, the Morletts closed in. They crawled along the pillars and slipped from cracks in the walls, their claws clicking on stone. They were everywhere, blotting out the gyre light.

"Go now, Brazier Veranquis," the Handmaid said, her voice turning to iron. "Our bargain is sealed. But my court grows hungry."

The Morletts snarled, the sound rising to a fever pitch.

"Our thanks, my lady," Folgar said quickly, already edging back. His hand clamped around Brazier's arm, tight as iron.

"There's no winning here," he hissed. "We go."

Brazier let the dwarf pull him, his feet dragging across the cracked tiles. His head swam, vision tunnelling. Around him, the chamber blurred, its shadows thick with teeth and hunger.

He stumbled down the pyramid, unable to feel the cut of stone under his boots. It was as if he were watching someone else scramble down the steps, someone that looked like him but wasn't, his mind unable to accept the reality that he had just given up one of his crew. He, Brazier Veranquis, had just signed away their freedom—maybe forever.

The thought that he might never see Matthias again brought reality crashing back to him so hard it caused a physical ache in his chest. At some point they'd made it to the edge of the city. Switch, or maybe Freyen, was saying something to him, or it could have been to Folgar. He didn't know. He couldn't bear to look at them. He just kept walking, head down, putting one foot in front of the other. If he stopped, if he looked into their eyes, he might never recover from the accusation and the disappointment he saw in them.

TWENTY-NINE KATHRYN

The hex sculpt showed converging forces. A fleet from Reantha drove southwest, while Theselan's ships surged northeast, cutting toward the same point. Behind them, the slower half of the rebel fleet, the Gyre Stars, pushed steadily southeast.

The *Tempest*, the *Crucible*, and the *Vanguard* hovered just a league from the northern tip of the Hyralian Gulf. And ahead of them all was the *Storm*. She was less than a mile from the Gulf's mouth, scrambling desperately toward safety. The black and silver filaments of its thrusters flared and churned in chaotic desperation, like insects in a disturbed hive.

Kathryn stared at the display. For years, the thought of Isdria Laanorath had filled her with terror, but now, chasing him down at the head of a fleet of ships changed Kathryn's perspective. Dread shifted to anticipation. Obsession transformed into something fierce and hungry, something a lot like excitement.

You're not out of this yet, she reminded herself. *If Gideon taught you anything, it's that things can still go wrong.*

And they could. Whoever commanded the two Spire forces had been slow to react; the three cruisers had already slipped past the point where they'd intercept. But the main rebel fleet wouldn't be so lucky. They would meet those forces head-on.

By alerting Reantha and Theselan, they'd forced the *Storm* off a certain escape route. But they'd also cut their own fleet off from the rest. No. She'd done that. It had been her decision. *And I'd make it again.*

She'd gambled. She'd sacrificed. And she'd created options. She'd carved out a path forward, and she'd keep doing that, again and again, until she had what she needed, until the mission was complete.

"Message from the Pheradies, sent fleet-wide," Jacob announced.

"On the hex," Kathryn said.

Korst's voice crackled from one of the wells.

"By now, you'll be aware of the situation facing the rebel fleet. If necessary, the Pheradies, the Vallidore, and the Orranthis will engage forces from Reantha and Theselan. You're to pursue the Storm into the Gulf, capture the vessel, and apprehend Isdria Laanorath. Await further instructions regarding the weapon and its destruction. Korst out."

The hex went flat.

"Get me two open tethers to the Tempest and the Crucible," Kathryn said. She'd already been in contact with Captain Greigor of the *Tempest* and Captain Olarin of the *Crucible* since retaking the nav deck. They'd been surprised at her earlier silence; she'd given a vague excuse about dealing with structural repairs. Admitting to a mutiny led by her First Officer within minutes of taking command was not a conversation she wanted to have just yet.

"Tethered," Jacob confirmed.

"Receiving, Captain," Greigor replied.

"Also receiving, Captain," came Olarin's voice.

In the background, she heard the muted, steady hum of their nav decks—clipped commands, quiet acknowledgments, the distant rumble of thrusters.

"Maintain formation into the Gulf," Kathryn ordered. "Then stagger pursuit into a reverse arrowhead. The Vanguard will bring up the rear, then initiate boarding under your covering fire. Olarin, have your war casters target her starboard hangar—carve us an opening. Once we're in, deploy both the Tempest's and the Crucible's boarding teams behind us."

"It would be our pleasure, Captain," Olarin said calmly.

"Captain Greigor," Kathryn continued, "focus gyranic attacks on the thrusters. Slow her down."

"We'll kneecap the bitch," Greigor replied. Kathryn couldn't help but smile. Greigor had the same impatient, hungry aggression Marcus Angelaux had displayed. If they turned out to be related, she wouldn't be the least bit surprised.

"My war casters have detected gyranic spikes in what appears to be the main hangar bay," Olarin said. "They believe that's where the weapon is being kept."

The hex flattened, then rescaled, presenting a magnified sculpt of the *Gloried Storm*. Its upper layers peeled back, filaments cascading to the command terminal, revealing a detailed cross-section. At the ship's centre, the bulbous chamber shaped like a toad's belly was surrounded by a labyrinth of corridors. Flanking it, two smaller hangar bays connected directly to this core chamber. A location marker pulsed deep inside, near the chamber's rear.

"Then that's exactly where we're headed," Kathryn said.

"We'll seize the starboard hangar bay, then fight our way into the central chamber. Isdria Laanorath won't stray far from the weapon."

"Some of those spikes are registering as messages," Olarin said.

"My navigator thinks they're sending communications into the Gulf."

Kathryn did not like the sound of that. Her mind immediately went to ambushes and enemy reinforcements.

"Does your navigator have any idea who the Storm is contacting?"

"Can't get a read on that. Nothing's coming out of the Gulf."

A variable Kathryn couldn't plan for. So she wouldn't.

"Be wary of additional enemy forces but still proceed to engage with the Storm. The Vanguard's forces will take the main hangar bay. Once we're in, we'll attempt to destroy it. If we can't, we'll secure the area and await further orders from the Pheradies. Captain Olarin—your forces will take the nav deck. Captain Greigor—yours will take the engines. Isdria Laanorath is a terrorist and a traitor, but he's not a coward. If he thinks he's losing, he'll overload the core and blow the ship. We can't let him do that."

"Aye, Captain," Olarin acknowledged.

"Aye, Captain," Greigor echoed.

"Good hunting, then," Kathryn said.

"Vanguard out."

Jacob dropped the tether, and the hex fell silent.

Kathryn took in the nav deck crew. Avery stood to her right, one eye swelling shut, bruises already darkening. He'd been freed from the brig, along with most of the engineering team. Karland stood across from her, quiet but steady, and between them, the ship's lone war caster slouched with fatigue. Strands of her brown hair were coming free of its bun, and the rings beneath her eyes Kathryn had noticed in the vulnerum had turned a shade darker. Her name, Kathryn had since discovered, was Josette Clever, and Kathryn had ordered her to bolster the ship's gyranic defences and nothing else.

Josette had laughed bitterly, replying, "As if there was anything else I could do."

They both knew she was almost completely drained, and drawing on any more of the gyre was likely to come at a significant personal cost. But what else could either of them do? Such was the fate of most war casters—a lesson drilled into them during the Academy. The quiet acceptance in her tired eyes told Kathryn she had made peace with that.

Senya stood behind them, stationed at one of the terminals, coordinating repairs alongside two members of Royer and Faber's teams. The idea of appointing a new First Officer had felt inappropriate so soon after the mistake she'd made with Gideon, but it hadn't mattered. Avery and Karland had naturally stepped into the void, filling the role together.

They'd cleared the bodies from the nav deck, but the scars remained: the doorway was still missing its doors, repeater-bolt impacts peppered the walls and decking, scratches marked where Senya had dragged her tower shield toward the command terminal, and panelling had been damaged in the engagement at Thela.

She felt like a soldier going into battle with a rusted sword. But at some point, it had become her sword. She'd grown used to its weight and trusted the feel of its grip beneath her fingers. Its dents and scratches weren't weaknesses; they were reminders. She'd fought for this ship. It was hers now.

She felt the shadow of her mother's presence then. It was a flicker of doubt, like the final flames of dying embers. Kathryn glanced around the deck, but Admiral Thrace made no appearance.

"The Storm has crossed into the Gulf," Jacob reported.

"We're five minutes out."

"Once the Crucible breaches, pull us directly alongside the *Storm's* starboard hull to shield the landers' approach," Kathryn ordered.

Then she turned to those around the command terminal.

"I'll be aboard one of those landers. Mr. Hurst, you will have acting command of the Vanguard."

Avery's good eye widened slightly, surprise flashing across his face. Karland and the war caster glanced briefly at Kathryn, but neither challenged her decision.

"Yes, sir," Avery replied firmly.

"Given the damage we've sustained," Kathryn continued, "you may need to retreat once we're aboard the Storm. That call is yours to make."

"And if you need to fall back from the Storm?" Avery asked cautiously.

"We'll retreat to the Crucible or the Tempest," Kathryn said.

"We outnumber the Sorel Tan; there's no need to hold our ground unnecessarily."

Avery nodded. "Understood, sir."

She turned to Karland.

"Let Sergeant Faber know I'll be joining his landing team."

Karland placed his hand in the hex and connected to the

hangar bay to relay her message.

"Primary bulkhead repairs complete, sir," one of the women behind the terminals reported. Kathryn thought her name was Devlyn Monteil. "Secondary repairs still ongoing."

"Keep non-essential maintenance crews on standby," Kathryn ordered. "We may need rapid response if we take additional hull damage."

"Yes, sir," Monteil replied, immediately relaying instructions through the hex to crews around the ship.

Karland removed his hand from the hex well.

"All boarding teams are assembled in the hangar bay, Captain. They're awaiting your orders."

Kathryn nodded once.

"Good."

On the hex, their three ships had reached the mouth of a primary tunnel, stopping less than an inch from the Gulf's wall. Stretching beyond lay a vast, scabrous landscape, an alien vista of jutting growths, swollen nodules, and massive fungal blooms. Twisted, gyre-infected limbs and scaled feelers thicker than spire-class frigates rose to scrape at the ceiling, swaying in slow, hypnotic patterns above rounded mushroom caps, some easily as large as the *Vanguard* itself. A fungal forest corrupted and warped by millennia of sorcery, teemed with goblin war-bands, witches, and the vicious surface crawlers that used the Gulf as their nesting grounds.

Navarch military doctrine dictated only one rule of engagement for either of Formaria's two Gulfs—the Doctrine of No Return: Due to extreme hostility from subterranean flora and fauna, personnel are strictly prohibited from disembarking naval vessels once deployed. Rescue attempts will not be conducted for personnel who violate this protocol.

Kathryn was reasonably sure she'd remembered that right almost word-for-word. But even if she chose to violate it now, it wasn't as though the Navarch would rush to their rescue. The *Tempest*, the *Crucible*, and the *Vanguard* were on their own. *Still more friends than you had two days ago*, she thought, and something about that realisation reignited Kathryn's sense of anticipation.

She'd left Ilantia alone, friendless, and all but shunned by her colleagues, making desperate decisions and reckless gambles that had nearly left her imprisoned or dead. Now she stood at the head of a fleet. The path ahead felt clear, with opportunities lining up like courtiers before a king, while Isdria Laanorath had run out of options. *But don't get ahead of yourself*, she reminded herself sharply.

"Passing into the Gulf now," Jacob reported.

Kathryn straightened.

"Mr. Hurst, issue general quarters."

Avery nodded once, placed his hand in the hex well. His eyelids fluttered briefly, then one of the free wells beside her trembled. Throughout the ship, terminals would be doing the same.

"All hands, action stations. Action stations," Avery's voice resonated from the hex. "Prepare to engage."

On the hex, the *Vanguard*, trailing just behind the *Crucible* and the *Tempest*, slipped out of the tunnel and into the eerie, warped landscape of the Gulf, like wolves entering an ancient and corrupted forest.

Then chaos erupted.

Several things happened at once. The hex display crumbled, dissolving like sand washed away by rain. It twisted, shifted, struggling to reform, becoming a rippling, undulating sea of meaningless patterns. The war caster winced, pressing one hand hard against her temple as if struck by sudden agony. Blood poured unchecked from her nose. And Kathryn's vision blurred. She was seized by a sudden, violent dizziness, as if she'd taken a blow to the head but without the pain.

Her vision swam, nausea rising sharply, bile crawling up her throat. Without thinking, she gripped the edges of the command terminal, squeezing her eyes shut. In the darkness behind her eyelids, columns of blue fire erupted. A Mirrovinjin face loomed before her, ravaged by decay, and the stench of rot pouring from the ruin of its skull. Pure, raw terror sliced through her veins, freezing her muscles, locking her breath. She forced her eyes open. Someone was beside her. She smelled Senya's scent and felt Karland's strong grip beneath her arm. They were speaking—shouting—but the ringing in her ears drowned out their words.

Avery and Josette had vanished. For a brief, panicked moment, Kathryn's mind thought some dark sorcery had simply obliterated them. Then she caught sight of Avery kneeling beside the war caster, helping her struggle shakily to her feet. Then who was standing at the opposite side of the command terminal?

She was lean and imposing, her posture rigid enough to crack bronzite. She wore a Navarch-blue doublet with gleaming admiral's epaulettes, her chest adorned with medals. Her mother stood directly across from her.

"Captain," Senya's voice came distant and muffled, like hearing her through water. "Captain, can you hear me?"

Sound flooded in all at once, like waves crashing against stone. Avery was asking if Josette could stand. Senya and Karland were urgently trying to get her attention, asking if she was alright. Deck officers shouted reports, demanding engine statuses, hex stability, hull integrity. Jacob was saying something, but too quietly to hear. And her mother stood utterly still, a smug grin spreading slowly across her face, her shoulders loose and her hands relaxed. There was no ruler this time, no anger, only satisfaction. Kathryn had gotten something wrong, something important, and her mother revelled in it.

"I'm fine," Kathryn said, pushing Senya and Karland away. Her voice barely rose above the noise on the nav deck. She tried again, louder, harsher: "I'm fine."

Whatever small protests Senya might've made were lost beneath the noise. Kathryn's entire attention was fixed on the hex display, where the sprawling, fungus-choked expanse of the Gulf unfolded before her.

The three rebel ships pressed forward in pursuit, but the single, lone shape of the *Gloried Storm* they'd been chasing moments before had become three, each breaking off in a separate direction.

Kathryn waited for one of them to falter, for its hull to

shimmer, fracture, or reveal some flaw that would betray it as an illusion, a figment of the Gulf's warping sorceries. But none of them did. All three looked perfectly real and perfectly identical.

"Sir," Jacob said, voice sharper and clearer than she'd ever heard from him. "I have tether requests from the Tempest and the Crucible."

Kathryn didn't take her eyes off the hex.

"Tell me what I'm looking at first."

"It feels like interference from the Gulf," Jacob said, but there was uncertainty clouding his voice. "Gyranic distortions are affecting our hex systems."

"It's coming from the Storm," Josette said, wiping blood from her nose.

She stood mere inches from the ghostly presence of Kathryn's mother, oblivious to the apparition. Kathryn forced herself to focus on Josette, resisting with every muscle the urge to glance at her mother's mocking smile.

"Either the Gulf is interacting with the weapon aboard the ship, or they've deliberately activated it somehow." The war caster coughed sharply into her hand, glanced down, then wiped blood across her gambeson.

"Either way," Josette continued, her voice strained, "it's emitting high levels of Obliquency."

"Can you withstand it?" Kathryn asked.

Josette met her eyes.

"I don't have a choice."

"Sir," Jacob pressed again, urgency sharpening his tone. "The Tempest and the Crucible are still waiting."

Kneeling behind the ghost of her mother, Kathryn couldn't stop herself from glancing up when the apparition spoke.

"You were always so certain of yourself," her mother said. "You tried to hide it, but I could always tell—you thought you knew better."

Her voice was calm, sharp, and inevitable.

"And now look where it's got you."

The illusion looked so real, so solid, that Kathryn's mind faltered for a moment, shocked into stillness. Her mother might have been standing there on the nav deck in the flesh.

"On the hex," Kathryn said, forcing the words through her lips. She tried to keep her voice level. She tried not to let it shake. *You are so close. Do not let this stop you from getting that damn elf.*

The two wells in front of her trembled in sync. Greigor's voice came through first.

"Sir, I assume you're seeing the same abyss-damned problem we are?"

"I am, Captain," Kathryn replied.

She kept her gaze pinned on the hex display, even though her mother's shape lingered just at the edge of her vision, like the silhouette of a demon in a dream she couldn't wake from.

"My war caster believes it's the weapon on the Storm, reacting with the Gulf."

"My war caster has told me the same thing," Greigor said.

"As did mine," Olarin added.

"Then we have no option but to split and pursue each vessel independently," Kathryn said. She let herself fall into the rhythm of command, the practiced momentum of decision-making, the discipline of thinking five moves ahead. Her brow creased in concentration.

"One of those ships is the real Storm. The other two are illusions. Whichever of us makes contact with the real vessel will need to hold position until the others can reinforce. Assign gully teams to your hulls—I have a feeling that's the only way we'll know which one is real."

"Aye, Captain," Olarin said.

"Aye, Captain," Greigor echoed.

The hex wells fell flat. On the sculpt, the *Tempest* veered portside, chasing the *Storm* that had broken northeast. The *Crucible* pulled starboard, hunting the one headed southeast. The *Vanguard* maintained its trajectory, cutting straight east in pursuit of the middle vessel.

"Mr. Agathor," Kathryn said. "Get a team up onto the hull—they're our eyes out here."

"Sir," Karland acknowledged.

"Gamble after gamble," her mother's voice hissed

opposite her, low and venomous. Rage simmered beneath the surface, boiling at the edges. "I knew you would turn out like this. I sensed it the day they gave you to me. Always thinking you knew better. That you were smarter than the admiral who trained generations of officers. Generations of the best."

Kathryn kept her eyes on the hex, tracking the three diverging ships, forcing herself to stay two moves ahead, thinking tactically and strategically—anything to avoid acknowledging the poison dripping from the other side of the command terminal.

"And what are you going to do if you reach the Storm first?"

The voice was quieter now. It wasn't a threat or a scream, but something worse. It was calculated and knowing. Kathryn's eyes flicked up before she could stop herself. Her mother stared with that same predatory calm. Panic cracked through Kathryn's concentration. Suddenly, a pressure gripped the back of her skull. It was cold and invisible, like a hand pressing down from above. A faint ringing filled her ears, dulling the rest of the nav deck to a background haze.

"I'm picking up increased activity in the Gulf," Jacob's voice cut through.

The pressure loosened. Kathryn shook her head, forcing herself back into the present. The weight upon her skull receded but didn't vanish. It lingered, like an invisible current flowing beneath the surface of her thoughts.

"Black abyss," Avery muttered. He was staring at the hex display, voice low with awe, or dread. Maybe it was both.

The tendrils and feelers rising from the fungal growths, which had drifted moments ago like riverweed in a slow current, now spasmed and jerked as if struck by lightning. Their movements were skittish and violent.

"What am I looking at?" Kathryn asked.

Her hands gripped the edges of the command terminal, needing to feel something real beneath her fingers, something solid to anchor her against the strange, creeping pressure still clawing at the back of her skull. Her eyes stayed locked on the hex, because if she looked anywhere else, she might see her.

The question had been for Jacob. But it was Josette who answered.

"It's eminat—" she started, then stopped.

Kathryn looked up. Blood was pouring from Josette's nose and splashing onto the hex terminal in thick droplets.

"Damn it," Josette muttered. There was no wince, no sign of pain, but that was somehow worse.

"There should be bandages in here," Kathryn said to Senya.

"Err, yes sir," Senya stammered. She turned one way, then another, before hurrying toward a wall panel.

Josette wiped at her face with her sleeve. Her voice came thick and distorted through the blood.

"It's emanating from the Storm. Massive surges of Aeturnic and gyranic sorcery. The Gulf's just… reacting to it."

Kathryn stared at the hex, at the chaos unfolding across the fungal nightmare outside, and thought: *Aren't we all.*

"I'm picking up more activity, four leagues south of our position," Jacob said.

The hex display rippled, then shifted, reforming into a rolling sculpt of the fungal expanse broken by flat, shadowy depressions marking underground lakes.

Jacob extended his mind outward, threading it through the noise of the Gulf. The sculpt stabilised momentarily, centring on a distant, indistinct section of terrain. This far from the ship, and under the Gulf's interference, the hex struggled to maintain its shape. It rendered the view as a blur of vague tendrils and looming caps, uncertain outlines bleeding into one another.

But then Kathryn saw it.

Amid the warped chaos, things moved: small clusters of filaments zipped and darted across the terrain like a swarm of insects. They were fast and erratic, like wasps. But if they were that visible on the hex… if the system scaled them at this size—

"Cicadrons," Avery said quietly, voice tight, the hatred in it unmistakable.

The giant wasp-like creatures—hundreds, maybe thousands—bobbed and wove through the fungal growth, disappearing and reappearing like ghosts in mist. There was enough to bring down a cruiser, maybe even three.

"A good captain knows when the odds are against them," her mother's voice echoed, low and firm. The pressure returned, clawing at Kathryn's skull. The ringing in her ears surged. "Tactical withdrawal when continued engagement serves no strategic benefit. A good captain understands regroup and counter are as vital as any offensive manoeuvre."

Her voice came to Kathryn as though spoken in a dream. It was stern, practiced, and meant to be memorised. Kathryn gritted her teeth.

"A good captain is resilient in the face of changing circumstances," she muttered. "A good captain doesn't balk at a fight."

"Captain?" Avery asked, hesitant.

She ignored him.

"Maintain course, Mr. Philadore," she said sharply, forcing volume into her voice to drown out the pressure. "Send a message to the Tempest and the Crucible. Advise them of inbound hostiles and instruct them to continue pursuit. Mission objective remains unchanged."

"I've never seen a swarm that big," Avery murmured, dazed.

"It's like they've been called," Senya said, her wide brown eyes fixed on the hex. "Like they've been called to the Storm."

"The weapon could be acting as a lodestone," Josette said, voice thick with fatigue. "Goblins are drawn to Aeturnic sorcery."

"It won't matter what they're doing here," Kathryn said, raising her voice until it rang across the nav deck, louder than the ringing in her ears, louder than the phantom weight still pressing at the edges of her mind. "It won't matter if there's a hundred of them, or a thousand. By the time they reach us, there'll be three Gyre Stars sitting in this Gulf, adding a swarm of Cicadrons to their kill count."

She let her gaze sweep the deck. She let her crew feel her conviction.

"We are soldiers of Formaria," she said. "We have fought and won against enemies who've outnumbered us a hundred to one, for a thousand years. We will fight, and we will win today."

She could feel their eyes on her.

Karland stood straighter.

"Yes, sir."

Avery nodded once and glanced toward Senya.

"Yes, sir," they said, nearly in unison, joined by the quiet affirmations of the officers behind them.

One of the hex wells beside Karland pulsed. He pressed his hand into the filaments, then withdrew it a moment later. When he spoke, there was something in his voice, a steeliness beneath the words. Maybe it was just what she wanted to hear, maybe not.

"Message from the gully teams," Karland said. "They think we've got the real Storm."

What happens if you reach the Storm first?

We hold out, she told herself, bracing for what was to come. *Until the Tempest and the Crucible arrive.*

"Mr. Philadore," Kathryn said. "Send word to the Tempest and the Crucible—let them know we have visual confirmation on the real Storm. Have them check with their gully teams to verify."

"Yes, sir," Jacob said, already moving.

"If that's the real Storm," Avery said, narrowing his eyes at the sculpt, "why aren't they firing on us yet? We're well within range of their aft repeaters."

Kathryn watched the hex as the *Vanguard* continued closing the last mile between itself and the enemy ship. Avery was right.

"Because firing would give them away," she said. "And they know it."

"Tempest confirms no visual on their target," Jacob reported. His chin dipped slightly to one side, eyes flickering under half-lowered lids. "Crucible the same. Both are shifting to our heading. Four minutes until they're alongside us."

On the hex, the sculpt reformed. The *Tempest* and *Crucible* curved back toward the *Vanguard*; their formation now a broad arrowhead with the *Vanguard* at the tip. A second later, tiny needles erupted from the *Storm's* aft repeaters in a hail of repeater fire. The Sorel Tan knew they'd been found.

Kathryn didn't glance across the command terminal. She felt her mother there like a furnace, all searing heat and judgmental silence. The pressure thickened again and the ringing swelled like far-off bells.

"Bring your team in, Mr. Agathor," Kathryn said.

Karland pressed his hand into the hex to relay her orders as the *Storm's* repeater fire rang out in a series of sharp clangs along their hull. Avery and Senya both glanced upward, but Kathryn remained locked on the display, her heart hammering in time with the rising pitch in her ears.

"Umm," Senya said, her voice small but bright with energy, "would you like me to give the order to fire back?"

She was clearly trying, and failing, not to sound eager. Avery glanced at her, the edge of a smile tugging at his mouth. The unexpected enthusiasm broke through the rising tension, and Kathryn felt her own lips curve into a smile in response.

"The Vanguard lost its bow repeaters during the fight at Thela," she said. "We've got nothing to fire back with until our mid and aft repeaters are in range."

Senya fidgeted, hands dancing nervously before she shrugged and waved it off.

"No, yeah—I knew that, sir," she said, glancing awkwardly past Kathryn's shoulders toward the wall.

"Mr. Philadore," Kathryn said, keeping her tone even. "Bring us below their hull line. Minimise their repeaters' line of sight."

She turned to Senya.

"Once we're in range, target their lower hull repeaters first. Then shift to the portside hull batteries."

"Yes sir," Senya replied, already moving back to her terminal and trying not to grin like a child.

On the hex sculpt, the *Vanguard* closed the last sliver of distance, less than an inch from the *Storm's* representation. Half an inch out, the *Vanguard* began to dip, sliding below its target's hull like a shadow slinking beneath a leviathan. The tapping along the hull intensified into a tight, rapid rhythm. Then a grunt from the other side of the command terminal broke through the tension.

Kathryn looked over to see Josette's face twisted in concentration, her eyes squeezed shut, her hands clenched into fists, and a vein throbbing visibly along her temple.

"They've initiated their magical barrage," Jacob said. His voice had gone cold.

"Maintain course," Kathryn ordered. "Once we're beneath their hull, reroute any spare power to our forward plating."

On the hex, the *Vanguard* slipped completely beneath the *Storm*, brushing aside fungal feelers and towering mushroom caps like strands of kelp. The way the two ships curved together looked more like a slow mating ritual between deep-sea giants than a battle manoeuvre.

"Open fire when ready, Ms. Kilburn," Kathryn said.

"Yes, sir," Senya answered, excitement buried just deep enough to pass for professionalism.

The decking lurched beneath Kathryn's feet, a shuddering ripple that sent her hand grasping for the edge of the command terminal. Karland and Avery mirrored the movement instinctively, steadying themselves as the *Vanguard* absorbed another barrage.

Josette was bleeding freely now. Her skin had gone ice white, and deep violet rings bloomed beneath her eyes. She looked like she was standing in a storm without shelter, taking the full force of the *Storm's* cadre of war casters.

Kathryn glanced toward the *Tempest* and *Crucible* on the hex, willing them to close the gap faster.

Another impact rocked the ship. She felt the spatial anchor struggling to hold them stable. The ringing in Kathryn's ears rose again, sharper and shriller. She could feel her mother's silent presence and the weight of judgment coiling around her ribs, squeezing them tight. Kathryn forced air into her lungs, but her heart hammered too fast. A quiet voice whispered in the back of her mind: *You won't make it. Whatever's in you, whatever this is, it'll break you before you reach Isdria.*

"Tempest and Crucible have opened fire," Avery said. He was leaning against the terminal, a bead of sweat rolling down the side of his face, his forearms straining against the edge.

On the hex, strings of filaments lanced outward—repeater turrets on both ships unleashing a barrage of needle-like bolts that struck the *Storm's* hull in a crashing wave. For a brief moment, Kathryn felt a flash of hope that cut through her haze like sunlight through fog.

Then a thunderous impact slammed through the nav deck. She was thrown forward. Her hands slipped from the terminal, skidding through the hex filaments. She crashed into the edge of the hex display, ribs slamming into the lip of the terminal. Pain bloomed across her chest. She let out an involuntary oomph as the air was forced from her lungs.

Avery and Karland were thrown to the decking. Josette had collapsed, her body crumpled somewhere beyond Kathryn's line of sight. The gyre channels running the length of the walls, floor, and ceiling flickered, then dimmed to a sullen, sickly blue. One of the wall panels to her right tore free and crashed down with a sharp *clang*. Only the hex display remained unchanged, its depiction of the battle still raging across the filaments.

A groan echoed through the *Vanguard's* bones. It was a low warning that turned into something sharper, the sound of metal under strain, of joints tearing. It was the kind of noise a ship makes when it's on the verge of breaking.

Around her, the rest of the nav deck came alive with her officers' groans and coughing as they struggled to right themselves. The hex wells chattered with urgent, overlapping voices from throughout the ship, spilling damage reports and cries for help. Kathryn didn't need to hear the requests to know many of them wouldn't be answered.

She moved quickly around the command terminal,

reaching out to help Avery to his feet as the gyre channels flickered again. The blue faded entirely, leaving behind translucent white veins pulsing with cold, crystalline light. The pulses rippled outward, washing over the nav deck in a ghostly moonlight glow, throwing strange shadows against every surface.

Josette's body lay sprawled beside the nav pit, unmoving. Blood trickled from her nose and ears. The silver light from the gyre channels cast her in a cold glow, as though she were already somewhere else.

In the nav pit, Jacob sat slumped forward, arms limp at his sides, chin resting against his chest. Kathryn stepped toward him. She moved over Josette's still form, knees dipping into the filament basin like sinking into fine sand, and slid an arm around Jacob's thin shoulders.

His body folded into hers.

There was no tension in him, none of the unconscious resistance of the living. He was just slack weight, and bones that felt too sharp beneath his uniform. Holding him was like cradling a child who'd gone far too long without food or warmth.

She turned his face toward her. His mouth hung open. His head lolled loosely onto her shoulder. She pressed her fingers to his neck, though she already knew what she would find. There was no pulse.

A hollow ache cracked open in her chest. It was too raw to resist. It was too sudden to stop. She barely knew Jacob. She hadn't even seen his face properly until now. And it was stupid, but all she could think, through the pressure building behind her eyes, through the ringing that drowned out half her thoughts, was that she'd lost another one. She'd lost another crew member who had, for the briefest time, trusted her and followed her, and who had been one of hers. And Josette... She didn't need to check to know she'd lost her too.

"Sir, message from the Crucible," Avery said. His voice was tight. "They've blown a hole in the Storm's hangar bay shield doors—they've got a way in!"

"I'm getting reports from all over the ship," Karland said, frantic now, the tension bleeding through every word.

"Structural damage runs from the upper hull all the way to the lower hull."

As if the ship wanted to confirm it, another deep groan rippled through the nav deck like the dying breath of some ancient, wounded animal.

"Chief Enginator is reporting thruster failures, sir," Devlyn called out from behind her. "Internal gyre system is down by seventy percent—and climbing."

Kathryn barely had time to register that before Avery spoke: "Sir… the hex is giving me an automated script…" He trailed off. He didn't need to finish it. She already knew what it would say.

"Complete system-wide failure expected," he said quietly. "Abandon ship order recommended."

Kathryn laid Jacob's body down in the hex pit with care, cradling his head so it wouldn't strike the filaments. She eased him to rest. He looked peaceful, like a man caught in the middle of a deep, dreamless sleep.

She stood.

She came face to face with her mother, standing across from her, unchanged and impossible, blonde hair bound painfully tight, every sharp edge of her face like a sculpture. But the features were softer now. There was a glint in her eye, a slight curl to her thin, bloodless lips. It looked almost like satisfaction. And the pressure radiating off her was like a leaden weight. Kathryn's limbs felt heavy, her chest tight, as if she were being squeezed from the inside out. Her body reacted the way it had since she was a child: heart pounding, muscles tensed, every nerve screaming danger.

Only this time, something was different. For the first time in her life, Kathryn imagined striking her. She imagined driving her fist into that immaculate face, drawing her blade and cutting straight down, clavicle to nave, and ruining that perfect uniform.

And with that thought, something changed. It didn't frighten her. It didn't shame her. It just settled into her mind with a kind of clarity. And for the first time, the anger wasn't tangled in fear or the echoes of a frightened child. It was hatred, cold and clean.

"Mr. Hurst," she said, her voice steady as she stared directly into her mother's eyes. "Inform the Crucible and the Tempest we are abandoning ship. Assemble retrieval teams and have all wounded moved to the hangar bays for immediate evacuation."

"Yes, sir," Avery said.

"Mr. Agathor," Kathryn continued, voice unwavering. "Boarding parties are authorised. Hit the breach point. Make sure there's a lander waiting for us."

"Yes, sir," Karland replied without hesitation.

The smile on her mother's face faltered. The corners of her lips twitched downward. The hawkish glare returned, piercing and cold. But Kathryn no longer cared. It had no power now. It meant nothing. She raised her voice, cutting through the nav deck, cutting through the ringing and the oppressive weight.

"Issue final orders to your teams to assemble in the hangar bays," she called out. "Then arm up—we're taking the fight to the Storm."

THIRTY
BRAZIER

Brazier walked ten feet ahead of the group, torch in hand. Folgar had given it to him without a word. He was close enough to see the bobbing lights behind him, to catch glimpses of shadows moving through the undergrowth, but far enough that their voices were no more than a soft murmur. To Brazier, they were a distant sound that felt like it belonged to another world. They'd given him space; space to walk alone, space to wrestle with himself.

The Brazier of yesterday would have called it indulgent. He'd have scorned this kind of brooding solitude, dismissed it as weakness. His brother's voice would have filled his head with sharp-edged lessons in pragmatism and discipline: Keep moving forward, no self-pity, no reflection, only the mission. But the Brazier of today didn't care about yesterday's rules—not tonight, not after the deal he'd made.

Walking the dark forest path, torchlight casting wild shadows along the trunks, he almost hoped one of Yeggardania's creatures would come for him, something savage, with teeth and claws, something he could fight.

But nothing came.

The forest was silent, and the silence felt like a mockery.

It was the same kind of silence he imagined Matthias had slipped into, vanished into.

They reached the steps of Calaxis without trouble. There were no ambushes or nightmares waiting in the dark. Folgar's surface team opened the gates at the sight of them, and they climbed the stairs to the platform leading down into the spire. It was only then, under the cold torchlight flickering off the pale grey alloy, that Brazier lifted his head and met their eyes.

Freyen caught his gaze first, and gave him a smile. It was warm and bright, almost enough to mask the flicker of pity he thought he saw behind it.

She'd done her best to scrape the muck of the Immuratum from her hair, but a grey crust still clung to her hairline, cracked and brittle. Brazier knew that smile well enough by now to see past it. She meant it, but it carried weight beneath the surface.

Switch didn't bother with a mask. She met his eyes, crossbow braced against her mechanical elbow, one fist planted on her hip, and raised an eyebrow. Her entire demeanour seemed to convey a single, unspoken message: Well? Did you enjoy your lonely little sulk, you big baby?

It almost made him laugh.

To his surprise, beneath the fatigue in their faces, the grime, the exhaustion, the sheer weight of the day, there was no anger. There was no resentment. There was none of the judgement he'd been bracing for since the moment he gave Matthias up.

There was just weariness.

Folgar reappeared from behind the semi-octagonal terminal, where he'd been speaking to someone over the hex.

"Karenna's waiting for you in the maintenance bays," he said to Brazier. "We've got a lift prepped to take you straight there."

"And the Anchorite?" Switch asked.

"She's all patched up," Folgar replied.

Switch gave a tight nod of approval, mixed with something like pride.

Folgar's eyes returned to Brazier. "I'll keep watch up here. Check in with your navigator when I can."

"Thank you," Brazier said, dipping his chin in acknowledgment.

Switch pointed a mechanical finger at Folgar. "Make sure that witch keeps to her end of the bargain."

"There's no fear of that," Folgar said, and for once there was no bravado in his voice, just hard certainty. "Reneging on deals isn't how their kind work."

The lift arrived with a low mechanical hum, and the octagonal platform rising up out of the well like a summoned creature.

"Bring some food for him," Freyen said, as they stepped aboard, patting Folgar on the arm. "When you take the toad his ale. Abyss knows what the Handmaid thinks passes for a meal."

"I'll bring a spare barrel, too," Folgar replied, with a ghost of a grin. "Maybe some real whiskey, if Karenna can get her hands on it."

The lift shuddered as it began its descent, walls blurring into streaks of grey and purple as they sped down into the heart of the spire. The temperature dropped with it, and a cold breath rose up from the depths.

"She won't kill him," Atlas said, out of nowhere.

Brazier turned toward the Rex Populaire's navigator but didn't answer. The words sat heavy in his chest, pulling at the fear he'd kept nailed down during the long march back through Yeggardania. It wasn't just guilt he'd been carrying. It was the weight of what if.

What if Matthias had already served his purpose? What

if the Handmaid moved on, disappeared into the endless depths of Yeggardania, taking Matthias with her? What if the task she'd given him had no end?

"She won't," Atlas pressed, like she could see the flicker of doubt behind his eyes. "A Lucidian is too rare. Too valuable to something like the Handmaid. And Folgar's right—they don't break their word. It's not in their nature."

Brazier thought about asking how she knew that, then decided he didn't care. Did he believe the Handmaid would honour the deal? No, not really, despite what Folgar had said. But he believed he would try to get Matthias back. And right now, belief was all he had to hold on to.

"Even if it was," Brazier said, voice low, tight with steel, "we wouldn't give her the chance."

Brazier hadn't worked out how he was going to follow through on that statement, but he knew it was true. It had been true from the moment he'd made the bargain with the Handmaid. He'd just been too distracted by his self-hatred to realise it yet.

"If you're thinking about a little return visit," Vandemir rumbled from behind him, "to make sure she keeps her word…"

Brazier turned to him. Vandemir stood with his massive Gorefelder resting point-down between his boots, his hands folded over the hilt, his eyes burning with quiet fire.

"Then we'd be honoured to join you," Vandemir finished.

Brazier held his gaze a moment, weighing the promise behind it.

"Not sure what I'm planning yet," he admitted. "But if it comes to a fight… you'll be the first I call."

The lift slowed, gave a mechanical jolt as it slotted into place, and the chute doors parted in front of them. The maintenance bay looked almost exactly as they'd left it. The gyre channels ran up the walls, pulsing with steady blue light. The bronzite frame circled the central pit, catching the glow like a halo. Piles of spare parts were stacked in neat, fast-dwindling mountains. And there, in the middle of it all, was the *Anchorite.*

She looked better, noticeably better. Even at a glance, Brazier could tell they'd done good work. Scorch marks and impact scars still ran across her hull like battle tattoos, but the missing thrusters had been replaced, and new repeaters glinted under the gyre light. She was still battered, but she looked ready to hunt again.

Karenna stood waiting for them, just outside the lift. She wore her same grease-stained coveralls, sleeves rolled up, weathered hands working at a rag that had long since given up on being clean. Her face was drawn with exhaustion, but when she saw them, a small smile crept through the fatigue.

"How's she looking?" Brazier asked, as they stepped out onto the bay.

Karenna fell in beside them, walking toward the *Anchorite* like it was her oldest friend.

"As good as we could make her, given the time," she said. "She ain't pretty, but she'll fly. Most of the replacement parts are calibrated, but Matthias'll need to adjust some protocols."

She glanced around the group, her eyes narrowing slightly. "Speaking of which…"

The words hung in the air, heavy as a weight. The only sound was the muffled thrum of ship engines and the clang of cargo operations bleeding down from the hangar bay above.

Karenna's eyes sharpened as the silence stretched. The realisation dawned in them.

"He's still alive," Brazier said. He forced the words out, knowing how hollow they sounded. "But we… had to leave him."

He tried not to wince as he said it.

Karenna's gaze didn't waver. She gave a slow, knowing nod, as if she'd already guessed the answer and had only been waiting for him to confirm it.

"If there's one dwarf who can survive Yeggardania," she said quietly, almost to herself, "it's Matthias Phaser. You can be sure of that."

"We don't plan on letting him survive it for long," Brazier replied. "We'll see you soon."

Karenna gave Switch and Freyen quick, fierce hugs, then offered a respectful nod to the rest of the Rex Populaire.

"Watch that throughput," Karenna called after Switch, voice gruff but fond. "She'll kick, to begin with."

"Thanks, Karenna," Switch called back, raising her augmented hand in a casual salute.

They climbed the boarding ramp, the gyre lights catching the hull of the *Anchorite*, painting her in streaks of oceanic blue, as though she were already streaking back toward a fight.

Aboard the ship, they laid Solon and Bertrand in the vulnerum, folding their hands over their chests like soldiers lain to rest. Their weapons were stowed in the racks, and then they made their way to the nav deck.

The *Anchorite* was a Navarch warship, made for a crew of six plus a squad of elite troopers. But after three months running with just four people, having twice that crammed inside made the ship feel as small as a lander. By the time they all squeezed onto the nav deck, crowding around the command terminal, it felt as though the ship had shrunk two sizes overnight.

Atlas rounded the terminal to the nav pit, then stopped, turning back to Brazier like she'd forgotten something.

"May I?" she asked, gesturing to the pit.

"We're going to struggle if you don't," Brazier said, nodding her in.

Atlas kicked off her boots, stepped barefoot into the pit, and knelt. She spread her arms, palms wide, and the hex around her knees bloomed to life.

A low vibration ran through the decking as the thrusters engaged. Overhead, the maintenance bay doors cracked open with a mechanical clatter, the echo ringing down the chamber. The hex sculpt rose with a shiver, projecting the Spire and its surrounding tunnels. They watched the miniature *Anchorite* pull away from the hangar, sailing east into the dark artery of tunnels.

"Got an urgent message," Atlas said, then corrected herself. "Multiple updates. All from the Pheradies, with Admiral Korst's command script."

"Transfer the last one to the hex," Brazier said.

A well beside Freyen's hand pulsed alive. Korst's voice spluttered out: "Anchorite, this is the Pheradies. As I speak, the Vanguard, the Crucible, and the Tempest are thirty minutes out from the Hyralian Gulf in pursuit of the Gloried Storm. Their engagement is imminent. The Pheradies and remainder of the fleet are three leagues northwest, following course. We anticipate engagement delays. Confirm receipt and respond with a situation report as soon as able. If you have secured the means of destroying the weapon, now is the time."

The message cut out. The hex fell flat.

"When did we get that message?" Brazier asked.

"Ten minutes ago," Atlas replied.

"Four-hour delay?" Brazier asked.

"Maybe longer," Atlas said. "The coordinates script tags them cutting in from the northwest, right at the tip of the Gulf."

"Then that's where we're going," Brazier said without

hesitation.

"We're ten hours out from the Hyralian Gulf, even on a good run," Freyen pointed out. "Whatever happens there will be done before we arrive."

"Then we get a message to the Vanguard," Switch said. "We tell Kathryn exactly what she needs to do."

"Better to send it to the Pheradies for relay," Atlas countered. "Less chance of it getting scrambled by Gulf interference if it's bounced from closer in."

"That's still a four-hour delay," Brazier said, running the numbers in his head and hating every one of them.

Vandemir, steady as a rock behind them, gave a low grunt. "Not to piss all over your plan, Captain," he said, his Harothellian accent rolling through the nav deck. "But you really think your harbinger's going to stop believing in ghost ships because of one message?"

Brazier didn't answer right away. He thought of Kathryn Stryker, of her steel-eyed conviction, of the weight she carried like it was welded to her spine. He'd known her only briefly, but that had been enough. She was stubborn, really stubborn.

"It's not likely," Brazier admitted. "But it's the only choice we have. Send the message. And get there as fast as we can."

"I might be able to help with that last part," Atlas said.

"You know a shortcut to the Hyralian Gulf?" Switch quipped.

"Nope," Atlas replied. "But I can get us there in half the time if I cascade the gyre system and combine it with a surge protocol in the engines. Little trick I picked up."

Brazier didn't have the faintest clue what that meant. But Switch clearly did. She stiffened like Atlas had just used her real name.

"That's not a trick," Switch snapped. "That's flooding

the core and burning out the reductor heads."

"That's the plan," Atlas said, grinning like she'd won a bet no one else had placed.

Switch's fists balled at her sides, and for a heartbeat, Brazier thought he might have to step between them.

"That is not the plan," Switch growled. "You do that, you'll fry the whole gyre system and get maybe one sprawl out of it before we're dead in the void."

"Not if you know how to ride it out," Atlas said, and winked.

"No one knows how to ride it out," Switch shot back, pure disbelief in her voice.

"Ms. Hale could make a ship sing and dance around her little finger," Vandemir said from behind them. "I've seen her do it."

Switch turned to Brazier, daring him with her glare to side with her, daring him to say yes.

"Let's try it," Brazier said.

Switch's jaw tightened. She shook her head and stormed off the nav deck. As the doors hissed shut behind her, Brazier was pretty sure he caught the words, "Just like having another Matthias," under her breath.

"You might want to hold onto something," Atlas said, cheerful as ever. "Power surge might override the spatial anchor."

"Never known it not to override the spatial anchor when you do this," Olivier muttered, already bracing against the command terminal.

The others followed suit, clutching the edge like priests hanging onto a Formarian relic.

A low rumble growled underfoot. The gyre channels burst into brilliant blue, lighting up the nav deck bright as daylight, as a rising whine shivered through the ship. It felt like thunder rolling under their feet—a wave of force swelling from deep inside the hull.

Brazier's gut flipped as the weight fell out from under him, like an invisible rope tethering him to the deck had just been cut. Only his grip on the terminal kept him from tumbling across the nav deck. Around him, the others were locked to the terminal with white-knuckled grips, faces set, eyes wide. In his mind, he apologised to his recently repaired ship.

On the hex, the *Anchorite* streaked across the void like a falling star, a blaze of light ripping through the darkness. The speed knotted tension in Brazier's chest, a primitive panic rising under his ribs. Nearly a millennium of Fromryr flight engineering told him this was normal. But his animal brain didn't care. It screamed that moving this fast could only result in a painful death.

"Best not to look at it or think about it," Vandemir said, turning his head away from the display. "Won't do you any good."

Brazier couldn't help himself. His eyes stayed glued to the hex, watching the *Anchorite* hurtle toward Maw Veraxies like it was tethered to some invisible slingshot.

"Inertial mutagenis is in the vulnerum," he called out. As the only dwarf there, he was the only one who wouldn't need it.

"Should have thought about that before we set the engines on fire," Loraine muttered, staggering toward the doors like a drunk. Freyen followed, her Kneldierian dexterity making it look almost easy, even as the ship shuddered beneath their feet.

"Once we're in the Maw, I can re-engage the anchor at full capacity!" Atlas shouted over the rising whine of the *Anchorite's* thruster discs. "You'll just have to hold on until then!"

Brazier's gaze jumped from the hex to Godenforte, who

gripped the command terminal like it was an anchor in a storm. His huge thumbs hooked over the edge, fingers curling into the hex wells. And for the first time since they'd met, Brazier saw the big man smiling.

"There's no good time to say this," Vandemir said, and it took Brazier a second to realise he was speaking to him. "But thank you for what you did in Yeggardania. For the exchange you made. I know what it cost you. And I'm in your debt."

His eyes were bright under the blazing gyre light.

"The Rex Populaire is your debt," Vandemir went on. "And we pay our debts."

"Good," Brazier said without hesitation. "Because I'll likely call it in."

"You just say when and where," Vandemir replied.

Before Brazier could say any more, the decking lurched beneath them. The thruster's hum spiked into a shriek, rattling through the ship. The gyre lights flared so blindingly he had to squint, ducking his head toward the hex.

"We're on a straight run!" Atlas yelled from the pit. "I'm taking it up a notch!"

Godenforte's grin split wider and a laugh burst from his chest, deep and rolling. Olivier was laughing too, a wild whoop joining the chaos. Vandemir threw his head back and howled like a wolf.

Brazier clung to the command terminal, heart thudding like a war drum in his chest. But even as the ship bucked beneath them, even as the thrusters screamed like they might tear free from the hull, he felt a grin creeping across his face.

He didn't hear the nav deck doors open behind him. He only noticed when Loraine almost tumbled into Godenforte, clutching a bundle of vials to her chest, her hand scrabbling for purchase along the command terminal.

Freyen was next, catching herself on Brazier's arm. Her

fingers locked tight around his bicep, and even through the storm of adrenaline and ship-quaking fear, the touch sent a sharp spark through him.

There was a heavy clank at his other side. Brazier glanced down to see Switch's augmented hand latched onto the hex well, her knuckles white with tension. He followed her glare to Atlas in the nav pit, her expression a sculpture of unimpressed fury.

"How are the reductors?" Brazier asked.

Switch turned her head toward him with slow, deliberate scorn. Even with the ship rocking beneath them, she managed a perfect look of withering disbelief.

"I don't know, Captain," she said. "Because you can't access a ship's reductors while the ship is under sprawl."

Brazier was spared from his embarrassment by Loraine and Freyen, who were fumbling to hand out the vials of Inertial Mutagenis. They passed them shakily to Vandemir, Godenforte, and Olivier. Vandemir uncorked his with his teeth and spat the cork into a hex well. Freyen held her vial out to Brazier. He popped the cork with his free hand, the other still white-knuckled on the terminal.

They all tipped their heads back and drained the potion. A ripple of tension passed through the crew; every one of them but Switch and Brazier jolted as the IM took hold.

Then they crossed the relative horizon. Brazier felt the familiar hollowing in his gut, that strange numbness as they punched into the Maw. The ship shuddered once more, then the storm settled.

A long, collective exhale swept across the deck as the scream of the thrusters dropped to a steady hum. The vibrations in the decking faded, and Brazier loosened his grip on the terminal.

"Reducing engine output while maintaining velocity," Atlas reported. "Enjoy the peace while it lasts."

On the hex, the *Anchorite* raced like an iron insect over a desert of black and silver sand, a streak of fury hurtling through the void.

"So, Captain," Vandemir said. "While we can all talk without cracking our teeth, it might be a good opportunity to discuss the plan for what we do once we arrive at the Gulf."

Brazier had given it only a small amount of thought, mainly because any plan he formed could change in an instant depending on what they found when they received an update from the *Pheradies* or reached the Gulf. His mind had also been distracted by Matthias. In fact, he hadn't stopped thinking about his navigator since stepping out of the Handmaid's lair and had now come to a very certain conclusion.

"This is what we're going to do," Brazier said, voice sharp with conviction. "We're going to find Kathryn. We're going to destroy Duessa. Then we fly back to Calaxis—not alone, but alongside one of the rebel fleet's cruisers, which will be filled with a full company of Angelaux troops."

The others were watching him now. The energy on the deck sharpened.

"And then," he went on, "we're going to march into Yeggardania and take Matthias back."

Switch gave a humourless laugh. "You think the King and the admirals are just going to hand us a ship and a battalion of soldiers?"

"They will," Brazier said. "If they ever want to hire us in the future. That's the deal I'll give Marcus and Admiral Korst. And they won't say no. The next time we see the Handmaid, it'll be at the head of an army."

There was a moment of silence. Then Vandemir's grin spread like a sunrise.

"You know something, Brazier Veranquis," he said, voice a rumble of admiration. "I had a feeling I'd enjoy working with you from the moment we met."

Brazier let out a slow breath, eyes flicking to the hex display and the *Anchorite* racing across empty space. There was one fight behind them, and one fight ahead, and one promise he was going to keep, no matter what it cost.

THIRTY-ONE KATHRYN

The lander shuddered as something nearby tore itself apart. The sound hit like a metal drum, deep, resonant, and carried on a pressure wave that climbed up through her boots, thudded into her knees, and rattled through the hand she'd wrapped around an overhead brace.

It didn't knock anyone down. The explosion was just far enough away for that. But it was close enough to remind them they were in a kill zone.

It could've been the *Gloried Storm* taking a hit. It could've been another lander full of her people, blown to shrapnel and fire before ever making contact. The thought came and went, like a ghost brushing her spine. She pushed it aside before it could take root. Guilt wouldn't help them now. It was just another distraction. Like her mother's voice in her head, she didn't need it, not anymore.

And somehow, she didn't. Despite Gideon, despite the losses he'd inflicted, despite the *Vanguard* broken and adrift behind them, the voice no longer crept in. There was no judgment, no quiet glee, no whispered failure at the edge of every breath. In making decisions, in sticking to her gut, in following through, in leading, the voice had quieted.

She didn't know why, only that it had, and that she'd

carry on like this to make sure it didn't come back.

Another boom followed. It was closer this time. The lander jumped in its descent, as the pilot jerked, chin snapping down like he meant to protect his throat. It was reflexive, primal—an instinctual response to shield the most vulnerable parts of his body. Conveyed through inorganic bronzite shell and magical hex reduction, it was an organic reaction translated into mechanical response. She wondered if the Formarians had known that would happen when they built the ships or if it was just a quirk of Fromryian physiology interacting with technology never meant for them. Like everything the Formarians had left behind, the answers were long gone. All they had now were ancient relics and enemies to use them against.

Behind her, someone exhaled, long, slow, and a little too loud. They were probably trying to settle their nerves. She didn't think it was Karland or Avery, but stress blurred identity. Whoever it was, they were forcing themselves to forget that a war caster might already be tracking their gyranic signature, that at any moment, the air could rip open around them and they'd vanish in a smear of fire and pressure. It was a stupid kind of fear. It was the kind of fear that didn't reward caution or discipline. You either drew the wrong lot, or someone else did.

She'd learned to make peace with that years ago. It was the kind of acceptance that came with repetition, like sword practice, training yourself to take a hit. Or maybe it had roots farther back, before the Navy when her mother taught her what being powerless felt like—with words and the ruler.

The fear of pain had always been worse than the pain itself, and once she'd learned that, the fear became manageable and predictable. It became something she could compartmentalise and push aside when it tried to crawl up her spine. She'd learned to box it out and shift into action.

She'd learned to think clearly and create options, like a blade adjusting mid-stroke.

Maybe that had been her mother's plan all along. Maybe her mother had been shaping her for this, not out of love, but design. Her plan had been to forge something sharp and useful: a tool.

And maybe that should have made her feel angry or used. Instead, she wasn't sure she didn't feel a little grateful. Everyone had to fight in the Eternal War. That was the cost of being Fromryr. It was better to go into it a honed weapon than a wide-eyed child. She felt like she'd known that once and was only just remembering it again.

"Entering the Gloried Storm's hangar bay now," the pilot called over his shoulder. "Be advised—landing zone is contested."

"Of course it's bloody contested," Sergeant Faber replied, dry and unbothered. "We're the ones contesting it."

That earned a round of laughter. Some of it was real, some of it was just people trying not to vomit tension.

Kathryn activated her repeater's gyre cartridge. It clicked and smoked. Around her, eight more weapons flared to life, filling the lander with ocean-blue glows that danced across mail and battle-scarred plate. On the four tower shields, the etched Angelaux doves shimmered in motion, caught mid-wingbeat like something out of a dream.

"Our objective is the north end of the main hangar bay," Kathryn said, raising her voice over the whine of descent. "Stay tight. Keep moving. If you get pinned down in the secondary bay, no one's coming for you."

A crisp wave of "Yes, sirs" followed. Then the lander bucked, its anti-sprawl a guttural whine. The hatch door slammed upward, and the noise of battle crashed over them, incoming fire, screaming, the rhythmic bark of repeaters, and steel against steel—sharp and cruel.

Arrows slammed into their shields as the tower shield line rotated and took the brunt. Faber's voice boomed over the din.

"Move, move, move!"

They spilled from the lander onto the deck plating, boots striking hard. The tower shield team ducked and set the line just in time to absorb another barrage. Arrows pinged and rattled off curved steel. A second later, Faber snapped another order.

"Cover right!"

The shield wall pivoted toward a partially destroyed lander, a scorched hull jutting up from its haunches. Kathryn scanned her flanks. Landers were scattered like discarded toys. Bronzite crates were torn open. Burned-out maintenance rigs stood limp. It was impossible to orient herself. Everything was chaos in motion. And above them, the hangar's curved gold-bronze wall arced like a rib cage.

"Set down! Forty-five left facing!" Faber called, and the squad packed tight to the lander's starboard.

Another flurry of arrows, sharp and angry. They thudded into shields and ricocheted off the next lander's hull with the cold, ringing sound of deadly intent.

Karland dropped to a crouch beside her, snapped his crossbow to the left, and let loose three bolts. Kathryn saw them fly past ochre uniforms before the Sorel Tan ducked back behind crates.

"Enemy left!" she called, before spinning to scan their right.

"Next lander on my mark!" Faber barked. "Cover behind!"

"Covering!" Kathryn shouted, loosing several bolts in the same direction as Karland.

"Move, move, move!"

The line surged forward, a wall of shields and armour

moving like a single creature. Karland and Avery laid suppressing fire behind them. Kathryn ran low and fast, eyes darting to the right flank. There were four landers, one of them blasted apart like a beetle cracked open. She clocked the damage and then the absence of bodies.

That mercy was short-lived. Ahead, where the line pushed forward, Angelaux bodies lay thick across the hangar floor.

Faber brought them to a halt beside the stern of another lander, the heat still radiating off its hull. Kathryn crouched behind it, the metal still pulsing from the descent, the smell of burned gyre ice heavy in the air.

Ahead, maybe fifty Angelaux soldiers were pinned at a makeshift barricade of carts, crates, and whatever else they'd dragged into a rough line. Across from them, fifty feet of open ground led to a command tower held by Sorel T'an archers and overlooking a set of double doors, leading into the *Storm's* primary hangar. Between the carts and the double doors was nothing but empty floor: a killing field between the Angelaux forces and where they needed to get to.

She scanned through a narrow gap between crates. Bodies littered the open stretch. Angelaux soldiers were pierced by arrows and sprawled like discarded dolls. A few had been dragged back, but they were limp, bleeding out in the shadow of cover.

Sergeant Royer crouched near the front line, wedging his repeater onto the lip of a crate and firing blind at the command tower. As soon as he ducked, an arrow sliced through the space where his hand had just been, skittering off the floor with a sharp tang.

"They're pinning us down and flanking left!" Royer called, waving them over.

"Tell us something we don't know!" Faber shouted back,

not breaking his cover.

Kathryn moved up to Faber's shoulder, ducking beside him behind the bulk of a tower shield. Karland and Avery kept up suppressing fire behind them, bolts crackling into the landers where Sorel Tan skirmishers probed their rear.

"Hold this position," she said, voice low and firm. "Push them off our rear."

Faber gave a curt nod.

Kathryn tucked her crossbow in tight and moved, sprinting low across the deck. She slid in beside Royer and two dark-haired soldiers. They gave her quick nods as she knelt beside them.

"These crates," she said, jerking her head toward the one Royer was crouched behind. "Can we move them?"

Royer glanced at it, almost confused, as if he was only just seeing it for the first time.

"We can."

"Good. We're going to roll them forward, use them as shields," Kathryn said. "Line them up along the command tower's flank and create a line to the doors. Advance in staggered bursts."

Royer's eyes lit up as the plan fell into place.

"How many of us do you want?"

"Thirty. The rest stay here and hold the landing zone. Reinforcements from the Crucible and Tempest are coming. We need that corridor open."

"Yes, sir," Royer said, already moving down the line, relaying orders.

"Faber!" Kathryn waved him over.

The sergeant broke from cover at a sprint. Arrows thunked into the plating behind him. Half a step slower and he'd have been skewered. He hit the ground beside her, panting.

She laid it out fast.

"We move crates into position, build a mobile defence line to the right of the tower, then breach the inner chamber. Your job is to hold this zone. Keep the lane open."

Faber's eyes narrowed.

"And the wounded?"

"Find a lander. Get them inside."

To their right, one of Royer's squads was already moving. A soldier shoved a crate forward while two others covered their flank. Repeater bolts punched through the air toward the southern end of the bay. More Sorel Tan were moving in, flanking the landing zone.

"Shield wall on the left flank!" Kathryn shouted, voice rising above the echoing chaos of the hangar. A call echoed down the line, and moments later, four soldiers lugging tower shields began creeping forward, shields angled like slabs of fortified steel. They stopped in front of her and Faber with a series of heavy thunks.

"We're forming a line to the inner bay doors with these carts," Kathryn said to the nearest of them, a stocky man with deep wrinkles across his brow and a nose that looked like it had lost more than one argument. "Our left flank's going to be wide open while we do it."

The soldier glanced up at the slowly advancing carts, judging distance and exposure. Then he nodded once.

"We've got it, sir," he said in a thick Pontivar accent. He turned to his squadmates. "You heard the captain. Lock it down."

The four men moved in sync, shields up, spreading into a wall of bronzite that covered the exposed soldiers. Arrows thudded into their towers but didn't punch through. The Sorel Tan were pushing, but not hard enough.

"Once the carts are in place, send those shields up the line," Kathryn said to Faber. "We'll need them when we breach."

"Yes, sir," he replied. "See you in there."

"I'll leave you a few to kill," she said.

Faber grinned and took off at a crouch, sprinting back through the staggered formation toward the lander, where their rear guard kept up steady repeater fire against the Sorel Tan pressing in from the south.

Royer appeared at her elbow and grabbed the edge of the next cart. "Push it forward," he told one of his team kneeling behind it. Together, they began wheeling it toward the three others already forming a crude line of cover. The shield team flanked them instantly, sliding into place to guard the move.

"You two," Kathryn said, pointing to a pair of soldiers crouched beside her. "Get that cart up and into formation."

They nodded and moved. Kathryn followed, positioning herself behind them, popping up just long enough to fire several bolts toward the command tower. Sorel Tan shapes darted and ducked behind their own cover, their return fire vicious and quick. Arrows snapped against bronzite and rebounded off the decking.

She helped guide the next cart into the line, sliding it tight behind the last one in the chain. The shield crew moved with her, shielding the next advance.

"Royer!" she shouted. "Push them up!"

The line inched forward. The gap between them and the double doors was closing.

"Keep them coming!" Kathryn called.

A ginger-bearded soldier with a shaved scalp leaned hard into the next cart, muscles straining as he shoved it forward. They were nearly in position when the man jerked and went rigid, a thick arrow sprouting from his thigh just above the armour plate.

He froze, pain not yet registering. Then his mouth opened in a strangled cry and he collapsed to the deck with a heavy grunt.

The shield wall folded around him, closing ranks to prevent a follow-up shot. Kathryn shoved her crossbow at the nearest woman. “Take this.”

Then she sprinted out into the open—no hesitation, no second thoughts. She reached the man, hooked an arm under his armpit, and lifted. He was heavier than she’d expected, but adrenaline did its job. Together, half-dragging, half-staggering, they made it back behind the cart line. She dropped him down beside one of his squadmates. He grunted in pain, a guttural noise from deep in his chest, as the arrow shaft clipped the arm of a nearby soldier.

“Snap it off!” the soldier said through clenched teeth, slumped against the cart, sweat already streaming down his temple.

Kathryn didn’t hesitate. She grabbed the arrow shaft with both hands and snapped it cleanly, leaving only a two-inch nib protruding from his thigh. The man let out a hissing breath. Saliva sprayed his beard as he nodded his thanks.

In another world, without war casters or anomancy, it would have been a death sentence. But here, it was triage. A war caster could widen the wound, extract the barb, and close arteries in a single gesture. It meant a soldier with an arrow embedded in their leg could last the fight with the almost certain knowledge they’d be fully healed once the battle was done. It was just a shame all the Fromryr’s enemies had the same capabilities too.

“We’ve got to keep this line moving,” Kathryn said, looking between him and the two soldiers crouched beside him. The ginger-haired man gave her a sharp nod, then rolled away from the cart, clearing the way for the next push forward.

Kathryn turned to the cart over from her and took her repeater back from the woman she’d handed it to.

“Keep them coming!” Kathryn shouted. But they were

already doing it. The carts were crawling forward, one after the other, into the no-man's-land between the crates and the command tower. A line of cover, crude but effective, was forming under withering arrow fire. Then came the shout.

"We've got incoming!" one of the shield-bearers bellowed, voice cutting through the noise.

Kathryn pivoted to the edge of the cart and looked. Fifteen Sorel Tan, maybe more, were rushing across the open ground. Their shields were shaped like gold leaves, their falchions bouncing at their hips. Their charge was fast, tight, and aimed to shatter the formation before it could fully lock in. It was exactly the move she would have made in their position.

And it was going to hurt.

"Incoming, left flank!" Kathryn bellowed, her voice raw. "Defensive fire, left!"

She hit the decking hard, chest down, her repeater coming up. She picked a target, one of the Sorel Tan rushing their line. She aimed low. The first two bolts missed. The third punched into the elf's ankle. He went down hard, a rag-doll collapse that sent his falchion skittering across the floor.

A breath later, the sound erupted behind her, *twang, click, twang, click*, dozens of crossbows firing in rhythm. The lines of fire arced over her, visible just at the top of her vision. Another wave came from her left—cover fire from the carts that hadn't yet moved. The Sorel Tan formation broke apart like dropped pottery, bodies folding mid-run, falchions slipping from fingers, blood pooling under fallen shields.

The momentary bloom of satisfaction in her chest was obliterated by a jolt of raw fear. A Sorel Tan soldier appeared from around the far side of the cart, falchion raised. Kathryn caught his eyes, seeing the flicker of the decision about to be made. He saw her, prone and exposed: the easiest kill.

She didn't scream. She didn't have time. Her brain filled

in the pain before it ever arrived, the razor drag of steel across her neck, fast and cold. Her muscles froze. Her body braced for the killing blow.

A curse rang out behind her. Then—*thunk, thunk, thunk*—three bolts fired in rapid succession. Something heavy landed in front of her.

The elf lay there, half-collapsed, legs sprawled, three bolts in a line down his chest. Blood leaked from his mouth in thick ropes. His eyes locked on hers. They were focused, burning with the last embers of determination.

And somehow, impossibly, he moved. His torso folded upward. The sword in his hand rose in a final, spasming swing. Another bolt hit him point-blank, right in the open mouth. The bolt punched through and rang off the cart behind him with a metallic tap.

He collapsed. This time for good.

Kathryn stared at the corpse, her breath loud in her ears, her arms buzzing with delayed adrenaline. The elf's final act had nearly ended her.

She turned her head and saw the soldier who had saved her—a woman, seated with her repeater resting between her legs, blinking like she hadn't fully caught up to the moment. Her face wore the same stunned expression Kathryn imagined was on her own.

A shadow crossed over her. A soldier leaned in from above.

"Sir, we're moving," he said.

Kathryn reached out and slapped the leg of the woman who'd just saved her life. The soldier blinked down at her like she hadn't even known Kathryn was there.

"We're moving," Kathryn repeated, dragging herself into a crouch.

The woman nodded slowly, the fog lifting from her eyes. She knelt, shouldering her crossbow.

"And thank you," Kathryn said.

"Anytime, sir," the woman replied, and together they heaved the cart forward, gripping the side handles and throwing their backs into the push. The dead elf's body flopped backward as the cart he'd been slumped against rolled forward.

Ahead, Royer shoved the lead cart into motion, barking over his shoulder. "Keep it moving!"

Kathryn crouched behind the cart's handle, pushing it forward while glancing back down the line. Arrows sliced the air overhead. Most of the carts were in position now, rolling toward the inner hangar doors. Behind them, Faber's team was still holding the landing zone, but barely. They were outnumbered, with maybe four tower shields standing between them and the Sorel Tan. And she needed those shields at the front, and soon.

Now would be a really good time for reinforcements, she thought grimly, and gave the cart another heave.

The Angelaux soldiers ahead of her moved in sync, two per cart, one firing over the top whenever they could. The noise was a rhythmic chaos: the ping of arrows on steel, the snap and click of repeaters, the dull shrieks of pain as bolts found flesh. The air was thick with the sharp, acetone smell of overheating gyre cartridges. And underneath it all was the hum, the mental white noise of a fight at full tilt.

She rode it. She let the roar of battle become background, ambient, like the silence before sleep. Her head moved on instinct. She checked her flanks, scanned for movement, making sure no one had been left behind. And somewhere, under the layer of tactical detachment, she realised something strange: she was enjoying herself. Surrounded by allies, focused, and in control. This was what she was made for.

Royer's voice snapped her back.

"Bring up the shields!"

Kathryn echoed the call. "Shields! Front!"

Twenty soldiers with tower shields rushed up the line, metal clanking.

"Faber!" she shouted. "Shields forward!"

The last four defenders from the landing zone sprinted to catch up. Two more soldiers passed her, iron bars on their backs, chains slung over their shoulders, hammers clinking with every step.

"Suppressing fire on the tower!" she yelled down the line.

She followed the breachers to the front as the tower shield unit formed up five deep into a tight wall. Forest green and burnished steel, their formation looked like an armoured insect crawling toward the doors. Arrows slammed into them with vicious, constant percussion.

"Shields high!" Royer shouted. "Protect the breachers!"

The men with the iron bars surged to the sealed double doors. Kathryn pushed forward, grabbing a chain hook, yanking with the others as the bars were hammered between the doors. They heaved together, shoulders tight, feet sliding on the decking, the doors parting slowly, painfully.

Breaking open sealed doors was usually a job given to dwarves, whose average strength nearly doubled that of the strongest human. It took two men on either side to part the doors. Kathryn pushed through and helped them slot in the chain hooks, then pulled on the chains with the others, parting the doors another few inches.

They opened another inch, then two.

Arrows whistled through the gap. The central shield took the brunt of it, clanging and sticking into the wood.

"Door breaker in!" Royer shouted, jamming a thick cylindrical device into the opening. "Prepare to receive fire!"

Kathryn dropped the chain and ducked into the second

line of the shield wall. The hiss came first, like steam escaping through cracked stone. Then there was a pop. The door breaker extended with a mechanical groan, forcing the double doors apart. The door mechanism failed with a sharp crack, and the breaker clattered to the decking.

The doors rolled open under their own weight.

And hell followed.

Three volleys of arrows came crashing through the widening gap. The sound was deafening, like a hailstorm. The tower shields held, but they buckled under the force. One soldier grunted as a bolt pierced the edge of his shield and grazed his shoulder. Another screamed as a shaft found the joint in his pauldron.

Kathryn gritted her teeth, crouched low, and waited for the moment she knew was coming—the instant between volleys when they could break through.

“Advance!” Royer shouted.

Kathryn caught a glimpse of their surroundings above the shield wall, just long enough to see the corridor sweeping left and right beyond the doors. Then she ducked back down. The Sorel Tan stationed beyond them were scattering, breaking into a retreat down the right-hand curve.

“About right turn, ninety degrees!” Royer bellowed.

The formation pivoted with the grinding steadiness of a siege engine, shields up, boots clanking across the deck. Kathryn felt the itch between her shoulder blades, the awful anticipation of open air behind them.

“Form tight on our rear!” she yelled.

The rear ranks immediately compressed, some turning to walk backward, overlapping their shields to form a full shell. Royer shot her a sharp glance: Who’s giving the orders here?

She gave him a sheepish shrug just as a cry went up from behind.

“Enemy rear!”

"Shields lock tight!" Royer shouted.

A second later, arrows slammed into both ends of the formation with a teeth-rattling crash: wood splintered and metal rang. Someone grunted in pain.

"Open front!" Royer called the second the storm eased. "Fire!"

Kathryn shoved her repeater through a narrow gap in the shield wall, aimed blind, and fired. She didn't know if she hit anything.

"Lock formation!"

The gaps sealed. Darkness pressed in around her. The heat rising from bodies packed shoulder to shoulder made the air feel thick and wet. Someone groaned, and Kathryn saw the shaft of an arrow protruding from their arm.

"Wounded back!" Royer ordered.

The man was shuffled down the line, disappearing into the protected middle rows.

"Advance!" came the next command.

The shield wall pushed forward under the weight of another volley from the rear. Kathryn nearly tripped over a Sorel Tan corpse, a cluster of bolts protruding from its chest. The soldier beside her grabbed her elbow to steady her. There was another body, then another. They stepped over the dead, under fire the whole time.

Kathryn risked a glance ahead. The corridor ended in another set of large double doors. And beyond them, she knew, was the chamber.

"Doors on our left," she said.

"I see them," Royer replied without turning, sweat streaming from under his helm, his voice hoarse from barking commands.

"Halt!" Royer called, five paces from the threshold. "Crossbows rear! Open rear!"

Shields parted with the rasp of wood on metal.

"Fire!"

A wave of repeater fire roared backward through the gap.

"Lock formation!"

Shields slammed shut again.

"Make them think twice before coming up on our arse," Royer muttered, then: "Advance!"

The formation surged forward, coming to a halt in front of the doors.

"New facing, left!"

The entire unit rotated cleanly, and Kathryn found herself in the middle of the right side.

"Breachers front!"

The soldiers with bars and chains shoved forward, muscles tense, sweat-streaked. Kathryn stepped up with them.

"I've only got one of these left," Royer said, holding out a door breaker.

"We don't need more," she said. "This is the last one."

Even as she spoke, the breachers wedged the bars between the door seams. Groaning metal echoed down the corridor. Chains snapped into place, and six soldiers strained against them. The doors gave, parting just wide enough for a hand to slip through.

Then it all went to black hell. The doors opened fully: someone had activated them on the other side.

Two breachers lost their footing and fell forward. Another soldier lunged to catch them, breaking formation. Royer shouted, "Lock shields front!" but it came a breath too late.

Arrows poured through the gap like floodwaters through a broken dam.

The breachers didn't scream. They died too fast for that. The man who broke formation caught five arrows to the neck and chest. The shafts punched clean through his flesh and armour. He dropped like a puppet cut from its strings, and behind him, more soldiers collapsed—struck in the arms, the face, the gut.

"Close the gap!" Royer roared.

Soldiers scrambled over bodies to seal the breach. Kathryn counted at least ten dead. Ten more were groaning, clutching wounds. Nearly a fifth of their force had gone in seconds.

"Advance! Step as one!"

And to Royer's credit, he didn't falter. There was no hesitation, just forward, into the chamber, before the next volley came.

The room they entered was massive—large enough to fit a Cauldron-class frigate with room to spare. The walls curved into a dome high above. On the right, Kathryn glimpsed what looked like a raised dais or command platform, but she had no time to dwell on it.

Because directly ahead of them was a wall of Sorel Tan. It was at least fifty wide and two deep: a solid line of one hundred elves with shields and spears, waiting.

"Enemy left!" someone yelled.

Kathryn rose on her toes, craning to see.

It was another Sorel Tan formation, another hundred, closing fast.

The first volley landed like hammer blows against their left flank. Shields shuddered. Soldiers grimaced under the weight of it, faces screwed tight against the thunderclap of incoming death.

Another volley slammed into the formation, just as brutal, just as jarring.

"What in the abyss is that?" someone muttered from her right. A helmeted head shifted, peeking between shields toward the upper edge of the chamber.

"By all that's holy in the dark," someone else said.

Kathryn followed the glance, and froze.

There, rising above the battlefield on a bronze-gold dais, was a throne. And on that throne sat a corpse in a forest-green robe threaded with gold. Its arms draped over the throne's rests. Its skin was the colour of bruised ash: hollow cheeks, eyes sunk so deep they were just pits of shadow. What little hair remained hung limp like old thread.

It was the Queen of Dreams. A god of the Aeturnum, the myth that had become part of Kathryn's reality. She couldn't tear her eyes from it. She couldn't look away.

"Concentrate!" Royer barked, his voice breaking the hold over her. "Advance as one!"

Kathryn's gaze returned to the shield in front of her. The formation pressed forward, the hiss and thud of arrows blending into a steady, maddening rhythm. Shields groaned. Some cracked. The seams whined with every impact.

"Steady advance!" Royer called again, forcing calm into the line.

Twenty feet from the Sorel Tan front, an elf shouted an order, and the entire enemy line fell back fifteen more feet. Another volley thundered in from the left, shattering against the flank shields.

They'll run out of arrows, Kathryn told herself. *They will.*

The elves reformed and loosed again. Directly ahead, a soldier's shield fractured, a shaft punching through just shy of his nose.

"Rotate front," Kathryn snapped, grabbing the man's shoulder. "Fresh shield forward!"

Without missing a beat, the soldier beside him dropped his overhead shield and stepped in. The formation flexed like clockwork.

"Rotate left!" someone called down the line.

There was more movement, more arrows. Kathryn flinched at the sound of them punching through the formation. Someone screamed.

"Close the gap!" a voice shouted.

Then there was another cry. The rattle of armour as someone hit the deck.

"Hold tight!" Royer thundered. "Lock shields!"

The formation compressed. Kathryn felt steel press hard against her shoulders, gardbraces grinding. Still, the arrows came—volley after volley, whittling them down. Royer didn't give the order to return fire, and she didn't blame him. Even a brief gap in the wall would mean another corpse on the ground. This was what the Sorel Tan wanted: pressure, attrition, collapse.

The shield in front of her shattered. An arrow punched through, slipping beneath a gardbrace and finding flesh. The woman holding it screamed.

"Rotate front!" Kathryn shouted.

Hands pulled the injured soldier back. Another stepped in with a shield. In the half-second gap, Kathryn raised her crossbow, fired at the elves, and hoped. Pain slammed into her chest like a hammer blow. She staggered.

For a terrible moment, she thought it was over. Her fingers clawed at her armour, searching for a shaft, for the bloom of blood, but all she found was a dent in her breastplate, right over the sternum. Her heart still pounded. Her lungs still pulled in air.

She was alive.

"Rotate left!"

Another volley—she couldn't tell from which direction anymore.

"Rotate front!"

"Rotate left!"

Screams echoed across the chamber. Kathryn turned, scanning their flanks. Their overhead shields were gone. One soldier was wrapping a blood-soaked bandage around another's shoulder. The woman swayed, barely upright.

Ten others looked just like her, bleeding, fading.

They were losing. The realisation hit her somewhere under her sternum. She was so close, so close to ending it, to getting Isdria Laanorath. And they were going to die here. It wouldn't be in the clash of steel, not blade-to-blade, but behind shields, suffocating under arrow fire, picked off like rats in a barrel. There would be no justice, just pain and attrition. It was an ending that felt cruel, undignified and deeply unfair.

Fair was never part of this, a voice whispered in her head. *Life has never been fair. You make your own options—remember.*

If she was going to die here, it wouldn't be caged behind a shield. It would be on her terms. She caught Royer's eye.

"Change of tactics!" she shouted.

His expression twisted in confusion. Another volley slammed into the line. He flinched as arrows rattled the shields, then peeked through a crack in the wood ahead of him. When he turned back, the look had changed to grim understanding. He gave a sharp nod, jaw set like stone. The soldiers around him were watching, hungry for whatever came next—anything but another volley.

"Formation ready swords!" Royer called out.

Kathryn unslung her crossbow and dropped it to the floor. Steel whispered from scabbards.

"Ready!" came fifty voices, hoarse but resolute.

"Prepare to charge!" Royer shouted.

There was a second of tension.

"Break and charge!"

The line shattered.

They surged forward, a tide of steel and fury crashing toward the enemy. For a heartbeat, it felt like they had the elves off guard. It felt like hope.

Then the volley came.

Arrows fell like a wave of razors. The man ahead of her took half a dozen shafts through his chest and legs and collapsed to the floor. Screams erupted around her. Shields dropped. Bodies fell. The left flank screamed as another volley ripped through them.

And then Kathryn was the front line.

The Sorel Tan were drawing again. Their bows rose as one. There was no more time. She ran faster. She pumped her legs. She screamed—not a word, just a cry torn from the gut. She closed in, five feet, three, two—

She hit them like a hammer.

She didn't raise her sword. She just launched herself over a kneeling elf, crashing shoulder-first into the second row. A bowstring snapped next to her ear. Someone grunted.

She tumbled hard, her ribs slamming into armoured limbs. Cold decking met her palms. She rolled. Her sword arm was pinned under her body. She twisted, ripped it free, and stabbed hard. The blade punched into a thigh.

The elf howled.

She stabbed again, into the back of the leg, then into a reaching hand. Steel tore through flesh and bone. The elf screamed.

Another Sorel Tan loomed over her, falchion raised high.

She brought her sword up just in time, catching the blade on her own. There was another blow, then another. Her arm trembled. Her panic surged. She kicked wildly and hit something solid. The elf buckled, falling onto her leg.

Before he could recover, she grabbed a fistful of his gambeson, yanked him down, and thrust her sword into the gap beneath his arm.

She screamed as she did it. The elf sagged against her. Her sword slipped free as he crumpled. She shoved at him, kicked him off, then crawled backwards, heart hammering in her throat. She could taste metal.

Around her, the battle had collapsed into chaos. The Sorel Tan line was shattered. It was just bodies, clashing steel, tangled limbs, and screams. Angelaux green and steel mixed with Sorel Tan ochre in a blur of violence.

She rolled to her belly, planting a hand to push herself up and felt her glove sink into something soft, a body. The elf she'd stabbed was still crawling, dragging himself forward in a pitiful spasm of survival. Kathryn surged up and over him, climbing his back like an animal. He bucked beneath her, flailing, but her weight, and his thin, wiry frame, kept him pinned.

She grabbed the hilt of his falchion, yanked it free from its scabbard. The weapon came awkward in her grip, reversed and slippery with blood. Still crouched over him, she jammed the blade down at the back of his neck.

The steel bit through hair and skin. He screamed. She bore down harder, adjusted her grip, and sawed, like cutting through rope.

Blood fountained into his hair, over her hands. The tendons gave with a sickening pop. She felt bile rise but kept going, hacking at the meat of his neck until he stilled under her.

Her hands slipped on the gore-slick hilt as she stumbled backward, spinning around on one knee, panting hard. Her heart was a hammer in her chest.

Then the panic hit.

The line was broken. What remained of the Angelaux force fought in ragged knots, overwhelmed by ochre-brown-clad soldiers. Repeater fire had slowed to a trickle. The battle was lost.

And then she saw him.

It was Isdria Laanorath. The ghost from her nightmares. The architect of her horrors. Towering at the base of the dais, his blade flashing through the chest of a soldier too slow to parry. His face twisted with disdain, as if killing were beneath him.

Hate ignited inside her, searing up through her ribs. She started forward, but something else pulled her gaze up, past Isdria, to the golden throne behind him. And the figure seated on it.

The Queen of Dreams.

Duessa sat draped in tattered green. Her greyed flesh hung like parchment from her bones, her lips pale and bloodless. Her eyes glowed like molten rubies. Kathryn froze. She couldn't look away. She couldn't think. The fire in those eyes wasn't rage. It was seduction, a whispering promise. Kathryn felt herself tipping inward, as if her mind were being poured into a dream made of silk and wine and forgetting. The fight drained from her bones. A voice cut through it like a knife.

"Enchanting, isn't she?"

The spell broke. Kathryn staggered back a half step, blinking herself awake.

She knew the voice.

Gabriel stood nearby, weight shifted onto one leg like he was waiting for a drink at an inn. His armour was smeared in gore. His blade hung loose at his side, casual, forgotten. But it was his eyes that pinned her. They were blue as a gyre light, full of mischief and calculation, and there was something else in them, something deeply wrong.

"The Queen of Dreams, brought out of her slumber," he said. "After all these long years. Redcrosse would be turning in his grave. Would be raging at the moon after all the effort he put into banishing her from this world."

He stepped forward, slow and measured.

"I had a feeling we'd meet again," he said, his voice rising to carry over the screams and steel. "Someone so persistent would never give up, I told myself. But then it occurred to me that was too simplistic an explanation. You're drawn here."

He nodded toward Isdria, who had now turned to bark an order to his troops. "Drawn to him." He tilted his chin toward Duessa on the throne. "To her, like a wolf to fresh blood. Like Morletts to the dead."

He cocked his head, gaze narrowing.

"Like a harbinger to the source."

He said the words softly, but they echoed in her skull. Cold settled on the back of her neck. She didn't reply. She just tightened her grip on the falchion, blinked blood out of her eye, and waited.

"You're the first, aren't you?" Gabriel said. "The one that failed."

There was something in his voice—mocking, but curious too. It was like he was studying a broken artefact. It made her wish she still had her short sword. The falchion she held now was too long, too front-heavy. The grip felt like it had been made for a larger hand. But she wouldn't have time to find the blade she'd buried in one of the corpses.

Gabriel sprung.

One moment he stood relaxed, weight cocked like someone mid-conversation. The next, the poise evaporated, replaced by sudden, terrible grace. He launched at her like a coil wire snapping loose.

She barely brought her falchion up in time. Steel met steel with a shuddering clang. Then she was retreating, caught in a blur of parries and sidesteps, each defensive move driven by instinct more than thought. Gabriel flowed with her, a shadow she couldn't escape. Left, right, thrust, parry, step back, pivot, deflect; he read her like a hex display.

He knew every move and every counter, and every counter to the counter.

She tried to break the rhythm—pivoted hard, sidestepped wide. It worked. Gabriel's back was to the battlefield now. Kathryn caught a fleeting glimpse of what remained and her stomach dropped.

The Angelaux formation was gone.

The shield wall had shattered. Small knots of survivors fought on, but the weight of the dead told the story. And yet, the Sorel Tan hadn't fared much better. The ground was thick with their bodies too. Red and brown smears across the chamber floor. It looked like the remnants of a funeral pyre someone had tried to light and abandoned halfway.

There were no reinforcements in sight. And with Gabriel in front of her, she'd never reach Isdria. He was standing untouched, his face unreadable, a blade in his hand, watching the slaughter unfold like a general inspecting his troops.

You won't make it, the voice said. *But you can still die trying.*

Kathryn charged.

The falchion swung wide, a cleave from the right, then the left. She put everything into her strikes, throwing the sword around her body like it weighed nothing, battering Gabriel's guard. His blade snapped up, deflecting her wild momentum, his feet adjusting. He caught her rhythm again, stepped in, and feinted.

She over-committed. He turned her blade aside, slipped inside her reach, and stabbed. Pain tore through her thigh just above the knee. She cried out, stumbled. Gabriel grabbed her wrist, torqued her arm, and used her own leverage to snap the blade from her grip.

She dropped. Her sword clattered beside her, useless.

Gabriel stood over her, looking down with bored detachment. He wasn't winded. He wasn't even sweating. Then he did something completely unexpected. He unbuttoned one of the pouches on his bandolier and took out an empty vial. Uncorking it, he held it to the flat of his blade, allowing Kathryn's blood to dribble into it.

Utterly stunned at the act, all Kathryn could do was stare up at the man as he recorked the vial, now filled with a tiny amount of her blood.

Gabriel put it back in his pouch and glanced past her, to the battlefield, then up at the dome above them, like something there amused him. A thin smile tugged at the corner of his mouth.

"This'll all be over soon," he said, quiet, almost intimately. "Though probably not in the way you were expecting."

He turned and walked away, toward Isdria. The Sorel Tan captain stood alone now, his face calm and cold as stone.

"We need to leave," Isdria said. "The source has done its work. It's no longer useful."

"Soon," Gabriel replied, nodding back toward Kathryn. "But one of your little mistakes is still alive."

Isdria turned. That single eye found her, full of disdain.

"Your first mistake, if memory serves," Gabriel said, enjoying every word. "We used to call her the failed experiment."

Isdria's expression shifted into something uglier. It was hatred carved into flesh. He stepped toward her.

Gabriel caught his arm. "No," he said. "Let me. Cleaning up your messes has become something of a specialty of mine."

He stalked toward her. Kathryn scrambled back, over bodies and fallen shields slick with blood. Her hand found something—wood, steel, the hilt of a sword—and she seized it, pushing herself to her feet, spinning to face him.

She'd die on her feet. She'd die fighting.

But Gabriel was already there. He raised his blade so the flat touched the underside of her chin. It wasn't hard, just enough to make the point. Whatever weapon she'd grabbed hung loose in her grip, forgotten.

Gabriel was smiling a predator's grin, wide and slow. His eyes gleamed with it, catching the light of the chamber like green glass under water. He held the blade steady, like a man savouring the moment before a kill. Kathryn braced for the bite of steel, for the flash of pain.

And then she heard it.

It was a low rumble, like distant thunder rolling toward them across the floor. She heard stomping boots, a voice barked an order, sharp and human, not elven.

"We're out of time!" Isdria shouted, the panic in his voice shattering whatever calm he'd had. "Be done with it, Gabriel! End this!"

Kathryn's eyes glanced toward the Sorel Tan captain, and her blood ran cold.

Gabriel was behind him.

His blade was drawn, he stood in the same casual poise with the same knowing grin. But Gabriel was also in front of her, still there, still smiling, and still holding the sword to her throat.

She looked down the blade's length. The steel shimmered. Smoke curled off it in thin, black tendrils, like rising mist. It was the same kind of smoke she'd seen back in the surface drift, the same illusion, the same trick.

The Gabriel in front of her wasn't real.

"Oh, don't worry," both Gabriels said in unison, voices overlapping like a twisted chorus. "I'll end it."

Isdria turned, too slow, far too slow.

The real Gabriel, with his blade already drawn, drove it through the captain's back. The point burst from Isdria's sternum in a wet punch. The elf gasped, hands scrabbling at the steel, his face frozen in a mask of disbelief and dying horror.

Behind her, the sound swelled. There was running boots, shouted orders, a new rhythm to the chaos. The reinforcements had arrived.

And the fake Gabriel vanished, dissolving into ribbons of smoke that twisted and evaporated before her eyes.

THIRTY-TWO
BRAZIER

Brazier hadn't known a ship could make the kind of noises the *Anchorite* was currently making. Somewhere between a shrill whine and a strangled whistle, it reminded him uncomfortably of a dying animal calling out for its mother. He had no idea how much damage they were doing to the ship, but he couldn't help but feel a stab of guilt at how they were treating her. If Switch's expression was anything to go by, they were committing a long, drawn-out murder.

Somewhere around the halfway mark between Veraxies and the Hyralian Gulf, Atlas had announced, far too cheerfully, that all the thruster discs would need replacing. To avoid looking at Switch, Brazier had made a show of studying the hex, suddenly deeply invested in the topographical anomalies of the current tunnel system.

That illusion had lasted right up until the *Anchorite* gave a violent shudder that didn't stop. It was the kind of vibration that made his teeth ache and his thoughts literally jitter inside his head.

Switch's real hand had punched into the hex well faster than a hot poker through snow. Moments later, she'd growled something about the weapons system decoupling its primary protocols and secondary isolations cascading through the rest of the ship.

Brazier hadn't even bothered to pretend he knew what she was talking about and simply trusted the look on his face to convey his confusion.

"Everything is falling apart," Switch had told him.

"Is there a way to prevent that?" Brazier had asked, already bracing for the scolding he knew was coming.

"I can maybe prevent that," she'd snapped, jabbing her metal thumb into her own chest. "But if this"—she'd pointed a finger so hard at the back of Atlas's head he imagined he'd see a dent in it—"keeps going on, then there won't be a ship left to save."

She'd stormed off the nav deck, doors hissing closed behind her.

"You'd think we were going to fall out of the air or something," Atlas had muttered then, her voice juddering with the same bone-deep vibration that had become the *Anchorite's* new musical procession.

For once, Switch and Brazier were in perfect agreement. It did feel like they were going to fall out of the air. He couldn't feel his teeth anymore, his wrists went numb if he held the command terminal too long, and there was a constant buzz in his bones like the ship was trying to hum its way through his skeleton.

It was just one more reason why he missed Matthias. Maybe he was biased, but he was pretty sure his navigator could've done everything Atlas was doing, just without risking the ship's spontaneous disintegration.

Now, less than a league out from the Hyralian Gulf, Brazier had perfected the fine art of standing upright while the deck did everything it could to buck him like a drunken horse.

"Update and location script from the Pheradies," Atlas said.

"On the hex," Brazier replied.

The command display surged, reforming into a new sculpt. The generic representation of the Gulf was gone, replaced by a knot of ships converging in the north—three Gyre Stars forming a loose V, closing around two smaller cruisers with another two stacked above and below. It looked like a flower opening in slow motion, with the *Gloried Storm* clenched tight at its core.

Korst's clipped, stern voice followed: "As we understand it, the Vanguard has sustained existential damage, with all hands abandoning ship. The wounded have been transferred to the Crucible, but Captain Stryker, along with all able soldiers, has led a boarding action against the Gloried Storm. We have been unable to relay your message to her. We believe she is heading for the Storm's primary chamber, and we have prepped boarding teams, with all officers and sergeants instructed to locate and secure her."

Brazier's fingers curled around the edge of the hex well. The numbing pain from the vibrations was just a distant feeling now. Kathryn was even harder to reach. The thing he'd really hoped wouldn't happen, was happening.

"Prep a hex message for the Pheradies," he said. They were almost at the Gulf, but the three-minute delay from its interference still killed any chance of real-time tethering.

He leaned into the well and spoke: "Understood, Pheradies. We'll bring the Anchorite onto the Storm and join you in that search." Then, with more confidence than he felt: "We'll end this today. Anchorite out."

The well went flat.

"Message sent," Atlas confirmed. "We're approaching the tunnel exit now. Slowing her down."

Brazier closed his eyes and muttered a quick prayer to the abyss, not that he really believed in that sort of thing. The ship's whine softened to a familiar thrum. The deck settled under his boots. The *Anchorite* sounded like herself again. He pulled the flask from his belt, grateful he could finally take a sip without spilling it all over himself.

"Get me a ship-wide tether," he said, sliding the flask back into place. A well pulsed on his right.

"We're about to cross into the Gulf. Kathryn Stryker has boarded the Gloried Storm, and is believed to still be aboard. So that's where we're going. Arm up and join me on the nav deck."

It took several minutes, but eventually the remaining members of the Rex Populaire, and Freyen and Switch, gathered around the command terminal. The blood, gore, and abyss-knew-what clinging to all of them looked like layers of war paint. It was strangely fitting, given what they were about to do.

Freyen handed him a repeater and three spare magazines. He slung the crossbow over his shoulder, palm resting briefly on the flight chamber, and clipped the magazines to his belt.

On the hex, the *Anchorite* slipped from the tunnel and into the Gulf. A tremor passed through the filaments, like a shiver rippling through the spine of the display. The sculpt distorted, struggling to hold its shape against the Gulf's interference.

"Okay, let's see what we're working with," Atlas said, her head tracking left to right. "Looks like we've got a breach on the Storm's starboard hangar. That's where the action's at."

On the sculpt, Brazier spotted landers peeling off from the three Gyre Stars, angling hard for the *Storm's* starboard bay.

"Then that's where we're going," he said.

"Yeah, except we're not the only ones who want to get into the Storm," Switch said. She leaned over the command terminal and pointed, moving her real finger in a circle to indicate the general area to the left of the *Storm* and over one of the cruisers.

What Brazier had taken for a quirk of the Gulf's interference now looked a lot like some kind of swarm. Tiny, bean-shaped filament clusters moved with eerie precision, flooding over the cruiser's hull and swarming the *Gloried Storm's* flank. They weren't heading for the same breach, they were crawling over the portside hangar and vanishing into its hull like termites.

Repeaters on one of the Gyre Stars swung toward them, shredding the filament clusters with tiny needles. But it wasn't enough, not nearly enough, not for that many.

"Darkest depths of the abyss," Vandemir muttered, leaning over the command display.

"That's a cicadron swarm," Olivier said, voice tight.

"'Swarm' is a wholly inadequate term for what we're looking at," Vandemir replied.

"Do you think the goblins know about the weapon?" Freyen asked.

"I think any explanation is on the table at this point," Brazier said.

"It's the blood," Vandemir said, eyes shadowed under a heavy brow. "Black-damned scavengers can smell a feeding ground from the other side of the underground. They're not here for the weapon. They're here for their next meal."

Brazier fought the instinct to rake a hand through his beard, mainly because he was fairly certain it was still caked with grime and other unidentifiable fluids. Finding Kathryn Stryker was already going to mean cutting through Sorel Tan elite. A horde of goblins wasn't on his wish list. *It's never easy*, he thought, remembering Switch's words.

And even if they did get through this, finding Kathryn and stopping Duessa, there'd still be Matthias, still

Yeggardania, and still the Handmaid and her flesh-hungry court.

If they got through it all he was going to get drunk for a week. He was going to buy real whisky and real ale, probably from Folgar, and they were all, the entire crew of the *Anchorite*, going to sit in one of Karenna's private wings and get roaring drunk. They would listen to Karenna's war stories. They would watch Folgar flirt badly. Switch and Matthias would insult each other like siblings. And Freyen would be at his side.

That picture alone gave him the push he needed.

"It doesn't change the mission," he said. "If we have to fight through a goblin army to reach Stryker, then that's what we do. This ends with her. She's the priority."

"Aye, Captain," Vandemir said. A wolfish grin spread across his face as if Brazier had just handed him the best assignment of his life.

"We're entering engagement range," Atlas said.

He could hear it now, the steady thrum of capital-ship engines, low and deep like leviathans shifting in the black, and the dry, percussive chatter of hull-mounted repeaters cycling through salvos.

On the hex, the *Anchorite* threaded the space between the *Pheradies* and the *Orranthis*, then dipped low, banking hard for the *Storm's* portside hangar bay. The air turned to pressure, then roar, then teeth-clattering vibration as they entered the breach.

The hex reformed into a jagged cross-section of the hangar, a crescent of landing pads and repair stations, now cluttered with landers crammed in at whatever angle their pilots had managed. A single command tower jutted up like a broken tooth, overlooking a set of thick double doors built into the inner hull wall. A trail of carts snaked toward it, like ants marching into a nest.

"Looks like we've got a secure landing zone," Atlas said. "But hostiles on the command tower."

"Could've done something about that if we still had a weapons system," Switch muttered.

Either Atlas didn't hear her or pretended she didn't. "Setting us down south of the zone. Ass-backwards approach so we're not eating arrows the second the ramp drops."

Brazier thought that was the most sensible idea he'd heard from the navigator since meeting her.

The *Anchorite* slowed, thrusters whining as it spun 180 degrees and dropped into a tight space between two landers. The manoeuvre gave them partial cover, and partial was better than nothing.

Brazier activated his gyre cartridge. Switch, Freyen, and Olivier followed. Atlas climbed out of the nav pit, pulling on her boots. Olivier handed her a crossbow, and she slung it over her shoulder without a word.

"Let's go get Kathryn and destroy a Lord of the Eternal Hunt," Brazier said.

The boarding ramp dropped with a solid thunk. Brazier moved first, crossbow raised level with his chin, eyes sweeping left and right for threats. The acrid smell of scorched bronzite and spent gyre ice hit him like a slap.

He veered left, moving between two landers, using their bulk for cover. Ahead, he caught a glimpse of the command tower—Sorel Tan elves in high positions, loosing arrows down onto the chaos below. Return fire from repeaters flew through the air.

He started forward, then the crossbows snapped up around him.

La'Voline soldiers appeared, red and green gambesons beneath gleaming steel breastplates. Their bronzite repeaters were levelled from behind landing gear and thruster arms.

"Friendlies!" Brazier shouted, lowering his crossbow.

"Names, ranks, and crew!" came the barked reply.

"Vandemir Vonclaire!" the captain roared back. "Of the Rex Populaire. And if you shoot us, the King of Sephera will kiss your cheeks before tossing you into the abyss."

"Vonclaire!" another voice shouted. "Bloody, black-damned Vonclaire!"

A squat man barrelled out from behind a lander, his stomach bulging against a polished breastplate that glinted under the blue light. His helm shone like a signal flare.

"Geraldore," Vandemir said, his tone the picture of cheer.

"You thieving old scoundrel!" Geraldore snapped, jabbing a stubby finger at Vandemir as he stomped forward in short, furious strides. He looked more like an angry money lender than a soldier. "You black-damned dog of a robber!"

"Perhaps we can discuss whatever proverbial bone it is you wish to pick with me another time," Vandemir said pleasantly, accentuating the sing-song Harothellian accent.

Geraldore halted in front of them, puffing.

"You owe me thirty knortes."

"In case it's escaped your notice," Vandemir said, gesturing broadly, "we're in the middle of a battle. Might we table this for later?"

"What, another eight months?"

"Preferably."

"We need to find Captain Kathryn Stryker," Brazier cut in, pushing the conversation back to something resembling useful. "Now."

Geraldore gave him a disinterested once-over. "You and everyone else."

Brazier stepped into his space. "We have information that can help destroy the weapon. And finding Stryker is key to that."

That got Geraldore's attention. His gaze sharpened.

"We think she's pushing for the main chamber," he said. "Reinforcements are en route. Who are you?"

"We're going with them," Brazier said flatly.

"As part of a mission on behalf of the King," Vandemir added. "Wouldn't want to delay royal business, would we?"

Geraldore's jaw clenched. His nostrils flared. Then he sighed.

"This way."

He turned and stomped off, cutting right between two more landers. Brazier and the rest fell in behind, their boots clanking across the decking. Ahead, another lander sat further out in the open, just in front of the ragged chain of carts that led to the inner chamber's doors—wide open like a mouth waiting to swallow them whole. La'Voline soldiers huddled behind the crates, ducking up and out just long enough to release a few bolts before diving back into cover.

"Through those doors is the main chamber," Geraldore said, jabbing a finger at the yawning double doors ahead. "Landing zone's mostly clear. We've got most of them pinned in the tower, but if you've got any brains at all, you'll keep your heads down."

He turned to Vandemir. "Don't bloody die in there," he added, with all the warmth of a tax collector, then turned and vanished back toward the makeshift landing zone.

Brazier leaned out, eyes scanning the stretch between them and the carts. There was fifteen feet of open decking, maybe a little more. The Sorel Tan archers in the tower were focused on the defenders behind the carts, but that didn't mean they wouldn't pivot fast.

He turned to the others. "We make for the carts. Freyen and I cover. Move on my call."

Vandemir gave a curt nod and stepped forward.

"Go!" Brazier barked.

Vandemir bolted across the gap, boots pounding. The

others followed behind him. Brazier raised his repeater and let off half a magazine at the tower. Freyen followed suit beside him, her fire just as wild and just as distracting.

"Go," he said, and Freyen took off, sprinting low and fast, diving behind the carts. The others popped up and added their fire to the chaos, buying Brazier his opening.

He broke cover, sprinted, and dropped hard into a slide beside Freyen, the bolts still hissing overhead.

Vandemir was already moving, crouched low, giant sword tucked under his arm. Brazier gave him six feet of space. Any closer and he'd risk losing an eye.

La'Voline soldiers glanced up as they passed, eyes questioning but not stopping them. The red and green of the Rex Populaire's armour said enough.

The closer they got to the doors, the more intense the exchange. Repeaters twanged near the threshold. La'Voline marksmen leaned from behind the last carts and the doorframe, trading fire with the tower. From the look of it, the corridor beyond was in their hands, but only just.

"You want to get in here?" a woman shouted from the corridor. She knelt behind a man pressed into the doorway, loosing bolts at the command tower above. He threw himself back just as two arrows shot by exactly where his chest had been a heartbeat before. Behind them, another soldier crouched over a fourth, flat on his back and groaning, tying off a bandage around the arrow shaft buried deep in his thigh.

"Aye, we do," Vandemir said.

Brazier reached back and tapped the shoulder of a La'Voline soldier crouched behind the cart. "Can you cover us?"

The man nodded and smacked the arm of his comrade. "Cover on our mark."

The second soldier gave a terse nod.

"Whenever you're ready!" the woman called.

Vandemir looked to Brazier and nodded.

"Covering fire!" Brazier bellowed.

Along the cart line, soldiers rose and opened up. The two at the doorway swung out and fired, bolts whistling overhead: *Twang, click, twang, click*. The bay filled with the thunder of repeating crossbows.

Brazier and the others sprinted across the open gap into the corridor, and stepped straight into a massacre.

To the left, bodies sprawled across the decking. Sorel Tan in ochre and tan, collapsed over crates and barricades, limbs twisted and splintered with bolts. To the right were more corpses. A field surgeon was working fast, dragging wounded Angelaux and La'Voline soldiers and lining them up against the wall.

The corridor curved, and at the far end, a loose wall of La'Voline shields moved forward in a steady press, shields scraping together. Brazier broke into a jog.

"I've never seen this many dead Sorel Tan," Olivier said, eyes wide.

"I've never seen this many Sorel Tan," Loraine replied. "Alive or dead."

"Keep an eye out for a blonde woman," Brazier said, scanning every fallen face with a silent hope that Kathryn wasn't one of them.

He picked his way forward, stepping over the bodies and viscera, deeper into the corridor, toward the moving formation. The further they went, the tighter the knot in his gut. They were late. He could feel it in his bones. And even if they weren't too late, then something else would be wrong. Something always was.

Somewhere at the back of his mind, his self-conscious knew he was just projecting his feelings of failing Matthias. It was guilt for leaving him behind, for trading him away. But knowing it didn't change anything. The weight of it still pressed into his chest like armour that no longer fit.

Not seeing Kathryn among the corridor's dead eased the knot in Brazier's chest, but only slightly. The formation ahead surged, shields banging forward as one.

"They're moving into the inner chamber," Vandemir said, tall enough to see above the wave of La'Voline troops.

Boots thundered. Orders were barked. The last of the soldiers poured through the double doors like sand through an hourglass.

"Stay together," Brazier said, already moving. "Priority's Kathryn."

They gave quick nods, weapons up, and followed him through. The chamber swallowed them whole.

Ahead, the La'Voline vanguard spread like a wave, crashing toward Sorel Tan lines. Blades clashed along with the scream of war cries and the din of combat.

To their left there was emptiness, towering walls that curved up to a domed ceiling, vast and echoing. And to the right—

Brazier nearly lost his footing.

A woman sat upon a throne of bronzite, her body draped in a forest green tunic threaded with gold. Her arms were outstretched, fingers lost on the throne's edges. She was the painting from the demon's book, brought to life.

Only worse.

Where the illustration had shown beauty corrupted by malice, the real thing was rot incarnate. Her skin was grey and pitted, her cheeks sunken. Her eyes were swallowed by shadow, and her hair hung in thin strands over a half-bare skull. She didn't move. She just watched, indifferent and eternal.

"By all that's dark in the abyss," Vandemir muttered. "That's her."

"Is that—" Atlas started, but couldn't finish.

"I could bury an arrow in the bitch from here," Loraine said, notching her bowstring as if it was already decided.

"Happy to take a turn after you," Switch added, raising her crossbow.

"Let's assume she doesn't go down with conventional weapons," Brazier said, patting the air in front of Loraine's bow. "We follow the plan. Find Kathryn. Break the spell the way the book told us. If that doesn't work, then yes, shoot until your arms fall off."

They kept moving. Brazier didn't look back at Duessa. He didn't want to know if she was watching.

Brazier slowed them as they neared the thick of the fighting. La'Voline soldiers pressed forward, encircling Sorel Tan fighters who clustered in small, desperate knots. The decking was strewn with bodies. They were mostly Angelaux soldiers, their white and green gambesons soaked through with blood. Brazier's chest tightened. This was the strike force Kathryn had come in with.

"She's here somewhere," he said, low but certain.

They moved as a unit, instinctively falling into a loose wedge as they picked their way through the dead. The battle raged in pockets all around them, bolts cracking, blades ringing. Every nerve in Brazier's body screamed danger. He had to keep overriding it, forcing himself to focus, to move.

The Sorel Tan were losing. He could see it in the way their lines staggered, the hesitation in their strikes. The tide was turning.

And then he saw him.

Gabriel.

Moving with that same eerie calm, sword hanging loose at his side. He walked straight toward a blonde woman scrambling backward over corpses, hands clawing for purchase, retreating one desperate movement at a time. Her gambeson was torn, her breastplate smeared with blood.

It was Kathryn.

Brazier raised his crossbow at Gabriel but couldn't get a shot. Too many La'Voline soldiers were in the way.

He sucked in air between clenched teeth. "I see her."

Freyen was already moving. "I've got eyes on her."

"The witch hunter and the woman on the floor," Brazier barked to Vandemir and the Rex Populaire as they surged forward.

"We see them," Vandemir said.

They broke into a run, weaving through the thinning press of La'Voline troops. A Sorel Tan elf came out of nowhere from their right, falchion raised. Vandemir pivoted, blade already coming up in a sweeping arc.

But it didn't matter.

An arrow punched clean through the elf's neck. Blood sprayed. The elf collapsed without a sound.

Loraine winked at her captain and said something that was probably sarcastic. But Brazier had all but forgotten the moment. He didn't register anything beyond what was happening twenty feet ahead.

Kathryn was on her feet, falchion gripped tight in her right hand. But Gabriel already had the tip of his sword pressed against her throat. One inch forward, that was all it would take. One quick thrust and all of this would be for nothing. Brazier lifted his repeater. He was too slow, too late, but he raised it anyway. Because what else could he do?

Then everything changed.

He saw the second Gabriel. They all saw him. He was standing behind Isdria. Freyen and Switch were close now, flanking Brazier, weapons ready, frozen by a sight they knew all too well.

The first Gabriel, the one holding the sword to Kathryn's neck, turned toward Brazier, flashed him a smile, and winked.

Smoke curled along his blade. Tendrils snaked from his shoulders, his chest, his mouth. Then, like parchment catching fire, he unravelled and disintegrated in a twisting coil of black vapour.

And behind Isdria, the real Gabriel moved.

He stepped up to the elf. His sword punched through Isdria's back, the tip bursting out from his belly, staining his gambeson red. Isdria's blade clattered to the deck. His hands clutched around the steel jutting from his gut, face twisted in pain. The sneer was gone, all that remained was raw disbelief.

Gabriel thrust forward, then pulled the blade free.

Isdria dropped to his knees. Hands pressed against the wound, the shock turning to confusion as he turned to look at Gabriel, now standing over his shoulder.

The witch hunter stepped in close, grabbed a fistful of the elf's long hair, and yanked his head back.

"You always said you'd die for your cause," Gabriel said, voice almost casual. "I'm just helping you follow through."

And then he drove the sword down into Isdria's neck.

Isdria gasped, then choked, blood spilling from his mouth in thick gouts as Gabriel tore the blade free. Arterial spray painted the air. The elf's body crumpled, hitting the deck with a thud.

Gabriel unhooked a pouch from his bandolier and drew a small vial. He uncorked it, touched the rim to his blade, and let Isdria's blood drip inside. When it was half full, he stoppered it and tucked it away.

Brazier stared, caught somewhere between stunned confusion and the impulse to act. He didn't know what he'd just seen, but he knew he needed Gabriel in irons. The witch hunter's testimony would matter to Varkoneth. It would matter to the crew of the *Anchorite*.

He took a step, then another. The others moved with him.

And that's when the inner doors at the far end of the chamber groaned open.

Brazier stopped cold. His stomach dropped.

He'd forgotten.

In the rush to find Kathryn, he'd completely forgotten about the goblins. Hundreds of them poured through the doors, a wave of snarling, screeching fury. Their skin was the green of spoiled fruit, their black hair matted or braided in crude knots, yellow eyes burning. They wore leather rags, rusted steel, and carried jagged axes, spears, and scavenged shields. They looked vaguely like a landslide.

Someone behind Brazier was shouting—"Form up! Shield wall! Form up!"

But Gabriel raised a hand. It was just a gesture, simple and calm. And the goblins slowed. They didn't stop, but their pace dropped to a crawl. Their snarling mouths still dripped spit, their eyes still burned, but unmistakably, they obeyed.

"What in the darkest, dankest abyss?" Switch muttered.

"He controls them," Freyen said. Her voice was tight, disbelieving.

"We shooting these things or what?" Loraine asked, already halfway to drawing.

"I, for one," Vandemir said, calm as a man drinking ale by an inn's hearth, "am very interested in seeing how this plays out."

He turned, raising his voice over the thrum of panic.

"Hold your fire!" he bellowed. "Hold your fire!"

"Who the abyss is giving that order?" someone yelled back.

"Captain Vonclaire of the Rex Populaire," Vandemir replied without missing a beat. "I speak with the King's authority."

There was a murmur. Brazier thought he caught the phrase, "The black gall of that man."

Then another voice: "Hold your fire!"

Across the blood-slick deck, Gabriel turned to Brazier and raised his sword, its tip aimed directly at him.

"Isdria was wrong, you know," Gabriel shouted, gesturing to the elf's body. "He was wrong about your brother. About your father. Your family wasn't disgraced. They were betrayed by the Ecclessius."

Brazier stared at him, stunned.

"Your father discovered a plot to remove Eluthienn," Gabriel continued. "A conspiracy deep in the Ravinican court. He wanted to warn the King of Ravinica, but the Ecclessius couldn't allow that. So they executed him to silence him. But not before your father told Torquen. And Torquen... he didn't betray Formaria. He sold the Luceron to the Sorel Tan not for coin, but so you'd have the future the Ecclessius tried to strip from you."

Of all the people, Brazier hadn't expected to hear those words from this man, and least of all in the middle of a war zone. He stood frozen, shocked, not just by who was speaking, or when, but by the weight of what was being said. For years, Brazier had lived under the weight of that story: the execution, the silence around his father's death, and his brother's disappearance. Torquen had never explained and Brazier had stopped asking. It had been better to believe his father wasn't a traitor than confront the possibility that he was.

All of it had calcified into a story he told himself to survive. Now Gabriel was telling him that story, the one that had kept him going all this time, was true.

But Brazier couldn't trust it. He couldn't trust Gabriel, not for a second. But why lie? And why was he being told this here? And now?

"How would you even know that?" Brazier shouted back. He couldn't think of anything else to say.

Gabriel looked at him.

"Because I was there," he said. "Aboard the Luceron. Not as Gabriel. As Talius Asher, a man the Ecclessius built. But I wasn't really him, just like I'm not really Gabriel."

Smoke began curling up Gabriel's body, slow and dark, like soot rising from burning parchment. It thickened, wrapping his limbs in writhing tendrils until he was cloaked in a living shadow. Then he began to shrink. It was slow at first, then in jerking collapses, until he was no taller than the goblins behind him.

The smoke peeled away. Skin emerged. It was yellow-green and cracked like old leather. A hand took shape, then a face, a mouth full of crooked teeth and a long beaked nose. Rusted-copper eyes flared open.

Where Gabriel had stood, now stood a goblin.

But not just any goblin. This one was older, more sunken. Its skin looked like parchment stretched over bone. Its ears and nose were unnaturally long. Warts clustered like fungus across its jaw.

And Brazier realised he'd never seen an old goblin before.

The creature twisted its neck, letting out a wet, cracking pop. Then it smiled. A red tongue swept its teeth. It clicked its jaws once, twice. All around the chamber, the La'Voline soldiers froze, staring.

The goblin turned its head, its voice sharp, nasally, and edged with scorn but with the unmistakable mockery that had belonged to Gabriel.

"It took me so long to learn your language," it said. "Not because I didn't understand, but because our mouths were never built for your vowels. Still, I learned. I took the name my family gave me and made it yours."

It lifted its pointed chin.

"Bork the Borken. That's who I am. And I will see my

family take its place in this world."

His gaze slid to Kathryn, still standing, still breathing, but pale with exhaustion and disbelief.

"She's yours now, Brazier Veranquis," Bork said. "Tell her the truth. Strip away the illusion. Destroy the lie my sister wove with her dreams."

Then his voice shifted, lower and harsher: "But for the tale, the true tale, it's already too late. You will not be able to undo it."

He released a sharp sound that was half snarl, half whistle, and aimed over his shoulder. A goblin echoed the call. The army moved as one. They flowed back through the inner doors like a tide in retreat.

No one followed. No one spoke. They stood in silence, watching. The chamber was thick with the sweet smell of spent ice and the tang of blood, and the wretched dark thing that had been the witch hunter Gabriel disappeared with the rest of the goblins.

They had won. The Sorel Tan had been defeated. They had the *Gloried Storm* and the weapon. Kathryn had survived.

But Brazier didn't feel like a victor. Gabriel's words sat uncomfortably in the pit of his stomach, churning with distrust and a sense of manipulation. He felt like a story had been told about him without his consent. And now he was left to pick up the pieces and decide if it would define him or if he would write something new.

But that was for later. First, he needed to tell Kathryn the truth, and, he realised with some unease, break the story that she'd told herself.

THIRTY-THREE KATHRYN

Kathryn stood frozen, watching the goblins retreat through the chamber doors. The falchion hung loose at her side. The wound along her thigh throbbed. Every other muscle ached, and her mind slipped between exhaustion and confusion.

Gabriel, or Bork the Borken, or whatever he was now, was gone. Isdria Laanorath lay sprawled on the decking, blood pooling beneath him, his once-smirking mouth slack. Her hindbrain, the ancient piece built for killing and surviving, kept whispering that she'd won. The enemy was dead. The threat had been removed. But it didn't feel like a victory.

Bork's words lingered in her mind, heavy as bronzite: the truth, the lie Brazier knew, and a sense that something greater had slipped past them, unseen. She had the strange notion they'd won the battle but lost the war, whatever war that might be.

Or maybe it was simpler. Maybe she felt hollow because she wouldn't be dragging Isdria Laanorath back to the Navarch in irons. She wouldn't stand before the Admiralty and force them to see the truth with their own eyes. She wouldn't force them to admit they were wrong as Isdria confessed.

She probed the shallow cut that had snuck around her armour, thinking maybe she was just tired—so tired she couldn't tell one feeling from the next.

Either way, dead or alive, it didn't really matter. With so many reports of Mirrovinjin ships and the capture of the *Storm*, the Sorel Tan's involvement could be proven beyond a doubt. The Navarch would finally believe her.

But it didn't mean they would accept her back into the navy. She wouldn't be reinstated as an officer. Abhorrence still ran in her veins. She still needed Veskanca, and she wasn't confident they'd help her find it. That, Kathryn decided, was what made the victory seem hollow.

She started forward, a strange need rising in her to look into Isdria's lifeless eye, to see for herself that it was really over, when a hand closed around her arm.

She turned to find Brazier standing there, looking up at her. He was only an inch shorter, but he seemed somehow smaller in the moment. Freyen and Switch flanked him, grim and dirty.

They looked like they hadn't seen a bath in a month. Brazier's beard was stiff with dried grime, streaks of sweat cutting pale lines down his temples. Switch looked worse, if that was possible, like she'd jumped in a river of whatever was sticking to Brazier.

Kathryn, filthy and sweat-soaked herself, felt an unexpected jolt of kinship. By the looks of things, they'd all been through the abyss, and they'd all made it out in one piece, mostly.

"You made it out of the Immuratum, then?" she said, trying for lightness.

She regretted it immediately. A shadow crossed Switch and Freyen's faces like a cloud passing over the sun.

And then she remembered the other dwarf, Matthias. He

wasn't here. It was possible he was on the *Anchorite*, but from the looks on their faces, Kathryn guessed that wasn't the case.

Brazier's face, though, showed something else. It was more than just grief. It was the tight, brittle look of someone about to say something important and not knowing how.

"Did you find out how to kill that thing?" she asked, nodding past him toward the throne and the corpse that sat in it.

Behind them, those La'Voline soldiers not helping their wounded had turned their attention to the throne. They were talking in hushed tones, as if they didn't want to disturb the being sat atop it. But whatever pull the Queen of Dreams had on her didn't seem to affect them.

Brazier hadn't taken his eyes from her.

"We found the Library of the Nine," he said. "And we found the book there. The book that explains how to destroy the Lords of the Eternal Hunt."

Kathryn shifted her weight onto her unwounded leg, using the falchion as a makeshift walking stick. "Convenient book. I hope you took it with you?"

"Wasn't really an option," Brazier said, still looking at her with that grave look.

Kathryn decided she was going to stop making jokes. They didn't seem to be landing.

"Duessa's magic works through harbingers," Brazier said.

Kathryn flinched at the word without meaning to.

"Harbingers spread her sorcery through stories," Brazier went on, as if he hadn't noticed. She got the sense that what he was telling her was very important to him.

"Stories that aren't true. But once they're believed, they become true. And the more people believe, the stronger she gets."

Kathryn frowned. Her mind jumped back to the chair, the blue fire, the Mirrovinjin, Isdria looming over her like a spectre. Her heart stuttered just thinking about it. But neither Isdria nor the Mirrovinjin had ever told her a story. She thought back to the Cawdora surface drift and the tortured gnome. No one had said a word to him either.

"You sure you're getting this right?" she asked, harsher than she meant to. "I wasn't told any stories about the ships. I saw it with my own eyes."

Brazier's eyes were focused on her with unblinking intensity. "The ships are the story," he said. "The Sorel Tan made you believe they were real. And that belief made them real. It's not about words. It's about what you saw."

Kathryn had to stop herself from laughing. But when she saw Brazier was serious, something began to turn at the back of her mind, something that felt a lot like doubt. Her hand was going numb around the grip of her stolen sword, and she didn't know when she'd started shaking her head, but she couldn't stop now.

"We found a girl," Freyen said. "She believed in the Mirrovinjin ships too. When we believed her, one appeared. But when we were picked up by the Eclipse? Their crew knew the ships weren't real. And the illusion vanished."

Kathryn stood in shock for several seconds. When the meaning eventually sank in, it cut deeper than any blade. She nearly staggered under the weight of it, her mind flashing back to Erin Carmowright, the Navarch Liaison. He'd believed her. And Demina had believed him. If what Freyen was saying was true, then that belief had birthed the first Mirrovinjin ship off Ilantia.

And the gnome, he hadn't been told anything. He'd just believed. And he'd told her about the ships, before one had arrived. When she'd accepted that, one had appeared.

Kathryn felt something crack inside her. She had fought

so hard to hold her story together, to stand against the doubt and the alienation. Her defiance had become her armour. And now it peeled away, brittle and useless.

It felt like betrayal and shame, like waking up to find everything she had built her life on had been a dream someone else wrote for her. It was as if she hadn't really been in control, someone else had. Oddly, it was the same thing she felt whenever she tried not to think about how her mother had shaped her life. How she tried not to ask herself whether the navy and her captaincy were the things that she, Kathryn, wanted, or whether they had been decided for her long ago, by someone who hated her.

A shout broke the moment. Kathryn's head snapped up. Behind Brazier, the La'Voline soldiers were moving fast, pulling into a shield wall.

And then she saw why.

The corpse still sitting on the golden throne began to twitch. Its limbs spasmed, jerking in sharp, unnatural bursts like something trying to break free. Its jaw dropped open, a grotesque rattle escaping into the air. The sound built, rising from a whisper to a death scream.

The corpse's glowing eye sockets stared straight at her, a deep molten red and sharp as crystal.

But she was no longer looking at its eyes. She was watching the flesh peel away. Flakes of dead skin rose into the air like ash caught on a phantom wind, revealing muscle, then bone, and finally nothing at all.

The body gave a final, rattling gasp, and Duessa, Queen of Dreams, and Lord of the Eternal Hunt, dissolved into dust.

#

Three days later, half the rebel fleet still drifted across the northern quadrant of the Gulf, silent sentinels circling the shattered wreck of the *Vanguard of Winter*. The ship lay like the corpse of some drowned god, tangled in the massive feelers and cavern-grown ropes of the surrounding fungal reefs. Nothing approached it. With Gyre Stars and cruisers stationed above and around, nothing dared.

Inside, repair teams crawled the ship's husk like ants across broken stone. Progress was slow. There were too few hands and too many dead. The scale of damage meant every hour brought a new list of impossible asks. Kathryn had petitioned to join them. Her wounds had been magically healed, the bruises and lacerations now just memories etched into scar tissue, but restlessness gnawed at her. She wanted to be useful. She needed to do something.

But Korst had denied the request. The admiral had ordered her to stay aboard the *Pheradies* until she and Sourant could complete a formal debrief with the *Anchorite's* crew.

So she spent the first day visiting what remained of the *Vanguard's* crew. Royer had died in the *Storm's* main chamber, cut down in that final, doomed charge against the Sorel Tan lines. She'd been the one to find his body, strewn beneath a pile of splintered shields and broken armour. Grief and guilt came in equal measure.

She'd tried to help carry him out. She'd nearly collapsed doing so. Her own wounds, and the weight of it all, were too much. She'd almost been carried out herself after that. Brazier and the others helped her limp back to the landing zone.

But Faber, Karland, and Avery had made it. That first night on the *Pheradies*, they'd raised mugs to Royer, to the others, and to survival. They got blisteringly drunk. The kind of drunk that wasn't about forgetting but about enduring. And while the sadness never left, it felt a little less sharp with company. Grief shared was better than grief alone.

The next morning, head pounding and mouth dry as a tunnel floor, she made her way to the *Anchorite*. She found its crew in much the same state. They welcomed her with nods, smiles, and a few words, and she quickly fell into a rhythm with them, repairing what could be saved. She stayed all day but declined to join them for supper. It was clear they were mourning Matthias. Whatever camaraderie they offered, that loss wasn't hers to share. She felt like an intruder at someone else's funeral, and so she didn't mind leaving.

The next two days, she wandered the halls of the *Pheradies*. Eventually, she found purpose in the hangar bays, helping logistics crews move plating and parts to and from the repair lines. The work was brutal, lugging bronzite panels and fragmented conduits, but it quieted her thoughts. The ache in her arms was easier to carry than the weight in her chest.

And then, something strange happened.

She slept.

There was no blue fire or visions of dark ships. There was no waking up clawing at the sweat-drenched sheets. She had two nights without nightmares. It was followed by two mornings of silence where once there had been the scratchy, venomous voice of her mother whispering from the back of her mind. She suffered no hallucinations. There was no tug in her chest dragging her toward Isdria. There was just peace.

That's when she realised Duessa was gone. She wasn't just destroyed; she was gone. The abhorrence, the madness, the constant edge of collapse had lifted. Kathryn didn't hear her mother anymore. She didn't see her. There were no judgments, no recriminations. There was just stillness and herself.

And she didn't need Veskanca anymore. She'd asked one of the ship's war casters to test her for abhorrence. There was none. It had left her system without a trace, as if she'd never suffered from it in the first place. She was still marvelling at that.

And now, at last, the summons had come. The debrief was underway. Kathryn sat on the deep green couches of the admiral's quarters aboard the *Pheradies*, waiting to hear what came next.

Sourant and Korst shared one couch, a foot of distance between them. The captain of the *Eclipse* sat rigid, hands planted on his thighs, back locked straight as a mast. His mug of tea sat untouched on the bronzite table, thin wisps of steam curling up and fading into the low-lit room.

Korst was the opposite. She lounged into the curve of the couch, one arm thrown casually over the back, one boot kicked up onto the seat at an angle, the spotless black leather catching the light. Her tea rested easy on her thigh. From the large bridge of her forehead to the lazy tilt of her smile, the dwarf radiated warmth and ease—the kind Kathryn had no trouble seeing through. Intelligence officers were good at that kind of thing: soft fronts, steel cores.

Korst smiled at Kathryn, and Kathryn smiled back.

Across from them, the crew of the *Anchorite* sat shoulder to shoulder. They were freshly bathed and freshly dressed, looking less like survivors and more like people again. Brazier in a dark, short-cut gambeson and trousers. Freyen in a deep green shirt under a worn leather jacket. Switch in black enginator's coveralls, both her flesh-and-blood and mechanical arms bare.

They were all present, except the one who wasn't.

The navigator's absence pressed against them like a quiet, invisible presence. Brazier carried it the most. It was etched into new lines across his forehead and the corners of his eyes. Something had changed in the dwarf. He wasn't old yet, but he no longer looked young either.

Kathryn knew the look. She'd seen it on Sourant, and on Korst. She'd seen it on every commander who lived long enough to realise the job took pieces of them, one by one. Usually, they realised after the fact.

And then there was her. She wasn't sitting with Sourant and Korst. But she wasn't quite sitting with Brazier and the others either. She perched on the edge of two worlds, fitting into neither. Once, that would have bothered her. Now, it just seemed... normal. Since walking off the *Gloried Storm*, her life had become bigger somehow, her horizon broader. She wasn't quite sure why yet, but things like making friends didn't quite matter as much.

Sourant broke the silence.

"We apprehended several of Isdria Laanorath's senior officers as they tried to flee," he said. "His Majesty Marcus Angelaux, aboard the Orranthis, is taking them and the Storm to neutral ground. They'll meet with Ecclessiarchal agents there."

Brazier rubbed the back of his head absently, like he expected to find something hiding there.

"The Ecclessius accepts that Varkoneth conspired with the Sorel Tan?" he asked.

"We shared the Storm's hex logs with the Ecclessius and the great houses," Sourant said. "It shows the Storm docking at Thela under a false signature. Records of multiple meetings with Rosantz vessels. Rosantz personnel boarding the ship."

"It was enough to convince the Navarch to blockade Thela," Korst added, blowing across the surface of her tea. "The Cauldron's surrendered."

At any other point in time, the idea that a great house had been toppled and its capital surrendered would have shocked Kathryn to her core. Now it was just one shocking event in a long list of shocking events. It just didn't have the same impact.

"And the other great houses didn't need much convincing to rally to Marcus," Sourant said, the corner of his mouth twitching. "Varkoneth Rosantz isn't exactly well liked."

Kathryn also knew that one house's decline was another's ascension. Liking or not liking Varkoneth Rosantz had little to do with supporting House Rosantz's downfall.

"But you were wrong about the Grand Ecclessian," Brazier said. "About his involvement."

So that's why Brazier had suspected the Church. Because Marcus had. Because they all had.

Sourant nodded. The fact didn't seem to bother him either way.

"We were," he said. "But we'll still need your testimonies."

"You're still planning to move against the Grand Ecclessian?" Freyen asked.

Kathryn blinked at the shift. She hadn't seen that one coming. From the way Sourant and Korst avoided looking at her, Kathryn guessed she'd just walked into a conversation that wasn't meant for her ears.

"He betrayed an ally," Korst said, voice easy but with a careful edge. "And failed, spectacularly, to do the one job the Church is supposed to do."

When the rest of the room just stared at her, she added, almost amused, "Keeping the Royal Houses in line. Varkoneth nearly broke Formaria in half, and the Grand Ecclessian let it happen on his watch. That kind of failure doesn't go unchecked."

"But first," Sourant said, "we have to deal with Varkoneth. Which means there may be a delay before you can give your testimonies."

"And a delay in receiving our pardons," Freyen said, raising an eyebrow and blowing on her tea like she was perfectly fine with the idea but wanted to keep the record straight.

"And our medals," Switch added, tapping a mechanical finger against her chin in mock thoughtfulness. "And the Anchorite. Let's not forget legal ownership of the Anchorite."

"All of that," Sourant said smoothly. "As agreed."

He picked up his mug and rested it on his thigh.

"In the meantime," he continued, "we'll escort you to Pontifax. You and the Anchorite will be kept hidden there until we can move forward."

"No," Brazier said.

It was one word, but it changed the temperature of the room like a blast of cold air.

Kathryn felt the invisible ripple of it. Even Korst sat forward slightly, mug resting forgotten against her leg. Sourant, about to take a sip of tea, rested his mug between his thighs.

"A member of my crew is being held by the entity, the Handmaid, in Yeggardania," Brazier said. His voice was low, measured, and about as flexible as a locked door. "We're going to get him."

Sourant and Korst exchanged the kind of look that said they'd predicted this exact moment.

"And if we told you," Korst said carefully, "we could send forces to retrieve him—"

"I'd thank you for the offer," Brazier said. "And tell you we're going with them."

Korst's mouth quirked up into something almost like a smile. "We thought this might happen. You'll have a full company as escort."

Brazier looked caught off guard, like he'd prepared for a long, bloody argument only to find the other side submitting.

"And we'd prefer you let the soldiers do the fighting,"

Sourant added dryly.

Switch scratched at the couch with her mechanical hand, then shook her head. "Yeah, we'd prefer that too. Funny how that never seems to work out, though."

"Our officer in Calaxis sent an update," Korst said. "Your navigator is still alive. Still working for the Handmaid."

The tension left Brazier like air escaping a vent. He leaned back into the seat. Switch and Freyen both turned to him.

"Thank you," Brazier said, clearly relieved.

"There was also a message," Korst said. "Bit of an odd one. He said to tell you: 'the toad is still a toad.'"

Kathryn felt a frown pull across her forehead, but Brazier just exhaled through his nose and shook his head, like it was exactly the kind of thing he'd expected to hear.

"The Handmaid's lover," Brazier said, confusing Kathryn further. "She thought if we destroyed Duessa, it would break the magic binding him. But that's not how Duessa's magic works."

Sourant looked like someone had slapped him across the face with a dead fish. It was shock, and a little disgust. Kathryn didn't blame him. The conversation had taken a very odd turn.

Korst just sipped her tea.

"That would've been during the time of Redcrosse," Korst said. "Hundreds, maybe a thousand years ago."

Brazier looked like he was considering that.

"In the library," he said after a pause, "the book implied that once a tale is complete, fully believed by those it's told to, the sorcery behind it becomes permanent. It can't be undone."

"So everyone back then believed the Handmaid's lover was cursed," Korst said, her voice tight with realisation.

Brazier shrugged.

"But people believed the Mirrovinjin ships were real," Sourant said. Kathryn winced. It was a tiny, automatic twitch she couldn't stop. If anyone noticed, they were polite enough to pretend otherwise.

"Enough people doubted it, though," Brazier said. "The lie wasn't complete. It didn't take root fully."

"Everyone who hears the lie must believe it," Switch said. "So if even one person doubts, the magic can still be broken."

"Seems that way," Brazier agreed. Then he frowned, remembering something. His brow furrowed deeper.

"There was something else," he said. "The book called the harbingers an *entwined* harbinger crop. Each illusion is tied to a specific set of harbingers."

Then his eyes widened.

"Not all tales can be undone," he said. "Only those linked to the entwined harbinger crop."

"And the crop that turned the Handmaid's lover into a toad died out centuries ago," Freyen said grimly.

"So the Handmaid's stuck with a toad for a boyfriend," Switch said. Then her face twisted into genuine horror. "How do they even make that work?"

Before anyone had to find an answer to that nightmare of a question, the command terminal pulsed to life.

"Tether request for Admiral Korst," the voice announced.

Sourant pushed to his feet without a word, giving Korst room to pass. She moved to the terminal, her boots soft against the bronzite floor.

Kathryn shifted on the couch, something tugging at her gut.

"The shi—" she started, then caught herself. Everyone turned their heads toward her.

"The illusions," she corrected quickly, her gaze locking with Sourant's. "There haven't been any more sightings?"

"None," Sourant said, a small and encouraging smile forming. "And those that were reported before have vanished. Not a trace of them left."

Kathryn nodded, her pulse suddenly hammering in her ears. She had seen Duessa dissolve into ash with her own eyes. War casters, Guilfier among them, had confirmed it too: The Aeturnic sorcery aboard the *Storm* and across Formaria had faded. Even so, some stubborn part of her still needed to hear it out loud. She needed it confirmed.

"It worked," Sourant said, his smile deepening with warmth. "You did it. I only wish we'd told you the ships weren't real when we first met you. I assumed Brazier would have mentioned that."

"He did," Kathryn said, trying to hide how foolish she felt. "I just didn't believe him."

"You are quite stubborn," Switch said to Kathryn. Kathryn couldn't tell if she was joking or not.

"You're one to talk," Freyen said, and both Switch and Brazier laughed. Kathryn found herself smiling, despite herself.

The warm moment remained for only a heartbeat before Korst disconnected the tether. Kathryn caught the change instantly, the frown pulling at Korst's features, the tight set of her shoulders.

Something was wrong.

"What did the goblin tell you before he retreated?" Korst asked, fixing Brazier with a stare that stripped away any trace of warmth. Her voice had gone cold, almost clinical.

"He said it's already too late for the true tale," Brazier said. He shrugged. "I didn't know what he meant by that."

Korst nodded once, a tight motion. "I received a message back from Admiral Adremar," she said, and for the first time, Kathryn saw something close to real shock on the dwarf's face. Worry pulled down the heavy line of her brow.

"He sent a team to investigate the Gyre Gate south of Calaxis Major." She hesitated, visibly bracing herself. "It's been rebuilt."

The room froze. Kathryn's skin went cold, and her hands felt slick with sweat. It was like someone telling her a fatal illness she'd fought through had returned, and worse than before.

"Isdria said they were using Duessa's sorcery to rebuild one of the gates," Brazier said, his voice low.

"But Duessa is dead," Sourant said, sounding more like he was trying to convince himself than anyone else. "The illusions are gone."

Brazier stared at the bronzite table between them, as if it might provide the answers.

"Unless there was another crop of harbingers," he said. "A crop that believed a lie told to them about the gates being rebuilt."

"But if Duessa's destroyed," Sourant pressed, "shouldn't the sorcery vanish with her?"

"Not if the lie was fully believed," Brazier said. His voice was grim now. "If everyone who heard it accepted it as true, then the sorcery becomes permanent."

"Wait," Switch said, cutting in. "Why bother with the fake ships at all? Why not just convince a few idiots into believing the gate was rebuilt and call it a day?"

"Because they needed Duessa to be powerful enough first," Kathryn said. The words tumbled out, clear and awful. She could hear the slight tremor in her voice as realisation set in. "That's what Isdria and Bork were talking about in the Cawdora Drift. The source had to grow stronger. Every new harbinger crop made her more powerful."

"The true tale has already been told," Brazier said. "The Mirrovinjin illusions—they were just a way to make Duessa powerful enough to embed the real story."

"And we can't track down that crop of harbingers and undo it," Korst said. "Duessa's gone. The sorcery is... locked in."

"And after a thousand years on our own," Brazier said, "we now have an open Gyre Gate."

"Did Admiral Adremar confirm if it's active?" Sourant asked, though even as he spoke, he sounded like he knew the answer wouldn't matter.

"Would anyone even know what an active gate looked like?" Korst replied, the weariness in her voice making her sound a decade older. She shook her head slowly. Kathryn half-expected her to sink her face into her hands right there.

"Why would Bork want the gates reopened?" Switch asked, her forehead creasing. "Even for a goblin, that's another level of suicidal. It's bad for everything living in Formaria."

Korst sighed. She exchanged a glance with Sourant. He slid over to make room for her to sit on the couch.

"We've been tracking the creature calling itself Bork the Borken ever since Eluthienn warned the High Lords of Thendergaarden that it was Bork who reawakened Lokul," she said. Kathryn felt her eyes widen at the comment. It momentarily distracted her from the panic still clutching her heart.

"The Grand Ecclessian dismissed the idea," Korst said. "But we didn't."

"We?" Brazier said. "As in the rebel fleet?"

Korst nodded once. "That was our original purpose," she said. "Investigating Bork. It's become apparent that he's an unusual goblin."

"They're all pretty unusual," Switch muttered.

Korst smiled faintly. "Agreed. But Bork is different. He wants a home for the goblin species. And he believes that by weakening Formaria, he can make us vulnerable enough to supplant us. Which is why we believe he did reawaken Lokul—and why he later reawakened Duessa."

"But the vampires would've turned on the goblins," Freyen said. "Same with whatever else comes through the Gyre Gates."

"Bork never intended for Lokul and his offspring to be unleashed on Formaria," Korst said. "His goal was to force us to ally with Eluthienn. Lokul was just the reason for that alliance. If Formaria allied with Eluthienn, then after the prince retook Ravinica, we would have been drawn into a war against Fiondagaard. Distracted. Bleeding resources. And most importantly—vulnerable."

"But Gabriel, Bork, killed Eluthienn," Freyen said. "Wouldn't that destroy his plan?"

"It did," Korst said. "But I suspect Bork couldn't afford to break character as Gabriel. Gabriel's orders were clear: if Lyander failed to kill Eluthienn, Gabriel had to finish it. If Bork hadn't, he would have blown his cover and probably years of preparation with it."

Kathryn was entirely lost now, but didn't want to interrupt. Her panic had turned to outright amazement at what she was hearing.

"So he reawakens Lokul, sets up this alliance, and then gets forced to pull it all apart because the Grand Ecclessian didn't hold up his end of the deal," Switch said, incredulous.

"Exactly," Korst said. "Bork gambled. He lost. And now he's moved to his next strategy."

The silence that followed was heavy in the air.

"And the Gyre Gate?" Brazier asked. "Varkoneth thought opening it would bring our ancient cousins back. That he'd welcome them as King of Formaria. What does Bork gain from that?"

"Chaos," Korst said. "Pure and simple."

Brazier frowned, but it was Sourant who spoke next.

"The Gyre Gates didn't just connect us to other worlds," he said. "They bound us to the Immuratum."

Korst nodded. "Destroying the Gates cut us off from the demon realms. But now, Bork has restored that connection—or at least partially."

Switch looked like she wanted to argue, but Korst raised a hand. "Not all connections were severed completely, obviously. There were still breaches."

"It'll be chaos for the goblins too," Freyen said.

"But that's the point," Korst said. "Fighting, killing, warfare, that's what the elves bred them for. To be cunning and vicious. But perpetually divided so they'd never be strong enough to unite."

"Until Bork," Brazier said.

Korst nodded.

"Bork understands his race can't win an outright fight against a united people like the Fromryr," she said. "So he's introducing outside variables. Breaking the unity we depend on. Causing chaos."

During her time in the navy, Kathryn had sat through multiple intelligence briefs on the self-styled goblin king. Korst's claims sounded exactly like the character that had been described to her years ago. But one thing still bothered her enough to interrupt.

"Bork can shapeshift?" she said, the memory of what she'd seen aboard the *Storm* flashing back with sickening clarity. "Only a handful of our most senior war casters can achieve that."

"It should be impossible for a goblin," Korst said. She glanced briefly at Sourant, who stayed carefully neutral.

Korst turned back to the others. "Our theory, and we're fairly confident in it, is that Bork *is* one of the Lords of the Eternal Hunt. One of the manifestations."

Kathryn felt herself go very still. What Korst had said

about the goblin king infiltrating the witch hunter Coven had been almost unbelievable. What she was saying now bordered on the absurd. The problem was, the Admiral was saying it with absolute seriousness.

"Most theories claim the Lords are created when actions in the real world reach a certain... magnitude," Korst said. "Acts so massive, so consequential, they birth entities embodying those acts."

"And what does Bork personify?" Switch asked. "All the worst shits every Fromryr has ever taken."

At any other time, Kathryn would have found that funny. But right now, she was hanging on every word Korst said. She didn't even want to breathe too loud in case she missed something.

"Bork embodies hubris," Korst continued. "The arrogance of the elves in believing they could create an entire species just to hunt and kill, to train their own warriors. That act, that cruelty and pride... birthed Bork."

"But it still doesn't explain how he can shapeshift," Kathryn said.

Korst shrugged. "The Lords are creatures of immense and ancient power. Lokul could turn others into vampires. Duessa spun lies into reality. Bork can shapeshift, and unite a race that was never meant to be anything but fractured."

Brazier's frown deepened. The kind of frown that said he wasn't quite convinced.

"Bork let Eluthienn kill Lokul," Brazier said. "And let us destroy Duessa. If he's one of them, he sure doesn't act like it."

"He hates them," Korst said without hesitation. "Hates and fears them. As all the Lords hate and fear one another. They were never meant to share power. Each one wants this realm for themselves. Lokul was a threat to Bork, just as Duessa was. He couldn't allow either to rise again."

Brazier leaned back, crossing his arms over his chest. "We saw him take Isdria's blood on the Storm," he said. "Caught it in a vial. And he took mine."

"And mine," Kathryn added.

Brazier turned to her, surprised, but Korst spoke: "That could be how he mimics others. Maybe he uses the blood to take on their shape."

"But why bother taking Isdria's form? Or yours?" Freyen asked, turning to Brazier, then Kathryn. "Everyone knows Isdria is dead now. And how would mimicking either of you help Bork's cause?"

Brazier shook his head. "Maybe it's not just the body," he said. "Maybe it gives him their memories too. For all the good my memories would do him."

"Or mine," Kathryn said, creeping concern worming through her. She did not like the idea that a goblin could turn into her. But she didn't see how it could benefit Bork, other than being able to pass as a human.

"We'll ensure this is passed on to Navarch intelligence," Sourant said. "It may even help us catch him, if he turns into one of you, and we know you're somewhere else."

Kathryn didn't add that would mean the Navarch had her location constantly.

"This would also explain a lot," Korst said. "He was convincing as Gabriel. Too convincing." She took a breath, then said, "Gabriel, the real Gabriel, was hunting Bork."

"Hunting him?" Switch said. "That didn't go well, then."

"No," Korst said, sighing. "Gabriel spent years in the Aeturnum, hunting blood shamans and warlocks. He was the best the Coven ever produced. Deadlier than any witch hunter before him. But he spent so long in the darkness, we should have known something had changed. Some even suspected."

"Isn't that against the Ecclessius' own laws?" Kathryn

asked. "No more than a month at a time?"

"The Lord Huntsman argued in Gabriel's favour," Korst said. "Gabriel was the golden boy. Untouchable. They trusted him implicitly."

"What do you think happened?" Freyen asked quietly.

Korst shrugged, looking weary. "I think Bork got to him before Gabriel ever got close. We tried to interrogate him when he returned. The war casters said he reeked of Abhorrence. But Anselhelm protected him. Wouldn't hear of it."

Brazier's voice was cautious. "You don't think Anselhelm was involved?"

"No," Korst said, shaking her head firmly. "He was fooled, the same as the rest of us."

"So you'll look for Bork now?" Freyen asked.

"We've been looking for Bork for years," Korst said. "The Storm is probably the closest we've ever been to finding him."

She shook her head. "And now we've got his mess to contend with as well, which is exactly what he wants."

"What will you do about the Gate?" Brazier asked. "And the Grand Ecclessian?"

"I have to return to Thendergaarden," Korst said. "The High Lords are already convening. But the Grand Ecclessian will have to wait."

"The other houses won't want to move against Cadarrasta with the threat of a reopened Gyre Gate," Sourant said.

"And the Grand Ecclessian will use it to rally support," Korst said. "He'll call for unity. Use the threat to tighten his grip."

"Is it wise for you to return to the capital?" Sourant asked.

"It would raise too much suspicion if I didn't," Korst said.

Kathryn leaned forward. "I'm going with you," she said. The words landed like a shot across the bow. All eyes turned to her.

"I want your recommendations," she continued, meeting Korst's gaze. "For reinstatement. As a Navarch captain."

"You'll have them," Korst said, smiling faintly. "But there's a place in intelligence too, if you want it."

The half-joke wasn't lost on Kathryn. She smiled back.

"I was going to ask if you wanted to come with us," Brazier said, tilting his head slightly.

"Yeah," Switch added. "You're pretty handy in a fight. Not too subtle, though."

Kathryn's smile widened, surprising herself at how good it felt, despite everything.

"No," she said. "I think it's time I got my own ship again."

A smile broke across Brazier's face, one that reached all the way to his eyes. He knew exactly how she felt.

Another storm was gathering. But for now, for this brief moment, it felt like a long night had finally ended. She'd savour the feeling as long as she could, because somewhere beyond it, a new fight was waiting. Kathryn didn't know what that fight held but whatever it was, she was walking into it with her eyes wide open.

There would be no more lies, no more stories written by others. From here on out, she'd write her own.

Epistolar message Fion to Vallorandyl

A telling in Vallorandyl.

The teller is Emries von Cadst, Duke of Ylstgaar, Adjutant to the Fion Throne, and Marshal of the Western Front.

The witness is Vermillies Sidtch, Lord Regent of Ravinica and Absolver General.

The telling is of the Lord Regents utter foolishness and lack of prudence. Your incompetence has led us directly into the goblin's snare, the foul creature known as Bork the Borken. Using the elf's blood, he deceived you utterly, planting seeds of calamity, which in turn has led us to be this tale's victim.

Our acceptance of his deceit has directly enabled the Gyre Gate's rebuilding, a folly beyond measure, a threat surpassing all prior dangers to the empire. We were its intended target, Vermillies. Once Duessa's powers were strong enough, we were the ones meant to believe the Gyre Gate would be rebuilt. And so it has come to pass.

You should have listened to the tale in its entirety before ensnaring me in its deception. But your eagerness to please overcame any shred of discernment you possess. Your errors undermine our conquests and threaten the emperor's dominion itself.

I now bear the grim duty of informing the emperor, yet our involvement must remain hidden. Hidden at all costs lest we face execution. Vermillies, your reckless failures imperil us all. Pray fervently to whatever deity might listen, that our conquest of Ravinica prevails swiftly. Only absolute victory can redeem your errors. May fortune favour us, for the storm gathering on the horizon promises devastation. Stand ready, Lord Regent, our survival, and indeed the empire's survival, depend upon it. The teller is Emries von Cadst, Duke of Ylstgaar. The witness is Vermillies Sidtch, Lord Regent, and no others.

The End

Glossary

<u>Races</u>

Constructii – Humanoid constructs, presumed built by the Formarians **Dwen'hiema** – Dwarves

Fenn – Reptilian humanoids

Formarians – Unknown, presumed extinct

Goblins – Humanoids, typically green skinned

Humans – Humans

Ilvalien – Elves

Kneldier – Gnomes

Mirrovinjin – Humanoid, typically pale-skinned with four arms

Rakkan – Humanoids, typically black or dark red skinned, sometimes allied to the Mirrovinjin

Skavrii – Large humanoids, typically with black carapace-like skin, allied to the Mirrovinjin

Trolls – Large humanoids, skin colour and features varies

<u>Factions, groups, and orders</u>

Artificium - Order of Enginators

Conclave – Order of Witch-Hunters, Order Abhorrentia

Ecclessius – De facto rulers of the Fromryr, religious organisation

Fal'Hannians – Largest mercenary organisation in Aetraya

Fromryr – Allied races of elves, dwarves, gnomes, and humans inhabiting Formaria

Gyranic Coven – Order of Mages

High Council – The leaders of the Fromryr, made up of monarchs, the High Lords of Thendergaarden and members of the Ordained Conglomerate

High Lords of Thendergaarden – Heads of the Navarch, Navigorum, Gyranic Coven, Conclave, and

Knights Redcrosse

Knights Redcrosse – Elite military order of the Ecclessius

Lords of the Eternal Hunt – Aeturnic deities, considered mythical

Navarch – Fromryian navy

Navigorum – Order of Navigators, also refers to nav deck

Ordained Conglomerate – The leaders of the Ecclessius

Sorel Tan – Banished elves dedicated to the restoration of the Gyre Gates, considered terrorists

Chaos and Darkness

Aeturnum – Darkness realm

Immuratum – Chaos realm

Abhorrence – Aeturnic corruption

Malignance – Immuratic corruption

Aeturni – Monster

Immurati – Demon

Gyranic sorcery

Anomancy – Healing

Abjurancy – Defensive

Evocancy – Offensive

Obliquency – Manipulation

Symulacrancy – Imitation

Settlements, structures & features

Cauldron – Second largest settlement

Cradle – Fourth largest settlement

Cove – Smallest settlement

Gyre Gates – Portals to other worlds, all destroyed during the Sundering

Maw – Spatial and temporal space distinct from the

rest of Formaria

Relative horizon – Boundary separating Maws from the rest of Formaria

Spire – Third largest, outpost rather than settlement

Surface drift – Large flows of gyranic sorcery pouring through breaches from Yeggardania

Vault – Largest settlement

Gyre ship classes and type

Ship classes refers to size – Maw, Vault, Cauldron, Spire, Cradle (there is no Cove class)

Ship type refers to function – Gyre Star, Cruiser, Frigate, Destroyer, Miner, Transporter, Lander

Fromryian Royal Houses

Angelaux – Capital: Pontifax

Couronne – Capital: Helispont

Dillendwan – Capital: Thendergaarden

Fontain – Capital: Taranis

Guildain – Capital: Asteron

Laanorath – Capital: Etherlain

La'Voline – Capital: Sephera

Rosantz – Capital: Thela

Yarranstar – Capital: Everaux

About the author

Sam Middleton is a science fiction and fantasy writer. He graduated from the University of Sheffield in 2014 with a Bachelor of Arts degree in English Literature. After graduating he pursued a career in business writing and communications before becoming a freelance writer and author. Find out more about what he's up to, at www.instagram.com/sammiddletonbooks/

Printed in Dunstable, United Kingdom

70049166R00288